P9-CDS-474

ALSO BY WILLIAM BOYD

NOVELS

A Good Man in Africa
An Ice-Cream War
Stars and Bars
The New Confessions
Brazzaville Beach
The Blue Afternoon
Armadillo
Nat Tate: An American Artist 1928–1960
Any Human Heart
Restless
Ordinary Thunderstorms
Waiting for Sunrise
Solo
Sweet Caress: The Many Lives of Amory Clay
Love Is Blind

SHORT STORY COLLECTIONS

On the Yankee Station
The Destiny of Nathalie "X"
Fascination
The Dream Lover
The Dreams of Bethany Mellmoth

PLAYS

School Ties
Six Parties
Longing
The Argument

NON-FICTION

Bamboo

Trio

TRIO

A novel

William Boyd

Alfred A. Knopf
NEW YORK 2021

THIS IS A BORZOI BOOK PUBLISHED BY ALFRED A. KNOPF

Copyright © 2021 by William Boyd

All rights reserved. Published in the United States by Alfred A. Knopf, a division of Penguin Random House LLC, New York, and distributed in Canada by Penguin Random House Canada Limited, Toronto.
Originally published in hardcover in Great Britain by Viking, a division of Penguin Random House Ltd., London, in 2020.

www.aaknopf.com

Knopf, Borzoi Books, and the colophon are registered trademarks of Penguin Random House LLC.

Library of Congress Cataloging-in-Publication Data
Names: Boyd, William, [date]- author.
Title: Trio / William Boyd.
Description: First edition. | New York : Alfred A. Knopf, [2021]
Identifiers: LCCN 2020038400 | ISBN 9780593318232 (hardcover) |
ISBN 9780593318249 (ebook)
Subjects: GSAFD: Black humor (Literature) |
Humorous fiction. | LCGFT: Novels.
Classification: LCC PR6052.O9192 T75 2021 | DDC 823/.914—dc23
LC record available at https://lccn.loc.gov/2020038400

This is a work of fiction. Names, characters, places, and incidents either are the product of the author's imagination or are used fictitiously. Any resemblance to actual persons, living or dead, events, or locales is entirely coincidental.

Jacket image: (movie camera) CSA Archive / Getty Image
Jacket design by Megan Wilson

Manufactured in the United States of America
First American Edition

For Susan

Most people live their real, most interesting life under the cover of secrecy.

—ANTON CHEKHOV

There is only one serious philosophical problem and that is suicide. Deciding whether or not life is worth living is to answer the fundamental question in philosophy. All other questions follow from that.

—ALBERT CAMUS

DUPLICITY

Brighton, England

1968

I

Elfrida Wing stirred, grunted and shifted sleepily in her bed as the summer's angled morning sun brightened the room, printing a skewed rectangle of lemony-gold light onto the olive-green-flecked wallpaper close by her pillow. Elfrida, wakened by the glare inching towards her, opened her eyes and considered the wallpaper, bringing it into focus with some difficulty, trying to force her comatose brain to work, to think. As usual, on waking she felt absolutely terrible. In front of her eyes, small sharp leaves seemed to be depicted there, in a stylised manner, she decided—or were they birds? Bird shapes? Or perhaps they were simply daubs and splatters of olive green that brought leaves and birds to mind.

No matter. Leaves, birds or random flecks—who really cared in the great scheme of things? She eased herself out of bed and slowly pulled on her dressing gown over her pyjamas. She slipped down the stairs as quietly as possible, wincing at each creak, hand securely gripping the banister, trying to ignore the awful hill-cracking headache that, now she was upright, had begun thumping behind her eyes, making them bulge rhythmically in sympathy, or so she felt. Then she remembered Reggie was long gone, up at first light, off to his film. She could relax.

She paused, coughed, then farted noisily and finished her descent of the staircase with careless din, striding into the kitchen and flinging open the fridge door looking for her orange juice. She scissored off the top of a carton and poured herself half a tumblerful before turning to the condiment cupboard and removing the bottle of Sarson's White Vinegar that she kept there behind the pack of sugar. She added a sizeable slug to her orange juice. Sometimes she wished vodka had more flavour, like gin, but she recognised at the same time that its very neutrality was her greatest ally. Vodka and tap water in a tumbler was her daily tipple when Reggie was around. He never questioned her near-constant thirst, luckily, and never wondered why there was always a considerable stock of Sarson's White Vinegar in the cupboard. Elfrida sat down at the kitchen table and sipped at her vodka and orange juice, finishing it quickly, and then poured herself another, feeling the buzz, the reassuring hit. Her headache was disappearing already.

The title of a novel came mysteriously, unbidden, into her head—*The Zigzag Man.* She could almost see the cover in her mind's eye. A clever use of the two zeds; perhaps different colours for the "zig" and the "zag" . . . She poured herself more orange juice and went back to the cupboard for the Sarson's, emptying the last half-inch into the glass. Better buy another bottle of voddy, she told herself. Or two. She found her notebook and wrote the title down. *The Zigzag Man* by Elfrida Wing. She had noted dozens of titles for potential novels, she saw, flicking back through the pages. There they were: *The Summer of the Wasps, Freezy, The Acrobat, Drop Dead Gorgeous, A Week in Madrid, The Golden Rule, Dark Eulogy, Jazz, Spring Equinox, The Lightning Process, Cool Sun, Mystery in a Small Town, Estranged, Artists' Entrance, Berlin to Hamburg, The Windrow, The Riviera Gap, A Safe Onward Journey, Falling Away*—title after title of unwritten novels. And now *The Zigzag Man* could be added to their number. Titles were the easy bit—writing the novel was the awful challenge. She sipped her juice, feeling sad, all of a sudden. It was now over ten years since her last novel had been published, she remembered ruefully: *The Big Show,* published in the spring of 1958. Ten long years and not a word of fiction written—just list after list of titles. She finished her juice feeling a numbness overwhelm her, tears stinging her eyes. Stop thinking about bloody novels, she told herself, angrily. Have another drink.

2

Talbot Kydd woke abruptly from his dream. In his dream he had been standing on a wide beach and a young man, naked, was walking out of the modest surf, waving at him. He sat up, still half asleep, still in a dream-daze, taking in his surroundings. Yes, he was in a hotel, of course, not at home. Another hotel—sometimes he thought he had spent half his life in hotels. Anyway, he didn't really care: the room was generously large and the bathroom functioned perfectly. It was all he needed for his stay. London was close, that was the main thing.

Now he swung his legs out of the bed and stood up, slowly, blinking, and rubbed his face, hearing his alarm go off. Six o'clock. What an absurd time to start your day, he thought, as he always did when his impossible job made these demands. He stood, stretched carefully, raising his arms above his head for a few seconds as if trying to touch the ceiling, hearing joints crack satisfyingly, and then pottered through to the bathroom.

As he lay in his bath, steam rising, he thought again of the dream he'd been having. Was it a dream or was it a memory? Pleasingly erotic, anyway, and about a young man, pale and limber . . . Or was it Kit, his brother? Or was it someone he'd actually photographed, perhaps, one of his models? He could remember the body but not the face. He tried to recover more details but the dream-memories wouldn't coalesce and the young man remained immovably generic—alluring, slim, unidentifiable.

He shaved, he dressed—classic charcoal-grey suit, white shirt, his East Sussex Light Infantry regimental tie—and ran his two brushes through the near-white wings of hair above his ears. The bathroom ceiling lights gleamed brightly on his freckled baldness. Bald at twenty-five, his father had once observed: I do hope you're my child. It had been an unkind remark to make to a young man self-conscious about his early hair loss, Talbot thought, recalling his father, who had dense straw-coloured hair, driven back from his forehead in tight waves, like a man facing into a gale. But then kindness was not a virtue you'd ever associate with Peverell Kydd so perhaps the slur was evidence of genuine suspicion . . .

He took the stairs down to the dining room and breakfast, expunging thoughts of the old bastard from his mind. Peverell Kydd, dead two decades now. Good. Fuck him and his shade.

He was almost alone in the dining room of the Grand as it was so early. A middle-aged couple in tweeds; a plump man with hair down to his shoulders, smoking, were his three companions. Talbot ordered and consumed his habitual kipper, drank four cups of tea, ate two slices of white toast and raspberry jam, all the while idly watching a rhomboid of sunlight on the maroon carpet slowly turn itself into an isosceles triangle. A sunny day—perfect for Beachy Head.

He had nearly finished his fifth cup of tea when his line producer, Joe Swire, appeared and ordered a pot of coffee from the pretty young waitress with the port-wine birthmark on her neck. Why did he notice such smirches, Talbot wondered, and not celebrate the young waitress's guileless beauty instead? And here was Joe, opposite him, a handsome young man whose good looks were marred by poor teeth, soft and snaggled.

"Break it to me gently, Joe," Talbot said as Joe consulted his clipboard with the day's schedule and business.

"The Applebys have postponed," Joe began.

"Excellent."

"But they've asked for another copy of Troy's contract."

"Why? They have it. They countersigned it."

"I don't know, boss. And Tony's off sick."

"Which Tony?"

"The DoP."

"What's wrong with him?"

"Touch of flu."

"Again? What'll we do?"

"Frank will cover."

"Frank?"

"The camera operator."

"That Frank—right. Is RT happy?"

"Seems to be."

They chatted on for a while, going over the schedule and anticipating potential problems. Talbot realised that he over-relied on Joe's expertise to ensure the film ran smoothly. He didn't enjoy the pettifogging nuts-and-bolts business of making a film, it wasn't his forte. Which is why he hired someone like Joe, of course, to manfully shoulder what really should have been his burden. Talbot knew he should try harder and show more interest, such as remembering people's names. It was one of Peverell Kydd's salient pieces of advice. If you remember their names and what they do they'll think you're a god—or a demi-god, at least. As with most of his father's proffered wise counsel Talbot was reluctant to take it. Whatever you choose to do in your life, my boy, don't, repeat, don't have anything to do with the film business, you're absolutely not the right type of person, so his father had declared. And yet here he was—a film producer with more than a dozen films to his name. Just like his father—although not a legend, definitely not, and certainly not as rich.

Talbot sat back and exhaled. Why did he feel sour and cantankerous today? he wondered. The sun was shining, they were in week five, close to halfway through the filming schedule; there had been crises, of course, but nothing calamitous. He was wealthy enough, contentedly married, in good health, his children grown up and thriving, after their fashion . . . So what was chafing at him?

"You all right, boss?" Joe asked, as if he could sense Talbot's darkening mood.

"Yes, yes. All's well with the world. Shall we go to work?"

3

Anny Viklund woke up and, as she did every morning as consciousness slowly returned, she wondered if this day was going to be the day that she died. Why did that morbid question come so quickly to her mind every single morning? Why was her first thought that this day, just begun, might be her last day on earth? Stupid. Don't think these thoughts, stupid. She lay there for a few moments, concentrating, then slowly became aware of the young man sleeping soundly next to her. Troy. Yes, of course, Troy had stayed the night . . . She rubbed her eyes. He had been so sweet, she remembered, and the sex had been good and energetic—exactly what she had wanted—what she'd needed.

She slipped out of bed and walked, naked, into the bathroom. She peered at her face in the mirror, always a bit shocked to see her newly cropped ink-black hair with its short fringe. So stark and transforming. Maybe she'd leave it like that and never be a blonde again. She urinated and cleaned her teeth and wandered back into the bedroom.

Troy was sitting on her side of the bed, rummaging at his thick brown hair with stiff fingers. He smiled, seeing her come back in.

"That was a bit of all right last night, wasn't it?" he said, obviously pleased with himself.

"You think so?" She climbed back onto the bed, hugging her knees to her.

Troy pointed at his morning erection.

"He's ready for more, I'd say." He leant over and kissed her left kneecap.

"We're due on set in an hour," she said. "They won't know where you are."

"Shit. Yeah. Good point." Troy frowned. He looked at her. "How come your pubic hair is a different colour from the hair on your head? Eh?"

Anny smiled. This, she now realised, was the sort of question Troy asked.

"My hair is dyed. The hair on my head."

"Natural blonde, then? Like it."

"My family is from Sweden."

"Yeah. But you're an American."

"It doesn't affect my ancestry."

Troy stood and wandered around the suite looking for his clothes.

"Better get back to my room," he said, vaguely.

Anny watched him dress. He was twenty-four, she knew, making him almost four years younger than she was. Maybe that was why she had slept with him. I've slept with too many old men, she thought—first Mavrocordato, then Cornell, then Jacques—I've forgotten what it was like with a young man. He was cute, Troy, almost innocent, she decided—yes, he still thought life was full of fun. She bowed her head, resting her brow on her knees. The act reminded her at once of Jacques. It was one of his sayings: the world is composed of people who bow their heads and people who don't . . . Where was Jacques, anyway? Paris? No, he had said something about going to Africa to meet a deposed president in exile. What was his name? Nkrumah. Yes. Very Jacques. A trip to Africa to meet a president—she kept forgetting how famous Jacques was in France. She unbowed her head. Troy was standing there, dressed in his jeans and his suede jacket, staring at her.

"You all right?" he asked.

"Yes, of course. I enjoyed myself. I'm very happy."

He sat down on the bed and kissed her.

"What'll we do?"

"We can't tell anyone," she said. "Nobody must know."

"But I want to see you again. A lot." He gently touched her cheek with his fingers. "You're terrific, Anny. I really like you. I've never met anyone like you."

"Then we have to be very careful. Be discreet. No one can know. No one must guess or have a suspicion." She thought further. "When we're shooting on set we just have to be professional—you know, like friends."

"Kind of difficult. Now."

"No one can know, Troy. My life is too complicated."

He shrugged. "All right. Have it your way—we'll be very careful. We're actors, after all. Well, you are." He looked at her shrewdly. "You're not married, are you?"

"I'm divorced. But I have . . . Another friend."

"In America?"

"In Paris."

"That's all right then." Troy smiled. "Out of sight is out of mind, as they say."

"Out of sight, but very much in mind."

Suddenly she grabbed the back of his neck and pulled his head towards hers, kissing him strongly.

They broke apart. Troy looked a bit stunned.

"Go," she said.

"Anny, I can—"

"Go."

"No."

4

Talbot looked at Reggie Tipton and smiled, trying to ignore his sour mood, trying to be friendly, trying to be convivially understanding, though he was actually thinking what an insufferable, deluded, self-important little man Reggie was.

"I thought—forgive me—that we were meant to be at Beachy Head this morning," Talbot said, evenly.

"We will be. I just need to get this pick-up."

"What pick-up? It wasn't on the schedule, Joe says."

"Last-minute thought of mine. Joe's up to speed, now. Just Anny—big close-up. Thinking, she doesn't have to say anything." He joined up his thumbs and forefingers to make a notional rectangle and held it up to his face—as if, Talbot thought, I couldn't quite grasp the concept of a "big" close-up. He really could be tiresome, Reggie.

"One big close-up. One shot, no more than ten minutes. Trust me, Talbot. We'll get everything done today."

"Fair enough, you're the director. Where is Anny, by the way?"

"Hair and make-up. She was late. Unfortunately."

"Do we know why?" Talbot still maintained a faint smile.

"No. Or at least I don't know. She was told the pick-up time, the car was there. We called her room—she didn't answer. We waited. She came down an hour later."

"I see. Is she all right?"

Reggie scoffed. "How can Anny Viklund be 'all right,' given her history? She's behaving *fairly* well—we're lucky—that's the best we can hope for."

"You cast her."

"Sorry, Talbot, that's not fair. I was under massive pressure to cast her, from you and Yorgos."

"Not true. Yorgos wanted her, for some reason. I wanted Suzy Kendall. Or Judy Geeson."

"Suzy Kendall would have worked. Could have been great . . ." Reggie frowned, as if imagining his film in a parallel universe.

"Or if not her, that singer. Whatshername," Talbot said.

"Lulu?"

"No. Sandra Shaw."

"Sandie Shaw . . . Can she act?"

"Reggie, it's not difficult," Talbot said. "At least not in this film. She'd have been perfect, Sandie Shaw—opposite Troy Blaze. Damn sight cheaper than Anny Viklund."

"It *is* difficult, acting, actually," Reggie said, a little petulantly. He lowered his voice and drew Talbot a few paces away from the camera crew.

"Talbot, would you do me a huge favour and not call me 'Reggie' on the set? If you must use a name please call me Rodrigo. Please. It's important to me. I've changed my driving licence, passport, everything—it's how I want to be known, professionally, anyway. It's very important to me."

"I'll try and remember. Sorry. It's all very odd, I must say. I've known you as 'Reggie' for years."

"I'm credited on this film as Rodrigo Tipton. It's a whole new beginning for me—everything might change."

"All right, all right. *Rodrigo.*"

"Thank you." Reggie/Rodrigo sighed. "Anyway, I suppose it is pretty amazing to have Anny Viklund in a little British film. Did you see how much money *The Yellow Mountain* has made? Tens of millions. And she looks stunning. And Troy seems to get on with her. There are lots of pluses." He held up his right hand and rubbed the tips of his fingers together. "It'll pay off at the box office."

"It had better." Talbot stopped smiling.

13

"Hello, darling, what's brought you here?" Reggie said, looking over Talbot's shoulder.

Talbot turned to see Reggie's wife, Elfrida, approaching. The oddest woman, he always thought. Tall, slim, she seemed to be trying to hide her face behind her thick dark hair. She had a fringe down to her eyelashes and her ears and cheeks were concealed by two chin-length curtains of hair brushed forward like a sort of hair-helmet. She often wore heavy black-rimmed spectacles that made the barrier seem even more impenetrable, though, oddly again, her lips were always painted a lurid red. An intelligent woman, obviously, but very strange. He wondered how she and Reggie ever came to be married.

"Elfrida, lovely to see you." Talbot shook her hand. He had read and enjoyed one of her novels, years ago—couldn't recall the title.

"Talbot, hello, hello," she replied, her red lips parting in a quick smile. She had a husky voice as if she were a heavy smoker but he'd never seen her with a cigarette.

"I've run out of money," she said to Reggie. "And the chequebook's run out of cheques."

"Excuse us, Talbot," Reggie said.

Talbot watched them walk away, talking quietly to each other. Elfrida was as tall as Reggie, if not slightly taller. Couples, he thought, how curious they are. He shook the idea away, thinking suddenly of the couple he made with Naomi—no more curious than Reggie Tipton and Elfrida Wing, he supposed.

He wandered off to find Joe and seek an answer to the question of when the hell were they ever going to get to Beachy Head? As he searched for Joe amongst the vans, caravans and the lorries of the set, he slowly realised that almost every transistor radio in the unit was tuned to the same radio station playing the same absurd song. He seemed to be moving from aural zone to aural zone when the song would die away, then, as he passed another group of lounging men, waiting, smoking, drinking coffee, it flared up, playing once more. Something about a cake and a park, and melting green sweet icing flowing down. Oh, no! How long was the damn thing? He kept hearing the same refrain. A park, belonging to a Mr. MacArthur, where a cake had been left out in the rain, and something about a recipe that could not be found. Oh, no! He was no admirer of modern "pop" music but this one seemed unusually abstruse, from what he could understand of the snatched lyrics.

There was Joe.

"Joe! Save me from this madness," he said. "Take me to Beachy Head."

5

Elfrida stood at the bar of the snug in the Repulse and ordered another gin and tonic. It was the pub she preferred in Brighton, two streets back from the Esplanade. Smallish, with a saloon bar as well as the snug, and decoratively unfavoured, it boasted only drab, neutral colours: browns, greens, dark grey—nothing themed, nothing garish. No music blaring, no gambling machines or toys for men to play. It was named the Repulse after an early nineteenth-century first-rate ship of the line that went down with all hands in some remote naval battle in the East Java Sea or somewhere—somewhere far from England, anyway, forever commemorated here in a modest Brighton pub, paid for by subscriptions raised by the widows of the crew. There was a framed parchment document in the short corridor on the way to the saloon bar that explained the history. Nice idea, Elfrida thought; a fit way of remembering the drowned menfolk. A place where you could drown your sorrows . . . She thought she'd quite like a pub as a memorial. Better than a row of books on a shelf. A little pub somewhere with a sign: "The Elfrida Wing." She took her drink back to her table in the corner, toying with the idea, imagining the pub—her stylised portrait on the sign, bright flowers in window boxes, benches outside, a little beer garden at the back . . .

The snug bar was quiet, afternoon closing time wasn't far off, and there were just three other drinkers, all men, apart from herself. She had a sip of her G and T and then searched her handbag (now heavy with a new bottle of vodka) for her notebook. She opened it in front of her and rummaged for her fountain pen. She had no intention of writing anything, she just wanted to look like she was busy with something, thinking—not a drinker, drinking. She doodled some spirals on a new page and then some squares and cross-hatched them dark.

Out of the corner of her eye she was aware of a man who seemed to be looking at her; a man of her age, in his forties, wearing a suit and tie and reading a book. He kept glancing at her. She pushed at her hair and her fringe and then put on her glasses. Maybe he recognises me, she thought, how ghastly. Maybe he'd read one of her novels and was thinking to himself, "Could that be Elfrida Wing over there?" Then she saw him swallow the last inch of his half-pint, stand up and cross the room towards her. She concentrated on her notebook.

"Excuse me, sorry for interrupting, but are you by any chance Elfrida Wing?"

Elfrida looked up.

"No. My name's Jennifer Tipton."

"Sorry. It's just that you look like her. Like her photo, I mean."

"Who is this Elspeth Wing?"

"Elfrida. She's a rather wonderful novelist. I've read all her novels."

"I'm a midwife," she said. "Apologies." She pointed at her gin. "It's my day off."

He smiled at her dubiously, as if not at all convinced.

"I wish I could write a novel," Elfrida said. That much was true.

"Well, sorry to bother you," the man said again. "Enjoy your day off." And he sauntered out of the pub, glancing quickly back at her as he stepped out through the door.

The encounter disturbed her. To think that even after ten years of silence on her part, after ten years of resolute writer's block, loyal, devoted readers might still recognise her. Terrifying. She had been much photographed and interviewed, particularly after the success of her last novel, she recalled, and then the film and then when she and Reggie got married in Islington town hall. Reggie had arranged for lots of photographers. Reggie wore white and she wore black—it seemed to amuse people. Something about her face, her "public" image—a young woman writer enjoying the acclaim—seemed to linger in people's minds. Novelists should be—are—the least recognised of minor celebrities, she thought, almost invisible. Conductors, artists, dancers, athletes, magicians, sportsmen, weather-forecasters, quiz-show hosts are far more familiar. But certain novelists seem to remain in the public consciousness. Perhaps it was her hairstyle—her fringe. Maybe she should change that? She finished her gin and went back to the bar to order another.

She sat on in the gloomy pub, drinking, waiting for the call of "last orders," thinking about the man and what he'd said. "A rather wonderful novelist." She supposed he had read her first novel, *Mrs. Bristow's Day.* How she hated that novel, now. It was short, around 160 pages, and related the day—in great, textured detail—in the life of an ordinary middle-aged woman, the eponymous Mrs. Bristow, who was married and had three grown-up sons, and was simply getting on with the business of living until she died. She goes shopping; she has a bit of a row over a constantly barking dog with a woman who is a neighbour; she goes to a dental appointment. In the dentist's waiting room she reads magazines and thinks about her sons, where they are and what they're up to. She has an old filling repaired in a molar then she returns home, pausing to buy an evening paper. Back at her house she prepares her husband's tea, waiting for him to return from work, then glances at the headlines, pondering the news at home and abroad. She hears a noise and goes to investigate and discovers a young man, an intruder who has broken in through the scullery window. In a panic he attacks Mrs. Bristow and kills her.

The problem that then emerged, she realised, wasn't the novel's surprising success. It did exceptionally well for a first novel and she was only just twenty-five, relatively fresh from Cambridge (Girton College)—no, the problem was that a famous literary critic, in his enthusiastic review, dubbed her "the new Virginia Woolf," as if *Mrs. Bristow's Day* was a clever, modern reworking of Woolf's *Mrs. Dalloway.* She hadn't thought anything of it at first, she hadn't even read *Mrs. Dalloway,* but when the epithet was repeated on the publication of her second novel, *Excesses* ("Elfrida Wing, widely regarded as the new Virginia Woolf, chalks up a second triumph with *Excesses*") she began to be a little irritated. Other critics repeated the comparison, thoughtlessly—recklessly, she felt. It was as if Virginia Woolf's ghost was somehow haunting her life. Mention Elfrida Wing and someone would inevitably say, "Ah, the new Virginia Woolf." It was on the publication of her third novel, *The Big Show,* that she realised that her name was going to be yoked to Virginia Woolf's for the rest of her writing life. "Elfrida Wing, celebrated and acclaimed as the rightful heir to Virginia Woolf, stuns with *The Big Show.*"

What made it worse was that she didn't particularly like Virginia Woolf's novels. She had read *Mrs. Dalloway,* by this time, and was underwhelmed. She found the novels overwrought and fey. She could see no similarity between her spirit, intellect and style as a novelist and Virginia Woolf's. But not so for every critic who reviewed her books. Nor her growing army of loyal readers, because the publishers repeated the claim—in bold—on her paperbacks. She began to hate the sight of her own novels. And that was why she stopped writing, she supposed. It was all Virginia Woolf's fault.

She took a mouthful of her gin and tonic and closed her eyes as she registered the benign, the sublime, effect. Who would have thought that the berries of the humble shrub that was the juniper could inspire this elixir? She felt her head reel, satisfyingly, drew another square in her notebook and shaded it in.

Perhaps, she thought, as she drew a series of arrows, large and small, she was making excuses for what was simply a complete lack of inspiration. Had she merely run out of fictional steam after three successful novels? Maybe—maybe—it had nothing to do with being regarded as the new Virginia Woolf at all . . .

After *The Big Show* had been published (sixteen translations, paperback rights sold for a good five-figure sum) she had met Reggie Tipton. Reggie, a very up-and-coming young film director, wanted to make a film of *The Big Show.* The film rights were acquired for a higher five-figure sum and for a while Elfrida realised she was actually quite rich. She bought a small house in the Vale of Health in Hampstead and she and Reggie had an affair, of course. Reggie's eventual film, now known simply as *Show!,* starred Melanie Todd and Sebastian Brandt but even their starry candlepower couldn't make it a success. It sold many more books for her, however, and she became even richer. Then Reggie left his wife (and children) and she and Reggie married. And then she had her miscarriage. Everything had gone wrong after that, yes, that was the crisis point.

She thought back to those days with some hesitation, reluctant to stir memories. Reggie, when she met him, was married to a humourless, pretentious woman called Marion ("The single biggest grotesque mistake of my life," he had confessed to Elfrida at the beginning of their affair). Reggie and Marion Tipton had two daughters, Butterfly and Evergreen, eight and six. When Reggie formally separated from Marion, moved in with Elfrida and divorce proceedings began, she noticed that his allotted quota of visits to the girls steadily diminished. When Butterfly was sixteen she wrote to her father saying she never wanted to see him again. Reggie had shown Elfrida the letter, not seeming too perturbed. Elfrida was more shocked at its cold, unforgiving tone than he was. He continued to see Evergreen from time to time until she too was persuaded by Marion's undying bitterness to cut all ties to her father. Reggie—secure in the castle of his ego—took it surprisingly well.

For her part, Elfrida always had something of a guilty conscience. She hated the idea that she was in some significant way responsible for this festering pool of unhappiness in the Tipton family, but the heady, alluring energies of their affair overwhelmed all other emotions. And then, shortly after they were married, when she became pregnant herself, she rather hoped that Reggie's new child would console him for the loss of the other two. But she miscarried in the third month. The resulting hospitalisation and her subsequent year-long mini-nervous breakdown, she now realised, was the watershed in their marriage. She slowly became aware that Reggie was actually somewhat relieved not to be a father again. Her miscarriage, as she put it to herself, led to a corresponding mismarriage. They tried for another child but without success and Reggie seemed to be losing even his faint interest in the idea, anyway, and so the dream of being a mother died. Nothing was ever the same again; Reggie began to have affairs and she stopped writing.

"Last orders please!" the barmaid cried.

Elfrida finished her gin and went to the bar to order a final drink and a packet of peanuts. That would have to do for lunch.

6

Anny and Troy sat in the banana-yellow Mini on the cliff of Beachy Head, in a warm stupor of sunlight, looking out at the refulgent English Channel, glinting silver. High in the sky above them a perfectly straight white contrail split the blue.

"Nobody suspects a thing," Troy said. "You're brilliant. You're so calm. What's the word? Impressive."

"Impressive or impassive?"

"Both. Yeah. You look so cool with those sunglasses on. No one could tell you were madly in love with me."

"Ha-ha."

Troy had his hand on her leg, slipping his fingers under her short skirt, and she could feel the heat of his palm on the inside of her thigh through the mesh of her ivory-coloured tights.

In front of them was an entire film crew surrounding a large camera mounted on a crane. Even though it was a sunny day, powerful arc lights burned strongly. The first assistant director was shouting at them through a loudhailer.

"Turning over! Action!"

Anny and Troy climbed out of their respective doors, joined hands and ran towards the camera. When they separated—each of them going a different side of the camera—they stopped. Anny knew that the next scene, shot from behind, would feature their stunt doubles who, hand in hand, would leap over the cliff and fall six feet into a net rigged below the turf's edge. It would be the penultimate scene of the film.

As for the final scene of the film, Anny had no idea how they would do it. According to the script, instead of falling to their deaths Anny's and Troy's characters would fly miraculously upward into the heavens, disappearing from sight—like those rockets they launched from Cape Kennedy, Anny thought, lost to view forever.

Rodrigo Tipton stepped round from behind the camera and wandered over.

"Fab," he said. "Can we do it just once more without the shades, please, Anny?"

"I don't want to do it without sunglasses," she said without really thinking.

"We probably won't use it but it might be an interesting option. Just to have it in the can, you know." Rodrigo smiled.

Anny thought about refusing—normally she would have refused—but for some reason having Troy beside her made her think again.

"OK."

After she had done the run to the cliff edge twice more without sunglasses Rodrigo said everything was great and now they would do the scene with the stunt doubles. Their day was over. Anny quietly told Troy that he should go and she would stay on a while. It would look better if they didn't leave together. Troy agreed.

"Yeah, but I'll come to your room tonight," Troy said. "Midnight."

"No."

"Yes. No one'll see me."

"I might not be there at midnight."

"You'll be there, babe."

He wandered off to his car and driver. Anny asked her assistant, Shirley, to get her a cup of tea as she stood behind the camera with Rodrigo watching the alternative Anny Viklund and Troy Blaze fling themselves off Beachy Head. What a way to go, she thought, remembering her macabre early-morning question to herself. Maybe, in a funny sort of way, it had in fact happened. She had indeed "died" today. The idea was strangely liberating and she began to think about Troy and his visit tonight. He was very sure of himself, but in a nice way, one that—"How's everything going, Anny?"

She turned to see who was speaking and saw a tall, bald man ambling over towards her. It was the producer, she realised. Tony? Terence? She had only met him once or twice so she decided not to risk a guess and said simply that everything was great, really good, thanks, everyone was being so nice.

"Good, excellent, very pleased," Tony or Terence said. He had one of those classic clipped, dry English accents, she thought. How do they speak like that, hardly moving their lips? No one can really know what they're thinking or feeling, everything sounds the same. He might as well have said, "Bad, terrible, I'm shocked."

He stepped a little closer to her and lowered his voice.

"We had a strange phone call in the office this morning. It was the police. They asked if a man called Cornell Weekes had tried to contact you."

Anny felt sweat form instantly in her armpits and on the palms of her hands. Just hearing his name had that effect on her. Cornell: her demon-lover, her one-time guru, her nemesis.

"No."

"Cornell Weekes is your husband, isn't he?"

"Cornell Weekes is my ex-husband."

"Ah. Right."

"He's in prison," she said.

"Not any more, apparently."

"What do you mean?"

"I don't know the details . . ." He pronounced the word "deetays," she thought, seeing him glance around to make sure no one could overhear. "But it seems that he absconded during a routine parole hearing. They think he made his way to Canada. To Montreal."

Anny began to calm down.

"Why would they think he was in England?" she said. "He was in prison in California."

The tall, bald man smiled in a kindly way.

"Apparently they found a map of London in the hotel room he was staying in. In Montreal." He shrugged. "A logical assumption. Why *was* your ex-husband in prison, if I may ask?"

"He tried to blow up a federal building."

"Right." He scratched his nose. "I'm sure it was a routine enquiry, you know."

"Cornell is a weird kind of fucked-up guy, but there's no way he'd come to England. He's never been to England."

"Reassuring." The man gestured at the film crew. "It's all going so well." He turned back and looked at her shrewdly. He must be sixty or seventy, she thought, like my grandpa. He was still quite a handsome man, she saw, lean and upright, despite being old and bald.

"My name is Talbot, by the way. Talbot Kydd."

7

At the end of the day Talbot sat in the office with Joe.

"What's up tomorrow?"

"We've got Sylvia Slaye and Ferdie Meares in for their costume fittings."

"Jesus Christ. Both on the same day? Is that wise?"

"Yes, boss. Short and sweet. Two birds with one stone is the idea. They've already sent in a list of their 'requests.'"

Talbot squared his shoulders reflexively as if expecting a blow, thinking. Old troupers. Former big stars. Now fading stars. Difficult people. The worst. He lit a cigarette.

"Joe, tell me. Do we have any idea how the last scene is going to be filmed?"

"Ah. Well. There's been talk of . . . Of animation. Some animation. Somewhere. In some shape or form." Joe almost squirmed in his seat as he said the words.

He was a decent young chap, Talbot thought. Should keep him on, somehow.

"We can't afford animation," Talbot said, calmly. "And animation would be so wrong, anyway. All wrong at the end of this film in particular."

"You'll have to talk to Reggie—sorry, Rodrigo—guv'nor. He seems to have some sort of animated fantasy sequence in mind."

"But it's not in the script. It's not budgeted for."

"The script's being rewritten."

"*What?* No, it fucking isn't!"

"Sorry. It was just that I heard Rodrigo was bringing in Janet Headstone. So I sort of assumed . . ."

"News to me."

"Apparently Yorgos gave him the thumbs-up."

Talbot felt his anger build. Yorgos was his producing partner. What were these people playing at? He exhaled. One day at a time. Stay calm, he told himself, there is always a simpler explanation to be found, somewhere.

He went to the cupboard, took out his bottle of whisky and poured himself an inch into a glass—all in the interests of reaching this new mental state of calm indifference, of Zen-like remove from the irritating, scratchy details of the life of a film producer.

How wise the Japanese were, he thought to himself, remembering that there were two words in Japanese to describe the self. Or so he thought: who had told him this? Apparently there was a word for the self that existed in the private realm and another, completely different, word for the self that existed in the world. Why didn't the English language have this sensible division? He abandoned his public self and, sipping at his whisky, retrieved his private self, happy to be absorbed in the plans he had made for the weekend. The travails of *Ladder to the Moon* would be erased from his mind—his private self would hold sway for a day or two.

8

Anny lay still in Troy's arms. His breathing was shallow and regular, his breath warm on her right shoulder, and she wondered if he was asleep. She had a slight headache and felt wide awake even though it must be past two in the morning now, she thought. She shouldn't have drunk the red wine that he'd brought. When she mixed alcohol with her pills it always made her sleepless—and those pills were meant to help her sleep.

The news about Cornell and his escape had really disturbed her—made her feel jumpy and suddenly insecure. And concerned. How had he escaped? And why were the British police calling the production office? Cornell had never been to England in his life, as far as she knew, so why would he now make this his destination? Because he knew she was in England, she supposed. The film had been announced, she had been photographed arriving at Heathrow airport. Cornell would have known: he followed her career, even though he claimed he wasn't interested in "movies." She brought his face to mind, effortlessly—lean and handsome, frown-lines permanently seamed in his forehead, deep between his eyes. How he used to spit out that word—"movies!" His features were so vivid even though she hadn't seen him since their divorce, an event she could hardly remember. They had kind of stumbled into divorcing each other, she thought. Why had they divorced? She remembered a fight in which she called Cornell a "sheepish anarchist." The slur had enraged him and he'd left home for a few days. When he returned he apologised but then insisted she quit the movie she was about to shoot, *Hotel Nights,* and she refused, asking him how he thought they would live without her fee. So he left home again, calling her a traitor. Then he spontaneously filed for divorce and, weary of the turmoil, she agreed, and it duly happened. She didn't hate Cornell, she realised, she just didn't have it in her to cope with him and his impossible ideals. She didn't have the energy to be married to Cornell.

But the trouble was, since the divorce, since the bomb outrage, her name was now always being linked with his. Every article or interview about her always mentioned her marriage to the "urban terrorist," Cornell Weekes. She told journalists that their marriage had lasted a few months, well short of a year, but it seemed to make no difference—Cornell Weekes was now inextricably part of her biography. She inhaled and bit her lip, feeling like crying all of a sudden. Why had she married him? What had she been thinking? Yes, he was handsome and had that charisma that visionary people seemed to possess, as he talked endlessly about "the American Reich," whatever that was. She had been so young when she met him, twenty-three years old, but Mavrocordato's *Aquarius Days* had just come out and suddenly she was a big star, a name. The unheard-of girl from Minnesota. Film after film offered, the money flowing in. Then Cornell Weekes stepped into her life.

He wasn't in the movie business, that was it. He hated the movies and Hollywood—the entertainment division of the American Reich, he said. He was older, grey-haired—wise, or so it seemed to her until she wised up in turn. And he reminded her of her father. That should have been the warning, that should have been the—

"Anny?" Troy said softly. "Can I ask you something personal? What's your real name?"

Another Troy question. This time she was glad of it, happy to be stupidly distracted. She turned in the bed to face him, pleased he was awake.

"Anny Viklund. It's my real name. Anny Makjen Viklund. Why?"

"Most people I know—in this business—don't use their real names. Same with me." He began to list them: Billy Fury, Cliff Richard, Adam Faith, Danny Storm, Tommy Steele, Bobby Hero, Georgie Fame, Mickie Most.

She kissed him gently.

"You know, I never for one second thought Troy Blaze was your real name," she said. "Though I like it."

"Well, it's better than my real name. Tell you that for nothing."

"What's your real name?"

"I don't want you to know. I want to be Troy to you."

"You'll always be Troy to me. What is your real name?"

"Nigel Farthingly."

"I like it. Maybe I'll start calling you Nigel."

"I should never have told you."

"I'm just kidding. Nigel." She kissed him again. "Sorry. Troy. I can see that it might be kind of hard being a pop star called Nigel Farthingly."

"Exactly. That's why the Applebys made me change it."

"Who're the Applebys?"

"My managers. Jimmy and Bob Appleby."

"Is that their real name?"

"Oh, yes."

His hand was on her breast, fingers touching the nipple. She reached down to feel him. Hard, rigid. A young man—so different from Cornell who always said he had "libido issues" as a result of his unhappy adolescence. He never went into details.

"I can't sleep," Anny said, putting on a baby voice. "What will we do?"

9

After she'd left the Repulse, Elfrida had bought a bottle of Tio Pepe amontillado sherry from an off-licence—part of her clever Reggie subterfuge, or so she reckoned. She had a taxi take her back to the house in Rottingdean that the film company had rented for Reggie. It was inconvenient living in a village at the edge of Brighton: taxis had to be called all the time as she didn't have a driving licence and she wondered why Reggie had agreed to this particular accommodation. When she had complained to him about the hassle and the bother that living in Rottingdean necessitated he had said just ring the production office and they'll send a unit car—it's all in the budget. But she never liked using unit cars—the drivers were all intensely curious eavesdroppers and compulsive gossips. They sat around all day exchanging bits of fruity information, she knew. How could she ask a unit car to come and collect her from the Repulse?

In fact the house was fine—better than fine. It was a big three-storey Victorian villa, grey brick with red-brick trimmings, called, oddly, "Peelings." Maybe a family called Peel had built and lived in it, she wondered. Peelings was set in a sizeable garden with two huge monkey puzzle trees at the front. There were five bedrooms and three bathrooms, a capacious sitting room and dining room, a "modern" kitchen—even a billiard room—all far too big for two people and, what with Reggie's near-constant absence on the film, most of the time she felt she was living in this vast villa on her own, like some dowager in her dower house being kept out of the way of the family.

Good point, she said to herself, that was probably precisely why he'd chosen Peelings—so she could be kept at a distance. Usually when he made a film or a TV programme they stayed in a hotel but with this film with its stupid title—*Emily Bracegirdle's Extremely Useful Ladder to the Moon*—he had said it was a question of prestige. It would cost the production a lot to house him like this and consequently they'd treat him with more respect, so he claimed. You have to play all the angles, darling, he had added—whatever that meant.

Elfrida sat for a while in the garden on a bench in the shade of a big chestnut, drinking some of her new vodka that she'd decanted into the Sarson's bottle, as she read a letter forwarded from London from her brother, Anselm. It was his annual round robin to family and friends (always despatched on his birthday) and she could barely read beyond the first page such was the remorseless, breezy tedium of Anselm's life as an eminent orthopaedic surgeon in Vancouver. Much of the letter was given up to the sporting exploits of his two sons, Jerold and Roldan, her strapping nephews, who seemed never off the pitch or the court or the slopes or the rink. After the death of their parents—within three months of each other in the limbo period leading up to the publication of her first novel—Elfrida imagined that she and Anselm (he was seven years older) would draw closer, inevitably. But he promptly emigrated to Canada, married, and Jerold and Roldan swiftly appeared. They rarely saw each other and family bonds were preserved out of duty, not fondness. Hence this round-robin letter. He could have been writing to his bank manager, she thought, and crumpled it up, throwing it on the lawn at her feet.

However, letter-reading inspired letter-writing and she fetched pen and paper and wrote to her literary agent and to her editor at Muir & Melhuish requesting an appointment for the following week. She bluntly told her agent, Calder McPhail, that she needed money. She was deliberately candid—they had known each other a long time—and she was emboldened by her vodka and tap water on top of her lunchtime gins. She said to both agent and editor that she wanted an advance on a new novel that she had almost completed, called *The Zigzag Man.* That'll make them sit up, she thought.

She watched the television news in the evening, made herself some supper—baked beans on toast—and then, at about eight o'clock when she was expecting Reggie to return she poured herself a small glass of Tio Pepe, leaving the barely touched bottle ostentatiously on the sideboard and, at the same time, made herself an exceptionally powerful vodka and water, a quadruple, in a tall tumbler. Consequently, when Reggie did return, late, after ten o'clock, she felt wonderfully sure of herself.

She switched off the TV when he came into the room and stood up, steadily, and looked at him coldly, intently.

"So," she said. "Who exactly is it that you're fucking on *this* film?"

10

The next morning, after his usual breakfast, Talbot felt suddenly dyspeptic. Back in his room he glugged at his bottle of Previzole, hoping that the chalky fluid might work its magic, worrying that his bloody ulcer was playing up again. It was nothing to do with his daily kipper, he knew—it was the forthcoming confrontation with Reggie over the hiring of Janet Headstone and the mooted rewrite that was making his stomach acids swirl and bubble and torment his duodenum.

He was fully aware of who Janet Headstone was but he had never actually met her. She was a young, brash, self-styled "cockney" novelist and the novels she wrote were racy contemporary working-class stories set in the East End of London. The school of "kitchen sink," Talbot thought, remarkably enduring. One of Janet Headstone's novels—*Down Canada Water*—had been made into a film (starring Samantha Frost) and had become a sizeable cult success, if such an oxymoron were possible, with its young cockney lovers, impossibly handsome and beautiful, ideally fashionable and poor. Janet Headstone had written the script and was suddenly a sought-after name in the British film industry when it was perceived that something "trendy" and cutting-edge "groovy" was required. A blousy, pretty young woman with a noticeable gap in her front teeth, she was often featured in tabloid newspapers, out on the town with various cool and notorious actors, footballers, TV personalities and the like. As far as he was concerned, Talbot had loathed *Down Canada Water* and he couldn't understand what this conspiracy between Yorgos and Reggie was hoping to achieve. Hiring someone like Janet Headstone for *Emily Bracegirdle's Extremely Useful Ladder to the Moon* seemed perverse, a mismatch.

He instructed Joe to bring Reggie over to the production office whenever there was a break for a new set-up. This was not a conversation that could take place with the risk of any of the crew overhearing or even seeing it. Talbot stepped out into the back garden of the production office and had another swig of Previzole. His stomach was on fire. The production office was in a two-storeyed semi-detached house in Napier Street. It was pebble-dashed and had a bit of mock-Tudorbethan half-timbering on its upper floor. It was perfectly comfortable and conveniently placed for most of their Brighton locations. The garden was a bit unkempt and rather too many plastic chairs had been left out in it—most of the production meetings were al fresco in this sunny summer. Talbot wandered around and restored an upended deckchair to normality. He was thinking: what would Peverell Kydd have done in a situation like this? He would probably fire Reggie, for starters; then maybe sue his partner, Yorgos. He didn't mess about, old Peverell. Another trait his son hadn't inherited. So what? Talbot said to himself: slash and burn is not my style. *Chacun à sa méthode.*

At around ten o'clock Reggie knocked on Talbot's office door—ajar—and wandered in. Talbot had him sit down, had Rosie bring them two cups of filthy coffee and they both lit cigarettes.

Talbot noticed that Reggie had a two-inch scratch on his cheek and three parallel scratches below it on his neck.

"What happened to you?" Talbot asked, pointing.

"Talk about inept. I was mowing the lawn, hit a molehill, tripped and fell into a wire fence."

"Since when did you ever mow a lawn?"

"I like gardening. It helps me think."

Talbot left it at that. The marks looked like nail scratches to him. Sharp fingernails raking down Reggie's face.

"So . . ." Talbot said, and left his "so" dangling in the air for a second or two.

"I somehow feel I'm about to be chastised," Reggie said.

"You probably should be chastised. What the hell is going on with Janet Headstone?"

"Ah, right. I get it. Janet Headstone."

"Precisely. Please explain."

"Look, I met her at a party," Reggie leant forward, "and I was telling her about our problems with the script. She said she'd love to help. Then, the next day, I had to see Yorgos about something and in the meeting mentioned Janet and he said, fantastico, she is genius, hire her for four weeks, just like that. I assumed he'd clear it with you."

"Well, he didn't. I've only just heard."

"Well, my apologies. You know Yorgos better than I do."

"I do indeed. How much is Janet Headstone being paid for her month's work?"

"I think . . . a thousand a week."

Talbot didn't allow his features to flinch an iota.

"That means you've lost two days' shooting."

"Yorgos said it could come out of the contingency fund."

"But this isn't a fucking contingency, Reggie. We have a script, a very good, very expensive script by Andrew Marvell, no less. What do you think he's going to say when he discovers Janet Headstone is rewriting him? He's a nightmare, a bully. Who's going to break the news to him? You?"

Reggie ignored the question.

"It's not rewriting, it's *extra* writing. Marvell wouldn't—couldn't—do the stuff Jan's thinking about."

"Oh, it's 'Jan,' is it?"

"Look, all right—we're chums. We've met a few times. We're on the same wavelength. She's delightful—fresh, different. You'd love her."

"Be that as it may. What I resent, Reggie, is that you didn't even think of coming to me—to see what I thought about the idea. You went over my head—or around my body—to Yorgos. He's the softest touch and you know it. It's disloyal."

"I'd never be disloyal to you, Talbot."

"But you just have been, my dear. We've got a new writer on this film I'm producing who costs a grand a week and I—me, the producer—am the last to know."

The rest of the meeting did not go so well. Talbot wanted to make Reggie "Rodrigo" Tipton squirm and he pretty much achieved his objective, he was glad to note. Reggie went back off to the set in a churlish and fractious mood. Talbot felt some mild vindication.

But he also felt the acid burn in his duodenum. Stress, confrontation, wasn't good for him but he knew that more confrontation was called for. Yorgos, this time. He told Joe he was going up to London and that he'd be back tomorrow morning.

He had the Alvis brought round from the Grand's garage and settled down for the drive up the A23. It was good to be behind the wheel, sensing the powerful thrum of the three-litre engine vibrating through the car's bodywork, admiring the wide silver bonnet in front of him "eating up" the road as the advertising brochures boasted. This model, the TF 21 drophead coupé, just a year old, could do 120 mph at full stretch. As it was, he overtook other cars and toiling lorries with effortless surges of acceleration. He smelt the new leather of the upholstered seats, his eyes flicking over the dials on the dashboard with their quivering needles like a fighter pilot on a low-level mission over hostile territory. Sometimes cars were simply wonderful: the Alvis at speed made him feel young again.

The offices of YSK Films Ltd were in Great Marlborough Street, one block to the south of Oxford Street. North Soho was how Talbot described the location when people asked him where he worked. YS was Yorgos Samsa and K was Kydd. Yorgos owned 51% of the company and, as he had once pointed out, if Talbot had insisted on his name going in first place the company would be called KYS—not an acronymic euphony to be sought, as Talbot immediately agreed. He was perfectly happy with YSK Films Ltd.

Yorgos Samsa rose from his desk as Talbot stepped into his office, his sallow face distorted in the widest of smiles. He kissed Talbot three times on his cheeks—left, right, left—and drew up a chair to the small coffee table in front of the window where informal meetings were held. Cigarettes were lit, coffee was provided. All seemed as it had always been—only the nagging semi-betrayal of Reggie and Janet Headstone tarnished the enviable good feeling between the two partners.

As a young man, barely in his twenties, Yorgos Samsa had fled Germany in 1933 on Hitler's accession to the Chancellorship and had made his way to England. That was one story. Talbot had overheard other conversations where Yorgos claimed to have been the sole survivor of a shipwreck in the Black Sea and had been offered a Nansen passport by the League of Nations; or else Yorgos had been the victim of a trumped-up court case in Transnistria, wherever that was, and had been obliged to escape Transnistrian injustice. Yorgos liked keeping his biography vague. In fact, Talbot had no clear idea what his nationality, or nationalities, was or were. He had sought an answer many times but the reply was always ambiguous: "I'm a fruit salad, Talbot, a bit of everything," or, "I come from here, I come from there," or "My parents were gypsies, Roma, they never told me." And so on. "Let's just say I'm a peculiar English gentleman—like you," Yorgos had told him once. And that was as much as Talbot had ever learned—he quickly stopped asking.

Yorgos was exceptionally fat, though his Savile Row tailors constructed immaculately cut, long-jacketed, double-breasted suits that made him look heftily solid rather than obese. His hair was dyed black and his wide face was pitted with the history of severe adolescent acne. He spoke almost excellent English with the faintest, unlocatable foreign accent. He liked to use colloquialisms as evidence of his fluency but his grasp of them was unsure.

In the 1930s, having arrived in England from somewhere in continental Europe, he secured employment in the accountancy department of Peverell Kydd's film company. His manifest talents with numbers had been spotted by Peverell and he had been swiftly promoted. When Talbot, on his father's death in 1948, had inherited the company the obvious right-hand man had to be Yorgos. And then, during a difficult financial crisis in the 1950s—Talbot married, school fees for two children, an exorbitant and unexpected tax demand and a contrary stepmother who had raided Talbot's trust fund—Yorgos had somehow raised the necessary cash to maintain solvency and the partnership was created, formally. YSK Films Ltd. was born and the company was divided with 51% in Yorgos's favour. Films were made, money was made, but the air of mystery persisted.

Before Talbot could even bring the subject up, Yorgos apologised for the Janet Headstone misunderstanding.

"It's entirely my fault, Talbot. I thought you had agreed with Reggie. I should have asked, checked." He slapped the back of one hand with the other, sharply. "Bad boy, Yorgos. But look—a horse can be led to water and we can strike gold. I'll make a small announcement to the press, to the trades: 'Janet Headstone hired to write for the *Ladder* film. Tony Blaze, Anny Viklund.' Talk-talk, chit-chatter. It's all good for us."

"Troy Blaze," Talbot said. "We'd better get that right or the Applebys will take out a contract."

"Troy, Troy, Troy. Old man's brain, Talbot."

Talbot had to agree that hiring Janet Headstone wasn't all bad news, necessarily.

"But what about Andrew Marvell?" he said. Marvell was the first writer. A difficult, impossible man.

"We just pay him more money. No credit for Headstone. He'll shut up his face. He's only interested in cash."

Yorgos went back to his desk and returned with a file.

"More important business," he said. "I have the contract for *Burning Leaves.* We own it, every job and tackle." He beamed. "You are a very, very clever man, Talbot. Your papa would be proud of you."

"Be that as it may."

Talbot opened the file to find a multi-page contract. There was a lawyer's letter paperclipped to the first page with a letterhead he didn't recognise.

"Who is—who are—Cordwainer, Goodforth and Bonvoisin?"

"Big international firm. They've done all the legal work."

"Why? What's wrong with John Saxonwood?" John Saxonwood was YSK Films' retained lawyer. An old army friend.

Yorgos leant forward and steepled his fingers.

"John Saxonwood can't practise law in California. He's fine for England but not for something as huge as *Burning Leaves.* This is the big one, Talbot, I tell you—the Pyramids, the *Titanic,* the Suez Canal. Everything changes for us, for YSK, with *Burning Leaves,* thanks to you."

After their meeting—all friends, more apologies proffered, everything settled—Talbot taxied to John Saxonwood's office in the City near the Bank of England. The place was shabby. In the waiting room parched spider plants were expiring on window ledges, year-old magazines were loosely stacked on a table, the carpet was stained. Talbot wondered if such neglect was deliberate, sending a message of some kind. One that he couldn't easily decrypt, anyway.

John Saxonwood offered him tea or whisky. Talbot thought it was time for alcohol.

"Very nice little Speyside malt I found near Forres," Saxonwood said. "Glen Feshan."

He shook a dead fly out of a tumbler and poured an inch of straw-coloured whisky into it.

"Slangevar."

Talbot took a sniff then a large sip before he ventured onto the subject of Cordwainer, Goodforth and Bonvoisin.

"I think I've encountered Goodforth. Sam M. Goodforth, if you please. American. Never heard of the others," Saxonwood said. "I can look them up. I don't think they're based in London." He wandered across to his office's bookshelves to search for some legal reference book.

John Saxonwood was very tall, six foot six, with gaunt, even features marred by a large broken nose, skewed to the left. He and Talbot had met in 1940, young subalterns in the East Sussex Light Infantry—"The Martlets," as the regiment was known—and had fought together and idled together throughout the Second World War as the Martlets had progressed through North Africa and on into Italy.

"Look, don't get me wrong," Saxonwood said as Talbot explained further. "I like Yorgos. You and he have made me a great deal of money over the years but he's talking nonsense. I can do deals in California—I do them all the time—I just hire a Californian lawyer. I could hire Goodforth if I wanted. So what's the problem? Doesn't add up."

Talbot explained further. "As you know, this play that we own—rather the film rights of this play that we own—is a very hot property."

"I know. I've seen it, remember? Is it still running?"

"Came off a month ago. More than a year on Broadway; now ten months in the West End. It's touring everywhere. Time for the film."

Saxonwood topped up their Glen Feshans.

"Well, don't sign anything unless I tell you to. Understood? I've got a funny, somewhat troubling feeling about all this. Makes my joints ache."

"Absolutely. I'll copy you in on everything."

"Delightful fellow though he is, he can be very persuasive, our Yorgos. Be warned."

"He's my partner, John. An old friend. He saved my bacon."

"That's exactly why you have to be extra careful."

"Listen, I found this play. Yorgos had nothing to do with it. We may be partners but *The Smell of Burning Leaves* was my discovery, entirely. I own it, morally speaking."

"'Morally speaking' isn't a term that lawyers recognise. Nor do film producers."

Talbot took a taxi back to the car park in Soho where he'd left the Alvis, still thinking about the strange set of circumstances that had brought him to *The Smell of Burning Leaves.*

In 1965 he had been in New York for a series of meetings. One weekend, on the Saturday, he had gone down to Greenwich Village and wandered along Christopher Street. As he strolled, he saw young men holding hands, men walking with their arms around each other's shoulders, laughing and relaxed. In a small bar he saw two men kissing openly. He felt like a ghost—a ghost from the past—or an alien: a tall, bald, suited Englishman, about to turn sixty, mingling with these young men who were now unconcernedly living, in public, what had been their secret lives before. He had felt strange—both liberated and ashamed: liberated to realise that there was nothing to stop him behaving like them if he really wanted to, and ashamed at the camouflage he had erected around himself for his protection: his demeanour, his wife, his children.

After he left the bar he took a wrong turning. It was early evening and in a side street he came across a small church that had been converted into a theatre. The play that was advertised was called *The Smell of Burning Leaves,* written by a woman called Fleur Schwartz. On a whim—he was still troubled by his Christopher Street revelation and needed distraction—he decided to buy a ticket.

Two hours later he knew he had witnessed something extraordinary. At least ten people in the small theatre—it sat about sixty, all told—had walked out noisily, outraged. That night he telephoned John Saxonwood at his home and said that on Monday morning, one way or another, YSK had to option the film rights of a play called *The Smell of Burning Leaves* by Fleur Schwartz. Money no object.

Fleur Schwartz, it turned out, was dead—a suicide at thirty-three—but her estate, in the shape of her mother, was more than happy—delighted—to grant an eighteen-month renewable option for $1,000 against a buy-out of $10,000. Talbot signed the contract a week later and paid the money. Three months later, Buck Lowry, no less, opened the play on Broadway—and the rest was theatre history. YSK was, as Yorgos put it, sitting on top of a river of gold.

What made *Burning Leaves* a scandalous, sell-out success was its subject. In a word: incest. In the play the central character, "Bud" Lagrange, develops an unhealthy sexual interest in his twenty-year-old daughter Esmerelda, who has returned to the family home after her divorce from her abusive husband, Freeborn. The milieu was white trash, Southern variety. It is high summer in some Louisiana hamlet, everyone is sweating, wearing the minimal amount of clothes that basic propriety demands. The title is explained during a conversation Bud has with a friend. He says that every time Esmerelda comes close to him he can smell her. What does she smell of? the friend asks. She smells of burning leaves, Bud replies. Eventually, after a series of increasingly fraught confrontations—Freeborn tries vainly, violently, to reclaim his bride—Bud's immoral cravings get the better of him and, one evening, drunk, he assaults his daughter at the climax of Act II and tries to rape her. Esmerelda kills her father with a kitchen knife. Standing above him, bloodied, knife in hand, she screams a feral scream of triumph. Curtain down.

Every producer, mogul, impresario and studio wanted the film rights—but they weren't available. They were owned by some small English—English!—film company in London. This totemic American play had been snapped up by the Limeys. Yorgos gleefully fielded and rejected the bids as hundreds of thousands of dollars were offered to buy the rights off YSK. At one stage when Warner Bros. raised their price to $1 million Talbot wondered if they should cash in and take their huge profit.

"No, no, no, Talbot," Yorgos said. "This happens only once in your life. The gift horse has galloped into our china shop and we will *not* look him in the mouth. We will do this, Talbot, you and me, and nobody else."

Talbot parked the Alvis by his wife's Austin 1100 on the wide gravelled forecourt of their house in Chiswick. It was brick-built, with a tile-hung upper storey and a small tower, making the roof nicely asymmetrical. The walls were embellished with various climbing plants (Virginia creeper, roses, carefully trimmed ivy) and it reeked of artistic class and solidity. Or, Talbot thought as he opened the front door, class, solidity and a bit of artistry visible in the blue-brick diapering and the timber-framed dormers.

Naomi, his wife, was on the phone in the kitchen. They blew kisses at each other as Talbot opened the fridge door looking for some tonics. He picked up a couple and moved through to the drawing room and found the gin amongst the grouped bottles on the sideboard. The wide doors to the garden were open but the sun was still blazing down and he didn't want heat. He made two gin and tonics—there was ice in the ice bucket—but he'd forgotten the lemon. He turned as Naomi came in holding a quartered lemon on a plate.

"Mind reader," Talbot said, kissing her cheek.

"You need one too, do you?" she said, picking up her drink.

"Slightly perturbing day," he said. "I'll tell you about it if it gets any more perturbing."

They hadn't seen each other for nearly two weeks, he realised, such had been the demands of the film, and Talbot was struck again, as if for the first time, by how large Naomi was becoming. A massive ledge of bosom, well-padded hips, an obvious double chin. She had never really been slender but she was clearly packing on the weight.

"How's school?" he said, sitting down and searching for a cigarette.

"Bloody. Everyone's longing for the summer holidays." She smiled. "Mustn't grumble. *C'est normal,* and all that. What about you? How's the 'fillum' going?"

"Actually, all going relatively well, considering. Which of course makes me worried. I think I hear distant thunder."

Their exchange made him realise, as it always did when they had been apart from each other for a while, how formal and semi-guarded their conversation could be. It was as if they had found themselves, strangers, sitting beside each other at a dinner party and were making small talk. Not man and wife married for twenty-six years.

"Something's fucking going on with Yorgos," he said, deliberately coarsening his vocabulary, all in an attempt to make their conversation seem more natural.

"Isn't there always something fucking going on with Yorgos?" Naomi said, with a thin smile, as if rising to the challenge. She didn't like Yorgos.

"Yes. But this seems unusually subversive. I haven't got to the bottom of it, yet. All to do with the play. I can't see what his plan is at the moment."

"Well, I'm sure you'll sort it out. You always do." She opened a glossy burr-walnut box sitting on the coffee table and took out a cigarette herself, screwing it into a short ebony holder. Talbot leant forward and clicked on his lighter for her.

"Humphrey's coming in an hour or so," she said, pluming smoke at the ceiling. "Let's all go out for supper."

Humphrey was their son.

"I've got to get back to Brighton, dammit. Night shoot. I'm expected."

"Well, he's here for a week. He has a concert at the Festival Hall next Saturday."

"Mustn't miss that," Talbot said. "Put it in the diary. I'll make sure I have to come up to town."

That pleased Naomi. She stood and went to the mantlepiece to fetch a postcard, handing it to him. Talbot saw a long thin waterfall in a verdant, lush forest. He turned it over and read its brief platitudes. It was from his daughter.

"What is Zoë doing in New Zealand?" he asked. "I thought she was in Singapore."

"She's teaching children to ski."

"Do they ski in New Zealand?"

"Apparently."

Talbot thought of Zoë when she was a little girl. Spry, adventurous, funny—always making him laugh. Now she was as far away from her family as was geographically possible, always travelling, always out of reach. At least Humphrey was still in the country—diffident, tortured Humphrey.

"Is Humphrey staying here?" he asked.

"Silly question. Of course he is—it's free."

He asked how Humphrey was getting on in Manchester. He played timpani for the Hallé Orchestra.

"He loves it, he says." Naomi ground out her cigarette in an ashtray. "Prefers it to London, he says."

Talbot poured himself another small gin. Careful. Driving.

"You're not overdoing it, are you, darling?" he asked. "You look a bit tired."

"Of course I'm overdoing it. The special headmistress tax—a millstone fitted to the neck, free of charge. I'm just like you: a kind of producer with a team of people who seem determined to let me down, one way or another, time and again."

Talbot laughed—genuinely. And Naomi laughed with him and for a moment the formality—the manufactured intimacy—disappeared and, as she laughed, he caught a shadowy glimpse of his wife as she was when he first met her in the early years of the war. My God, Talbot thought: how your life gallops by.

"I'd better be going," he said.

He kissed her goodbye at the front door, saying he'd telephone in a day or two, climbed into the Alvis and pulled away onto the main road—but did not turn towards Brighton, instead he headed for Primrose Hill.

He parked the Alvis some distance away around the corner and walked back to his flat, letting himself in through the garden door—his usual point of entry. That way he never confronted his neighbours, who were virtually unknown to him, anyway, and vice versa. He probably entered the building's front door once or twice a year.

He owned the downstairs maisonette of a large end-of-terrace early Victorian stucco house in a quiet street off King Henry's Road. It had a small garden with a door that gave on to a mews lane behind. He crossed the garden—a square of weedy lawn, with a border of hortensias and an ancient apple tree with a mossy wooden bench around the trunk—and let himself in through the back door. His bedroom, bathroom and darkroom were at this lower-ground-floor level. Upstairs, the ground floor, was roomier and grander. A kitchen-diner, a drawing room with two eight-paned windows that looked on to the street and the garden and another room that had been the master bedroom, he supposed. It was now designated as his "gallery."

The flat was sparsely but tastefully furnished. No curtains—the interior folding wooden shutters were in good condition—dark-stained floorboards with Persian rugs, a Knole sofa and a couple of loose-covered armchairs. There were a few black and white photographs on the walls—a contorted Bill Brandt nude on a beach, a Cartier-Bresson, an Ingrid Soames picture of two roses—but nothing really that would reveal the personality of the man who owned the property.

The name by the bell push for flat A said "Eastman." His neighbours (there were four flats carved out of the two floors above his) called him "Mr. Eastman" on their rare encounters, usually to do with communal repairs to guttering or roof. He was almost as anonymous as it was possible to be in this day and age, he supposed, and he took pains to ensure that this remained the status quo. No one knew when he came or went, thanks to the garden door. He had a telephone that rarely rang. He paid all utility bills by cash—he had even bought the flat for cash, £12,500, asking John Saxonwood to provide it, no questions asked. For all he knew the electoral register had him down as "Mr. Eastman." He never received any mail that he hadn't initiated. The key purpose of being Mr. Eastman of Primrose Hill was not so much that the set-up allowed him to be by himself but to discover what self he was, in fact. And, he wondered, what exactly was that "self" that he hid away so diligently, that private self? It was an ongoing experiment, and one he relished.

He switched on the lights—the shutters in the drawing room were almost permanently closed—and had a swift check around to see that all was in order. Then he unbuttoned his fly and took out his cock. He walked around the room and poured himself a whisky and drained it in one gulp. Then he took off all his clothes and folded them on an armchair. Naked, he poured himself another large Scotch, sat down on the other armchair and smoked a cigarette, thinking, imagining. When he felt the mood was right he found the keys in their secret hiding place and unlocked first, the padlock, and then the two mortice locks to the gallery and went inside. He locked the door behind him.

II

Anny Viklund waited at the bus stop, blinking in the harsh Brighton sunshine. That's why they call it Brighton, Troy had said, because of the brightness. It's very bright here because we're so close to the sea. Bright Town. She had laughed—but now he was gone, back to his trailer as her big scene with him was over, in the can.

She had had to slap his face, then jump out of their yellow Mini, give a wild flinging look around her and then run away, heedlessly. Now, alone in this strange town, Emily Bracegirdle had to board a bus and she had no money.

Anny looked around her—at this street in Brighton. She saw a cinema called the Curzon and an uneven row of buildings with shops at street level: a Wimpy Bar, a bank, a chemist and a piano shop. Small English cars whizzed by.

"Action!" the first assistant director shouted and the cream-and-red-liveried bus shuddered into life and headed towards the bus stop.

A curious crowd of local spectators held back by portable metal barriers looked on at this motion picture being shot in their town. Out of the corner of her eye Anny could see Rodrigo Tipton crouching behind the big camera set on its track.

The bus stopped and two extras boarded.

"Go, Anny!" Rodrigo shouted and Anny climbed onto the platform at the rear. The bus pulled away.

"Great! Cut! Let's do it once more."

As Anny stepped back off the bus she wondered if Troy would come to her room again tonight. He hadn't said anything after their face-slapping scene had ended—she hoped she hadn't hit him too hard—but she was looking forward to seeing him again. It was funny, but being with Troy at night, secretly, with no one having the least idea, was making this film—a film that she had never particularly wanted to do—the most enjoyable film-making experience of her career thus far.

The bus effortfully backed up to its starting position. Anny took her place beside the extras in the shelter of the bus stop. While they waited for everything to be reset she looked incuriously at the Brighton folk who had gathered to stare at these film stars and actors at work, men, women and children, silent, watching fixedly.

Then she saw Cornell Weekes.

12

Elfrida hadn't even had her first drink of the day when the idea came to her, just like that, naturally, spontaneously. She was on the point of reaching for the carton of orange juice when it arrived—a revelation, an answer, an antidote. Nothing to do with alcohol, just her brain working independently. How marvellous. She made herself an extra-strong Sarson's and orange, toasted herself, drank a couple of mouthfuls just to start the engine, as it were, and went in search of her notebook.

VIRGINIA WOOLF'S LAST DAY, she wrote in capitals. Then: THE LAST DAY OF VIRGINIA WOOLF. Maybe that was better, had more of an admonitory, classic ring to it. No need to make her mind up just yet, it was the concept that was key.

Not wasting any time, she called a taxi from the local Rottingdean firm that she used and told the driver to take her to the "best" bookshop in Brighton. In the event, the bookshop he chose turned out to be in Hove, Brighton's grander, statelier, sister town, off Portland Road, near the shabby, tired green space that was Davis Park. The Book Nook, as it was named, was a small shop and seemed too small for her purposes, she worried. Still, it was a start, she was actually taking steps.

Elfrida disliked bookshops since her writer's block had begun. They seemed to her to be threatening, mocking spaces, almost as if the profusion of books on display was a personal rebuke, a pointed slur and reminder of her endless inactivity. As she stepped inside she saw that the place strove to live up to its name. Not only were the high shelves crammed but every available surface, every nook and cranny, was piled with books, apparently randomly, though a quick glance told her that the shelves at least possessed some notional order as she saw labels advertising photography, art, travel.

The Book Nook was a long narrow bright shop lit by two big skylights. Shelves ran down each side and there was a thin refectory table in the middle where the books were piled, as well as on window ledges and various stools. At the far end was a high desk and behind it a young man sat reading. He wore a beret and had a pointed beard, waxed at the tip, Elfrida saw as she approached, and the tip had a jade, or at least a jade-coloured, bead threaded on to it.

Elfrida pretended to browse—she was the only customer and the young man took no notice of her, not even a "good morning," she observed with faint disapproval. She found the fiction section where there was a fair sampling of Mrs. Woolf's novels and, she spotted with some alarm, the distinctive magenta spine of *The Big Show.* She left it untouched and interrupted the young man to ask where she might find "biography" and was directed up an iron spiral staircase to a small mezzanine floor above the desk, equally crammed, where biography shared shelves with "local interest" and "cookery." Heading for W she found several volumes of Leonard Woolf's autobiography but saw, disappointingly, that volume four ended in 1939—two years too early. Damn.

She carefully clambered back down to the ground floor and told the young man that she was looking for a biography of Virginia Woolf.

"I don't think there is one, actually," he said. "Nobody's much interested in that Bloomsbury lot."

"Oh. How odd."

"There is Holroyd's biography of Lytton Strachey, volume one. Volume two's imminent. He knew Woolf. Strachey, I mean."

"Yes, but Strachey died in 1932," Elfrida said.

"Did he? Poor chap."

"And, do you see, I'm particularly interested in the . . . ah, the last year of Virginia Woolf's life. 1941."

The young man fiddled with the jade bead attached to his beard, frowning, thinking.

"There is *A Writer's Diary.* Her journals—edited by her husband."

"That might be exactly what I need. Have you got it?"

"It's out of print, published in the '50s. I could try and find it and order it."

"Marvellous. If you would. Very kind." Elfrida saw this as a good sign. She began to warm slightly to the taciturn young man.

"Maybe you'd best check out the obituaries," he said.

"Excellent idea."

"Why are you so interested in the end of Woolf's life, may I ask?"

"Well. Because I'm a teacher," Elfrida improvised. "A lecturer in English literature, actually, at . . ." She chose a distant institution, "the University of Aberdeen."

The young man sat up straight.

"In fact, come to think of it, I might have something."

He scampered clangingly up the spiral staircase and descended a minute later with a small pamphlet. He handed it to her.

"It's by a local author," he said. "Privately printed."

Elfrida looked at the title. *Virginia Woolf's East Sussex* by Maitland Bole. She flicked through it—sixty pages or so, blurry photographs, rather a good map.

"A local author?"

"He lives in Eastbourne."

"I'll take it. Do you know him?"

"He pops in from time to time with his stock. He churns out these pamphlets. You know, *Henry James's Rye, Literary Life in Romney Marsh, Kipling and Burwash,* et cetera."

"Fascinating." Elfrida handed over some change—the pamphlet cost four shillings and sixpence, a bit steep, she thought—still, it was a start, a symbol of her intent.

"I'll need a name and a phone number," the young man said, now staring at her fixedly.

"Why?"

"You're ordering a book," he said patiently. "I'll need to let you know when it arrives."

"Of course. Silly me."

He pushed a notepad and a pen at her across his desk and she wrote down her name—Jennifer Tipton, not Elfrida Wing—and the phone number of the Rottingdean house.

"Thank you for that," Elfrida said, suddenly very keen to leave. "Head fizzing with Virginia Woolf, at the moment. Thank you so much." She grabbed her pamphlet, smiled and turned away, feeling breathless all of a sudden. That was what happened when she went into a bookshop—she should keep away from them. She needed a drink.

Once settled in the Repulse, a double gin and tonic in front of her, Elfrida contemplated Maitland Bole's pamphlet. Virginia Woolf had committed suicide on Friday 28 March 1941 by drowning herself in the River Ouse in East Sussex. According to the detailed map in Bole's pamphlet, the Woolf house in the village of Rodmell was on the edge of the Ouse Valley. Bole wrote: "There are few more evocative and inspiring views than the valley of the Sussex Ouse between Lewes and Newhaven. At dawn the vast water meadows can take on a near-mystical character. 'O Albion, how do I love thee' is the thought that comes to my mind when, of an early morn, walking with my dog, Trebizond, the ethereal mists that waft gently in the golden rays of the rising sun turn the whole scene into a tableau of—"

Elfrida closed the pamphlet. She was feeling very strange, though she recognised the sensations. She was inspired, that's what it was, creative juices were beginning to flow, feeding her imagination. It was like one of those speeded-up sequences in television documentaries when drops of rain begin to dampen the parched craquelure of a dried-out riverbed: mud forms, water trickles, quickens, then becomes a torrent. *The Last Day of Virginia Woolf* was going to be her salvation, she knew it. In celebration, elated, she finished her gin and tonic in a series of large gulps. First things first. A trip to the village of Rodmell was a matter of urgency and then a pensive stroll along the banks of the River Ouse.

13

Just walk along the Prom, Rodrigo had told her, you won't notice or be aware of the cameras. Just do your own thing, stop, look out to sea. Take all the time you need. We'll have three cameras on you, long lenses. The people around you won't know you're being filmed. Are you sure? Anny asked. What if somebody recognises me? They won't, believe me, Rodrigo insisted. So Anny did as he instructed, she put on her sunglasses, stepped out of the car into Brighton's gull-clawed air, and walked along the esplanade from Waterloo Street to Regency Square and, just as Rodrigo had promised, nobody gawped at her, did a double take, or stopped her and asked for her autograph. Maybe it's my new black hair, she wondered. Or maybe I'm just not as famous here as I am in the States.

She sauntered along, stopping from time to time, looked at a revolving rack of postcards, paused to listen to a busker, skirted a whelk stall and wandered aimlessly along until she reached Shirley, her assistant, who guided her into her car that whisked her back to Waterloo Street to do it all over again. Rodrigo asked her not to stop at the busker as this whole sequence was designed to go under music, a song from the Beatles, or Dangerous Play, or the Pretty Things, Pink Floyd, the Rolling Stones, Antarctica, the Kinks or the Troggs, he said, confidently dropping names at random, or whoever they could afford.

Anny was happy to oblige and set off again, thinking that it was almost like being a normal person, walking like this, unrecognised and unpestered, amongst the holidaymakers, looking down at the shingle beach at the moms and the dads and the kids screaming in the shallow surf. At one stage in her stroll along the front she thought: I could be living a life like this—an ordinary person—if only Gianluca Mavrocordato hadn't cast me, fresh out of my sophomore year in college, in *Aquarius Days,* and thereby changed my life forever. The thought made her sad, suddenly. But in that case, she realised, she would never have met Troy Blaze. There were always compensations, if you looked hard enough.

After the third perambulation along the esplanade she was taken back to the unit base where she saw the tall producer, Talbot Kydd, waiting for her outside her caravan.

"Anny, good morning," he said, smiling politely. "Can I whisk you away for half an hour? Rather urgent."

"Why? What is it?"

"The police want to talk to you. About your husband. I thought it best to be discreet—so we should go to the production office."

At the production office—Anny was surprised to see it was an ordinary house in an ordinary street—she was shown into a front room, full of plastic chairs, where she declined the offer of a cup of coffee or tea. She felt calm: she had decided to say nothing. In fact, she was beginning to wonder if she had been hallucinating when she thought she had seen Cornell in the crowd that day when they were filming at the bus stop. She had looked away and looked back but there had been no sign of him. Autosuggestion, she supposed—triggered by the mention of his name. She lit a cigarette, had a couple of puffs, then put it out. An unordered cup of coffee was brought to her, nevertheless—it looked disgusting. It had brown congealed blobs of undissolved coffee powder floating on the surface.

The door opened and two men were shown in. One of them, she could tell instantly, was American—the cut of his jacket, the button-down shirt, the shiny penny loafers gave him away. The other was English, young, stout, with sideburns and a thin drooping moustache.

"Miss Viklund, thank you for seeing us," the Englishman said. "I'm Detective Inspector Desmondson, Special Branch."

"What's Special Branch?"

He didn't answer, just carried on with his introductions.

"This is Agent Radetski."

Agent Radetski was a small wiry man, also young, with a crew cut and a lopsided smile that he was trying to straighten as he offered his hand and showed her his badge with the other. She looked at it. Federal Bureau of Investigation. She felt her mouth go dry.

Desmondson arranged three plastic chairs in a rough triangle and they sat down.

Agent Radetski cleared his throat.

"I believe you're aware that your husband, Cornell Weekes, is a fugitive," he began.

"He's not my husband."

"Forgive me: your ex-husband."

"I haven't seen him for nearly two years. I really know nothing about him, what he's doing or his whereabouts. We're not in touch at all. I didn't even know he was in prison." This wasn't true but she wanted to erect the stoutest of stone walls around herself.

"We believe he's in England," Desmondson interjected. "We have fairly good, positive sightings of him landing at Dover on a ferry from France."

"He flew from Montreal to Lisbon, Portugal, a week or ten days ago," Radetski said. "That much we can be sure of."

"I don't care," Anny said. "You might as well tell me that Sirhan Sirhan was a fugitive. It means as much to me."

The two men glanced at each other.

"We're concerned that he may try to make contact here with you in Brighton," Radetski said. "Do you mind if I smoke?"

"Be my guest."

Both Radetski and Desmondson lit cigarettes.

"Why would he make contact with me?" Anny said, keeping her voice level. "We divorced. I've had nothing—nothing—to do with him since our divorce. He's sort of a non-person to me." She paused. "It was a strange divorce—but entirely his idea, not mine. He didn't want to be married to me any more—he hated me working in the movie business. That's where we are. Why would he make contact?"

"When you're on the run," Radetski said, patiently, as if talking to a backward child, "when you're on our 'most wanted' list, when Interpol has been alerted throughout Europe—you get desperate."

"Any port in a storm," DI Desmondson said, with a sympathetic smile.

"He won't come near me," Anny said with some vehemence. "I don't hate him, but too much has happened. Too much water under the bridge, if you know what I mean."

"I would just ask you to be on your guard," Radetski said.

"If you see him, if you see any trace of him, if he tries to contact you, please let us know." Desmondson leant forward and gave her his card. "Twenty-four hours a day."

She took it without looking at it.

"What exactly did he do?" she asked, feigning ignorance, the better to protect herself, she thought. "I know he set off a bomb."

Radetski sighed. "He planted three bombs, in fact. One outside a San Diego recruiting station for the U.S. military, one at the Pasadena Republican Party office, and one at the gatehouse of Fort Mitchell, Nevada. Only one detonated—at Fort Mitchell—two soldiers were wounded, one seriously—lost both his legs. The other bombs were disarmed—his fingerprints were all over them."

"Why? My God. Why would he do this? What was he—"

"There was a kind of press release, to coincide with the bombings, sent to the *LA Times* and the *San Francisco Chronicle.* He said he was declaring war against the American Reich and invited the population to rise up and join him."

Anny felt weak—a hollowing-out inside of her, as if her guts had been removed. Cornell—how fucked up could one person be?

"Is he insane?" she said quietly.

"I suspect not. But we won't know for sure until we apprehend him."

The meeting was over; the detectives carefully stubbed out their cigarettes and Agent Radetski asked Anny for her autograph—for his daughter.

14

"Is she all right?" Talbot asked Joe.

"She's gone a bit quiet," Joe said. "So we've pushed back her shooting today. I took her to the hotel. Rodrigo thought it best that she had the afternoon off. Big scene tomorrow."

"What's that?"

"The love scene with Troy."

"God. The nude scene?"

"There's still some debate about that," Joe said—but he couldn't hide his curiosity. "What exactly did the police say, boss?"

"This fellow on the run from the FBI, Cornell Weekes, may be heading to Brighton."

"Seriously?"

"Anny's the only person he knows in this country. They were married, briefly, apparently. It's a bit worrying . . ."

Joe looked impressed. "And that was an FBI agent, was it, in the office? Blimey."

"Just what we need—an FBI fugitive." He looked heavenwards, as if beseeching the gods of cinema to spare him.

"Oh, yes," Joe said. "Sylvia Slaye would like to see you."

Talbot felt his ulcer burn.

"Where is she?"

"Costumes."

Talbot walked over to the day's unit base that was set up in a municipal car park near Chapel Street. As he approached he saw the usual untidy cluster of vehicles—actors' trailers, catering and lavatory facilities, hair and make-up and costumes in their larger trucks with steps extending from the rear, and all manner of vans and lorries parked hither and thither, filled with arc lights and cables and camera equipment. A bit like a battalion headquarters, he always thought, with a very lazy adjutant, who hadn't heard of parallel lines.

He climbed the steps to costumes like a man going to the scaffold. He had worked with Sylvia Slaye before so he knew what to expect.

"I'm not decent, darling!" she shrieked as he came through the door.

Before he turned away he caught a glimpse of folds of white flesh, red panties and a red bra and a mop of peroxide-bleached hair emerging through the collar of a purple-sequinned dress.

"You can turn around now, you dirty old man, you."

He turned. Sylvia was tugging at and smoothing down the creases of her dress over her haunches. She hadn't lost any weight since their last meeting, he saw. She wrapped a pink feather boa round her neck.

"Ta-dah!" she exclaimed, flinging her arms wide.

They kissed. Talbot took a step back. The dress was far too tight for her plump frame and there was a lot of cleavage on display. The hem was short—mid-thigh.

"What do you think?" Sylvia said, striking a pose.

"You're meant to be a housewife, you know, Sylvia. You look like . . . You're too . . . glamorous."

"Come off it, Talbie. That's what they want from Sylvia Slaye—a bit of glamour in their sad little lives."

He smiled. He would have to have a word with Rodrigo. This was absurd.

She was now sitting down on a stool forcing her feet into stilettoes, the pressure of her extended arms deepening the deep crease between her breasts. To think she was known as the English Brigitte Bardot once, Talbot thought, remembering her in her heyday in the '50s when they had worked together on *Sudden Death in Soho.* She had specialised in gangsters' molls and doomed "ladies of the night" in a few cheap and lurid thrillers before she had struck box-office gold in a series of films about a character called Milly Jenkins. *Milly Jenkins*

Goes Camping, Milly Jenkins Gets Married, Milly Jenkins Joins the Army and half a dozen others, all saucy British comedies, packed with sexual innuendo and frequent glimpses of Sylvia's increasingly ample curves.

He remembered now—it was the Applebys who had insisted on Sylvia. The Applebys with their distant but potent and unignorable influence. Talbot offered Sylvia a hand as she rose unsteadily to her feet. She was playing Mrs. Bracegirdle, Emily's mother. Ferdie Meares was Mr. Bracegirdle.

"I always thought you were a mean, penny-pinching bastard, Talbot Kydd," a man's voice came from behind him.

As if on cue, Ferdie Meares wandered into costumes, his wide, insincere smile meant to indicate he was joking. He was wearing an orange-hued tweed suit as if he'd come up to town from some rural fastness. "I don't know what persuaded me to accept your miserable offer."

"You're at liberty to turn it down, Ferdie, dear chap. Nobody wants to force you to be in this film."

"And pass up the chance of our screen reunion? Do me a favour, sunshine." Meares went and stood by Sylvia, putting his arm around her and kissing her wetly on a cheek. He was an abnormally thin man with a weak chin, beaky nose and protruding eyes. He had been the put-upon foil of a comic duo in variety shows—Moore and Meares—that had ended on Moore's sudden and premature death. However, Ferdie went on to make a good living in films, playing the prissy, fussy comic fool in innumerable British movies—the ineffectual teacher, the officious clerk at the Labour Exchange, the inept soldier who couldn't march, and so on. A singularly unpleasant individual, Talbot thought, forcing a smile.

"Always happy to have you on board, Ferdie," he lied.

"I shall just have to get my reward in heaven," Meares said, smiling back with dead eyes.

"You wanted to see me, Sylvia," Talbot said, turning to her.

"Yes . . . We're not happy with our accommodation," she said. "Are we, Ferdie?"

"Nor our means of transportation, come to that," Ferdie added.

Talbot turned them over to Joe. They were only required for a couple of days' filming but they wanted suites in the Metropole and their own cars with drivers, permanently available. Neither perk was in their contracts, but what the hell. Talbot wandered back to the Grand feeling strangely depressed. Sylvia and Ferdie were all wrong, completely wrong, nobody would believe them as Anny Viklund's parents and, moreover, he knew that Reggie "Rodrigo" Tipton hadn't half the force of personality necessary to combat their massive egos and their proliferating demands. Perhaps they could be cut out in the edit, he thought, trying to console himself.

He had the Alvis brought round and, settled behind the wheel, headed east along the coast road towards Rye. He needed this time away from *Emily Bracegirdle's Extremely Useful Ladder to the Moon.* Back to my world, he thought, and an interlude of sanity.

15

"But you told me you were divorced," Troy said. "So why would he come looking for you?"

Anny closed her eyes, feeling like crying again.

"I don't fucking know. He's very confused. He planted three bombs. He's declared war against the U.S."

"Bloody hell," Troy said. "Why did you marry him? Sounds a complete nutter."

"He was different," Anny said. "He was like no one I'd ever met. Passionate about everything." Then in a spasm of honesty added, "He reminded me of my father."

She watched Troy frown, clearly trying to come to terms with this concept. They were lying in bed in Anny's suite, it was late, well after midnight. Troy had brought his usual bottle of wine with him but Anny hadn't drunk any. She had taken two Equanils after the interview with the detectives, she had been so shaken by their unwelcome news.

"What did your dad do?" Troy asked.

"What?"

"What was his job?"

"He was a pharmacist."

"What's that? Some kind of farmer?"

"You call them chemists, I think."

"Oh, yeah. Right. Was that in Sweden?"

"No. It was in a place called Lake Harbo, in Minnesota." She turned to face Troy and snuggled into him as he folded his arms around her. "In America. I'm American. My dad was a 'chemist' in Lake Harbo. He had his own shop—Viklund Pharmacy. The place is full of Swedish immigrants."

"Have you got any brothers or sisters?"

"I've got a brother, two years older than me: Lars."

"Weird name! Lars . . ."

"Yeah. Unlike Troy."

"What does he do?"

"He's in the army, in Vietnam."

Anny told Troy a short version of her history. Born in Lake Harbo, Minnesota in 1940, not far from Minneapolis. Father named Kurt; mother named Hilma. Everything was fine until Hilma had an affair with a man called Melker Eliasson and went back to Sweden with him. The war was over. Two years later Hilma Viklund died in a car crash. Anny, who had no tangible memory of her mother, and brother Lars were brought up by their aunt, Kurt's sister, Sigrid. Anny graduated from Lake Harbo High School and went to Rosenberg College to study Veterinary Science. She liked acting and was in the college's amateur dramatic society. One day, on a whim, she went to Minneapolis to audition for a film by Gianluca Mavrocordato. Mavrocordato chose her from 1,000 girls that he'd seen in his countrywide search for a new star. She played the lead in his film *Aquarius Days* and her life was changed forever.

"And here I am," she whispered, "in bed with the famous Troy Blaze."

"Sometimes you get lucky," Troy said and kissed her.

"You'd better go," she said. "We've got our big day tomorrow."

"Are you going to do it?"

"I've done it before. I did it in *Hotel Nights.* Rodrigo says they'll only see my ass, not my boobs. Big deal."

"I'll get naked as well, if you like."

"I like." Now she kissed him.

"But I might get carried away," he said.

"I doubt it—you've got twenty guys standing by the bed."

"Yeah. Suppose so." He thought for a while. "What exactly do you have to do?"

"Get out of bed—nude—and walk to the window and look out. Cut."

"I could come and stand with you at the window."

"That would be neat. Ask Rodrigo. I'm sure if the audience see your ass as well as mine we can't fail."

"I will. Yeah. You wait and see." Troy sat up and ruffled his hair with both hands. "Fuck it." He slipped out of bed and began to pull on his clothes, nodding to himself as if mulling something over, something important. He sat down again and took her hand.

"Listen," he said, "on our next day off would you like to come and meet my mum and dad?"

"Sure," she said, without thinking. Then she thought: why does Troy want me to meet his parents? She looked at him—he was smiling. She thought again: because that's the sort of thing Troy Blaze would do. There was no guile, no hidden plan. "Do they live near here?" she asked.

"A town called Swindon. We can get there and back in a day."

"That would be great," she said. "Really great," she added sincerely. "I'd like that, thank you. See Swindon and die."

16

Colonel Ivo Stuart-Hay MC, DSO and bar, lived in a rectory about two miles from Rye off the aptly named Military Road on the way to Appledore. It was a classic rectory of sand-coloured brick set in a landscaped park of six acres. The house was described in *The Buildings of England* as "severe and elegant" and had two storeys, five eight-paned bays and an off-centre Tuscan–Doric porch. Severe and elegant would also describe the colonel, Talbot thought, who was without doubt—in and out of uniform—the best-dressed man he had ever known.

Talbot pulled in to one side of the porch and, stepping out of the Alvis, looked out over the park, with its carefully grouped and positioned beeches, oaks and chestnuts, towards the stump of an ivy-choked deer tower that the colonel described as his "folly." It was very quiet, no sound of traffic from Military Road, the day was warm and a slow convoy of small high clouds dawdled east towards continental Europe. Maybe this was what he needed, Talbot wondered to himself, some sort of civilised retreat. The busy world wasn't far away—it had taken him just over two hours from Brighton—and you could venture forth to find it whenever the mood took you.

"Major Kydd, welcome."

Talbot turned to see the colonel's former army servant, George Trelawny, step out of the front door. Trelawny was a small, powerfully built man—in his fifties now, Talbot supposed—and was wearing a red-striped t-shirt and faded jeans.

They shook hands, familiarly. Talbot had met him several times since Trelawny had left the regiment but it was always something of a shock to see him out of uniform.

"The colonel's round at the back with the dogs. Shall we be goin'?" Trelawny had never lost his West Country burr.

They walked around the side of the rectory to find a big tarred and weatherboarded barn with a red-tiled roof. Half a dozen chicken-wire cages were built onto one side. In the cages, small black dogs scampered around in the sunshine.

"How's it all going, George?" Talbot asked.

"Can't breed enough of them," George said. "Got a two-year waiting list."

Talbot approached the nearest cage. Four French bulldogs rushed forward jumping up to put their paws on the wire, tongues lolling. Ugly little things, Talbot thought. He had once asked the colonel why, of all the dogs available to him in the world, he had decided to breed French bulldogs. They hardly ever bark, the colonel had said, simple as that. Talbot looked at the cages, calculating that there must be close to forty dogs running about. Low doors had been cut in the weatherboarding so they could retreat inside to the barn or be corralled there. They were indeed quiet dogs, he realised, only an enthusiastic panting, snuffling sound emanating from them. Made sense. Then Colonel Stuart-Hay emerged from the main barn door, Talbot managing to prevent himself from giving a reflexive salute. He'd served through the war with Stuart-Hay, commander of the 2nd Battalion of the East Sussex Light Infantry, until the colonel was wounded south of Rome. Talbot had been his intelligence officer and they, perforce, had spent many, many months in each other's company.

They shook hands. Stuart-Hay was wearing a navy blazer with cavalry twills and highly polished ankle-length riding boots. He had a red silk cravat at his throat, his wiry grey hair was parted on the left and combed flat with some kind of oil or Macassar. His black eyepatch only added to his lean and craggy allure. He must be almost seventy now, Talbot realised: central casting, he thought, a perfect member of the intellectual English warrior class—except in one crucial regard.

"How're you doing, Talbot?" Stuart-Hay asked with a grin. "Not ground you down yet?"

"Oh, they're trying."

As they walked back to the house Talbot told them about the visit of Special Branch and the FBI to the set.

"Not your everyday occurrence, I can see," Stuart-Hay said.

"Poor girl," Talbot said, "she's putting a brave face on it but I think she's very shaken up. Lot of extra stress for her."

Inside, the rectory reflected the severe and elegant taste that the facade possessed. Fawn parquet flooring with navy rugs, sensible, comfortable armchairs and sofas and a few unremarkable oil landscapes on the walls. The abiding impression, Talbot always thought, was one of almost manic cleanliness. George Trelawny's army training, he assumed. No dogs were allowed inside.

They sat in the drawing room and George mixed them all powerful martinis. The icy gin was exactly what Talbot required and it seemed to make the colonel unusually chatty. They gossiped about their army colleagues and the colonel demolished a new book that had recently appeared about the 8th Army in Italy—"95% rubbish" was the verdict. George disappeared into the kitchen to prepare lunch and he duly summoned them into the dining room.

They had smoked salmon to start, then roast lamb with peas and boiled potatoes, with a very good claret, Pichon-Longueville '58. Pudding was raspberries and cream and half a Stilton was brought out to go with the port. They spent ten minutes with pen and paper revisiting and analysing a skirmish that the battalion had been involved in at Wadi Musa in 1942—the colonel was finally writing his memoirs.

"I've all my old intelligence notes back in London," Talbot said. "I'd have brought them with me if I'd known."

"Actually, they might be very useful. Marvellous. The battalion history is so bloody vague—one wants precise numbers, actual names, what the weather was like."

"Long time ago, Ivo. We're all getting old, memory fading."

"True, but not entirely decrepit."

George stood up and said he was going to deliver two French bulldog pups to a buyer in Ramsgate. He should be back by six, he said.

"Nice to see you again, sir," he said to Talbot, then corrected himself. "Talbot."

He went over to the colonel and kissed him on the lips.

"Drive carefully, darling," the colonel said. "Remember there's nothing more dangerous than a country road."

After George had left the colonel topped up their glasses of port and they went back through to the drawing room. The colonel lit a small cigar, Talbot a cigarette.

"How's your 'life,' Talbot?" the colonel asked, knowingly. "How's your 'undeveloped heart,' as I think you once described it to me?"

Talbot picked up the inference.

"Oh, it's developing," he said, and allowed himself a suggestive smile.

"Glad to hear it."

"Nothing much has changed. I'm still taking my photographs. Some of the young chaps are very sweet."

"Women?"

"There are some models. One or two professionals. I haven't quite lost my taste. I'm very particular, though."

"Always were a dark horse, Talbot."

"We're all dark horses, aren't we? All mysteries."

The colonel considered this remark, with a slight frown on his face, as if he were giving it the benefit of serious thought.

"I suppose nothing lasts very long, though," the colonel said.

"No. A day or two at the most. A couple of them have come back but I don't encourage it. And that's for the best. How I like it."

"Well, we can do anything now," the colonel said. "Since the blessed Act."

"I know. I just wish it had a different name, you know. 'The 1967 Sexual Offences Act.' Why not 'Sexual Nature Act'? 'Sexual Orientation Act'? I never assumed I was giving 'offence.'" He paused. "It's still illegal in the military. Just as well we're all retired."

"Exactly," the colonel said. "Never really thought about it that way." He looked at Talbot, knowingly. "So—are you taking advantage of our new liberties?"

"I'm quite happy with my set-up. With my 'life.'"

"What about Naomi?"

"I don't think she has any real idea."

The colonel tapped ash off his cigar.

"She must have *some* idea, surely. Women have an instinct," he said. "She must know you're queer. My mother knew about me from the age of eight, she claimed. Though she never said a word. Told me on her deathbed."

"We live and let live, Naomi and I," Talbot said. "All very civilised."

The colonel poured himself another port. Talbot declined: he had to return to the film set, he said.

On the gravel outside the front door the colonel stopped him just as he was about to slide into the driver's seat of the Alvis.

"Last week I went with George to a club in Brighton—George took me—called the Icebox."

"The Icebox?"

"It was quite a revelation," the colonel said, thoughtfully. "To be in that place with our people, our 'folk,' as it were. No holds barred, no risk, no scandal. All legal. I never thought I'd live to see it."

"I suppose it is remarkable. The change in the law, I mean."

"You should go, Talbot. These young people—they're not like us, our generation. Scales fall from your eyes. Just pop in for ten minutes. It's very relaxed, not at all threatening or unbalancing, if you know what I mean. I found it . . ." The colonel searched for a word. "Rather wonderful, inspiring."

"Not sure if it's exactly my cup of tea." Talbot paused, trying to imagine the colonel in a place such as the Icebox, whatever it was like. He realised that he had no idea what constituted such a club; what he was imagining was culled from some film he had seen, pre-1967, of course. Then, emboldened by the direction their discussion had taken, he asked a question he'd never asked before.

"Please don't answer this if you don't want to, Ivo. Tell me to mind my own fucking business, but, during the war, were you and George . . . ?" He didn't finish.

"Of course," the colonel said, candidly. "We were very discreet, very, very careful, but we both knew at once what our . . . our feelings were for each other. I fell in love with him almost immediately. Simple as that."

"I see," Talbot said. "Personally, I never had, not for one split second, the faintest idea."

"Which was my—our—absolute intention." He smiled. "I never had the faintest idea about you, either, I have to tell you. Handsome devil, almost turned my head."

They laughed.

"Rather a marvellous story. And now you're both here, living together, working together," Talbot said.

"We couldn't be happier. I couldn't be happier. The world sometimes moves in mysteriously appropriate ways."

They shook hands.

"Nothing ventured, nothing gained, Talbot. Remember that. We're not here for long—make the most of it."

"I'll bear it in mind."

"Anyone you know want a Frenchie? Loyal little dogs. You can jump the queue. Good discount."

Talbot drove away, his head full of the subtext of the colonel's words. He had hoped this lunch would be a relaxing interlude, a trip down memory and military lane, but it had shaken him up, somewhat. Nothing ventured, nothing gained.

Suddenly, spontaneously, as he reached Rye, he turned east and drove past Rye harbour to Camber and Camber Sands. As he parked his car at the Sands' car park he could see that the tide was out and the immense beach stretched away before him, almost to the horizon, it seemed, like a huge segment of desert set down here on the south coast of England. Cloud shadows hurried across it, mottling the caramel sand. He took off his jacket and tie and tossed them in the rear seat. Then he walked down through the dunes and on to the beach, past the holidaying families and sunbathers and headed out across the sand flats towards the distant grey-blue stripe that was the Channel.

His young brother, John-Christopher Kydd, Flight Lt "Kit" Kydd, had been shot down opposite Rye by three Messerschmitt 109s, his Spitfire crashing full tilt into the Channel some three miles off Camber Sands. The plane and Kit's body had never been recovered, such was the velocity of the impact, the Spitfire's near-vertical dive thrusting the aircraft deep beneath the surface. It had been 22 July 1940. Almost twenty-eight years to the day, Talbot thought. Kit was twenty-three when he had been shot down.

Talbot walked on, past a solitary, frisky, yapping dog—some kind of terrier, lost—trailing its lead behind it, and then a man teaching his little boy how to fly a kite. He kept walking, feeling the occasional sunburst hot on his bare head. The tide was at its lowest ebb and it must have been nearly a mile, or more, to the sea's edge, where small waves unfolded with a muted, soothing crash.

Talbot stood there, looking at the waves, thinking of his brother, wondering how his life might have been different had Kit lived. Kit—blond, guileless, with his easy laugh. He was tall, taller than Talbot, and Talbot remembered how he had joked, the last time they were together, about the contortions required to climb into the cockpit of his Spitfire, how he had to be specially folded into position by his ground crew. Kit's sudden death seemed to draw the life out of their mother, dead herself within the year, allowing his father to embark on his next, disastrous marriage and a sequence of short-lived affairs. What if Kit had lived . . .

"Kit!" he yelled out to the restless, choppy waves. "Kit, I'm here! It's me! I'm here, Kit! I think about you! I remember you! I dream about you!"

His words were snatched away by the breezy gusts of wind and, immediately self-conscious, he glanced around to check if anyone had noticed this elderly man shouting at the sea. But he was alone on the edge of the vast beach, it seemed. He turned and trudged back across the sand to his car. He couldn't explain why, but he felt he had just done something valuable, however pointless it was to imagine a world where Kit still lived. The "what ifs" could stretch the length of Camber Sands itself, all its five miles. Live the life you were given, he told himself, recalling Ivo Stuart-Hay's words, and be the person you are. Easier said than done.

Back at the Grand he handed the car keys to the doorman and headed straight for the bar. The Icebox, that was the name of this club. He should find out where it was, just as an experiment, something new, to see whether anything had changed since the law was passed. As the colonel said: we're not here for long—make the most of it.

17

Was today the right day . . . ? Elfrida wondered to herself, feeling strangely nervous. She topped up her orange juice as a way of calming down. Maybe she should pause awhile—a few days—think things through a bit more. After all, she'd only just had the idea so perhaps she was being unduly precipitate. But, at the same time, she recognised the familiar symptom: procrastination, one of the baleful signs of her block, her long-lingering malaise. No, Elfrida, she urged herself, start, begin, get going. She recalled Guy de Maupassant's famous injunction. Just put black on white, ink on paper.

Steeling herself, she booked a Rottingdean taxi to take her to Rodmell, wait and return, hang the expense, and she went to gather up her notebook and Maitland Bole's pamphlet. She decanted a couple of inches of vodka into a small glass bottle in case she needed some extra encouragement and, seeing that the bottle was open, had a swig and then a second. What was that Russian saying? No bottle of vodka should be opened to serve just one drink—or something like that. Two servings a minimum. Who said that? Pushkin? Dostoevsky? No matter, she was paraphrasing, but, in any event, it seemed to her an eminently sensible folk-tradition.

The taxi had pulled up outside the front door and Elfrida had given an acknowledging wave when the telephone rang. She thought about not answering but then wondered if it might be Reggie—whom she had hardly spoken to since their fight—he might as well be filming abroad for all she saw of him, and so she answered.

"Hello?"

"Hello. Could I speak to Jennifer Tipton?"

"Sorry, you've got a wrong number. There's nobody by that—" She remembered, suddenly. "One moment." She cleared her throat. "Hello? Jennifer Tipton here."

"Hi. It's Huckleberry from the Book Nook. We've got your Virginia Woolf."

"Virginia Woolf?"

"You ordered *A Writer's Diary.* It arrived this morning."

"Oh. Yes, of course. Marvellous. I'll be right down."

She hung up. It was a sign. She suddenly felt joy-brimmed, joy-flushed, joy-sprung, as if she were in a poem by Gerard Manley Hopkins. The shade of Virginia Woolf was encouraging her to travel to Rodmell and drive a stake through her heart. She scampered out to her taxi. Procrastination be damned.

She had the disgruntled taxi driver detour to Hove and the Book Nook where she paid Huckleberry for Woolf's diaries. She flicked to the end as the final entries were what she was interested in, reading avidly as they journeyed on from Brighton to the Ouse Valley—not far away.

Elfrida told the taxi driver to park outside the village pub—the Abergavenny—thinking that she might look in for some refreshment later, after her researches. She wandered down a long narrow street towards the lower edge of the village and to Monk's House, Virginia and Leonard Woolf's country home, able to identify it easily thanks to Maitland Bole's excellent map. She stood and contemplated the surprisingly small house, barely visible because of the mass of overgrown vegetation around it. She saw flaky white weatherboarding and a gate. Tall bushes and trees obscured most of the view.

She paused a moment, trying to summon up the spirit of Virginia Woolf—and failing. To the right she saw a high-walled pathway to the church—St. Peter's. She walked up the path a few paces and, standing on tiptoe, peered over the wall to gain a view of the garden through the annoying foliage. It was a substantial garden, she saw, some few acres, she thought, and she could see an orchard beyond the flower beds. In front of her was a pond and a glassed-in sun porch. Some deckchairs and wooden seats were positioned on a patch of lawn and she spotted an ancient man in a beige linen jacket and panama hat deadheading dahlias. So, the place was occupied. She might presumptuously knock on the door later, she thought.

She headed for the church, skirting it and on to the graveyard's perimeter wall with its view of the water meadows beyond. She could make out the course of the river, or at least its high embankments, about half a mile away, very bare, not a tree or a bush in sight, and running straight, almost like a canal. She glanced back at Monk's House, though it was still largely obscured by trees and the orchard from this vantage point. Virginia would have walked across her garden and through the orchard to the garden gate in order to gain access to the fields leading down to the Ouse—no need to come via the church, of course. Elfrida sat on the wall, swung her legs over and dropped down the other side.

It took her less than ten minutes to make her way across the meadows to the river and she soon stood on the high embankment looking down on the slow-moving stream, wondering if this were perhaps the actual point where Virginia had filled her coat pocket with a heavy stone and then waded in. Where had she learned that fact about the stone? She searched her memory. That's right: Enid Bagnold had told her at a party, years ago. Funny how things sprang into your mind like that. Then she thought: had Virginia jumped in? The Ouse was tidal, she had learned from Bole's pamphlet, and at high tide was quite deep here, she estimated, maybe six feet. Easy to slip under, take some lung-filling breaths of water. She looked at Bole's map again. The next village, not far off, was Southease, a third of a mile away—and there was a bridge crossing the river at Southease. Surely she wouldn't have gone any further downstream towards Southease? People crossing the bridge might have spotted her. Where she was now standing on the west bank was as close to Monk's House as possible. Upstream was Lewes. No, somewhere on this very turfy stretch of embankment—a yard or three in either direction—was the exact spot where Virginia Woolf decided to enter the water and end her life.

She shivered. It was a pleasantly warm though cloudy day in July

1968. It would have been freezing on 28 March 1941, she imagined. She unscrewed her little bottle of vodka and raised it to the river in salutation, then had a couple of bracing swigs. She slipped it back in her handbag and turned and strode through the meadow towards the church, a strange new respect building in her for her fellow writer, now she had seen the spot with her own eyes. Whatever else it took to commit suicide by drowning there would be a distinct need for personal bravery, for courage. And icy pragmatism—that heavy stone in her pocket was there precisely to combat second thoughts. And, maybe—the notion struck her—maybe she couldn't even swim. Who knew these things? . . . Lord, Elfrida thought, finding it much harder to clamber back into the churchyard, surely there must be an easier way of ending your life and bringing the blessed release of oblivion?

She peered over the wall again, looking into the garden of Monk's House. The old fellow was now sitting in a deckchair reading a newspaper.

"Coo-ee!" Elfrida called. "Excuse me! Here I am by the wall!" She waved, parting the branches of a laburnum so she could be better seen.

It seemed to take the old man about two minutes to fold his newspaper, struggle out of his deckchair and slowly wander over. He doffed his hat, peering at her concernedly.

"Hello," he said. "Is everything all right?"

"Yes. Oh yes, I'm perfectly well. I was just wondering," she said, disingenuously, "if this was Virginia Woolf's house. By any faint chance."

"Yes, it was," he said. He was very thin and narrow-shouldered with a sunken, gaunt face beneath a mop of dense white hair and ears that seemed to grow out of his head at right angles, like the handles of a pot.

"I'm very interested in Virginia Woolf," Elfrida said.

"You're not alone."

"May I ask when you came to live here?"

"1919."

"Ah." Elfrida realised. "You must be Mr. Leonard Woolf."

"I am indeed."

Damn, Elfrida thought. I can hardly ask him what his wife did on her last day before she drowned herself. Frustrating. Play for time, that was the best tactic, at least she had his attention.

"I'm a novelist myself," Elfrida volunteered, to explain her presumption. "Often compared to your wife, Mrs. Woolf. My name's Elfrida Wing."

"I'm not familiar with your work. Apologies."

Well, why don't you ask me in for a cup of tea, she thought, and find out more? How many strange novelists go to all this trouble to make their way to Rodmell in a given year? None, she'd have wagered. She decided to be bold.

"I'm very interested in the details of Virginia Woolf's very last day—28 March 1941."

Mr. Woolf blinked rapidly at her, as if seeing her for the very first time. The corners of his mouth turned down as he stared at her. He looked as if he were about to spit.

"Good morning to you, Mrs. Tring," he said abruptly, throwing his newspaper down on a seat and stomping back into the house.

Fuck! Elfrida thought. Fool! I should have been more subtle, asked for a glass of water or something, she remonstrated with herself. She wandered angrily back up the lane towards the pub, the Abergavenny—odd Welsh name for a pub in East Sussex, she thought—noticing as she approached that her taxi was nowhere to be seen. Idle bastard.

She went in and ordered a large gin and tonic. The bar was wet with un-mopped rings of beer and the place seemed dirty and uncared for. Some long-haired local lads were playing a boisterous game of darts so she took herself off to the most distant corner, had a large gulp of her gin and opened *A Writer's Diary* in the hope that Virginia might be more forthcoming than old Leonard Woolf had been.

She read the very last entry again, dated 8 March, almost three weeks before she killed herself. The tone seemed quite sensible and balanced—no sign of mental disturbance. There was one sentence that held her attention. "I shall go down with my colours flying." Intriguing. Was that some kind of premonition? Then the final observations: "Must cook dinner. Haddock and sausage meat." What a disgusting mixture, Elfrida thought. Though it was interesting that she was going to cook it herself. No staff? Then she read on: "I think that it is true that one gains a certain hold on sausage and haddock by writing them down." Elfrida considered this gnomic remark for a few seconds. Perhaps it made sense only to another novelist. She felt a new spasm of inspiration. It was working. The visit to Rodmell and Monk's House had been an amazing intuition. She would gain a "certain hold" on Virginia Woolf and her last day—and thereby kick-start her own career into life again—*by writing it down.* Yes.

18

It started to rain in the afternoon and, as a result, they couldn't shoot outside and Rodrigo, mysteriously, called a halt to the day's filming.

"Don't you have 'rain cover'?" Anny asked him.

"I don't believe in rain cover," Rodrigo said, bafflingly. "It destroys spontaneity."

Anny went back to the hotel early but, even so, there was the usual small crowd of autograph hunters waiting at one side of the main door. Their numbers had been growing over the last week or so as if word had finally reached Brighton that a famous American film star was staying in their midst.

"Anny! Anny!" came the cries as she stepped out of the car. Anny, feeling benevolent, wandered over to her fans and started signing her name. There were about half a dozen hunters—all young women, curiously—and Anny, head down, signed away as the books were presented to her in sequence. But the last book was proffered by a man, she could tell from his big hands, and he opened his book on a fresh page.

I NEED YOUR HELP! was written there in big capital letters.

Anny looked up to see a bearded man in a woollen hat pulled down to his eyebrows. He wore spectacles and it was that unfamiliar detail that ever so slightly prolonged the split second that it took her to recognise her ex-husband. Cornell Weekes was indeed in England. And in Brighton. And standing in front of her.

Anny dropped her gaze back to the book.

"Jesus, Cornell, I don't believe it," she said, her voice heavy with disappointment. "They're looking for you here," she added quietly. "The FBI were here, talking to me about you."

"You have to help me, Anny. You're my only hope. I'm desperate."

She wrote her room number down.

"Come tonight," she said. "Call up. Try to look presentable."

She walked off and into the hotel without a backward glance.

In her room she swallowed two Equanils and a Seconal. Then she showered, placed the "Do Not Disturb" sign on the outside of the door and clambered into bed. She slept, waking at eight o'clock that evening, feeling groggy and thick-headed and took an Obetral to wake her up. They were marketed as diet-pills but everyone knew they were amphetamines in flimsy disguise. She dressed and ordered a ham and cheese sandwich and a pot of coffee from room service but, when it came, she realised she wasn't hungry, because of the Obetral. She drank two cups of coffee with lots of sugar and began to think about what she would do when Cornell showed up.

The call came about an hour later.

"We have a Mr. Ingmar Bergman here who says he has an appointment with Miss Viklund."

Ingmar Bergman was her favourite film director—Cornell knew that—she had often told him of her dream that one day she might be in a Bergman film—though it was a problem that she couldn't speak Swedish, she realised.

"Show him up," she said.

Cornell came awkwardly into the room, his usual mixture of chagrin and bravado emanating from him, as if he were angry that he had to come to her for help but recognising that he needed her, please, Anny. She saw he was wearing a tie and his hair was dyed black like hers. They did not shake hands or kiss. He took his spectacles off and slipped them in a pocket. His beard was trimmed and was greying, she saw, and thought that it suited him. With his gaunt face and his deep-set dark eyes he looked even more like the prophet-figure that he saw himself as—a seer in the wilderness of the twentieth century, the rest of the world ranged and railing against him.

He looked around the room and asked if he could eat her sandwich, seeing it sitting there untouched on its plate. Help yourself, she said, and he chomped it down in half a dozen bites—then poured himself a cup of cold coffee.

Suddenly he set the cup back on the tray and leant forward covering his face with his hands.

"I'm so tired, Anny," he said, his voice muffled by his palms. Then he began to cry, quietly, almost inaudibly, just the shuddering of his shoulders giving his misery away.

She looked at him, trying to ignore the wrench of love for this maddening man that now tugged at her, feeling that she wanted to take him in her arms and stroke his hair and whisper words of comfort in his ear. This was what it was like with Cornell, she realised—life as a wildly swinging pendulum: from love to anger, from affection to irritation, from warmth to fierce antagonism. And back again.

She stepped forward and laid a hand gently on his back.

"Please, Cornell," she said, feeling the tears warm in her own eyes. It was incredibly rare to see him so vulnerable. She had seen him cry only once or twice before, she remembered. He hated to cry, he had always told her, crying was a kind of defeat, the sign that you'd lost.

"You can't go on like this," she said.

He looked up, sniffed and rallied himself, wiping his eyes with the heels of his hands.

"I don't have any choice," he said. "I can't go back to that place. I'm running for my life, Anny. For my *life.*" The emphasis he gave to the word seemed to bring back his usual vigour. He looked at her and she removed her hand from his shoulder. All the old love she had been feeling for him seeped quickly away.

"This is the only time we can meet," she said, her voice brusque. "What do you want?"

"Money."

"Turn yourself in, Cornell. I beg you."

"How can you say that? I'm not going to fucking rot in prison for the rest of my life. I'd rather kill myself."

"Then maybe you *should* kill yourself. If life isn't worth living then it makes sense, you know, to kill yourself," she said harshly, then a second later regretted her tone. "Give yourself up. It might be the right thing—in the long term," she added, feebly.

"My life will be worth living—as soon as I get to Africa, to Mozambique."

"Mozambique? Isn't there some sort of war—an insurrection—going on there?"

"Exactly. A colonial power against a rebel army fighting to free their country. That's why I'll be safe. I have contacts in FRELIMO."

"Jesus." Anny saw the familiar mad zeal burn in his eyes. She sighed. "Why did you plant those bombs?"

"It's called an armed struggle. I'm a freedom fighter engaged in a war against an oppressive state."

"Just like FRELIMO. You should be right at home."

"It's not some kind of joke, Anny."

"I know. Tell that to the soldier with no legs thanks to your bomb."

"I know. I feel kind of bad for the guy . . ." Then he visibly stiffened himself. "You know what? He's a fucking professional soldier. There are risks that come with the profession. Injuries, fatalities. He was in combat. In a combat zone."

"Jesus, Cornell. He was in Nevada."

"The war is everywhere. The country's at war."

"He just didn't know it, right?"

"He knew it. There's a war going on, an undeclared war."

She felt weariness settle on her, like a shawl around her shoulders. There was never any arguing with Cornell.

"Why should I help you?" she said. "Do you have any idea how much trouble you could cause me?"

"We were man and wife." He corrected himself. "Husband and wife. That must mean something. We shared our lives. We had good times, Anny, you know that. We swore an oath."

"That was declared null and void after a few months."

"An amazing few months. Admit it, Anny. It was . . . special, different. I changed you. You owe me."

What could she say? She had no answer. She felt light-headed, now, recognising the effect Cornell had on her. It was a force, a mild but concentrated force of nature—like a cold-virus or an endless rainy day. He burned with an eternal flame of perceived injustice, everywhere, all the time. A parking meter was an injustice to him; putting your trash out was an affront to his liberty; having to stop at a red traffic light undermined his human rights. His relentless illogic triumphed over anything rational that aspired to be an alternative explanation, a brake, a contradiction. What she remembered of their married life was a near-constant sense of intellectual fatigue.

Symptoms that she was experiencing again, she noted, as she watched him talking—not listening to him—as he sat on the chair by the room-service trolley. She took in his new beard, his cheap suit, his unpolished shoes, his mismatched socks, one brown, one blue. How had she ever come to marry this man, this mild dipshit maniac? she asked herself for the thousandth time. And no answer came. Maybe it was that fatigue that made her decide to help him now, she thought. One last gesture. Anything to make him go away; anything to bring back calmness and tranquillity, to stop the eternal sense of agitation that being in the presence of Cornell Weekes provoked.

"How much do you need?"

"Five thousand dollars."

"Fuck! Cornell—"

"OK. Two thousand. I need to go back to Lisbon, then catch a plane to Lourenço Marques from there. Then you'll never hear from me again. Never see me again in your life. That's got to be worth two thousand bucks, no?"

He was right, she thought. The best 2,000 bucks she'd ever spend. The best. She made up her mind.

"I don't have that kind of cash on me."

"But you can get it, right? They must be paying you a fortune on this movie."

"I'll try." Her brain was racing but was muddled by the Obetral. "I'll ask the production office. The producer."

"How will you get it to me?"

She thought for a moment.

"Wait with the autograph hunters at the front door of the hotel each day. When I have the cash I'll slip it to you."

"OK. But don't delay, OK?"

He stood up and prowled round her suite, aggressively. The old Cornell Weekes seemed to be back. He fingered the thick curtains, weighed the heavy brass pull that opened and closed them.

"Living high on the hog, eh, Anny?" he said accusingly, sneeringly. "Life must be good."

"It's a job. It's what I do. They provide accommodation."

"You should be ashamed of yourself. It's disgusting."

"I'm not ashamed of myself, not for one second. Fuck you, Cornell! You're happy to benefit from my 'disgusting' job, oh, yeah—so you can go and fight the good fight in the jungles of Mozambique. Doesn't it strike you as ironic? A sacrifice of noble principles? You happy taking my filthy money? Why don't you go rob a bank, Mr. Freedom Fighter?"

"I have no choice. You do."

"Funny how it always works out that way. You're in the right. I'm in the wrong." She felt the weariness of arguing with him begin to afflict her again. It reminded her of their brief marriage and its unending tensions. Suddenly she longed for Troy—so simple, so straightforward.

"You know what? I think you should go," she said, striding to the door. "I'll get your money tomorrow or the next day." She held the door open for him. He stood there, hands on hips as if reluctant to leave.

"I suppose I should thank you," he said. "Thank you, Anny. I know it's not easy for you. But I've always felt that you and I had something—"

"I don't want your thanks, Cornell," she said wearily. "I want nothing from you, any more. This is the last thing I'll ever do for you. Ever."

As he passed her he leant forward and tried to kiss her and she punched him hard in the chest.

"Ouch! That fucking hurt!"

"Never ever try to touch me again."

"OK. OK. Gimme a break."

When he'd left she refused to let herself cry, remembering the Cornell edict: crying was a kind of defeat, a sign that she'd lost. But she had lost, she knew, or at least surrendered. What had she done? Wise voices in her head told her she was making a terrible mistake; but other voices from her heart told her she had had no option. She picked up a fork from the room-service trolley and pressed the tines into the muscle of her forearm, hurting herself, damaged nerve endings keeping her mind off Cornell Weekes. She pressed harder, harder. She drew the fork away and saw that she had made a neat red line of four suspension dots on her skin. Deep red. She watched the skin break and the bright blood-beads well up. Four gleaming red dots. She rubbed spit on them—inhaling, exhaling, inhaling, exhaling.

For a moment she thought about calling the English detective who'd given her his card but, somehow, she knew she couldn't turn Cornell in. Poor, sad, mixed-up Cornell. Let him flee to Africa, she thought, embroil himself in the new fantasy of liberating Mozambique from the yoke of Portuguese dictatorship. Cornell off to realise another impossible dream, righting more geopolitical wrongs. In a way, she thought, you had to admire someone like that. They burned brighter than ordinary mortals. Still, it would be money well spent. She began to feel calmer. It was the best thing to do, she reasoned: get him out of my life as quickly as possible.

Then she had another idea. She called the hotel switchboard and gave the operator a number in Paris.

"Allo? Oui?"

It was Jacques. He was back from Guinea. Suddenly obscure African countries were a part of her life. She felt her chest inflate with pleasure.

"It's me," she said. "You're back. Wonderful."

"I just returned." She listened to his deep voice as he told her about his meeting with Nkrumah and how Nkrumah had awarded him a decoration: the Order of the Star of Ghana.

"I thought he'd been deposed. In exile."

"Of course. But he still gave me this medal."

"Congratulations." She paused. "Cornell has been here."

"Putain!"

"Yes, *putain.* He wants money."

There was silence.

"Will he leave you alone?"

"I think so."

"Well, give it to him." He paused. "Look, I'm going to come over and see you. I miss my pretty little girl."

"I miss you too," she said. "When will you come? I still have a month of filming to go."

"I'll come in a few days. I'll call you. I have a few things to do here in Paris."

"OK. Can't wait."

"Je t'embrasse, chérie."

"Bisous." She hung up.

She sat there still for a while, thinking. Wondering if it was Cornell that had made her turn to Jacques. Replacing someone so vacillating, flighty and annoying with someone so sure of himself and his value system he seemed almost serene. Why did she do this sort of thing? What did it say about her as a person? What needs were being satisfied? Stop, stop, stop, she told herself. She felt a little tremble of panic running through her, as if her body was being vibrated by a machine, or as if there were some powerful engine thrumming in the room below. It was a sign that her life was becoming too complicated and she knew that wasn't good for her. First, the demands of the film and now Cornell turning up, and now Jacques saying he'd come over to visit. And Troy. Why was it that her life seemed to arrange itself like this—complication piling on complication? Maybe it was too much. Maybe Jacques shouldn't come . . . But then he'd be suspicious if she tried to put him off.

She took another Equanil and called Troy in his room. He said he'd be with her in two minutes.

19

"Oh, yes," Joe said at breakfast. "One other thing: Miss Viklund would like to see you, privately."

"That's odd," Talbot said. "Any idea what it's about?"

"Not a clue. She said she'd come to the office. She's got the morning off. Big scene with Sylvia and Ferdie this afternoon."

"Right." Talbot pushed his unfinished kipper away. He was feeling bilious again—best not to overstress his duodenum. He had an unpleasant premonition about the day ahead even though, looking out of the tall windows of the dining room, he could see the sun was shining.

Anny Viklund arrived at Napier Street just before ten. She was wearing sunglasses and she didn't remove them when she sat down opposite Talbot at his desk. He made sure the door was shut, offered her a choice of refreshments that she declined, asked if she minded if he smoked—she didn't—and he lit up.

"You wanted to see me," he said. "I do hope everything's all right."

"I need two thousand dollars in cash," she said.

She was extremely beautiful, Talbot registered, as he managed successfully to disguise his astonishment: smooth white skin, a firm chin with the hint of a cleft, a tiny, perfect tipped-up nose with flared nostrils, as if she were inhaling fiercely. The severe short black fringe somehow had the effect of concentrating one's attention on the near-flawlessness of her physiognomy. The effect was even more compelling when she suddenly removed her sunglasses and stared at him. Her eyes were a very pale, greyish-blue, her gaze almost startlingly intense.

"May I ask what the money's for?"

"It's a personal matter."

Drugs, Talbot thought wearily. She has to pay her dealer.

"It's not for drugs," she added, as if reading his mind. "I have all the drugs I could possibly need. I just have to buy something with cash. And as you can imagine it's not easy for me to access such a large amount of cash, here in Brighton."

"Let me buy it for you," Talbot said. "Whatever it is. I can write a cheque: it'll be so much easier."

"Can you buy me peace of mind with a cheque? I don't think so."

"Right. No. I see." Talbot drew on his cigarette, deciding not to pursue the matter further. It would be politic not to ask any more questions.

"Dollars are a problem. I'd have to go to a bank."

"Pounds will be fine. I just need cash."

He did a quick calculation. "Two thousand dollars is about eight hundred pounds. We might even have that in the safe. Excuse me a moment."

He ran upstairs to the accountancy department and asked for the safe to be opened. They had close to £1,500 in cash. Geoff Braintree, the accountant, was not happy as he counted out the money.

"What shall I put it down to?" he asked plaintively. "It's complex, Talbot. There's bookkeeping to be fixed."

"Personal loan to producer. Whatever, you'll think of something. I'll have it back to you in a couple of days. After the weekend."

He signed the chit and returned to his office and handed the four blocks of £10 notes to Anny. She put them in her handbag and replaced her sunglasses.

"Thank you, Talbot," she said. "I'm very grateful. More grateful than you can imagine."

She smiled, showing her small, impossibly white, expertly capped teeth. Talbot stubbed out the remains of his cigarette and walked her to the front door. She was an exceptionally tiny person, he noticed, as he loomed over her—as if she were a prototype or a maquette for a young woman, almost a different species, and the manufacturers had decided that something larger would be more appropriate for the rest of homo sapiens.

"What's coming up today?" he asked, keen to change the agenda. "Anything exciting?"

"I get to meet my 'parents' this afternoon," she said.

"Oh, yes. You'll love them," Talbot said, with forced enthusiasm. "Sylvia Slaye and Ferdie Meares. Old-school British actors. Fabulous."

"Have they done many movies?"

"Countless. And TV. Legends, national treasures, you know." He worried he'd gone a bit far, but too late now. He put a paternal hand on Anny's thin shoulder.

"Promise me you'll tell me the minute anything's worrying you, or causing the smallest problem," he said. "We're here to do absolutely anything you require."

"I'll be fine," she said. "Now I have the money. Everything's fine."

She said goodbye and climbed into the rear seat of her waiting car and it pulled away. What was that all about? he wondered, watching the car turn a corner out of sight. Peace of mind, she had said. Blackmail? Some sort of pay-off? Gambling? A debt? He stopped himself. None of my business, he thought, I've got enough on my plate.

His crowded plate became even more crowded after lunch when Geoff Braintree came downstairs with a sheaf of invoices and spread them on his desk.

"What's this?" Talbot asked.

"More film stock."

"We're making a film, Geoff. We need film stock."

"We could have made three films at the rate we're burning through this stuff. Way, way over budget."

"Is that Reggie's—sorry, Rodrigo's fault? Is he shooting miles of film?"

"You'd better ask Spencer," Geoff said. "I don't understand cinema."

"That's why you're such a good film accountant, Geoffrey."

After Geoff had left, Talbot put in a call to Spencer Osmond, their editor, who was in a cutting room in London—in Soho—trying to construct a rough assembly of everything that had been shot so far.

"Is Reggie shooting miles of film?" Talbot asked. "You know: take after take."

"No, actually," Spencer said. "Three or four takes on average. Doesn't print them all. There's the odd day when he goes a bit film-school auteur but on the whole he's behaving himself."

Talbot hung up. Someone was stealing their film stock and therefore, most likely, it was someone in the camera department. He felt the acid bite in his innards. He needed some time off—the weekend was just around the corner, thank God. He would investigate next week, discreetly. He needed to think about this carefully.

One hour later, Reggie called.

"Serious problems, Talbot."

"Fire away."

"Anny won't work with Sylvia and Ferdie."

"Why the fuck not?"

"She says, and I quote: 'These people could never be my parents.' She's adamant."

"It's called 'acting,' for God's sweet sake."

"She won't do the scene with them. Flat refusal."

"What do Sylvia and Ferdie say?"

"I've fobbed them off. Told them it was a technical problem to do with lenses. They don't know what's going on."

"Good. Well done. I'll be right over."

Talbot had a car take him to the bungalow on the outskirts of Shoreham-by-Sea that was doubling for the Bracegirdle family home. He told the driver to pull up behind the double-decker bus that was the crew's mobile canteen—he had no desire to bump into Ferdie or Sylvia. He found Reggie and together they made their way to Anny's trailer.

"Is she hysterical?" Talbot asked.

"Not in the least—surprisingly calm and rational."

Reggie knocked on the trailer door, announced who they were, and seconds later Anny let them both in. They sat down on the narrow bench seats. She did seem very composed, Talbot thought—almost serene, in fact—and unkindly wondered if she'd taken anything chemical to bring about this tranquillity.

"Anny, please. What's wrong with Sylvia and Ferdie?" Talbot asked, bluntly.

"I just can't believe these two people as my parents—Emily's parents," she said, reasonably. "Emily Bracegirdle would never have parents like that. It would be impossible to play the scene with them. I can't relate to them as people. I can't talk to them."

"We can't choose our parents, you know."

"But I'm being asked to act—act like they're my parents who created me, like that woman is my 'mother' who gave birth to me. I have to love them. It's completely impossible."

In a funny sort of way Talbot knew what she was talking about. There was indeed something grotesque, something rebarbatively Grand Guignol, about Sylvia Slaye and Ferdie Meares as a couple, as putative mother and father. But he had to put the opposing argument.

"But, surely if you—"

"It's like you presented me with a dog and a rat, or a spider and a flea, and you said—these are your parents."

"Bit extreme, Anny," Reggie said tentatively.

"I'm just trying to make you see what I'm feeling. I can't do it. I can't act that. It makes me sick. I'm sorry."

Talbot tried to reason but he knew a brick wall when he was confronted with one.

"Well, let's all have a think and maybe we'll come up with a solution," he said lamely. They smiled at each other and took their leave.

"I'm not doing this to be bad, or because I'm some neurotic actress," Anny said. "I'm doing it for the sake of our film. For its . . ." She paused and Talbot could sense her searching for a word. "Its veracity."

He and Reggie stood outside in silence, both looking at the ground as if a solution to their problem was to be found there amongst the muddy footprints and the crushed grass stems.

"Fucking veracity," Talbot said.

"Fucking disaster," Reggie said. "Could we recast?"

"No. Scandal, lawsuits, money, money, money. You know those two."

"Fucking disaster," Reggie repeated. "Never saw that coming. Not in a million years."

"Is there a pub near here?" Talbot asked.

"There is, actually."

They walked half a mile into Shoreham-by-Sea and found a pub called the Captain Bligh. Very apt, Talbot thought, given their own current mutiny. What would Captain Bligh have done if this had happened on the *Bounty*? he wondered. Fifty lashes of the cat all round.

The pub was gloomy and empty, having just opened for the evening session. It had a patterned carpet whose pattern was barely visible, tramped into grimy grey uniformity by the soles of a thousand drinkers' shoes. The ashtrays were still full of the lunchtime clientele's cigarette butts and the smell of stale smoke and sour beer hung in the air like fine moisture. A surly plump girl with a bubble perm poured them each a large whisky and they took their glasses over to a window seat where a view of Shoreham harbour and its houseboats was half obscured by dying geraniums in a window box.

"There's got to be some way round this," Reggie said. "Got to be."

"Can we cut the scene?" Talbot asked.

"No. It's crucial. It's when the Bracegirdles—the parents—discover that Emily's been having an affair with her driver—Troy. There's a huge big barney—screaming, shouting, throwing plates. You can imagine Sylvia and Ferdie going for broke. Everything subsequently pivots round it."

"What about rewriting? Can we write something different?" Talbot didn't really know what he was talking about but he saw Reggie's expression change. It brightened.

"In fact . . . That might be the answer . . ." Now he looked a bit awkward. "I meant to tell you, Talbot . . ." He cleared his throat. "But Janet's actually here. Has been for a week."

"Here in Brighton? Janet Headstone?"

"It was her idea—she's staying in a friend's house. In Kemp Town," he added.

"What's she doing?"

"She's working on a new ending. Ideas for a new ending. Versions, possibilities," he improvised quickly. "Maybe she could figure something out. She's bloody clever that way. Get us out of this pickle."

"I'd hardly call it a 'pickle,' Reggie. Still, we are paying her a grand a week. Might as well make her earn her keep."

"Let me give her a ring," Reggie said, and went to find a phone box.

Talbot stood and crossed the spongy carpet to the bar and ordered another whisky—the warm alcohol seemed to be soothing his gut, paradoxically. Local anaesthetic—he knew he'd suffer later.

They walked back to the set where they found everything was winding down, Anny's refusal to act with Sylvia and Ferdie prematurely ending the day's filming. Who pays for that? Talbot wondered, aggrieved, in the car that drove them to Kemp Town. They headed for the East Cliff, turning off Marine Parade just before reaching the surprising grandeur of Lewes Crescent and motored along Chesham Road, Reggie giving the driver confident directions, Talbot noticed. Clearly he had been here before.

Janet Headstone's friend's three-storey house was in the middle of a tree-lined terrace. The house was painted pale purple and the window frames were picked out in scarlet. There was a tall, dying limp-leaved yucca in the small front garden and an empty green plastic paddling pool. Janet Headstone opened the door to them both—Reggie giving her a peck on the cheek—and led them through to a modern kitchen-diner. They took their places around a scrubbed pine table set below a massive light recovered from some billiard hall. The walls were painted pillar-box red and the fridge seemed to be made from chrome. Strange tall spiky-looking plants in ceramic pots were arranged in a line on the window ledge behind the sink. Through the window was a garden full of toys and enough equipment for a small park: a slide, a jungle gym, a swing, a seesaw and a Wendy house.

Janet offered them beer or gin and vermouth. Talbot opted for the latter; Reggie chose the beer.

"Shall I fill Janet in on the backstory?" Reggie asked.

"Good idea," Talbot said. "Is there a serviceable loo, by any chance?"

Janet directed him to a bathroom upstairs. The inside of the bath had been painted blue and there were many etchings on the walls of a mildly pornographic nature. Talbot had a pee and tried to come up with a mental picture of the people who actually lived in this house—Janet's friends—and failed.

He came down the stairs slowly, feeling weary, wondering if gin and vermouth were a wise choice and, as he stepped onto the carpet, a large mirror in the hall at the foot of the stairs afforded him a clear, angled view of the kitchen through its open door. He saw Reggie and Janet locked in a clinging and passionate kiss; Reggie had a two-fisted grip on her buttocks, rucking up the hem of her dress. Reggie's face was clamped between Janet's hands, tongues flickered wetly.

He stepped back, coughed a couple of times and waited a few seconds before strolling nonchalantly back into the kitchen—Reggie and Janet were back in their places, Reggie swigging beer from the bottle, Janet plaiting her ponytail.

"Jan's had a brilliant idea," Reggie said, gesturing at her to tell Talbot.

"Do everything on the phone," she said, though to Talbot's ears it came out as *evryfink on vuh phaon.* She was very cockney, he realised.

"How would that work?" he asked.

"Scene one: Emily calls her mum and dad. Cut to Mum answering: hello, darlin'. Cut back to Emily. She says: I'm marrying—what's Troy's character's name again?"

"Ben."

"I'm marrying Ben, she says. Mum goes bananas. No you fucking ain't! Emily slams down the phone. Cut back to Mum and Dad and they rant and rage. They try to call her back. She doesn't answer. Dad throws the phone against the wall. Mum bursts into tears, et cetera, et cetera."

"It's brilliant," Reggie said. "Sylvia and Ferdie get to do their stuff—overact, throw things, weep and wail. Emily sits alone thinking about the bombshell she's dropped."

Talbot had to admit it was ingenious.

"Should work. Not even Anny Viklund can object to saying one line into a phone," he said.

"Exactly—everything's pretty much as written—but the three of them don't play the scene together."

Talbot thought. "Are there any other scenes between the three of them?"

"One other," Reggie said. "The engagement party in the pub. But we can do the same—Emily never shows up. Sylvia and Ferdie get to vent their fury again. Could be very funny. Emily elopes with Ben. Bingo."

"Will you run it by Anny?" Talbot said.

"First thing. She just doesn't want to interact with those two. She'll be happy with this solution. I know it."

"By the way, wasn't it Ferdie Meares who was done for indecent exposure?" Janet asked.

"Insufficient evidence," Talbot said. "Acquitted." He took a gulp of his gin and vermouth—it was warm. He asked if there was any ice but Janet said the freezer in the chrome fridge was broken.

Now it was Reggie's turn to go to the lavatory, leaving Talbot and

Janet alone. She stood up and went to fetch another bottle of beer. She was wearing a short black-and-white-striped dress that was a little tight on her, and white PVC bootees, Talbot noticed. A pretty woman who wasn't looking after herself, he thought: candles being burned at both ends and the middle. He was aware of the silence between them.

"Funny sort of house," Talbot said. "Who are your friends?"

"He's a drummer in a rock band called Higher Ground. Quite good, actually."

"Funny that. My son's a 'drummer.' Timpanist in the Hallé Orchestra."

"See? We move in different orbits, Talbot," Janet said, shrewdly.

"I don't know if I agree," Talbot said. "We're both working on the same film, both living temporarily in Brighton."

"Well, I'm going back to London this weekend. This street is a nightmare Fridays and Saturdays. There's a club at the end of the road. They all come out at four in the morning, screaming and shouting. Crazy queens."

Talbot said nothing, but allowed himself a slight smile.

"I think they've earned their fun, don't you?"

"Just because it's legal doesn't mean they can destroy my beauty sleep." She laughed.

"What's this club called?"

"Ah. The Ice something. The Ice Show. No, the Icebox."

"Maybe you should get a petition up amongst the neighbours."

"Not my style, Talbot, old mate." She smiled broadly at him.

Talbot wasn't sure if he liked Janet Headstone very much.

"I know you weren't too happy about me coming on board," she said, as if sensing his animus.

"Oh, I'm perfectly happy. I just wished I'd been told about it. I was kept out of the picture, that's what irritated me. Nothing to do with you."

"Yeah, exactly. Nothing to do with me. Reggie said Yorgos had cleared everything."

"All water under the bridge," he said, standing. "Anyway, Janet, I'm very grateful—you may just have saved our bacon."

"Worth her weight in gold," Reggie said coming back in, and put his hand on her shoulder, then snatched it away as if her skin were hot.

"I'd better get back," Talbot said. "Thanks again, Janet."

"See you around, Talbot. Wait till you see the ending I've got lined up."

Reggie walked him to the door.

"I'll wait on a bit," he said. "Block out the new pages with her. We'll regroup tomorrow. Forge on."

Talbot resisted the temptation to resort to innuendo. If Reggie Tipton wanted to fuck Janet Headstone that was his business. I wonder if Elfrida has any idea, he said to himself.

"Crisis over," Reggie said.

"*This* crisis," Talbot replied. "There'll be another one tomorrow, no doubt."

"Onwards and upwards," Reggie said, and opened the front door for him.

Talbot was driven back to the production office. Joe was there at his desk but otherwise the place was empty; the premature end to the day's shoot had given everyone an early night.

"Ah, boss, there you are," Joe said as Talbot came in. "Glad you're here. Sir Dorian Villiers called. Said it was urgent."

"The gods descend from Mount Olympus."

"I stood to attention. He wants you to call back." Joe handed him a scrap of paper with a number on it. Talbot took it from him, trying to hide his reluctance. What did Dorian Villiers want? He looked again at the scrap of paper. A Brighton number. And now Talbot remembered reading somewhere that Dorian had recently moved to Brighton with his most recent (third) wife, the Italian actress, Bruna Casanero.

He knew Dorian Villiers as they had worked together some years ago on a disastrous YSK film called *Cometh the Man,* a historical epic about King Alfred the Great. Dorian Villiers was generally regarded as the finest Shakespearean actor of his generation, up there with Burton, Olivier and Gielgud, but the talents that served him so well on stage did not transfer that successfully to the screen. His acting was mannered, declamatory and overemphatic. *Cometh the Man* had been an expensive film and expensively promoted but was a marked failure with the critics and the public. Bizarrely, despite this conspicuous turkey that they had managed to concoct, Dorian felt the experience had bonded him to Talbot, forcefully, indissolubly, interminably. He had said many times that Talbot was one of his dearest friends, one of the "few good men" still standing. Talbot and Naomi had spent two Christmases with the Villiers (when he was married to Vanessa Halton) at their huge manor house near Cambridge and Dorian was always inviting him to lunch or dine at his club when he was in town. Try as he might, duck and dive as much as he could, Talbot could not cool Dorian's ardency. And now he had come to live in Brighton . . . He picked up the phone and dialled.

"Dorian? It's Talbot."

"Well met by moonlight, Talbot, *mon brave*! You bastard—why didn't you tell me you were filming here in Brighton-town?"

"I thought you were still in Cambridge."

"That bitch from hell, Vanessa, stole that house from me—and all my goods and chattels."

Talbot could hear him light a cigarette.

"But here I am, Talbot darling, ensconced in good old Brighton-town and we are having—sweetheart Bruna and I—an anniversariyie partayie," he put on his cod-medieval accent, "to celebrate us being one year on from our glorious nuptials. We would like to invite you and as many of your fellow thespians as you can muster to join us."

He gave Talbot more details. Talbot promised to ask Reggie, Anny and Troy. They'd love to come, he was sure.

"What about Sylvia Slaye and Ferdie Meares?" Talbot suggested. "I think you know them."

"I will not have that disgusting flasher in my house but the good wench Sylvia is more than welcome, forsooth."

They talked some more. Dorian's secretary would send out formal invitations; the date would be confirmed, the venue, the dress code (black tie), the starting time and when carriages would be required.

"When the morn, in russet mantle clad, walks o'er the dew of yon high eastward hill, no doubt. It'll be the party of the year, Talbot. Can't wait to see you, my dear fellow."

Talbot hung up, a mild depression settling on him. No getting out of that one, for sure. Thank God tomorrow was Friday and the weekend was almost there. Which reminded him. He picked up the phone again and called Naomi.

"I can't make it home this weekend, darling," he lied. "So sorry. Crisis after crisis here. All hands to the pumps."

Naomi was silent for a moment.

"It's Humphrey's concert on Saturday night. Royal Festival Hall."

Shit, Talbot thought. He'd forgotten.

"I'll be there," he said. "I'll make sure. I'll drive up."

"Don't let him down," Naomi said flatly. "He's expecting you. It's important."

"I know. Don't worry—I'll be there."

They said goodnight and Talbot hung up and then slowly let his head fall until his brow was resting on his blotter. He was alone in the office—Joe had left before the call to Dorian Villiers. Now, he arched his back and stretched his arms wide in a tense crucifixion pose, spreading his fingers. There must be an easier way to earn a living, he thought.

The phone rang. I'm not answering that, he said to himself, not at this hour of the night. Go to hell.

He picked up the receiver.

"Talbot Kydd."

"Ah, Talbot, glad I tracked you down," John Saxonwood said.

"It's very late so it can't be good news," Talbot said, warily.

"I've had the contracts in for *The Smell of Burning Leaves.*"

"And?"

"Yorgos has stitched you up, old chum. Very, very cleverly. Your name's all over the place but—to my eyes—it looks like you won't own a thing."

20

There were two basic types of alcoholics, Elfrida realised, and she liked to categorise them as "Sippers" and "Benders." "Benders" were out of control—wholly appetite-driven, consummation was rapid and destructive, swift oblivion was the aim. Days would go by when "Benders" were on their bender—lost weekends—that usually ended with collapse, catatonia or death. "Sippers" on the other hand were more discreet and shrewd. They steadily topped themselves up throughout the day—sipping—aiming to maintain a constant level of potent, satisfying but—hopefully—unnoticeable inebriation. Unlike Benders, Sippers—while effectively very drunk—could still function, conduct a conversation and maybe even hold down a job.

Elfrida poured some vodka into her breakfast orange juice. She wasn't deluded or in any form of denial, not at all: she knew she was an alcoholic of the "Sipper" variety, and she also knew that the day that she started writing a new novel she would be sober again. That was her particular problem: creative impasse had driven her to drink. It wasn't her fault or some flaw in her character, no. Many other writers and artists had experienced the same predicament—Ernest Hemingway, Scott Fitzgerald, poor Edith Everly, Faulkner, Elizabeth Bishop, Dylan Thomas, Morris Hughes, Brendan Behan, Henry Green, sad Malcolm Lowry, Celia Tanson, Evelyn Waugh, Ian Fleming, George Vanderpoel and a good few others whose names she couldn't currently recall. It was a small exclusive club. Actually, not that small, come to think of it. Pondering her list she realised that most of them were "Benders." Odd, that.

Yes, she thought, feeling pleased with herself, matters were being brought in hand, steps were being taken, light was spottable at the tunnel's end, and so forth. She added another dash of vodka to her juice and went to find the telephone number of the Book Nook.

"Hello, I'd like to speak to Huckleberry, please."

"Huckleberry here."

"Huckleberry, good morning. It's Jennifer Tipton on the line."

"Sorry? Who?"

"You ordered Virginia Woolf's *A Writer's Diary* for me."

"Did I? Morning."

"And you sold me a copy of Maitland Bole's book. Or, rather, pamphlet."

"It's all coming back to me, Miss Tipton."

"Mrs."

"Mrs. Tipton. What can I do for you?"

She explained that she was telephoning for Maitland Bole's number, or address, if that were possible. She wanted to congratulate him on his pamphlet—it had been exceptionally useful in her researches into Virginia Woolf.

"I don't think I can really do that," Huckleberry said.

"Why not? You told me he lived in Eastbourne."

"He's a very private man, you see. I can't just give out his number. He'd be furious."

Elfrida had a moment of inspiration.

"Well," she said, "would you convey to him the information that I'd like to buy fifty copies of his pamphlet? Do give him my telephone number. I won't be furious."

"Oh. Right. I'll see if I can track him down."

Maitland Bole himself telephoned ten minutes later. He had a rattling voice, much interrupted by throat clearings and dry staccato coughs. It turned out that Bole no longer lived in Eastbourne but in London, in Fitzrovia, he volunteered, vaguely.

"Could we meet?" Elfrida asked. "I've got some questions for you, seeing as you're such an expert on Virginia—and I could give you a cheque for the pamphlets at the same time."

Bole suggested that they rendezvous at midday the next day at the main entrance to the Tate Gallery on Millbank. He had "private business" to transact there, he confided.

"Perfect. And may I take you for lunch?" Elfrida invited. "The Tate restaurant is one of my favourite places."

After a fusillade of coughs, Bole agreed.

"How will I know you?" he asked.

She thought for a second: how to describe herself? Tall, with thick dark hair cut in a heavy fringe, red lipstick? Hardly a stand-out in a crowd.

"I'll be carrying a copy of *To the Lighthouse.* How about that?"

"See you tomorrow, Mrs. Tipton."

Elfrida replaced the receiver on its cradle. Her heart was bumping as if she'd run up three flights of stairs. She was sure her life was about to change—and the wine list at the Tate restaurant was one of London's finest. She would woo Maitland Bole with the very best claret and extract the secrets of Virginia Woolf's last day from him.

She went upstairs and packed an overnight bag. She wasn't going to wait any longer—she'd catch a train up to London right away. And she had other business in the city. The morning's mail had brought enthusiastic letters from agent and editor, both "dying" to hear more about *The Zigzag Man.* She felt her fortunes were on the turn.

She wrote a note for Reggie—"Gone to London on business. Call me at home. Back next week. E."—and she telephoned for a taxi to take her to the station. Reggie would be happy—a whole weekend to fuck whatever tart he was fucking and no wife in view. Bliss.

21

There were a lot of fans that evening, Anny saw, a dozen or more: word must be spreading. She signed their autograph books, looking out for Cornell. She felt her rising panic again. The police hadn't returned but they might be watching. But then, she reasoned, how would they know when her day's shooting ended? Why should she stop for the autograph hunters—why not just stride into the hotel? She was safe, she decided, but this was the end, period.

Cornell duly arrived as the last fan left. He was wearing a brown raincoat, his spectacles and a tie, she saw. He almost looked distinguished.

"Hey," he said, not smiling. "Have you got it?"

"Nice to see you too, Cornell. Yes, I have it."

She reached into her handbag and found the money. She had wrapped a blue plastic bag around the flat bundles of notes so that it looked like she was handing over a sandwich. Cornell quickly slipped it in his coat pocket.

"Thank you, Anny," he said. "You just saved my life."

"Well, enjoy your life. Bon voyage." She paused. "By the way, it's in pounds, not dollars. Eight hundred pounds—which is two thousand dollars. If you want dollars you'll have to change them."

"Shit. I don't want to go to a bank."

"So change it at the airport. It's a gift, by the way. No need to pay me back. Goodbye."

She felt the pressure of his hand on her arm, stopping her from leaving.

"Can you get me any more? More would be a help," he said in his wheedling, sheepish voice.

It made her stern. "There's no more, Cornell. It's over. We're done, we're through. I cancel all your debts to me."

"Why are you so bitter, Anny?"

"You have the nerve to ask me that? Jesus."

"Can I see you again? I miss you."

"No. You divorced me, remember?"

She walked into the hotel feeling very strange. She refused to look back—but at the same time she realised that she would never see Cornell again, that a significant chapter of her life had just ended. She whirled round, looking for him—but he had gone. A bus had pulled up and a small party of tourists was disembarking. Where was Cornell? How would he cope in Mozambique? It was crazy—stop! She admonished herself. Get a grip. But she felt a heaviness in herself—almost a kind of grief, a bereavement. She hated herself for thinking this but she wanted to see him again—just once more.

She walked across the lobby to collect her key in a strange, confusing miasma of emotions. The unique Cornell Effect, she now recognised. She had sounded so sure of herself but standing there talking to him brought all the memories back, unsettling memories—the push and pull of their relationship, its tireless, tiring variation of attraction and rejection, of fondness and maddened irritation. And she was aware, at the same time, what a huge risk she had taken for him. Why, she asked herself as she picked up her keys from the front desk, why was she prepared to do such a thing for such an infuriating man? Was it some memory of the feelings she once had for him? Some pity she was expressing in witnessing his mad, awkward zeal, the crazy fucked-up principles that had driven him to this disastrous end point in his fraught, inept journey of political activism? Or was it just her nature—maybe it was that, her stupid instinctive response to the neediest of men? She had no answer that made any sense.

Later, when Troy came to her room she could see he felt something was wrong.

"What's up, babe?" he asked, gently. "Looking all nervy and strung up."

For a moment Anny felt like telling him of her last encounter with Cornell but decided against it. So she related the details of the Sylvia and Ferdie fiasco and how she had refused to act with them.

"Wow," Troy said. "Bit heavy. What a day you've had, my lovely. You won't be popular."

"You wouldn't act with me if you didn't like me, didn't respect me."

"I suppose so. What's going to happen?"

"I don't know. I just made my position clear to Rodrigo."

"You got to do what you've got to do, in this life," he said with a smile and began to undress.

Anny wondered, afterwards, why sex with Troy was so easy; why "making love" with him was so uncomplicated and mutually pleasurable. Maybe the answer was simple. Troy was always hard—always—there was never any issue with tumescence. That concern had been a constant problem with her other lovers, Mavrocordato and Cornell in particular. Even Jacques needed his little rituals—he would disappear into the bathroom for two minutes before they went to bed and he liked to drink a lot first. It was a bit hit and miss with Jacques: sometimes good, sometimes awkward, half-achieved. There was always that slight undercurrent of worry—like hearing a mosquito in a room—that somehow spoilt things. Too much brain involved, too much thinking. But not with Troy. All she had to do was take off her clothes and he was ready for action.

"We're like two animals, mating," she said to him.

"That's not a very nice thing to say."

"No, I mean we feel the need and we just, you know, do it."

"But you're beautiful, Anny. That's what turns me on. Your beautiful face, your incredible body. I can't resist. Anyway, animals only do it to breed."

"True," she said. "I take it back."

He jumped out of bed, his cock swinging, still heavy, she saw, still engorged, and he went looking for his bottle of wine.

"Want some?" he said, from across the room, holding up the bottle.

"No. I took my pills."

"Why do you take all those pills? You're not sick." He came over with his glass of wine and sat on the side of the bed.

"I need them—for when I'm worried. Or I can't sleep. Or I can't wake up."

"You're taking pills to cancel out the effect of the pills you've taken. Not clever. I don't take drugs."

"Alcohol is a drug," she said. "You've got a drug in your hand."

"No, it's not. Drinking is a natural act. Breathing smoke into your lungs, injecting yourself, sniffing powder up your nose or swallowing powerful chemicals is not natural. It's not in our nature. Drinking is—it's like eating, breathing, pissing."

"It's not like that," she said. "I don't want to get stoned. It's a safety net for me. I'm like a high-wire act. I need my net."

"I'll be your net," Troy said.

Anny was going to kiss him in gratitude but the phone rang. It was the front desk.

"Hello, Miss Viklund, we have a Mister Jacques Soldat here for you."

"OK. Could you send him up in five minutes? I just have to finish a meeting. Thank you."

She thought she was going to vomit.

"Send who up?" Troy said.

"My boyfriend from Paris. He's here."

"Fuck! What do we do?"

When she opened the door to Jacques five minutes later she was dressed. She kissed him and clung to him and whispered in his ear.

"We're just finishing a script meeting," she whispered. "He'll be gone in a minute."

She led Jacques from the hallway into the suite's sitting room. Troy sat at the table, also fully dressed, script open in front of him. Opposite him there was another open script—hers.

"Troy, this is Jacques. Jacques, Troy."

They shook hands.

"Heard a lot about you, man," Troy said. "Good to meet you."

"Enchanté."

Anny closed her script. She was finding it difficult to breathe. She wanted to take great lungfuls of air.

"Got a big scene tomorrow," Troy said. "Thought we'd better go through it on our own."

"I don't want to interrupt," Jacques said.

"We're pretty much done." Troy picked up the script. "See you tomorrow, Anny."

"See you."

"Nice to meet you, Jacques."

"It was a pleasure."

When Troy had gone Jacques took her in his arms, staring into her eyes, tilting her chin up with a finger.

"Why didn't you goddam tell me you were coming?" she said, firmly, pre-empting his awkward question.

"I wanted to surprise you."

"Well, it worked."

Jacques released her and poured himself a glass of wine from Troy's bottle.

"What happened with Cornell?" he asked.

"I gave him money."

"Enough?"

"I gave him what he asked for. I told him that was it. Finished." She heard her own voice, as if it was being broadcast from a radio—full of conviction, so assured. How could she do this? She was an actress, after all, she thought—as long as Jacques didn't know she was acting.

"Anyway," Jacques said. "I'm here now. All your troubles are over."

22

Within a minute—less—Talbot knew the girl was all wrong. Even to refer to her as a "girl" was something of a joke. He had placed the usual advertisement in the *Photographers' Journal.* "Young male or female models sought for medical textbook and fine-art magazines. Excellent physical condition essential." He had had three immediate responses—two male and one female—and had chosen the one, the supposed young female, with a London address. There was no point in bringing some lad down from Scotland or Yorkshire for a couple of hours in the studio.

The young woman who had presented herself at the garden gate at the appointed hour (as instructed) smiled and said, "Hi, I'm Lorraine." She was small and perilously thin with dyed black hair badly cut in that strange feathered style, he saw, and, Talbot reckoned, was closer to thirty than to twenty. She looked nothing like the photograph she had sent as evidence of her modelling suitability. He always insisted on a photograph as there was a particular type of girl he needed. The type of girl was vital—gamine verging on feral—and he could usually tell from the photos they sent. But this Lorraine looked entirely different from her promotional image and, he could see, she wasn't in excellent physical condition, either. Her pallor made the acne scars that dimpled her jawbone more obvious, a sad stippling of pink and blue spots, and the belt of her jeans was buckled below the improbable swell of a small pot belly for someone so manifestly skinny. Was she pregnant? He felt the sudden weariness of unforeseen disappointment descend on him; the mildly bitter realisation that the world has let you down again.

All the same he showed Lorraine into the house and into the drawing room, cursing his bad luck. He had to make this encounter end as soon as possible.

"I'm really sorry," Talbot said, "but my camera seems to be broken." He gestured at his Rolleiflex mounted on its stand. Everything was set up for the shoot—the linen backdrop, the 500-watt spot, the photoflood spot. "I'm going to have to get it fixed. Apologies."

"Don't you have another camera?"

"Of course, several. But they're not right for this job. Unfortunately."

He took out his wallet and gave Lorraine the £10 note, the fee they had agreed on.

She took the note, turned it over, scrutinised it, folded it and tucked it in a pocket, petulantly, almost sneeringly, Talbot thought.

"Well, waste of a Saturday for me," she said with some aggression. "Came all the way from Dagenham."

Talbot found a fiver in his pocket and handed it over.

"For your expenses. Just one of those damn things. Very sorry."

"Yeah." Lorraine looked at him knowingly. "We could still—you know—even if your camera's broke."

"I don't follow."

"I'm not stupid, Mr. Eastman. We all know what 'Young female models' means. I done this before, many times. We could have some fun. You've paid me. I've come all this way."

"I think," Talbot said, closing his eyes, "you've got the wrong end of the stick. I'm a professional photographer."

"Wrong end of the stick?" Lorraine repeated. "Let's have a look at your stick, then. There's all sorts of things I can do with a stick . . ."

"I think you'd better leave, if you don't mind."

Talbot showed her out, feigning outraged dignity, terse and silent. As he saw the sagging seat of her denim jeans—no buttocks there—he suddenly realised she must be a drug addict of some kind. *Caveat emptor.*

At the garden door Lorraine pointed a finger in his face and said, "Remember, I know where you live. You can't do this sort of thing."

"And I know who you are," Talbot replied, evenly, affecting unconcern. "And so will my solicitor, if I experience any problems with you." He recognised that he had this patrician, unprovable conviction that any threat of the "law" unnerved poor or working-class people.

"Fuck you, you perve, you old cunt," Lorraine said and wandered off down the road with her £15.

Talbot closed and locked the garden door, relief warming him, able to relax, now. It was very rare for his models to turn nasty or threatening. This had only happened twice before—both times with young men. It was disturbing to have a woman insult him. Advertising in bona fide photographic magazines seemed to be the ideal cover. There were dozens of similarly encoded advertisements on the back pages of these journals—for male and female models—all couched in terms of absolute probity, and all concealing the usual carnal motives, no doubt.

He was suddenly distracted by a series of metallic clangs and dull slaps of planks being dropped from a height, then a chorus of raucous shouts from the street. Looking up, he could see that the back of the next-door house had a shrouding of scaffolding. The noise must mean they were scaffolding the front, now. "As noisy as a gang of scaffolders," he thought, the simile coming into his head, for some reason. He went back inside and poured himself a large Scotch and soda, somewhat unnerved by his encounter with Lorraine. So much for his plans for this Saturday, this precious weekend. He had been looking forward to his photography session—you never knew what such encounters might bring in their train, that was an essential part of the thrill—but now he had an empty day to himself before he was due to head for the Royal Festival Hall and Humphrey's concert.

He searched among the few books he kept here at the flat and found a copy of *A Room With a View*. He had a sudden pang of memory about Zoë who had studied *A Passage to India* for O level. "It's by Em Forster," she had told him confidently. She had been a very sweet sixteen, all right, he thought, slow to leave her pre-teen child-self, as if reluctant to confront the adulthood heading remorselessly, speedily, for her. She had liked her father's company then, he remembered—they had seen a lot of each other. And then it all changed.

He topped up his Scotch, picked up his cigarettes and went back down to the garden and settled on the bench in the shade of the apple tree. Perhaps he'd pop out to the new Italian restaurant on Erskine Road later and have a plate of pasta.

He lit a cigarette and opened his book but seeing the printed page suddenly made him think of Yorgos and the *Burning Leaves* contract. He had deliberately pushed the matter to the back of his mind, thinking—surely—that John Saxonwood was over-reacting. The contract was in French, John had said, and, as far as he could tell, the film rights in the play were now assigned by YSK to a company based in Luxembourg called FUMODOR S.A. He, Talbot Kydd, was named as one of the directors of the company but was not the owner, or had not contributed a share to the sum of money—500,000 francs—that was required as an escrow deposit for all limited-liability companies in Luxembourg. And that, John said, was his concern. Who put up that money? Yorgos? Or Yorgos and some partners? Why wasn't he, Talbot, invited to contribute? There must be a simple explanation, Talbot said, let me talk to Yorgos. I'm not sleeping easy, John Saxonwood said.

Talbot thought about this turn of events. Hand on heart, he would swear on the proverbial stack of bibles that Yorgos Samsa would never knowingly attempt to deceive him, let alone defraud him. Maybe he was being naïve but Yorgos had saved his professional life on at least three occasions. Of course, he was something of a dodgy customer—he was a film producer, for God's sake—but this FUMODOR S.A. scheme must be something that would benefit YSK Films further down the line: tax efficiency, rebates, subventions, grants, something like that. And in any event he hadn't signed anything, so for the moment all was stasis. It could wait until he had a chance for a proper conversation, could look Yorgos squarely in the eye and discover precisely what his clever scheme was.

He read a few pages of *A Room With a View* before the sudden intrusion of music distracted him. That bloody song again—about the park and the cake in the rain and the missing recipe. He stood up and shaded his eyes: there was a shirtless man standing at the highest level of the scaffolding fiddling with what looked like a large portable radio and, at the same time, was yelling incoherent instructions to his colleagues at the front of the house. Something about the scaffolder's poise and musculature made Talbot stride into the flat and return seconds later with his Pentax, fitted with a long telephoto lens. Keeping to the shade cast by the apple tree to make him less obvious, Talbot focussed on the man. He was coming down slowly, tightening bolts at each level with some kind of spanner and shifting planks with short kicks of his boots so they sat more securely. He was shirtless because the day was warm and Talbot could see through his lens, as the man climbed down to another level, that he was young, thirty or so, lean and muscled with a tapered back, broad shoulders and flat discs of pectorals. As he tightened the bolts of the clamps that held the scaffolding poles Talbot could see the shift and flex of his muscles beneath his lightly tanned, slightly grubby skin.

Perfect, Talbot thought, admiringly. I'll let him play his silly music. If only Lorraine had looked as remotely *en forme* . . . He went back to his seat, set his camera down and picked up his book. He saw he'd turned down a page, a third of the way in, and opened the book there. He read a few lines:

> "Well," said he, "I cannot help it if they do disapprove of me. There are certain irremovable barriers between myself and them, and I must accept them."
>
> "We all have our limitations, I suppose," said wise Lucy.
>
> "Sometimes they are forced on us, though," said Cecil, who saw from her remark that she did not quite understand his position.
>
> "How?"
>
> "It makes a difference, doesn't it, whether we fence ourselves in, or whether we are fenced out by the barriers of others?"
>
> She thought a moment, and agreed that it did make a difference.

He yawned, and closed the book—he wasn't that interested, he realised, noticing that some of the hydrangeas in the border were beginning to wilt. He stood and walked over to a small paved area where he kept his few gardening tools in a wooden storage cupboard at the corner of the house where the garden wall formed a right angle with the darkroom. There was a water butt here, also, and he lifted the lid of the storage cupboard, found his watering can, filled it from the butt and gave the wilting hydrangeas their blessed draught of water. Might as well do the others, he supposed, and went back to the butt.

Later, he thought it was strange how time seemed to slow during an accident. Not slow motion, exactly, but as if segmented, like a series of jump cuts. He was aware of something small and dark falling fast at the periphery of his vision. Then there was a *smack* as it glanced off the top of the dividing wall between the gardens and then several panes of his darkroom window exploded and shards of glass fell around him, tinkling, clattering.

He reeled back, glass crunching under his feet, and saw lying on the ground one of the silver bolt and clamp devices that scaffolders use to fix their steel poles to each other. He stooped to pick it up, imagining for some reason that it might be hot to the touch, like some kind of meteorite.

"Are you OK?" came a shout from above.

He looked up to see the young scaffolder leaning out, peering down. Bizarrely, Talbot felt super-aware of the maddening song about the park and the icing and the cake in the rain—it was still interminably playing on the radio—and the absence of a recipe for the cake. He wondered suddenly if he was in shock.

"Were you hit?" the man called, switching the radio off.

"No," Talbot shouted up to him, gathering himself. "Just missed me."

"Don't move. I'll be right there, sir."

"There's a door off the mews," Talbot called to him. He held his hands out: they were trembling slightly. What would have happened if that clamp had hit his head? Incapacity? Instant death? . . .

He walked slowly to the garden door and opened it. He held up the clamp as the scaffolder appeared.

"It almost hit me," Talbot said. "You've got to be more careful."

The young man was breathing deeply, still shirtless, wearing dirty jeans and heavy boots. Talbot handed over the clamp. The man looked at it intently.

"How could that have fallen? I don't get it." He held it out as if in evidence. "Some arsehole must have left it on the walkway. I must have kicked it off."

"Don't ask me," Talbot said. "All I know is it fell off your scaffolding, somehow. Missed me, broke my window."

The man ran a hand through his hair. His nipples were small brown discs, erect, Talbot noticed. He was very lean with no subcutaneous fat on him at all, the muscles clearly defined—you could count his ribs. A little fuse of dark hair ran down from his navel and then under the belt that held his jeans. He had no hair on his torso. Talbot felt his chest tighten, his breathing suddenly shallower. Was it shock? Or was it an example of what he had come to call one of his *Tod in Venedig* moments?

"Can I have a look?"

They walked over to the shattered window.

"Accidents do happen, I suppose," Talbot conceded. "Lucky it didn't fall on my head. Anyway, you have your clamp-thing now."

"We call them couplers, actually."

"You have your coupler."

The scaffolder looked at him.

"You've cut your head."

Talbot touched his forehead and saw the blood gleam on the palp of his finger. He took his handkerchief out of his pocket and the scaffolder took it from him.

"Here, let me." He dabbed at Talbot's forehead. "Just a little cut. Sincere apologies." He had a marked London accent but was clearly educated to a degree, Talbot thought. The scaffolder handed back the handkerchief. Talbot, pocketing it, now realised that a mild shock had indeed set in. His legs felt weak and he could feel tremors running through his body.

"I think I'd better sit down."

The scaffolder took his elbow and guided him back to the seat under the apple tree. Sitting down was better.

"If you get a glazier in to fix that, sir, we'll pay for it, obviously. I'll report it to my boss."

"What? Right. It's a bit inconvenient as I'm not always here. We've got a caretaker, though."

"Have you got a phone number, sir? We can arrange everything."

Talbot tore a blank leaf from the endpapers of *A Room With a View,* took his pen out of his pocket and unthinkingly wrote down the phone number of the Grand at Brighton and his name. Then he scribbled over his name and the number so they were illegible and wrote down the number of the caretaker.

"I'm in Brighton during the week," he said. "Working there. I'm staying in a hotel. That's the caretaker's number—you can leave a message with his wife."

"Can I borrow the pen?"

The scaffolder tore a strip off the bottom of the leaf of paper and wrote down his details, handing them over. Talbot saw: Gary Hicksmith. Axelrod Scaffolding Ltd. And a phone number.

"If your caretaker calls the office, we'll sort everything out when it suits."

"Right. Thanks."

"I didn't catch your name, sir."

"Eastman."

"Mr. Eastman."

Gary wrote it down. Talbot stood up—he felt less shaky.

"Anything else I can do for you, Mr. Eastman?"

"No, thanks for asking. I'm fine now."

"I'll report this in and we'll wait for the call about the glazier. We'll pay for everything, of course." He shook his head, as if suddenly baffled by this turn of events. "This has never happened to me before. Never."

"Right, thank you." Talbot picked up his book. "I think I need a cup of tea."

The scaffolder picked up his camera and handed it to him.

"Nice camera."

"I'm a professional photographer."

"Oh. Great. Super." He paused. "Could have been worse." He grinned. "Thank heaven for small mercies, eh?"

"Just a broken window."

They both chuckled, their mutual relief expressing itself in shared laughter.

"I'll be in touch, Mr. Eastman. You're a scholar and a gentleman. You mind how you go."

Gary Hicksmith left and Talbot shut and locked the garden door behind him. He felt calmer now, the whole event and the subsequent encounter playing itself out in his head like a loop of film. The stupid song, the smash and splinter of glass. He could hardly recall Gary's face, he realised, only the details of his naked torso seemed to have registered. Darkish blond hair, blue eyes? . . . Even-featured, a trace of stubble, a chip off a front tooth . . .

He went back inside and poured himself a large whisky and took a gulp, feeling the burn in his throat and chest. Funny how these events can shake up your life, send it heading in unexpected directions. Glaziers, scaffolders . . . And now he knew what a "coupler" was. He reached into his pocket for his handkerchief and saw the still-bright stain of his blood. He remembered Gary's gesture: how he had taken the handkerchief from him and dabbed away the trickle from the cut. Strange, that. To take it upon himself to do that . . . "You're a scholar and a gentleman," he had said. How did that phrase arrive in a scaffolder's lexicon? He would arrange for the caretaker to call Axelrod Scaffolding Ltd. and make an appointment for the glazier to come round. Something told him that he should try to find a way to see Gary Hicksmith again. A strange compensation for the disappointments of Lorraine. Gary Hicksmith had stirred something in him.

He sipped at his whisky, thinking, agitated. He had hours to kill before he had to be at the concert that night. Somehow he felt that he needed to be active and distracted. He needed to drive, needed to be behind the wheel of the Alvis. He knew they were filming on the front at Brighton today. He would drive back to Brighton, he thought, yes, check on everything, then return to London. Motion, distraction, duty done—that's what he needed. He put his whisky down and picked up his car keys.

23

Maitland Bole was a full twenty-five minutes late, much to Elfrida's irritation. She was always over-punctual herself and found it difficult to tolerate sloppy timekeeping in others. She wandered up and down the steps of the Tate Gallery, whistling monotonally, a soft audible symbol of her displeasure, glancing at her watch, and, eventually frustrated, sat down on a bench and began to read *To the Lighthouse* simply to pass the time but recognising, a few pages in, that she'd forgotten how much she actually disliked the novel, with its footling detail and its breathy, neurasthenic apprehension of the world, all tingling awareness and high-cheekboned sensitivity. How in the name of all that was reasonable could anyone assume that she and Virginia Woolf had anything in common as novelists? A simple read of a page or two of one of her own novels would reveal—

"Mrs. Tipton?"

She looked up to see a small man in a crumpled grey suit with a bulging briefcase in his hand. He had a wispy, yellowy-white Abraham Lincoln beard, his upper lip shaved clean. What was the point of such a preposterous beard? Elfrida wondered, still annoyed by his tardiness. But she smiled politely, stood, greeted him, shook his hand and led him down to the Tate's basement restaurant.

Established in a corner, their backs to Rex Whistler's evocative and mysterious Arcadian mural, more pleasantries were exchanged—

weather conditions, travel, health—and they consulted the menu. Or, rather, Bole consulted the menu while Elfrida consulted the wine list.

"Burgundy or Bordeaux?" she asked.

"I don't drink," Bole said. "Doctor's orders."

"That's a shame. Not even a glass?"

"Daren't risk it. I might have a seizure—the medication I'm on."

"Poor you. Sorry to hear that. Well, I'll order a bottle just in case you change your mind."

She waffled on about the rare wine-drinking opportunities the Tate's restaurant provided but she could tell that Bole wasn't listening as he scrutinised his dining choices. Not off to the best of starts, Elfrida thought, and ordered a bottle of 1962 Gruaud-Larose. Then she chose pea soup and liver and bacon while Bole plumped for prawn cocktail and steak and kidney pie. He was more than happy with a glass of Thames water, he said, as Elfrida's bottle arrived. She tasted it and deemed it satisfactory. There were some advantages to dining with a teetotaller, she thought, encouraging the sommelier to pour her a generous glass.

"I've got your pamphlets in my briefcase," Bole said.

"Let me write you a cheque immediately," she said, thinking that a free lunch and a highly profitable monetary exchange rather put Maitland Bole in her debt—he could hardly refuse to answer her questions.

She took out her chequebook, wrote the cheque (£22 5s) and handed it over. No discount offered, she noticed, even though she was buying in bulk. Still, she had her own objectives this lunchtime and that's what she should concentrate on, she told herself. Bole took a plastic bag out of his briefcase that was packed with the pamphlets and handed them over. She tucked the bag under the table by her feet.

"You see," she said, "I'm particularly interested in the details of Virginia Woolf's very last day. I've seen the house, I've walked across the water meadows to the Ouse and stood on the bank looking at the water, and I've even had a conversation with Leonard Woolf." She took a sip of her wine. "I'm trying to imagine what she was thinking in those last hours of life—from the moment she woke up. The whole process would be simpler, and better, if I knew the details of her daily life, her domestic routine."

"Why?"

"Sorry?"

"Why are you interested in the last day of Virginia Woolf?"

"Because I'm going to write a novel about that last day." She spoke without thinking and wondered if she'd made a terrible error in announcing the fact. But, curiously, it seemed to make Bole relax.

"Well, if it's a *novel,*" he said, emphasising the word, as if it were some kind of unpleasant disease, "then you can just make the whole thing up. You don't need me."

"True in a sense," she said, carefully, "and I will speculate to a degree, obviously. But the more I know, the more details, facts, the better the fiction will be. Or so I happen to believe."

"Is that right?"

"Yes. In my experience."

"Are you a novelist?"

"No! Not at all. No, no. Goodness, no. I mean, as a reader. In my experience as a reader." She took a gulp of her wine—it really was delicious. And she was now exceptionally pleased she didn't have to share it with Bole.

"I'm starting out," she said, a little lamely. "Thinking of having a go at a novel."

Bole pushed his finished prawn cocktail to one side. He had a sizeable blob of Marie Rose settled amongst the wiry hairs of his chin-beard. She wondered if she should alert him to this—she didn't think she could eat on if it wasn't removed—and then, luckily, as if he could read her mind, he swiped it away with his napkin.

"That would be your fourth novel, Elfrida Wing, am I right?" Bole smiled as if he'd just won a prize.

You fool, Elfrida admonished herself. You stupid fool. Bole was in her world, a "man of letters" of some sort. Of course, there had been a chance he might recognise her, now she thought about it. Her dreams of total anonymity were never going to be realised as long as her novels were on a shelf somewhere, with a picture of her young self on the back flap.

"Yes," she said. "I apologise. A silly subterfuge."

"I'm an admirer," Bole said. "Particularly of *Excesses.* My favourite. So cunning, so wonderfully dark."

"Thank you."

"And now a novel about the last day of Virginia Woolf. I can't wait."

"There may be a bit of a wait, in fact. I'm just researching the idea."

"It's really none of my business," Bole said, "and I hope you don't mind my pointing this out. But do you think anyone's really that interested in Virginia Woolf, any more? My *Bloomsbury in East Sussex* is my worst-selling pamphlet by far. I think Woolf's a bit old hat, these days. There must be other writers you could tackle: Oliver Onions, Alfred Duggan, Edith Nesbit."

"I have a particular, personal interest in Virginia Woolf."

Bole shrugged.

"It's your decision, of course. But what about Henry James in Rye? Kipling? Ford Madox Ford?"

"It has to be Woolf. Sorry."

Bole leant forward, confidentially.

"Well, the first thing you should know is that they had separate bedrooms—Virginia and Leonard, that is—so she would have woken up alone."

"Really? Do tell. Do you mind if I take notes?" She found her notebook and pen and began to scribble away as Bole spoke. And he certainly did—she hardly needed to interpose a question—it was as if his prawn cocktail had made him garrulous. And as she made her notes she became aware that he seemed to have very precise information. He told her that in the morning Leonard Woolf always brought Virginia a cup of tea in bed, then she would have a bath and get dressed and the two of them would breakfast after Leonard had had his bath. He mentioned that Virginia Woolf worked in a wooden, purpose-built gazebo-shed in the garden and that, every day, around about nine o'clock, she would cross the garden to begin her morning's work. She had just finished her last novel in 1941, Bole added, *Between the Acts.*

On her last day of life, 28 March, she had returned to the house around eleven o'clock, unnoticed, because Leonard was working upstairs in his study, and left two letters on a table—or the chimney piece, he wasn't absolutely sure—one for Leonard and one for her sister, Vanessa. Then she had put on her wellington boots, and a fur coat, and picked up her stick as if she were going for a walk. She left the garden by the gate by the church and walked to the Ouse. It was high tide so the water would be very close to the edge of the embankment. She was spotted by a labourer as she headed to the river. That was about 11:30, or 11:40. This labourer was the last person to see her alive.

"Then she jumped in—or waded in, or slithered in—the banks are steep," Bole said. "Of course, as you're writing a novel you can choose. Maybe a leap would be more dramatic."

"Apparently she put a big stone in one pocket," Elfrida said.

"Really? How do you know that?"

"Enid . . ." She paused. "A friend of the family told me."

"Interesting," Bole said. "I didn't know that. Nice detail." He forked a piece of kidney into his mouth and started chewing vigorously, an action that made his beard bob disconcertingly, Elfrida thought, and she bent her head to concentrate on her liver and bacon. She wasn't very hungry, she realised. She poured herself another glass of Gruaud-Larose.

"It is an interesting detail," Elfrida said, "because it rather proves that her suicide wasn't something she did spontaneously. She clearly wanted to die and the large stone was meant to make second thoughts impossible."

"Good point," Bole said, frowning. "Or to make the end swifter."

"Exactly."

Bole resumed his narrative. Leonard Woolf came down to lunch at the usual time and found the letters.

"A suicide note?" Elfrida asked.

"I believe so. Whatever she wrote was enough to make him raise the alarm. But she'd disappeared. Gone."

"How awful," Elfrida said, suddenly transported to the banks of the Ouse. A fur coat, wellington boots, a large stone in a pocket.

"You don't happen to know what type of fur coat she was wearing, do you?" Elfrida asked.

"Sorry, no. Is it important?"

"Well, for a novelist it might be. Was it mink, musquash, rabbit? God is in the details, you know."

Bole looked at her, mystified.

"The body wasn't found for three weeks," Bole said. "Even though they dragged the river again and again."

"How do you know all this?" Elfrida said. "If you don't mind my asking."

"I spoke to her cook, Louie Everest. She was very forthcoming. Very happy to chat about it all."

"Louie Everest. What a name. So, she had staff."

"Only the one—Louie. She would pop in every day to cook lunch. The live-in maid had left at the end of 1940. Apparently—Louie told me this—Virginia Woolf actually liked doing housework. Really liked it."

"Now, that is interesting," Elfrida said. "Fascinating. What kind of housework?"

"What kinds of housework are there? Dusting, polishing, washing dishes, tidying, laundry. I don't suppose she had a vacuum cleaner in Monk's House."

"Not in 1941, no."

"Did they exist?" Bole seemed genuinely interested.

"Oh, yes. But they were luxury items. It was a bit of a social brag: 'We have a Hoover.'" Elfrida tried to imagine a Hoover in Monk's House. "She might have had a carpet sweeper, however," she said. "You know—push-pull."

Bole thought. "I can't quite see Virginia Woolf with a Bissell, can you?" He was beginning to seem quite animated—perhaps he was thinking of another pamphlet, Elfrida wondered: *Household Appliances in East Sussex Between the Wars.*

"I suppose a Hoover would be unlikely . . ." Elfrida tried again to picture Virginia Woolf doing housework. "Do you think she might have done some housework that day?"

"Who knows?" Bole said, dabbing at his mouth and horrible beard with his napkin. "If it's a novel you're writing you could have her doing a bit of dusting or polishing the silver."

Elfrida made a note: "Housework?"

Bole was looking at the menu again, considering a dessert. Elfrida topped herself up, realising the bottle was almost empty. She felt charged with a strange energy that she hadn't experienced in years. She knew what was going on. Her brain was working, exploring the possibilities of a fiction. Virginia Woolf was going to do some housework before she killed herself. Wonderful detail. She emptied the rest of the bottle into her glass.

"According to Louie Everest," Bole confided, "she was very affected by the war—in a bad way, I mean. Her house in London was bombed—destroyed—and the Ouse Valley was right under the flight path of the German raiders."

"The Battle of Britain," Elfrida said. "Of course."

"Bombs were dropped. Planes crashed."

"Must have been terrifying, sometimes."

"Oh yes, the wider conflict came to East Sussex," Bole said a little pompously. "I've written a pamphlet about it—*East Sussex at War.* Sells very well, if you're interested."

"I may very well be." Elfrida wondered if she dared to order more wine.

"As I said, bombs were dropped on villages—incendiaries—there were machine-gunnings of traffic and streets. Aircraft crashing—dead pilots and aircrew. Air-raid warnings all day and night. It got to her."

"Got on her nerves in a real sense. Yes, I can understand that."

"Louie Everest told me that it was obvious for about two months—since the beginning of 1941—that she was close to a crack-up. Another nervous breakdown. Louie knew the signs."

"My God, yes . . ." Elfrida thought: you find you're going mad and the world around you has gone mad. Why not jump in the river?

Bole ordered apple crumble and custard.

"Can I tempt you to a brandy? A cognac?" she asked.

"Lord, no! That would kill me off."

"I hope you don't mind if I partake." Elfrida smiled and signalled for a waiter. She was celebrating—the book in her head was taking shape. Life was suddenly worth living again.

24

The sun was shining but the day felt strangely cool, Anny thought. Maybe it was her proximity to the sea—green-blue, choppy, endless—that was making her shiver. It was only the English Channel, she knew, but from where she was sitting on Brighton's Esplanade the horizon promised its usual imitation of infinity. It could have been the sea, pistachio-coloured, with darker shroudings that hued the water, like blooms opening, dark sea-flowers opening below the waves, changing the light, changing the temperature . . .

She stopped herself. What was she thinking? She looked at the open script in her lap. There were a lot of lines to be remembered in this upcoming scene and she was having trouble retaining them in her mind, urge herself on as she might. She was sitting on a folding canvas chair amongst the usual clutter and paraphernalia of a film shoot—cameras, generators, sound recorders, a make-up tent, great coils of cable and stacked arc lights—positioned close to the entrance to Brighton's West Pier. She could see, twenty yards away, Jacques and Troy in earnest conversation, Jacques gesturing eloquently; Troy listening, head cocked, hands clasped behind his back, as if he were a student being hectored by his professor. What could they be talking about? she wondered, vaguely concerned. She looked down again at her script. This was the big reconciliation scene between Emily and Ben, hence the three pages of dialogue. It was ostensibly taking place forty-eight hours after Emily had slapped Ben's face, boarded a bus and disappeared. She subsequently experienced a series of strange, surreal encounters (yet to be filmed) and then had telephoned Ben and instructed him to meet her under the pier. She had tried to learn the lines last night and failed because of Jacques' arrival. His presence seemed to fill her hotel suite like perfume, like smoke.

After Troy had left they had ordered some food and more wine from room service. When they went to bed, eventually, she had told Jacques that her period was about to start. Jacques said fine, don't worry, *chérie,* and admitted he was very tired himself. The relief was immense. As she lay beside him in the dark, awake for hours, it seemed, listening to his gentle snores, she kept pushing away memories of herself and Troy and their lovemaking in that very bed a few hours previously. She pushed away guilt, also, and set her mind to neutral. No wonder she couldn't learn her lines, she thought, with everything that was going on, all the multiplying complications of her life. She stood and went to find Rodrigo.

Rodrigo was very understanding when she told him she had a bit of a migraine and that she was having trouble remembering her lines.

"It's not a problem, honeybun," Rodrigo said. "Most of this scene is in long shot. You and Troy can say anything you like—rhubarb, rhubarb, you know—and we'll dub it all in during post."

"What about the close-ups?"

"We'll write everything down on idiot boards. No, I don't mean that—I hate that expression. Sorry. We'll have your lines on boards behind the camera." He smiled benignly. "Actually, I prefer it this way. You get more spontaneity."

"Great. Thanks, Rodrigo. It's just like my head feels full of hot concrete."

"Migraines are a fucking nightmare. You leave everything to me, sweet angel."

She could now see that Jacques was wandering over to them. When she'd first introduced him to Rodrigo he claimed to have read Jacques' book, *Black Skin, White Heart.* "One of the great books," he had said. "*Exceptionel, incroyable.* A privilege to meet you, sir."

Jacques had always told her that he'd be a rich man if the number of people who claimed to have read his book had actually bought it and done so.

"How's it going?" he said, finding a chair and sitting down beside her. *"Ça va?"*

"What were you talking to Troy about?" she asked.

"Paris. He had no idea what had happened in May. No idea at all. It's like he's living on a different planet."

"He's a pop singer."

"It's not an excuse."

"You're too stern. Too implacable."

"I think I'll go back to the hotel," he said. "I'd forgotten how incredibly boring it is to be on a film set." He gestured. "What are all these people doing, standing around—eating, smoking, drinking coffee? And they're all being paid. It's like a circle of hell."

"You're too stern, I told you so," she repeated and encouraged him to go back. In the scene they were about to shoot she and Troy had to kiss and she wasn't sure she wanted Jacques to witness it. In their relationship—in the year or so of the intensity of their relationship—she hadn't made a film so this was something new to him. Jacques had been part of the solution to the monstrous success—and the monstrous intrusion in her life of the monstrous success—of *The Yellow Mountain*. When she was with Jacques she could almost forget that she was an actress, a "star." So *Ladder to the Moon* was the first time he had seen her at work. He kissed her on both cheeks, squeezed her hand, allowed his knuckles to brush her breasts and said he was going to explore this curious town, and looked about him, as if deciding which way to go. Just then Talbot Kydd appeared.

"Anny, good afternoon. Lovely day. All going well?"

"Perfect." She stood up and introduced Jacques.

"Talbot, this is my friend Jacques Soldat. He's visiting for a few days."

"Hello," Jacques said. They shook hands.

"Talbot's the producer of the film."

"Ah. The man with the real power," Jacques said.

She saw Talbot smile.

"It's a fantasy we like to encourage," he said.

"The fantasy of power," Jacques said. "It could be the title of my next book."

"La Fantaisie de Pouvoir," Talbot said. "Or would *'puissance'* be better? *'Hégémonie'*?"

"No: *'pouvoir.'* I'll steal it from you."

"Je vous en prie."

"I'm going for a promenade," Jacques said.

"*Un flâneur à Brighton.* Not such a good title."

The two men laughed. For some reason, Anny felt glad that they had met—they seemed to like each other, she thought. At least they responded to each other. Most people who met Jacques seemed in awe of him, like Rodrigo; they wanted to be acknowledged somehow, as fans, supplicants. Talbot didn't. She liked him for that.

Jacques said au revoir and wandered off and Talbot went to talk to Rodrigo. Then Shirley appeared and said Anny was wanted in hair and make-up for final checks.

An hour later she was standing under the West Pier, listening to the rattle and shift of the pebbles being rearranged by the small waves, as if some giant maracas were being gently shaken. She was wearing silver pointed boots, red flared trousers and a short purple kaftan shimmering with sequins and tiny mirrors stitched into the fabric. Rodrigo wanted her and Troy to wear the brightest clothes, all primary colours. The other characters' costumes verged on monotone—greys, browns, sludgy greens. It was "symbolic," he said, when she asked why, and added nothing more.

She shivered. There were arc lights on her but underneath the pier it was damp, seaweed hung from the metal piles supporting the boardwalk like wet beards, she thought. She could see small crabs moving about in the fronds and there was a strange smell in the air—fishy and industrial at the same time—as if diesel fumes were drifting down from some machinery above her head. She heard the shout of "Action!" and looked up the beach for Troy.

This was the long shot, the master shot with two cameras on them, so there were no crew near her. Troy was walking towards her, still a hundred yards away, vivid in his cerise hussar's jacket, white jeans and red boots. He had to walk a long distance along the shingle towards her—music would be playing over this scene, so Rodrigo had said. They would confront each other under the pier, talk, and then kiss and make up.

As she watched him steadily drawing near she felt a strange emotion begin to come over her—a kind of relief, a relaxation. Nobody else had ever made her feel so calm. Why did he have this effect on her?

Or maybe it was because Jacques had left on his promenade through Brighton.

Troy was here, now. He stopped.

" 'Ello, darlin'," he said, in a cockney accent. "We just have to talk nonsense, according to Rodrigo."

"What were you and Jacques discussing?"

"Oh, yeah. He was telling me about these amazing riots in Paris, in May. All these schoolkids and students rioting, trying to start a revolution. I must have missed it."

"Don't you watch television?"

"Of course I watch telly. *Top of the Pops.* Nature programmes. Lots of sport."

"What about the news?"

"I don't really like watching the news, to be honest. It depresses me."

"I know what you mean."

They stood there for a while facing each other, smiling. How stupid I am, Anny thought.

"I suppose it should look like we're having a bit of an argument," Troy said, and waved his arms about, randomly.

Anny pointed at him, then put her hands on her hips as if she was offended. As far as she could remember, Ben was apologising and Anny was to be unforgiving before she yielded.

"I miss you, Anny," Troy said. He drew a line with his finger across his eyebrows. "I'm up to here with unused spunk."

"That's disgusting," she said. "Is this how you charm me?"

"Can I sneak in tonight?"

"Jacques is staying with me. How can you 'sneak' in?"

"You could sneak into my room."

"He won't be here long. He has to go back to Paris."

Troy nodded. "Is the revolution over?"

"Seems to be. I'm not sure what's going on now."

"You're fucking beautiful, Anny. Anyone ever told you that?"

A shout came from the esplanade.

"OK! Kiss now!"

Troy stepped forward and took her in his arms. He kissed her neck.

"I've creamed my jeans," he said.

She turned his face and kissed him hard, her tongue deep in his mouth. He responded and held her tightly. Anny closed her eyes and surrendered herself to the moment, sensing the weakness in her spine, the lung-heave of desire, of oxygen-need.

"OK! Cut!"

They broke apart.

"That was a nice long one," Troy said. "I suppose it'll have to do for a while. Iron rations."

Anny wondered how long they had been kissing. Five seconds? Ten? Twenty?

She turned and looked up to the esplanade where the crew were beginning to shift all the equipment down onto the shingle for the close-ups. She felt her neck stiffen.

Jacques was standing there on the edge of the esplanade, his hands in his pockets, staring at her. Even at this distance she could feel his cold scrutiny. She waved at him and blew a kiss. It was a futile gesture, she was fully aware. Jacques would know, now. All doubts gone, all suspicions confirmed.

25

"Virginia Woolf stirred, grunted and shifted in her bed as the faint spring sunshine created a thin lemon-yellow rectangle on the wall of her bedroom. She sat up slowly, blinking, her arriving consciousness chasing away the dream she was having from her immediate memory. She could not grasp that fleeting, fleeing dream, try as she might, and then she remembered that this was going to be the last day of her life."

Elfrida put her pen down and exhaled. Now she saw that her penless right hand was shaking, vibrating, and she quickly picked up her vodka and tonic. She raised the glass to herself.

"Welcome back, Elfrida Wing," she said. She would stop drinking soon, she promised herself—perhaps when she had a full chapter done and the book was more of a reality; when more black was on white. Now she'd just started she didn't think the time was right to put the extra pressure of abstinence on herself.

And she had started—the dam had broken, the mists had cleared, day had followed night—and whatever other cliché would serve, she thought. She gave a little loud *whoop* of pleasure and then felt self-conscious.

She turned back a page of her notebook and looked at what she had written.

THE LAST DAY OF VIRGINIA WOOLF
a novel by
Elfrida Wing

She banged her fist on her desk, both elated and angry with herself. Why had it taken a decade of silence to produce these few dozen words, these three sentences? There was no rational answer—but time, circumstance and the aleatory, unfathomable workings of her mind had combined to deliver this . . . this recension. Was that the word? She went to her bookshelf and took out her dictionary. No, not really. "Recension" meant the editing of a text, or more generally, "a revised or distinct form of anything." Not quite. "Recessional," then. She checked: a hymn sung at the end of a church service. There was something hymn-like in what she had written, she supposed, it provoked a real form of rejoicing. But no, "transfiguration" was the word she needed. It had been a transfiguration, a transformation, something beautiful, sublime, had happened—a metamorphosis. Something dry and sterile had experienced a transfiguration and had become fecund, glorious and full of promise.

She screwed the cap back on her pen, picked up her glass and went downstairs. Softly, softly, one step at a time, she said to herself. She sat down in her sitting room a little overwhelmed at what had happened, sensing tears in her eyes. It had been such a long time. Foolish woman, she admonished. She was just happy to be back in her own house—her cosy white cottage in the Vale of Health in Hampstead—a house she had bought with all the money she had made from *The Big Show.*

Not entirely her home any more, really, given that Reggie had moved in after their marriage. It was full of his possessions, his stuff: posters of films he'd made or would have liked to have made—*The Exterminating Angel, Belle de Jour, La Dolce Vita, The Red Desert, Il Gobbo.* This was why he wanted to change his name to Rodrigo, she realised. Some preposterous hope that people would think he was half Italian or Spanish or Brazilian and that the new name would allow him to borrow, or steal, some of the allure of these foreign film-makers he so admired and envied. It was sad, she thought, sad as the crude abstract sculptures—unpolished curved pieces of welded metal—perched on windowsills and tables and the two black leather Eames chairs with stools that didn't suit the shabby, Arts and Crafty look of the sitting room at all, she thought. She took her glass into the kitchen for a transfiguring, celebratory refill. Reggie had paid to redo the kitchen, she admitted, all granite and pale blond wood—again not exactly to her taste. Maybe he was quietly colonising the house, she thought, unkindly. Maybe she should reclaim the lost ground now she was writing again: she'd been too compliant, too passive.

She topped up her drink and stepped out through the kitchen door into her small square of back garden. There was a round teak table with a parasol and four chairs set on a neat raised terrace of York stone, a patch of lawn and a high beech hedge. No flowers apart from a border of perennial purple geraniums running along the foot of the hedge. She pulled a chair into the sunlight and sat down, thinking about Reggie and their marriage.

She knew Reggie had affairs, especially when he was making a film. He wasn't an accomplished adulterer and she discovered his transgressions without really trying. She supposed she should be more bothered but she couldn't stir herself to protest, somehow. *Une épouse complaisante.* Another novel-title for her long list. Anyway, her own libido seemed pretty much shut down as well, these days. She found herself wondering what Leonard Woolf had thought about Virginia's affairs. Was he *un mari complaisant*? But then Virginia's affairs were all with women. Did that make a difference? Still, she thought, now her career as a novelist was functioning again perhaps everything would change and she'd kick Reggie out the next time she caught him in one of his nasty, furtive dalliances. Just like his first wife, Marion, who had instantly chucked him out when she'd discovered his affair with me, she thought. God, Marion Tipton, what a vengeful, hostile, unforgiving woman. Though, she considered, maybe she had grounds for her bitterness. Reggie's daughters had been young, six and eight. What were the girls' names? Stupid names: Butterfly and Evergreen. Imagine growing up as Evergreen Tipton . . . As Elfrida thought back to the months of the affair with Reggie it seemed as if she was contemplating a different person, another human being entirely. Oh, *that* Elfrida Wing . . .

She heard the phone ring in the house and wondered whether to answer it. All right, she thought, in the spirit of the recent transfiguration I will start answering the phone, and she strode back indoors. She picked up the receiver. It was one of her oldest and closest friends,

Jessica Fairfield. They had been at Cambridge together and Jessica had turned into a rather brilliant solicitor, so everyone told her; a senior partnership was imminent.

"There you are, darling. Glad I caught you," Jessica said. She had a deep voice, it could have been a man on the line.

They chatted for a bit, Elfrida making sure her lies were not too bold. Yes, everything generally wonderful, writing again, Reggie was fine, happy to be directing his silly film.

"Listen," Jessica said. "Are you busy tonight? Something's come up."

26

In the taxi on the way to the Royal Festival Hall Talbot found his mind returning repeatedly to his strange, unsought encounter with the young scaffolder, Gary Hicksmith. Was this natural or was there something growingly obsessive about this focus? Let it play out as it may, he thought, there was nothing to be gained by fantasising. He almost laughed out loud. There was *everything* to be gained by fantasising; surely fantasising kept you sane, interested in life, connected to events, to all manner of agreeable, hypothetical possibilities. Maybe, he considered further, the very ability to fantasise was a fundamental feature of our human nature. Animals didn't—couldn't—fantasise. Only *Homo sapiens* possessed that gift. We should cherish it.

He remembered his conversation with Anny's friend, Jacques Soldat, on the front at Brighton and their amused, ever so slightly spiky speculation about a book called *The Fantasy of Power.* Soldat had a strange, aggressive manner, as if he lived to provoke and was suspicious and slightly contemptuous of everyone he met. It was born of self-confidence, though, this attitude—of success, not chippiness, that debilitating English disease. He brought Soldat to mind. What did Anny see in a man like that—at least twenty years older than she was? They did themselves no favours, these young, vulnerable actresses. Cornell Weekes, the urban terrorist, and Jacques Soldat, the radical philosopher. Surely she could have met and chosen someone more appropriate . . . Anyway, it wasn't his problem.

He had telephoned Naomi to arrange where to meet and discovered she was laid up in bed with flu, so he was to go to the concert alone, she said. Fair enough, he thought, his weekend wasn't running to the plan he'd made so he might as well discard it entirely. Also, it would give him a chance to spend some time alone with Humphrey, "man to man," and determine the state of their relationship which, currently, to be honest with himself, he would describe as somewhat awkward and distant.

He picked up his ticket from the box office and wandered a while amongst the throng of concertgoers, wondering whether to have a drink now or at the interval. Interval, he thought. He bought a programme and saw that Richard Strauss's tone poem *Also Sprach Zarathustra* was to start the evening off followed by Grieg's *Peer Gynt Suite* and Rimsky-Korsakov's *Scheherazade.* He looked about him at his fellow members of the audience as he went upstairs to locate his seat in the auditorium and thought, as he always did when he found himself in a significant crowd, how simply odd other people were, how strange. Sometimes he wished—as if in another world that he controlled absolutely—that people should have labels on their backs describing who they were and what reasons they had for their presence: "Germanophile," "Failed Artist," "Bored," "Classical Music Enthusiast," "Trying to Impress," "Aimless Tourist," "Forlorn Lover," or whatever. And what would his label proclaim? "Father of the Timpanist." Perhaps he seemed just as odd to the others, this tall bald severe-looking middle-aged man, equally worthy of their curiosity and scrutiny.

He took his seat, to one side but with a good view of the orchestra, annoyed that he hadn't brought his binoculars. Opera glasses were no good, not sufficient magnification, he found. He had been to hundreds of concerts in his life and found the experience immeasurably improved if you could watch the players through the precisely focussed lenses of binoculars. It was voyeuristic, he knew, but to see in close-up the intensity of concentration and the range of facial expression and distortion was stimulating and diverting. And when the musicians weren't playing it was even more enticing: the covert scratching that took place, the adjustments of hair and costume, the whispers, the asides, the glances, the fiddling with the intricacies of the instrument, getting rid of saliva, moistening reeds, tiny twists of the pegs that tightened or loosened strings, one eye always on the score or the conductor—it was like being a peeping Tom in public, and uncensorable, wholly conscionable and permitted. For him it made the experience of concertgoing almost sensual, both an aural and visual indulgence.

He watched the orchestra sidle diffidently on stage, edging past the flimsy music stands to find their seats. Scores were checked and straightened and then the usual groaning, creaking and screeching sound grew as instruments were tested and tuned. He saw Humphrey shuffle in behind his four-wide kettledrum set and deliver a few tentative pianissimo thumps to the heads, adjusting the tuning posts, and Talbot wondered, for the four-hundredth time, no doubt, what in heaven's name had possessed his son to choose the timpani as his instrument?

He had asked him once and Humphrey had said, "Someone's got to do it"—it was a joke—and then he followed the remark up with a more sincere observation. "Imagine an orchestra without percussion—hard and soft. We convert and reconnect all those centuries of sophistication with the roots of music, Dad. Rhythm, percussion—the rock on which all music is based. The caveman beating on a log with a club. We add atavistic power." His words had all the studied artificiality of a prepared defence—no doubt he'd repeated them many times in answer to the same question—but they had made Talbot think. Maybe he was right. Timpani, the big drums, were the orchestra's pulsing, throbbing heart. A good phrase, he thought; maybe he'd try it out on Humphrey on the taxi ride home.

The conductor came on stage in his white tie and tails, bowed low, stepped onto his little podium and *Zarathustra* began—the slow growl of the basses, the contrabassoons, the organ and then the trumpets calling, rising to the octave, then the orchestra and now Humphrey—bam-boom-bam-boom—molto pesante—thirteen blows thundering out into the auditorium. Richard Strauss, the timpanist's favourite composer. For a minute or so Talbot felt a small flicker of paternal pride. The drums called out—muscular, thrilling, the beating heart of the orchestra—Humphrey leading the way. Talbot surrendered himself to the music.

Stirring stuff, Talbot thought, as he emerged from the auditorium at the interval, it would make the Grieg seem epicene and thin. He looked around and headed for the bar. He had pre-ordered a large Scotch and soda and, as he turned, he almost bumped into a woman who was also carrying her mid-concert sharpener. Gin and tonic, he guessed.

They looked at each other.

"Talbot, what a surprise."

"Elfrida. Exactly. Well met, lovely to see you. Isn't Strauss splendid? Almost makes me want to join the Nazi Party."

"I wouldn't go quite that far."

"I'm joking."

"Of course you are."

They exchanged a few more musical platitudes as if to expunge the bad start to their encounter.

"I came here with my friend, Jessica," Elfrida explained. "And then she started to feel faint just as we were about to take our seats so went home."

"We've both been abandoned. Naomi has flu."

"Naomi?"

"My wife."

"Of course. Do give her my best wishes for a speedy recovery."

As far as Talbot was aware, Elfrida and Naomi had never met.

"My son is in the orchestra. Timpani."

"How fascinating. Thumping away. Marvellous. He must love *Zarathustra*."

They both drank to fill the silence. Both lost in the awkward formality of their personas, Talbot thought, chronic social ill-at-easeness being the English middle-class status quo.

"Is Reggie here?" Talbot asked, stupidly, immediately wishing he hadn't.

"No. He won't leave Brighton, so he says. Not until the film is done."

Talbot knew this wasn't true. Reggie came up to London regularly to see the edit, the rough assembly of what he'd filmed. And to rendezvous with Janet Headstone, no doubt.

He and Elfrida wandered spontaneously away from the bar to a darker corner of the mezzanine, as if they were a couple, Talbot thought, controlled by unspoken assumptions and old habits, stuck with each other until the concert resumed, unable to think of a polite way of being alone.

As they talked on—politely, meaninglessly—Talbot looked more closely at Elfrida. He always forgot how tall she was—he didn't have her filed away in his mind as a tall person—and very slim, wearing a grey suit with an indigo blouse, flat patent shoes. Her lips were a vivid red and there was a tone in her voice as she talked—a constant—dry, reedy, verging on cynical, he would say. He suspected she was wary of him, anyway, quite apart from her inbuilt lack of social ease, as he was part of Reggie's world, not hers. She kept touching her hair, nervously, her fringe, the hanging sides, keeping the helmet in place with a quick brush of her fingers. What was she hiding from? he wondered. He glanced quickly at his watch—still ten minutes to go—asking himself when he could safely regain his seat. He was beginning to find the banal politesse of their conversation tiresome and awkward—no doubt she felt the same—but appearances must be kept up. Meeting the wife of a colleague you didn't expect to meet, and didn't particularly want to meet, provided its own mild social agonies.

Still, they talked on—about the Festival Hall itself, the pleasures of concertgoing, the Vietnam War, the house in Rottingdean, the particular strangeness of Brighton as a town. She seemed to relax a bit as she drank her gin and tonic. He wondered vaguely if a man (not him, obviously) would find Elfrida attractive, sexually attractive. He had no idea. She was clever, that was for sure, and she made him chuckle when she said that she thought Brighton functioned as a kind of rackety conscience-free zone for Londoners—like the Las Vegas of England, she said. It was well expressed and he knew what she meant: old norms of behaviour were more easily abandoned there, as if the town's reputed loucheness were contagious. And he found himself thinking that if Reggie, and the film, and his own role in the film, hadn't stood between them then he imagined that they might actually have come to enjoy each other's company, unreflectingly. Might have. Yet another parallel universe.

The bell rang to announce the end of the interval.

"Do you know," she said, "I think I might skip the second half. See how poor Jessica's getting on."

They made their farewells and Talbot watched her walk back to the bar. Strange woman, he said to himself. How many times had he made that observation about her? He wondered what observation she might make about him.

After the concert he met Humphrey at the stage door. They shook hands and he noted that Humphrey's handshake was weak, like holding an empty glove. How could you tell someone that? That they should firmly grip a hand when shaken? Impossible. They walked up to Waterloo Bridge to hail a taxi.

"Wonderful concert," Talbot said.

"I don't think we were quite at our best."

"Well, the punters seemed to enjoy it."

In the taxi Humphrey chose to sit in the jump-seat diagonally opposite rather than beside him, Talbot noticed, as he quietly scrutinised his son. Humphrey was now in his mid-twenties, his hair was neatly long, carefully combed to cover his ears, with a sideswiped fringe revealing a triangle of pale forehead. He had a patchy soft moustache that didn't suit him. A good head of hair, Talbot noted ruefully, but not handsome, missing out on the clean-cut, even features of the Kydds—nose a bit bulbous, and thin-lipped as well. He had been a pretty and charming little boy, Talbot recalled—his war baby, conceived and born during the conflict. And when Humphrey was little Talbot thought he could see in him a resemblance to Kit, his own brother, but that disappeared at pubescence. Talbot had married Naomi in 1941, while home on leave from Africa, and Humphrey was born before their first anniversary; Zoë following a year later. He thought of Zoë with something of a prick of loss. How your children change with adulthood! Two children, a boy and a girl, over and done with, Talbot thought. He actually couldn't remember how often he and Naomi had made love after Zoë's birth. They definitely had—there were many years when he still laboured under the delusion that he was perhaps 50% heterosexual.

"Are you staying tonight?" Humphrey asked.

"Of course. I came up specially to see—and hear—you play."

"Thank you."

"No need for thanks, Humph. I'm the one who should be thanking you. I felt very proud."

"Thanks again . . . Dad," he added.

"How are things in Manchester?"

"I really like it. I enjoy my life there."

"Anyone special?" He smiled to make the innuendo seem fond, not prurient.

"Not really. Nice bunch of mates in the orchestra, you know."

The thought entered his mind—and kept on going—that maybe Humphrey was queer. He decided not to speculate further.

They headed west through London for Chiswick, silent again. Humphrey lit a cigarette and smoked it awkwardly, as if he'd only just started smoking and hadn't mastered the technique. He puffed away, not really inhaling, making a lot of smoke. Talbot lit up as well—smoke fighting smoke—and began to talk about anything: plans they had made for changing the Chiswick garden, Naomi's struggles with the school board and the erratic and demanding progress of *Ladder to the Moon.* Humphrey appeared to be listening intently, nodding and smiling. Father and son engaged in genial conversation, Talbot thought, imagining some invisible witness watching them. Wasn't it curious how your children could become complete strangers to you?

27

Jacques returned to Paris the next day. However, nothing seemed to have changed, Anny considered, grateful, convinced she wasn't thinking wishfully. Maybe he had thought her kiss with Troy was just acting, what actors had to do—to make it seem real. They had been affectionate to each other when they were alone, there were no embarrassing conversations, they themselves kissed with real passion. In bed that night Anny took his cock in her hand and offered to bring him off but he said, No thank you, *ma puce,* I can do that myself with more expertise. He laughed—they both laughed—and he held her close. There was nothing untoward that she could spot, no hint of suspicion or distrust that she could discern, but she still had this strange feeling that he was quietly watching her, analysing and examining her, as if seeking to detect minute changes in her behaviour or demeanour. Neither of them made any reference to Troy or the filmed kiss.

Two hours after Jacques had left for London to catch his plane she was called by reception.

"Mr. Ingmar Bergman is here to see you."

Cornell was unshaven and his clothes were creased and rumpled as if he'd been sleeping on someone's floor. He also seemed significantly more agitated.

"This can't go on, Cornell," she said, wearily. "I told you I wouldn't see you again. They're looking for you. They're not stupid. They think you'll make contact with me. I'm not going to let you drag me down with you."

"Nobody's gonna drag you down," he said. "I'm gone—but I need some more cash. This documentation I need costs a fucking fortune. It's a nightmare."

"I don't want to know!" she shouted at him. "I don't want to know anything about the shithole you've dug for yourself! OK?"

"Give me a break, Anny! Do you know how tough my life is, right now? At this moment?"

"And whose fault is that? Huh?"

She strode into her bedroom and rummaged in her handbags, finding one purse and then another. There was money in them. She counted the dollars she had: $145. She returned to the sitting room and held the notes out for him, her arm stiff. He took them, a little shamefacedly, she thought. She had given money to him once, she reasoned, so it didn't make any difference if she gave him some more. She was complicit, one way or another. It made her feel a little sick—too late now.

"That's it," she said. "You cleaned me out."

"Could we order something to eat?" he asked. "I'm starving."

"No. Go away, Cornell, and don't come back, please. Fucking leave me alone. Get out of my life."

He looked at her darkly, hurt.

"There was always a mean, bitchy side to you. Look, I'll pay you back."

"Don't worry about the money, please. My pleasure. It's a gift—a parting gift."

She walked to the door and opened it.

Cornell had his hard-done-by, victim-of-life's-injustices look on his face as he shuffled out. He touched her cheek and she slapped his hand away.

"How about a goodbye kiss, babe?" he said, meekly.

She kissed him on the cheek. So help me God, she thought.

She closed the door behind him and locked it. She wasn't tearful, or even angry—she just had a bad feeling that it wasn't over. She was sure that, one way or another, Cornell Weekes was going to find a way to mess up her life.

She called Troy's room. He came over to her in five minutes, holding up his usual bottle of red wine as she opened the door to him. They kissed. She hugged him. Now she felt calm, felt the warmth of that strange security that Troy seemed to bring to her.

"Where's old Jacques-the-lad, eh?" he asked, taking a corkscrew out of his pocket.

"Back to Paris."

"He doesn't suspect, does he?"

"I don't know. I don't think so. He didn't say anything, anyway—though he was acting kind of strange. All sort of watchful. And then fucking Cornell came round wanting more money."

"You don't have much luck with your men, do you?" he said, pulling the cork from the bottle with a wet pop. He poured them both a glass and sat down at the table. He smiled. "Apart from me."

"I'll give you a trial run," she said. "You're off to a good start."

She began to take off her clothes.

"Day off tomorrow," Troy said. "Do you want to come and meet my mum and dad?"

"In Swindon?" She had remembered.

"In sunny Swindon."

She was naked. She came over and sat on his lap. Maybe this was what she needed—a glimpse of normal life. Troy's parents in Swindon. It would be the best therapy. He kissed her shoulder.

"What do you say?"

"I can't think of anything in the world I'd rather do," she said.

28

"Virginia Woolf. Hmmmm . . ." Calder McPhail drummed his fingers on the desk, frowning. "I thought you said the novel was called *The Zigzag Man.*"

"Well, it is," Elfrida said. "That's underway, as it were. But I had this new idea. *The Last Day of Virginia Woolf.* I've started it, well underway, also. I'll do *The Zigzag Man* next."

"That's good news, at any rate," Calder said. "Two novels underway. We like things to be underway." He seemed sceptical. "It has been a while."

"Not that long," Elfrida said. "It's only ten years. If I were an American novelist no one would think anything of it." She looked across the desk at her literary agent. She hadn't actually seen him in the flesh for . . . She calculated. God. Two years? He'd definitely got fatter, she thought—life must be good. Calder was in his fifties. He'd always been stout, a thick-set barrel of a man, but now his double chin lapped over his collar and he seemed a little flushed. Hypertension? He had a polite Edinburgh accent and a dry, reserved manner that mostly disguised his fully developed sense of humour and a propensity to sudden, intense short-lived rages. She was very fond of him, seeing him as a benign older-brother figure whom she could go to in any hour of need—for almost anything. Such as now. Calder sat back in his chair and exposed the medicine ball that was his belly as if reading her mind.

"I think," she said, as if the idea had just come to her, "an advance for both novels would be perfect. Stagger the payments, you know, every three months. It would spur me on."

"Tell me more," he said.

And Elfrida did. *The Last Day* would be an imagined, subjective exploration of the few hours that Virginia Woolf experienced between waking and dying by drowning on 28 March 1941. It would be scarifying, revelatory, audacious.

Calder seemed a little underwhelmed.

"Is anyone actually interested in Woolf these days?" Calder said. "I mean, seriously interested. She's a bit passé, no?"

"Well, I am. And I don't even particularly like her work. She's a fascinating instance of . . . Of a type of human being, a case study." She paused. "She's the most interesting woman writer of the twentieth century," she added boldly, not quite believing her own propaganda.

"I beg to differ," Calder said. "Wealthy, snobbish, over-privileged, physically unattractive, English intellectuals fucking each other. Nice houses, good interior decoration, hot and cold running servants. This is 1968, Elfrida. Look around you. Germany, France, the U.S.A., Vietnam. The world is on fire, changing. Don't go backwards."

"They are still *people,* Calder. Human beings . . ." Elfrida wondered what she would say next. "And people come to us, us novelists, looking for information."

"About what?"

"About other people. About all the other people in the world. What we're thinking, what we need, what we dream about, what we hate. What makes us tick, basically. People are opaque, utterly mysterious. Even those dearest to us are closed books. If you want to know what human beings are like, actually like, if you want to know what's going on in their heads behind those masks we all wear—then read a novel."

She stopped, a bit astounded at her peroration. She couldn't remember when she had last talked for so long, uninterrupted, so passionate, so relatively eloquent, by her standards. Was it the gin she had drunk before their meeting or was it her novelist's brain, suddenly active again after its decade's dormancy, like an animal stirring after hibernation?

"It sounds all a bit *recherché. The Zigzag Man* seems an easier sell. Tell me about that."

"*The Last Day* is the novel I'll write next," she said with what she hoped sounded like adamantine confidence. "Do me a two-book deal, there's a clever agent."

"I've done three two-book deals for you, Elfrida, and your publishers are still waiting for the contracted books. Are you familiar with the concept of the law of diminishing returns?"

She ignored him. "I haven't been well. But now I am. I'm fizzing with energy. Full of piss and vinegar."

He held up his pale hands, palms forward.

"All right, all right. I'll call Ginevra. Tell her the good news."

Ginevra Russell was her editor.

"Is she still alive?"

"Just about. Funnily enough, she asked exactly the same question about you, last week."

"Ha-ha. Liar."

"She did ask if I'd seen hide or hair of you. Same difference."

They talked on about Ginevra and her personal hygiene issues. Then they gossiped further and laughed a lot. Yes, Calder was her friend, Elfrida registered, an ally. Not just a tenpercenter, as Reggie referred to the Hollywood agents he had to deal with.

As she left, he warmly kissed her goodbye at the door, giving her a brief, untypical hug.

"You know I'll do my best," he said. "But don't expect mountains of cash. You've got quite a debt at Muir & Melhuish. It won't be easy."

"Nothing in life is easy, darling Calder. Soldier on."

29

John Saxonwood looked at the file in front of him and stirred the air above it with his fingers as if trying to dissipate some unpleasant smell.

"Smoke and mirrors, Talbot," he said. "And in medieval French legalese. No wonder I was suspicious."

"It must be some elaborate plan of Yorgos's," Talbot said. "I'll talk to him—he'll explain everything."

"You seem very confident that all is well."

"I am. He's full of schemes, Yorgos. He just hasn't fully filled me in on the details of this one."

"I look forward to eventual enlightenment. But, as far as I can tell, he's trying to defraud you."

"Impossible. Never. No, no, not Yorgos."

John spread his hands in surrender.

"I can only report what I see in front of me," he said. "I think you'll have to be a bit firmer than that. Screw him down."

"He's one of my oldest friends, John. He's saved the business at least twice. He's Zoë's godfather, for Christ's sake. Why should he be trying to defraud me?"

"Shall we say, 'money'? Or 'power'? Or 'influence'? When you're playing for these stakes friendship seems to slip down the ranking priorities."

Talbot gave up trying to persuade John of Yorgos's essential, if idiosyncratic, probity and took a copy of the contract and its translation away with him and taxied back to Primrose Hill—without reading a line—to pick up the Alvis. While he was in the flat he telephoned the caretaker who looked after the building and its fabric to check on the progress with the glazier who was booked in to fix the downstairs window. All was in hand, he was told.

Naomi had asked him how he had cut his forehead and he made up a story about a light falling from a gantry on set and showering everyone with shards of glass.

"My God," she said. "What if it had hit your eye?"

It was a fair point, he admitted, had it actually happened, and he thought again of his narrow escape from the falling coupler. But then life was full of narrow escapes and one was probably only aware of 10% of them, if that. He drove back to Brighton in a perplexed and darkening mood, feeling his duodenum beginning to burn. Some sort of confrontation with Yorgos was inevitable if they were going to sort out this curious business about the *Burning Leaves* contract. What was Yorgos playing at? What was really going on? He refused to underwrite John Saxonwood's pessimistic analysis. It was far more likely that this was some elaborate scheme that Yorgos had concocted and they were all going to make far more money as a result. All the same, he was conscious that he kept making the case for Yorgos—and not for himself. Was he in a state of denial? Perhaps, he conceded, but sometimes being in a state of denial was what was required. He turned his head right and left as he sped down the A23 towards Brighton, easing his neck muscles. Try to stay calm, he said to himself, if only for the sake of your ulcer. All this will pass.

Ferdie Meares was waiting for him in the production office when he arrived—clearly in a state about something. Talbot sat him down in his office and poured them both a Scotch, maintaining a polite smile on his face.

"What seems to be the problem, Ferdie? I can tell you're not happy."

"I'm not. I'm fucking furious."

"We don't like furious. What's the trouble?"

"It's my catchphrase."

"Your catchphrase . . . Remind me of it."

"'I'm excited! Are you?'"

"I remember now. And what's the issue?"

"Your so-called director, Rodrigo Arsehole Tipton, won't let me say it in my scenes."

"Well, maybe it's not appropriate."

"It's in my contract."

Talbot called for Ferdie's contract and checked. Sure enough, there it was in some subclause. Ferdie Meares was contractually permitted to utter his catchphrase—"I'm excited! Are you?"—on at least two occasions during the filming of the scenes in which he participated.

"I think you should have a quiet word with Rodrigo," Ferdie said.

"I will," Talbot said. "Consider it done."

"And why have my scenes with Anny Viklund been changed? I was looking forward to working with her."

"It's that kind of film, Ferdie. Fluid, ever-changing, in the spirit of the times we live in. It's 1968. Swingin' London and all that hoo-ha. We're making little alterations every day—everyone has to live with these changes."

"Does Andy Marvell know?"

"Why do you ask?"

"Because he's a friend. He's one of the reasons I agreed to do this film."

Lying bastard, Talbot thought.

"I think Andy's in LA," he said, vaguely.

"He won't be happy if you're tinkering with his script," Meares said and stood up. It was a covert threat, Talbot realised as he showed him out.

"I don't think your catchphrase was in Marvell's script, come to that."

"Andy won't be happy," Ferdie reiterated, just in case, Talbot thought. "No fucking fear. Not one little bit."

Talbot had a unit car drive him to the set. They were out in the countryside, between Burwash and Herstmonceux, picking up shots of the yellow Mini motoring through idyllic East Sussex. More opportunities for great music over, Reggie had said. Talbot found him watching a Test match on a portable TV near the camera lorry. Talbot explained the contractual situation regarding Ferdie Meares's catchphrase. Reggie refused point-blank to incorporate "I'm excited! Are you?" into any segment of *Ladder to the Moon.*

"No, Talbot, I'm sorry. It's demeaning. This is a serious film—not some pantomime in a provincial theatre."

"Just let him say it and then cut it out in the edit."

"But that means surrendering to the cunt that is Ferdie Meares."

"Lose a battle, win the war."

"He'll sue us. Safer to say 'no' now."

"He can't afford to sue us."

Talbot hoped he had persuaded Reggie that the way of least resistance was the only route to take on this occasion and left him to his cricket, wandering off to see if he could locate a cup of tea. He spotted Tony During, the director of photography, standing by a camera crane waiting for the Mini to come barrelling down a sunken cart track. He was a bearded man with a sallow complexion, who always looked under the weather. Talbot remembered that he'd just had flu.

"Hi, Tony," he said. "Feeling better?"

"Sorry, guv?"

"The flu."

"What? Ah, yeah, much better, thanks, guv."

He found Joe standing by the tea lady and her trolley, the steam from the urn thickened by the afternoon sunshine, like ectoplasm. Joe handed him a polystyrene cup of tea the colour of wet sand.

"Don't forget you've got a meeting at five," Joe said. "Back in the office."

"Who with?"

He lowered his voice. "The investigator."

"Ah, you found one. Good."

"He was in the Yellow Pages, as it happened. Wasn't difficult."

"Well, that's what the Yellow Pages're for, I suppose." He looked around. "Where are Troy and Anny?"

"They've got a day off. We're doing all this car stuff with their stand-ins."

"Right," he said. "I'd better get back then."

The investigator was waiting in the sitting room of the Napier Street office when Talbot arrived. He was young, in his thirties, gauntly handsome, pale and starveling thin, with dark tousled hair that came down to his shoulders. He was wearing a tight black suit and a bootlace tie. His shoes had very pointed toes. He was chewing gum.

He sat across the desk from Talbot, leant back and grandly crossed his legs after proffering his card.

Talbot glanced at it and handed it back.

"You can keep it, man," the investigator said.

Talbot looked at it again and placed it on his blotter. It read:

CRIMINALITY RISK CONSULTANT
"Are you on the borderline? We can help"
Kenneth Kincade (LLB)

"Thank you for coming to see us, Mr. Kincade," Talbot said.

"Please call me Ken."

Talbot noticed that Ken seemed to have a slight American accent.

"Are you American?" he asked.

"I'm from Brighton. Born and bred." The scuffed pointed toe of his visible winklepicker jigged up and down, metronomically.

"Excellent. I see you have a law degree."

"Almost. I dropped out in my third year. That's why I put brackets round the LLB." He made the shape of the brackets in the air with his forefingers.

Talbot nodded. Maybe Ken Kincade would work—he hadn't time to go looking for another investigator, anyway. He explained the situation, telling him of the significant theft of film stock, some hundreds if not thousands of pounds' worth having gone missing. The obvious suspect would be someone in the camera department.

"How many bozos in the department?" Kincade asked, frowning and still chewing.

"Four. The orders for film stock come from the camera department. It must be one of the crew."

"Stands to reason. Or all of them. Could be a conspiracy."

"I hadn't thought of that but I somehow doubt it," Talbot said. "I just want you to find out the guilty party. Then I'll take care of everything."

"Rough justice, eh?"

"I simply want to keep this under wraps."

"Capeesh. I'm twenty bucks a day, plus expenses."

"Bucks?"

"Pounds. Sorry. Two days up front if you don't mind."

Talbot went upstairs to the accountancy department where Geoffrey Braintree provided him with eight £5 notes. He handed them over to Kincade with the names and addresses of the members of the camera crew written on a piece of paper. Kincade counted the notes twice and pocketed them.

"Don't I have to put my moniker on a contract or something?"

"Let's keep this as informal as possible, if you agree," Talbot said, beginning to weary of Kincade's ridiculous argot. "All I need is a name."

"No es problemo, señor," Kincade said, touching a finger to his forehead in casual salute. "I'll send you an official receipt. You can tear it up if you want but I'm afraid it has to go on my books. Pleasure doing business with you, Mr. Kydd. I'll be in touch."

He left and Talbot wondered if what he was doing were wise. Too bad—he had to find out what was going on: damage limitation and all that. His phone rang.

"Hello?"

"Talbot, me old mucker. Jimmy Appleby here."

"How're things, Jimmy? What can I do for you?"

"Everything's diamond, Talbot. But Bob and I would like a quick meeting. Got an interesting proposition—think you'll like it. Guaranteed. Come and see us when you're next in town. Or maybe we'll come and see you."

"Whatever works."

"How's our baby boy doing?"

"Troy? 'Like a duck to water' is the expression, I believe."

"Lovely-jubbly. See you soon, Talbot."

Talbot hung up. A "proposition"? Why did that make him worried?

30

Mrs. Farthingly offered Anny another slice of Battenberg cake.

"No, thank you, Mrs. Farthingly, I've eaten too much already."

"Nonsense. Eat like a bird. Go on, have another slice. Such a skinny little thing, you are. There's more meat on a wren's shin, as we say in these parts. We need to fatten you up, young lady."

Anny, uncomprehending, took the proffered slice and put it on her side plate with the fish-paste sandwich and the buttered scone.

Mrs. Farthingly stared at her, warmly, full of benign interest. She was a small plump woman with pink-rouged cheeks and thin, perfectly white curly hair. She had a tic that made her blink in rapid spasms from time to time. Anny found this very disconcerting.

They were sitting facing each other on parallel sofas in the "back living room," as Mrs. Farthingly described it. Through French windows Anny could see a fish pond, a sundial and a thin length of lawn divided by a crazy-paving path that led down to a garden shed. Beyond the shed was a high railway embankment and every now and then a commuter train would rumble and sway past, in both directions.

"Now, as I was saying," Mrs. Farthingly resumed her analysis of her son's career. "Nigel's so pleased to be in this film. He's had only two singles out in the last year and neither one made the top thirty. And this is somebody with a platinum disc."

"Well, he's great in the film. A natural actor."

"That Paul Jones has been in a film. I think that's what gave Mr. Appleby the idea."

"Was that the film with Jean Shrimpton?" Anny was beginning to feel a bit faint, she realised.

"I wouldn't know, dear." Mrs. Farthingly cut herself a slice of Battenberg. "In 1966 Nigel was at the London Palladium. Do you know where his last concert was?"

"No."

"The Tower Club, Warrington."

"Is that bad?"

"Worse than bad. And then Mr. Appleby moved him from Decca to Parlophone, but they don't seem to care about him. He's not a group, you see. And it's all groups today. I told him—you need a pop group, son. Like Cliff or Manfred. He doesn't listen to me, no, no."

She smiled at her. Anny didn't know what to say.

"So who exactly are you in this film?" Mrs. Farthingly asked.

"I'm Emily, Emily Bracegirdle."

"Yes. And what's the story?"

"I'm meant to be a famous film star who's making a film in Brighton. And then I fall in love with my driver. A young man from Brighton."

"And that's Troy."

"Yes."

Mrs. Farthingly frowned.

"But you already are a film star making a film in Brighton."

"Yes."

"That doesn't seem very clever."

"I think it's about how art imitates life. And life imitates art. That's the point."

"What on earth is that meant to mean?"

Anny saw Troy and his father emerge from the shed and amble up the path towards them.

"Here come the menfolk," Mrs. Farthingly said, eyelashes batting. She stood and opened the French windows for them.

"You'll have some cake, won't you, Nigel?" she said as they entered.

"You bet. Thanks, Mum."

"Did Nigel tell you he bought us this house?" Mr. Farthingly said. "We used to live in a council flat."

"It's a great house," Anny said. She hadn't really taken it in when they arrived. Semi-detached, pebble-dashed, a huge pampas grass plant in the small front garden. She looked at Mrs. Farthingly who was still smiling at her.

"More tea, dear?"

"Could I have a glass of water, please?"

Nigel/Troy disappeared, heading for the kitchen to fetch her one.

"We could never have afforded a house like this," Mr. Farthingly said, emphatically. "Never in a million years."

"Not in this part of town, that's for certain," Mrs. Farthingly added.

"I see," Anny said. "Sure."

"Nigel bought it for us when his first album went platinum," Mr. Farthingly said. "One minute he's in a talent contest in Slough and the next he's got a platinum disc and signed to EMI."

"Decca," Mrs. Farthingly corrected. "'Up All Nite' it was called. N-i-t-e."

"I'm slowly getting to know Troy—I mean Nigel's music."

"If you can call it music!" Mrs. Farthingly scoffed.

"Would you like to hear the album?"

"Dad, leave it out," Troy said, coming back in and handing Anny her glass of water. "Anny doesn't want to listen to some old album. She's come to meet you."

"Mind you," Mrs. Farthingly said, "that LP changed our family fortunes."

"And he bought us a car," Mr. Farthingly said. "A Jaguar S-type. Silver-grey."

"That you never drive," Troy said, reprovingly.

"I don't like to risk it," Mr. Farthingly said. "Only for very special occasions."

"Where are you from, Anny?" Mrs. Farthingly asked.

"From Minnesota. In the U.S."

"And to think you've come all that way to make a film with Nigel."

"I have to say that Nigel is the only thing about this film that is keeping me sane."

"He's not a bad old fellow, our Nige," Mr. Farthingly said and cuffed his son on the thigh.

"Compared to his brother," Mrs. Farthingly said, her voice dry with disdain.

"Mum," Troy warned.

"His brother is in prison," Mrs. Farthingly said, flatly. "You might as well know, Anny. No secrets in this family."

"Let's not dig all that stuff up," Troy said. "Anny doesn't want to know about Godfrey."

"I didn't know you had a brother called Godfrey."

"Godfrey," Mr. Farthingly said the name slowly, then repeated it, "Godfrey is the black sheep of the family."

"Are you familiar with that expression, Anny?" Mrs. Farthingly asked.

"Yes. May I ask why he's in prison?"

Mrs. Farthingly sighed. "Because he's a sinner."

"He stole the lead off the roofs of over two hundred churches in the south of England and the West Country," Mr. Farthingly said.

"Then he sold it to scrap metal merchants," Troy said. "And used the money to buy drugs—speed, mostly—that he sold in pubs and clubs in Portsmouth and Southampton."

"And Bournemouth," Mrs. Farthingly added, disgusted. "My God . . . Heaven preserve us."

"Now you know why we call him the black sheep of the family," Mr. Farthingly said.

"Thank the good and merciful Lord above for Nigel," Mrs. Farthingly said.

"Godfrey is a lot older than Nigel, by the way," Mr. Farthingly said. "He's twelve years older."

"Nigel was my lucky baby," Mrs. Farthingly said. "I was forty when I conceived." She turned to her husband. "Imagine if Godfrey was our only child. Heavens!"

"Doesn't bear thinking of. Doesn't bear thinking of."

Everyone was silent for a few moments.

"Can we change the subject?" Troy said. "Let's stop talking about Godfrey. You'll make Anny depressed."

"Do you have any brothers or sisters?" Mrs. Farthingly asked.

"I have a brother. Lars. An older brother."

"He's not in prison, is he?"

"No. He's in the army. In Vietnam."

"Oh, my Lord!" Mrs. Farthingly squealed, both hands flying to her cheeks. "He's fighting in the war in Vietnam? Your brother?"

"Well, he's over there, but I don't know if he does any actual fighting."

"Godfrey should have joined the army," Mr. Farthingly said with unusual bitterness. "Should have done his National Service. They should never have stopped it. It would've made a man of him—but now he's just a common criminal."

"Have some more cake, Anny."

"No, thank you. I'm fine, thank you."

She offered more Battenberg to Troy who took a slice. Mrs. Farthingly turned back to Anny.

"Do you have a boyfriend, Anny?"

"Mum, please, that's a bit forward, that."

"That's OK." Anny smiled. "Yes, I do have a boyfriend," she said. "Nigel is my boyfriend."

31

"Do I have to go?" Elfrida asked.

"You don't *have* to—of course. But I think you should come," Reggie said. "It might look odd if you didn't."

"But I won't know anyone."

"So what? You might meet some interesting people. It's Dorian Villiers' party, for God's sake. It should be an interesting crowd, at the very least. For a novelist. Good copy."

"I don't need to go to a party to get good copy."

"All right. You do what you fucking well please. I don't care."

"All right, I'll come."

"You have to promise to sit with me," Anny said. "Promise me, Troy."

"I promise. But there may be a seating plan. Or, maybe there'll be a buffet."

"Just stay close."

"It's just a party, Anny. No big deal."

"I hate parties."

Talbot was fumbling with the knot on his bow tie when the telephone rang. Who had invented the bow tie? Why was it so confoundingly difficult to knot? He should have bought a ready-tied version but some vague, ingrained snobbery made him resort to a real one, however lopsided the thing looked when it was done. Maybe that was the point. He picked up the phone.

"Hello?"

"Talbot, my dear, we need to speak."

"I'm about to go to a party, Yorgos."

"I am coming down to see you. I explain my—our—very complicated deal for *Burning Leaves.* It will work for us, Talbot. We will be very rich."

"I have to say it all seems a bit odd."

"Exactly. Precisely. This is the plan. Odd, difficult, confusing. Wait till I explain for you everything we are doing. The early bird will find the pot of gold at the end of the rainbow."

"Great. Let me know when you're coming down."

Anny felt strange and a bit nervous sitting beside Troy in the back of the car on the way to the party—probably because she couldn't quite accustom herself to seeing him in a tuxedo. He seemed a different person, somehow—or at least visually. He looked older, and his handsomeness, his unique good looks, had become generic. He looked like any cool young guy in a tuxedo—no longer her particular Troy. Stop it, she told herself, and squeezed his hand. He turned and told her again how beautiful she looked. And she did look beautiful, she thought, or at least she had tried. She was wearing a black velvet dress with a low, scooped front, her breasts held, compacted and presented in a firm, perfect cleavage by a heavily wired brassiere. She had a red silk shawl around her shoulders and diamond studs in her ears. "Bloody hell," Troy had exclaimed when she emerged from her bedroom. "You look like some kind of fucking film star!" He said her breasts were like two scoops of vanilla ice cream and he stooped and kissed them in an act of "homdage," he said. She gently corrected him and thanked him on behalf of her breasts.

She glanced over at him as they motored through Brighton. He looked so different. She reached over and rubbed at his groin, feeling for his cock.

"Anny! Are you mad?"

"You look very handsome, Nigel. I couldn't resist."

"Stop it, girl. Behave."

She leant her head on his shoulder. She hated parties but maybe she'd enjoy this one.

Elfrida covertly drank half a pint of vodka before she and Reggie left for the party. She felt reeling drunk but she knew she could remain coherent as long as she didn't drink any more. It was a trick she had learned—and it worked. Don't go to a party to get drunk. Get drunk and then go to the party. She wore a bulky green satin dress that she had found in her wardrobe—what had possessed her to bring it?—it seemed dated, very 1950s, somehow, but she didn't give a fuck, so she said to herself. She put on heavier make-up and wore some ostentatious paste amethyst earrings. No one could say she hadn't made an effort.

As they gathered in the hall waiting for their taxi she saw that Reggie had opted for a red bow tie with his dinner jacket.

"Very counter-culture, darling," she said. "You look like a croupier in a seaside casino. Are you sure that's the impression you want to make?"

"Are you all right?"

"Right as rain."

"You're not going to disgrace me, are you?"

"Only if you disgrace me."

"Have you been drinking?"

"I had a sherry before my bath. Sorry, I forgot to ask for written permission."

"Sarcasm isn't your tone, darling."

"You should read one of my novels, one day. Might enlighten you."

He seemed tense, almost chippy, she thought. Usually he enjoyed parties—he always abandoned her so he could prowl around the rooms assessing the guests, seeking potential professional purchase and advancement. She picked up her clutch bag. Inside she had the number of the Rottingdean taxi firm that she used written on a card. If she wasn't enjoying herself she'd call and quietly leave. Reggie could make his own way home.

. . .

When Talbot arrived at Dorian's enormous, double-fronted, white stucco house just off Marine Parade, he realised he was too early. Servants were lighting two flaming braziers on either side of the pillared portico and, to his astonishment, an actual red carpet was being rolled down and fixed to the front steps.

He lit a cigarette and waited for the final touches to be made before he went in. However, he was hailed from the first-floor balcony by Dorian himself, flanked by giant Ionic pilasters, like a dictator addressing a crowd. He was leaning out, in white tie and tails, Talbot noticed, with some kind of diagonal red-sash decoration across his chest.

"Knock, knock, who's there i' the name of Beelzebub?"

"Very good of you to remember how I like a red carpet, Dorian," he called up.

"A most mirthful fellow. Don't linger out there. Come in, come in, for God's sweet sake, Talbot, darling man!"

Talbot felt a sudden depression enfold him. Bizarrely, he wished he were back in Chiswick having a kitchen supper with Naomi. Be careful, he told himself: eat little, drink less. Yorgos's telephone call had unsettled him, he knew. It wasn't typical of the man, very out of character, somehow. He put it to the back of his mind, flung his cigarette away and went up the red carpet and on into the great volumes of the hall. Chequerboard marble flooring; two entire garnitures of silver armour flanked the step to the grand staircase that divided itself against the rear wall beneath a life-sized swagger-portrait of Dorian as Falstaff in *Henry IV, Part I.* There were thickets of red poinsettias everywhere. How on earth had he found those in high summer? Two ranks of four serving maids stood holding trays of champagne flutes. Talbot forgot his vow of sobriety and took one. Dorian was clearly making a statement tonight.

Elfrida paused in front of a tray of fizzing flutes of champagne.

"Do you have anything soft?" she asked a waitress. "I don't drink, you see."

"There's a bar upstairs, ma'am, you can get a juice or something there."

“Thank you.” She led Reggie up the stairway, pausing to look at Dorian’s portrait.

“Who’s that?” she said. “Is he meant to be Falstaff?”

“It’s Dorian Villiers as Falstaff to be precise. Don’t you recognise him?”

“I thought it was Orson Welles.”

“He’s probably a guest.”

They could hear the surf-break, the wave-crash of excited conversation coming from the reception rooms on the first floor. Elfrida felt her familiar party-funk afflict her: all those strangers; all those hours of banal conversation with men and women she’d never see again. Why did people bother?

She closed her eyes and held on tightly to the banister, feeling her head swim. Maybe she’d overdone the prophylactic vodka, she wondered.

“Are you all right?” Reggie asked. “Have my glass of champagne.”

“No thanks. I’m just bracing myself.”

“You could just try and have some fun, Elfrida. It’s not a crime, you know.”

Anny and Troy climbed the stairs, Troy with a glass of champagne in his hand. Anny wasn’t drinking as she’d taken a couple of Equanil before she’d left and felt secure, now—in that ideal Equanil haze—clear-eyed yet muffled, somehow, as if she had an invisible force field around her, keeping her safe. She pointed at the portrait.

“Who’s that?”

“Haven’t a clue.”

They walked into the main drawing room. It was crowded with men and women in evening dress. The noise level of the conversation was considerable—Anny resisted the temptation to cover her ears with her hands. Through double doors there was another equally crowded smaller drawing room with crimson walls and many portraits hanging there.

Troy stopped a passing waiter with a canapé tray and ate three squares of smoked salmon one after the other.

“Smoked salmon. Bloody delicious. Have some, Anny.”

“No thanks, I’m not hungry.”

She looked around and saw Talbot talking to a man with a red sash across his chest. Talbot caught her eye and beckoned her and Troy over. Talbot kissed her on the cheek, to her surprise.

"Anny Viklund and Troy Blaze—our illustrious stars. This is Sir Dorian Villiers, our host."

Villiers bowed and kissed Anny's hand.

"How lovely to see you again," he said. He stepped back to take her in. "Radiant. Gorgeous. Incandescent. *Meravigliosa.*"

"Thank you, kind sir."

"I don't think I ever told you properly how thrilled I was to work with you in *The Monopoly Affair.* Ruddy bloody marvellous."

Anny smiled and said nothing. She glanced at Troy. Was this some kind of game?

"You must give my love to Porfirio," Villiers continued. "Tell the old bastard I miss him."

"Sure," Anny said.

Villiers spotted someone else across the room.

"Larry!" he bellowed. "Who the fuck invited you?"

He headed off to accost Larry. Talbot sipped his champagne.

"Great character," he said, with mild enthusiasm.

"Who does he think I am?" Anny asked.

"I think . . . I think it might be Melissa Blake," Talbot said. "Don't worry—he never listens to anyone. Let's see if we can find Rodrigo in this mob."

The three of them began to negotiate their way across the heaving, shifting room. Anny slipped her hand into Troy's.

Dorian's house had a full-sized ballroom at the rear with a sprung wooden floor. Ten tables for twelve were set up in it, each table with a floral centrepiece ringed by four candelabra, candles lit. It had taken Elfrida five minutes peering over shoulders at the placement easel to find her seat—miles from Reggie but she wasn't worried about not being near him. She was sitting between a foreign man who spoke exclusively in German to the woman on his left, and a quiet bespectacled fellow who pushed his food around his plate looking for fragments he could eat. He said he was Dorian's stockbroker. He apologised for eating so slowly.

"I've had about fifteen feet of my intestines removed," he explained. "I can hardly eat a thing, you see." He found a disc of carrot and popped it in his mouth and chewed carefully.

As Reggie was out of sight somewhere across the room Elfrida had moved on to white wine after her glass of orange juice. She put on her spectacles and contemplated the room, or what she could see of it from her table. She spotted Dirk Bogarde and Jill Bennett and someone she was pretty sure was Claudia Cardinale. Matthew Maxwell was on the next table and, she was convinced, so was Morgan von Hoffman.

"Isn't that Morgan von Hoffman over there?" she said to her stockbroker neighbour.

"I wouldn't have the faintest, sorry. Out of my depth."

She saw Talbot Kydd wandering by and waved at him. He came over.

"You're not leaving us, are you?" she asked.

"Just going to inspect the facilities."

"I did enjoy the concert the other night. How was the second half?"

"Splendid. Rather diminished by the Strauss."

She leant over the back of her chair and inclined her head. "By the way, is that Morgan von Hoffman over there? Table on the left."

Talbot glanced over.

"No. It's Max von Sydow."

"I thought I recognised him."

"I'll see you later," he said and moved on.

Elfrida turned to the stockbroker.

"It's Max von Sydow," she said. "At least I got the 'von' right."

"Who's he?"

"Doesn't matter." She saw a waiter passing and called for another glass of wine.

She thought back to her encounter with Talbot Kydd at the Royal Festival Hall. It had given her an unwelcome shock bumping into him like that—it was always a bit strange, not to say shattering, to suddenly meet someone out of familiar context. He'd been perfectly charming, though, of course—no doubt suffering from the same unwelcome shock as she. Charm, she thought: a very elusive English concept, very loaded. To her it meant closed, polite, coldly affable, able to make conversation about nothing. That summed up Talbot Kydd quite well, she reckoned.

She told the waiter to leave the bottle.

Yes, Talbot Kydd, always in a dark suit and tie, always well groomed. Yes, he was groomed—good word—groomed to impenetrability. She remembered Reggie had said that Talbot had enjoyed a "good war," whatever that meant. Surely you had a "good war" if you survived it, unmaimed. Simple as that. Of course, he'd been a soldier. That explained a lot. A soldier in the movie business—bizarre.

"Charming man," she said to the stockbroker.

"Absolutely. Sorry, who?"

"Talbot Kydd, the film producer."

"Oh, Talbot Kydd. Dorian loves him."

When Anny found her seat and discovered she wasn't sitting beside Troy she made him bring his name card over and swap it.

"Nobody will know," she said.

Troy looked at the card.

"You could have been sitting beside Eric Burdon," he said. "Now you've got me."

"You're the one I want, baby," she said. "When can we go back to the hotel?"

"We'd better wait until the meal's over. At least."

She put on her sunglasses while he went to put Eric Burdon's card where his had been. The candlelight was making her dizzy.

"Now everyone will know you're a film star," he said, returning and sitting down beside her.

A waiter put a glazed and shivering crab mousse in front of them. Troy had a taste.

"Not bad," he said. "Fishy." He forked the rest into his mouth.

"You can have mine," Anny said, passing it over.

Talbot was at Dorian's table, sitting beside Dorian's wife, Bruna Casanero, who, Talbot was surprised to see, was not only very beautiful but heavily pregnant. She must be at least thirty years younger than Dorian, Talbot calculated, and discovered she spoke good, heavily accented English. Her pregnant belly was extraordinarily neat, as if a small glass cloche or cantaloupe melon was stuffed under the crêpe de Chine of her azure dress. Dorian was across the table from her and he kept blowing kisses in their direction. Bruna found this very amusing.

Talbot noticed that Dorian had grown his hair to collar length and it was newly coloured an even butterscotch-beige—the better to take the years off, Talbot supposed. He had liked Dorian's previous, second wife, Vanessa, a shrewd sardonic woman who seemed to have Dorian's measure and would cut him off whenever his hyperbole seemed to be veering out of control.

Bruna was speaking to him.

"Sorry?"

"Have you children, Talbot?"

"A son and a daughter."

"And their names?"

"Humphrey and Zoë."

"This I like. I am naming my son Ercole. He is to be my firstborn. In English is Hercules."

"Right. You know he's a boy. Amazing."

"I know he is a boy." She pressed her hands on her neat dome. "Because he is calling to me."

"Hercules Villiers. What a name!"

Talbot pushed his uneaten cheesecake away a few inches as Dorian rapped loudly on a glass carafe—its clear crystal ring silencing the ballroom—and rose to his feet to scattered applause.

"As Chaucer said—or should have said if he had any bloody sense," Dorian began, his booming voice and legendary projection requiring no electronic amplification, "fain would ye come to this fair borough yclept Bright Towne, where ye may wench and wassail to your *haertès* content!"

Elfrida felt her head begin to nod. She had sat through some long speeches in her time but Dorian Villiers was breaking all records. He was now talking in appallingly accented Italian to his wife—*la molta piú bellissima sposa é mamma del mondo*, or some such rubbish. She could hardly bear to listen any more. She looked around for a waiter with a bottle of wine but all the serving staff seemed to have disappeared for the speech. Very wise—she was about to do the same, she decided. She slowly shifted back her chair, whispered, "Do excuse me," to the stockbroker and slipped away, leaving her clutch bag at her place, sign that her departure was temporary.

She found a waiter clearing glasses away in the crimson drawing room and he fetched her a glass of white wine. She needed the loo, she realised, and followed arrow-signs upstairs to the bedroom, bathroom and cloakroom floor of the Villiers mansion.

However, the lavatory she eventually found, off a wide corridor with pale blue carpeting, was occupied. Seconds after she'd tried the locked door it opened and a man appeared. He was in his forties, she supposed, and was wearing those fashionable round wire-rimmed spectacles. His thick dry greying hair was severely parted, just off-centre, like a white firebreak driven through dense forest, she thought. His velvet dinner jacket looked a bit threadbare and his bow tie was askew.

She apologised, he apologised, then he asked if she knew where the coats were kept. He had handed in a briefcase but it seemed to have disappeared.

"I came coatless," she said. "You're not leaving, are you? In the middle of the speeches?"

"I've got to get a train back to London," he said. "You don't happen to have a spare cigarette on you, by any chance?"

"Sorry. Non-smoker." She sipped her wine. There was something sympathetic about this man, she decided, in a downtrodden way, with his diffident scholar's look.

"Are you a friend of Dorian's?" he asked.

"Never met him. Are you?"

"I'm not sure if 'friend' is the right word. I gave him a good review about ten years ago and he now invites me to all his parties. All the time."

"A review?"

"I used to be a theatre critic in the past. I think he was in *Blithe Spirit*. I can't remember."

"A theatre critic! Fascinating."

"Yes." He repeated the word, quietly. "Fascinating."

"Are you still a theatre critic?" she asked.

"No. I was sacked. And now, actually, I'm a novelist. Not a very successful one but I somehow scrape a living."

"How intriguing. Would I have heard of you?"

"My name's Laurence Falconer."

"I have heard of you," Elfrida said, "I'm sure. Anyway, congratulations. Better to be a novelist than a theatre critic, I suppose."

"Dark and dirty work but someone has to do it."

"Have you written many novels?"

"Over twenty or so. At least. Thirty? I've lost count."

"Good Lord." Elfrida emptied her glass and set it down. "That's an *oeuvre*."

"I do use a few noms de plume. Keeps me out of mischief."

"Do you find it easy? Writing, I mean?"

He frowned. "I suppose . . . No, is the short answer. But it's sort of fulfilling."

"People forget how much sheer hard craft is involved."

He looked at her more closely, peering at her, as if trying to identify her. She realised she'd spoken unthinkingly.

"Do you write novels?"

She considered denying it, as she usually did, but thought, what the hell?

"I'm thinking about it. Writing a novel, I mean."

He put his hands in his pockets and exhaled noisily as he stared at her, swaying slightly. She realised he was very drunk. *In vino veritas.*

"It's a long and very bumpy road, as somebody once remarked," he said. "Probably another novelist."

"Bumpy roads, very bumpy roads, long ones, fair enough. As long as there are no mudslides or earthquakes."

"Oh, there may be the odd earthquake, but low on the Richter scale, usually."

"But there are compensations. In your experience?" Elfrida asked, smiling.

"You are the ultimate one-man band, I suppose. Not to be sniffed at, that."

"Yes. Sounds perfect."

He smiled at her, his eyes bright through his round lenses. She suddenly felt her bladder straining.

"Lovely to meet you, Laurence Falconer. Good luck. Excuse me."

She stepped into the lavatory and locked the door and leant back against it, exhilarated, almost shocked. Fancy meeting a fellow novelist. Maybe it was a sign.

"Can we go?" Anny said to Troy. "I'm so tired. He must have spoken for an hour."

"It was certainly over thirty minutes," Troy said, looking at his watch. "No notes either. He's a great actor."

"That doesn't excuse him. Let's split."

Troy was finishing her cheesecake.

"OK, babe. Give me a minute." He looked around. "We should say goodbye to Rodrigo."

"We'll see him tomorrow. It doesn't matter."

A man in a dark suit carrying a clipboard appeared at their table.

"Excuse me. Miss Viklund?"

"Yes? What is it?"

"I'm sorry to interrupt but there are two gentlemen downstairs who would like to speak to you."

Troy interjected.

"Sorry, man. Look—lots of people want to speak to Miss Viklund. This is a private party. Yeah? Tell them to approach the production office."

The man with the clipboard bent his head and whispered in Troy's ear as Anny looked on, bemused. Troy started nodding.

"Is there a private room?" Troy asked.

"Of course."

"What's going on, Troy?" Anny said—she'd never seen him look like this.

"I think we'd better go with this man, doll."

Elfrida returned to the ballroom. It was clear that the dinner was slowly breaking up after coffee and petits fours had been served. Men were lighting cigars, decanters of port were circulating, and people were beginning to drift back to the reception rooms for the party's endgame, whatever that might be. Elfrida found her table and saw that both her dining companions had left. She picked up her clutch bag and retrieved the card with the Rottingdean taxi firm's number on it. Now to find a telephone in this impossible house. Her brain was beginning to feel a bit muddy and slow. Better stop drinking wine, she said to herself, even though her mood was good, not to say high, after her encounter upstairs. She looked around and saw Talbot Kydd talking to a pregnant woman and wandered over. Talbot smiled politely as she approached.

"Elfrida—can I introduce you to Bruna Casanero?" Then he bolted.

Elfrida shook Bruna Casanero's proffered hand.

"I am the wife of Dorian," she said.

"Lovely to meet you," Elfrida said. "Is there a telephone nearby?"

"I show you," she said. "Come with me."

She followed Bruna as they weaved through the messy tables into a kind of pantry area where waiters were stacking plates and glasses. Bruna pointed to a wall-mounted telephone.

"You dial nine, you get line," she said.

"Thank you so much," she said. "I just want to call a taxi to take me home. I've had a wonderful evening." She pointed at Bruna's pregnant belly and said, "Maybe you should sit down, take the weight off your feet."

"No, I'm fine," she said. "Strong Italian woman. Do you have children?"

"I do," Elfrida said. "I have three daughters."

"And their names?"

"Selina, Serena and Sabrina."

Bruna looked at her fixedly, a half-smile on her face. It was a trick Elfrida used in response to the often-asked question. Sometimes she said she had three sons: Godfrey, Geoffrey and Gregory.

"I leave you to telephone," Bruna said and went back into the ballroom.

Elfrida helped herself to a handy half-full glass of wine and called for a taxi.

Talbot stepped out into the street and moved away from the surprisingly strong circle of warmth emanating from the still-glowing braziers. In a cool shadow he lit a cigarette and thought about the party. Had he enjoyed himself? No. Had he met anyone interesting? Certainly not. Had his life experience been remotely enhanced? In fact his life experience had been diminished by the patent waste of time. What had possessed Dorian to mount something so ostentatious, so lavish? Not a clue. *Cui bono?* No one. Then, he thought, maybe that harsh reckoning was true of all parties. Someone—some young person—had once said to him that the only reason to go to a party was to "score." To score sex, or drugs, drink, food, gossip, contacts, influence, advancement. If you didn't score, then that party had been a waste of your precious time. By that token he had had a pointless evening. Still, not every—

"Ah, Talbot, there you are. Thank Zeus. They told me you'd just left. Glad I caught you."

Dorian advanced into his patch of shadow beyond the glare of his portico's lights. He had a cigar in his hand and his red sash had slipped under his belly.

"I think I might stroll back to the hotel," Talbot said. "Bit of fresh air. What a lovely, special evening. Thanks, Dorian. What a night."

"Can I have a quick word, Talbot?"

"Of course."

Dorian drew him further away from the front door and its glow—guests were leaving now in significant numbers—and led him into deeper shadow.

"This film of yours, this moving picture, that you're shooting here in Brighton," Dorian said. "What's it called?"

"It's a very stupid film with a stupid title. *Emily Bracegirdle's Extremely Useful Ladder to the Moon.* We call it *Ladder to the Moon.* Or simply *Ladder.* Reduces the shame."

"Who cares? Film titles these days make no sense. The point is, Talbot, is there a part for me in your stupid film?"

Talbot took a breath.

"We're fully cast, Dorian. We're halfway through the shoot."

"So what? A cameo role. I can be someone's rich uncle. Visiting royalty. Evil mastermind. You name it."

"It's just not that kind of film. You'd hate it."

Dorian sucked heavily on his cigar and its end burned an angry, cindery red. He tossed it away into the gutter.

"Let me put it this way, Talbot, old friend. Excuse my lack of subtlety, but I need to make—need to lay my hands on—a legitimate five thousand pounds by the end of next week. It seems to me that the only feasible way that objective can be achieved is if you give me a part in your film and pay me five grand. Simple as that."

Talbot paused, then said, "How come you can throw a party like this one and still need five thousand pounds? You must have spent—"

"No, I didn't *spend.* I ordered, I demanded, I arranged. Bills will come in, in due course, and one day I may pay them. But currently, my need is very clear. Five thousand pounds by the end of next week. I can't put it more plainly than that."

Talbot thought again for a few moments before replying, recognising that this request hid some stranger, darker, profounder crisis in the Villiers household. He decided not to enquire further about the crisis, whatever it was.

"I'd do it like a shot, Dorian. But—excuse *my* lack of subtlety—if I suddenly put you in this film it will fuck everything up."

"There's nothing you can't fix, Talbot." He put a big hand on Talbot's shoulder. "You're one of my oldest friends. I would owe you everything. I'm asking you for this favour as a friend, one of my dearest friends. If you don't do this for me then everything's going to go tits up. And I mean everything."

"Dorian, listen, you know I would—"

"I'll be there Monday morning. A couple of days' work. Five thou. Everything lovely again. Bless you."

He leant forward and kissed Talbot on the cheek, Talbot smelling his sour cigar breath, and then he walked back to his vast house. What the fuck has he done? Talbot thought. What kind of desperate, shocking mess is he in? He closed his eyes and felt his stomach acids begin to churn.

Elfrida was told by the Rottingdean despatcher that the taxi would be waiting for her outside in fifteen minutes. Perfect, she thought, just time for a final glass of wine. She wandered back into the ballroom, emptying now, and saw the stars of Reggie's film—what were they called? Angie and Tim?—following a man carrying a clipboard out of the room. She found a half-empty bottle of red wine and a cleanish glass that she filled before making her way into the crimson drawing room. It was smoky and noisy, still busy with guests reluctant to leave, keen to hang on to the atmosphere of revelry and indulgence. She looked around, sipping at her wine, thinking that this room was like a chapel dedicated to the greater glory of St. Dorian Villiers. There were many portraits of the great man and many black and white photographs and playbills advertising performances of his most famous roles—Lear, Tamburlaine, Archie Rice, Prospero, James Tyrone, Macbeth and, of course, many Falstaffs.

She peered closely at a framed poster for a play she didn't recognise, *White Shadow, White Wave,* and she saw, reflected in a corner of its glass, almost like a tableau, a couple sitting in a corner, knee to knee, the man leaning forward to light the woman's cigarette. A second later she realised the man was Reggie. She turned, put her wine down on a side table, and wandered over, steering herself around groups of boisterous people. Maybe Reggie would come back with her; there was no point in ordering two taxis, seeing as the party was so clearly over.

"There you are, darling," she said. "Taxi'll be here in five minutes. Do you want to come back with me?"

Reggie stood up and the woman with him stood also.

"Oh. Elfrida. Talbot told me you'd already gone. Do you know Janet Headstone? She's doing some extra work on our script. Thank God."

Elfrida saw a young blonde woman in her thirties, her hair wound up in a loose chignon, wearing a shimmering turquoise dress, tight across her heavy bust with a chasm of cleavage on display. They shook hands.

"How do you do," Elfrida said.

"Really lovely to meet you."

She had one of those twangy London accents, Elfrida noticed, all glottal-stop. To mee' you.

"See you tomorrow, Jan," Reggie said, picking up his cigarettes and lighter.

"Safe home," Janet said.

Elfrida and Reggie left the room and headed for the staircase.

"She's saved our lives, has Janet. Very smart cookie."

"Really? Lucky you."

Elfrida said nothing more, her brain in turmoil, concentrating on descending the staircase without falling over. Now she knew who it was.

. . .

The man with the clipboard led Anny and Troy into a small dining room on the ground floor to the left of the staircase. The table was laid for breakfast. Sitting at it were Detective Inspector Desmondson and Agent Radetski of the FBI.

Anny felt a bolus of vomit rise in her throat.

Troy stepped forward, taking control.

"What's going on here, fellas? We're at a party. You can't just—"

"May I ask who you are, sir? We want to speak to Miss Viklund privately," Desmondson said.

"He's a friend," Anny interrupted. "I want him to stay."

Desmondson glanced at Radetski, who nodded.

"Fine with us."

"What do you want?" Anny said.

"We have news of your husband, Cornell Weekes."

"He's my ex-husband. I keep telling you."

"Apologies."

"What about him?" Anny's throat felt parched, now. Not a trace of saliva.

"Have you seen him recently?" Radetski asked.

"No. Not for months and months. Over a year. More."

"He was arrested earlier this evening at Southampton docks," Radetski said. "He was about to board a ferry to Spain. He had a considerable amount of money on him."

"What's all this got to do with me?" Anny said.

"Yeah, exactly," Troy added, supportively.

"Because." Radetski paused and glanced at Desmondson. "Because he said that the person who gave him this money was you."

SURRENDER

I

"What's going on, Talbot? It's outrageous," Reggie said, plaintively. Faux-plaintively, Talbot thought, this sort of thing happened all the time in the wonderful world of movie-making.

"It's no mystery," Talbot said. "We need to create a cameo role for Dorian Villiers."

"Why the fuck?"

"Because it will help the film in its film life. Having his name attached—you know: 'with Dorian Villiers'—will help sell the film to the world. The sales people are excited, over the moon," he lied.

"What does Yorgos say?"

"He's delighted, couldn't be happier." That much was true. Talbot had phoned him and put the suggestion to him and he instantly agreed—agreed to Dorian's hefty fee, also. "Cheap at the price," he said. In fact Talbot had floated the idea precisely to gauge Yorgos's response knowing that the nature of the response would confirm or cancel his suspicions. The speed of Yorgos's acquiescence duly provided the sign, and it did indeed increase his suspicions. Something was going on, Yorgos wanted to keep Talbot happy. And they still had to survive their face-to-face regarding the contract for *Burning Leaves.* Talbot now had the feeling he could ask for anything and Yorgos would accommodate him—anything to keep him sweet. It was worrying.

He and Reggie were sitting in Talbot's office at the end of the day's shooting. Talbot fetched his bottle of whisky and poured them both a glass.

"Well, you're the boss," Reggie said a little sulkily. "What kind of a role could Dorian have?"

"I don't know. He could be some kind of fantasy figure, an apparition, some creature of Emily Bracegirdle's imagination." He suddenly had an idea. "Why don't we ask Janet to dream up something? We're talking two or three pages, a couple of days' filming, maximum. Janet writes it, we shoot it, if it's no good we might not use it. Dorian only wants to be paid for work done."

"Tax?" Reggie asked, knowingly.

"It could be anything."

"Well, you can ask Janet," Reggie said. "I refuse. It's your idea."

"All right, I will. With pleasure. By the way, it's not an 'idea,' it's a scheme, a tactic. This way we get a movie giant in our film. Nothing to lose, everything to win."

Reggie didn't look convinced.

"I'll swing by Janet's this evening," Talbot continued. "She can dash something off. We're paying her all this money, she might as well earn it."

"Janet Headstone has already saved this film."

"Then writing a couple of extra pages for Dorian Villiers will be like . . ." He searched for a simile. "Like falling off a log."

Reggie was thinking. "I suppose 'with Dorian Villiers' does add a certain cachet."

"Exactly. Worth every penny."

"Just how many pennies are we paying the old bastard?"

"Still negotiating," Talbot lied again. "Will you call Janet and tell her to expect me around seven?"

Talbot was late when he arrived at Janet Headstone's house in Kemp Town—it was closer to eight o'clock so he told the driver not to wait. He rang the doorbell and Janet answered, wearing a red and black kimono above bare feet. He noticed her toenails were painted black. She was very pleased to see him, somewhat to his surprise, and as they wandered through to the kitchen, chatting, he wondered if she was a bit "high." He could never be sure with drugs—what people smoked or injected or sniffed or what pills were popped. They sat down round the pine table and Janet made them both gin and tonics, Talbot trying not to have seemed to have noticed the roll and sway of her heavy breasts beneath the silk of the kimono, the lapels of which were beginning to gape alarmingly. She was definitely "stoned," he decided. She lit a cigarette as Talbot told her about the Dorian Villiers situation and the need to create a small role for him.

"Where did this brilliant notion spring from?" she asked.

"It was an idea we had—seeing as Dorian's actually in Brighton, living here. Capitalise."

"And he can be anything?"

"Anything that fits into a couple of days' filming."

"Is Rodrigo happy?"

"I wouldn't say he's on cloud nine but he hasn't said no."

Janet thought. "Villiers could be an old tramp—some old dosser Emily meets when she goes on the run."

"Ah. I don't think we actually want him in a scene with Emily—with Anny, I mean. Maybe he could be some sort of apparition—something in one of our dream sequences. A wizard, you know. A spectre."

"What if he was the ghost of her grandfather?"

"Not bad."

"We've got that bit where Emily's wandering around in the dark, lost, looking for somewhere to sleep. It's raining, she's hungry. She huddles in a doorway—goes to sleep."

"And is troubled by a dream of her old grandad."

Janet waved her cigarette around.

"Some sort of sleazy old geezer, admonishing her," she improvised. "The ghost of the past. You know, maybe cursing her or something."

"Like it."

She stood up and paced about the kitchen, continuing her extemporisation, the speed of her progress up and down the room, to and fro, causing the skirt of her kimono to separate, revealing her pale sturdy legs and thighs. Talbot was half-listening, finding himself wondering if she and Reggie were having a full-blown affair. Quite probably, he reckoned, Reggie's reputation encouraged the surmise. He just hoped poor Elfrida didn't find out until after their film was finished.

Janet sat down with a bump that made the table shiver.

"Couple of pages should do it. Nice long monologue," she said.

"As long as it's enough for two full days' work for Dorian. If we shoot a lot then we can always use bits in flashback if we want."

"Got you. When do you need this by?"

"Sometime tomorrow would be ideal. Then we can get him in next week." Talbot had managed to push Dorian back by a couple of days. He didn't want a cheque, he wanted cash and Talbot said that would take a little longer. I'll sort everything out with my agent, Dorian had said. Best to keep it between us at the moment.

"Are you sure Rodrigo's happy? It sounds like something he'd hate," Janet asked.

"I think he's becoming used to the idea. He can see the commercial advantages," Talbot said carefully, knowing Janet would telephone him as soon as she could. He finished his drink and said he should be going. Janet walked him to the door and, to his surprise, kissed him goodbye.

"We must try and work together," she said. "I mean, properly. Make a proper film together."

"Any day. A pure pleasure."

"I've written this script. It's a bit autobiographical. Actually, it's very autobiographical." The thought made her laugh, quite heartily. "I'd love you to read it."

"Send it along," Talbot said, feeling a familiar weariness descend on him, as he envisaged significant portions of his future involved with Janet Headstone's autobiographical film script.

"What's it called?" he asked, trying to show willing.

"Turmoil." She pointed at him, her forefinger unsteady, wavering in front of his eyes. "It'll be fucking brilliant, Talbot."

Outside, Talbot lit a cigarette. *Turmoil*—good title for a film about his life, currently. He felt that his life, his professional life, was beginning to accelerate out of control. Or crumble away, like a sandcastle undermined by a rising tide. A rising tide of complications and then more complications. This film, *Ladder to the Moon,* was like weather: both unpredictable and unavoidable. You had no idea what the next day would bring, but it would bring something: wind, rain, sun, storms, drought. The simple overriding ambition was to survive, to maintain some degree of normality. He needed another drink. Surely there must be a pub somewhere in the neighbourhood . . .

He looked towards the small shopping parade at the end of the street where his eye was caught by a glimmer of white neon glowing in the encroaching duskiness of the summer evening and he wandered towards it.

The Icebox.

He stood outside, wondering whether to go in. There was a door set below a 3-D, white-neon square box. The name of the club was actually burned into the wood of the door, the letters charred, as if by some sizzling-hot writing implement. Or a red-hot poker, he thought, wryly. A man came out and hurried away, head down. Talbot caught the door before it closed and stepped inside. Stairs led down to a basement landing and to one of those heavy maroon velvet curtains that you found in entryways of French brasseries. Talbot paused again—and then pushed through the thick folds.

Inside the club, soft, jazzy music was playing and the lighting was dim and blue-tinged, somehow, to reflect the club's name, he assumed. Along one wall was a lengthy bar and tables were arranged around a small wooden dance floor. Beyond the tables against the rear wall were circular booths upholstered in navy blue, but barely lit. It was a cross between a pub and a nightclub, he supposed: you could have a pint of beer or dance or canoodle in the shadowy darkness of the booths, driven by whatever urge had brought you here.

He wandered over to the bar. It was early and there were very few customers. The bluey lighting made everyone's face a curious, leached-out monochrome. It was almost like being in a black and white film, he thought; the atmosphere encouraging the idea that this wasn't quite the real world, that you were performing somehow, that it wasn't really you.

For a moment Talbot thought about turning around and heading back out to the street and the Grand Hotel but the barman—a tubby fellow in a bow tie and a waistcoat—had spotted him and welcomed him with a cheery "Evening, sir, what can I do you for?"

Talbot said hello, both curious and excited in a strange way, and ordered a Scotch and soda. Who was it who had said that the sense of one's own uniqueness in this crowded world was absolutely banal in the end? . . . But there *was* something that made you unique, surely—your sexual life. What you responded to in another person, what your sexual triggers were. Who could analyse this accurately? What explained the attraction of the particular geometry of a face and the myriad examples of human form—the sex, the smells, lips, legs, breasts, buttocks, penises, vaginas, thinness, fatness, hair, the colour and length of hair, the absence of hair, teeth, nails, eyes, and on and on—was unique to you, the person who found all these differing aspects of another person, this precise congruence of detail, stirring and arousing. Why this one—and not that one? Maybe the answer to that question was the key to your human nature, that led you to its unique identity, its idiosyncratic verity, and was therefore the very opposite of banal. Sometimes it could take you by surprise—the curious alchemy of an individual you encountered could trigger emotions and feelings that you thought you were indifferent to, or resistant to. Maybe that was why he felt excited, here in the Icebox. This was the Brave New World for a man like him, of his age and experience, everything was different now—he could be ambushed at any turn and disarmed, his undeveloped heart redeveloped.

Two young men stood at the end of the bar and glanced at him for a second as his eye roved over and past them. Maybe the cold blue light was the masterstroke—everyone looked odder, more otherworldly, in the arctic glow. Shed your old identity and your old inhibitions was the message he was receiving.

He sipped his whisky and continued his scrutiny. Maybe half a dozen men were in the club, some young with long hair and moustaches, some middle-aged. There was an elderly man sitting at a table wearing a covert coat and a bowler hat staring at his drink as if it contained some answer to his particular problem.

"Not seen you in here before, sir," the barman said. "Live in Brighton?"

"Passing through," Talbot said.

"Aren't we all, Talbot?" came a familiar voice from behind him.

He turned, to see George Trelawny standing there. He looked instantly for the colonel but sensed almost immediately that George was alone. They shook hands. George was wearing black jeans and an untucked floral-motifed shirt with a long floppy collar. He took his place by the bar beside Talbot, smiling. Talbot registered again his stockiness, his bullish, barrel physique—a strong, small man.

"Thought I might bump into you here one day," he said.

"Really? What're you drinking, George?"

George asked for a brandy and ginger that was duly served up and Talbot asked if the colonel would be joining them.

"No. Not tonight. He has to be in the mood. However, I pop down myself from time to time—he doesn't mind."

"I remembered he'd mentioned this place," Talbot said, as if he had to excuse his presence here, somehow. "I had a meeting up the road, funnily enough. Thought I'd check it out."

George took two large gulps of his brandy and lit a cigarette.

"It's a very good club. You make what you want of it. No pressure on you."

"What exactly does that mean?"

"You can come in for a drink on your own—like we've done. Or you can come in with a friend and not be 'bothered.' Or you can come in here to meet new people."

"I see."

George glanced at the two young men at the other end of the bar.

"If you got talking to someone, for example, and you wanted to talk to them more privately, you can go downstairs. There's a big basement. And the lavatories."

Talbot took this information in with a vague smile. This was Brighton's answer to Christopher Street, he supposed.

"What about you, sir? I mean, Talbot?"

Everyone was equal in the Icebox, Talbot realised.

"What about me?" he said.

"Are you here for a drink? Or something else?"

"I suppose you could say I'm on a recce, of sorts . . . And a drink, of course. I had a trying meeting. Film business, you know. It can be tiresome."

"Ah, yes, the films." He paused for a moment, seemed about to speak, then thought the better of it—and then decided to speak. "Did you ever see that film with Dirk Bogarde?"

"I've seen many. *Doctor in the House*?"

"No. That one where he played a lawyer. Posh lawyer. And some young lad was blackmailing him."

"Yes. It was called *Victim.*"

"That's the one. You remind me of him from time to time—that Dirk Bogarde. Just sometimes. A certain expression on your face."

"He's much younger than me—and with a full head of glossy hair." Talbot signalled for another whisky.

"You don't look like him—but sometimes I see the same expression. Sorry, I'm not making much sense."

"You mean I look like a 'victim'?" Talbot said, trying not to sound hostile.

"No. Not at all. The opposite. It's more like . . ." George protested and searched his mind for the right expression and Talbot waited out his inarticulacy. "The look you have on your face, sometimes, it's like . . . Like you're seeing through everything. Know what I mean? Bogarde has that look as well. Like you know what's true—and what's lies."

Now Talbot took out his cigarettes and lit one, giving himself time to think. He really didn't have the slightest idea what George was talking about.

"Well, if you're paying me a compliment, George," he said, "I'll happily take it. Funnily enough," he said, drawing the smoke deep into his lungs, "I had a chat with Dirk Bogarde just last night. Met him at a party. Delightful man. Very open, intelligent, amusing."

"The circles you move in, sir. Sorry, Talbot." He corrected himself again and smiled, knowingly. "If you'll excuse me—I see my friend has arrived."

He squeezed Talbot's arm above the elbow, quite hard, still smiling. Talbot registered the familiarity, the subtext, of the gesture. In the twenty-odd years he had known Corporal George Trelawny he had never touched him like this. Ever.

"See you around, Talbot. Take it easy."

"Give my best to Ivo," Talbot said, vaguely, and watched George go to the maroon curtain to greet a young man in a suit and tie, carrying a briefcase. They installed themselves in a booth at the rear. Talbot finished his drink quickly and left.

2

It was most odd, Elfrida thought, but when she was at home in London she had absolutely no idea how much she drank, not the faintest. Whereas in Brighton, in Rottingdean, she measured out her life in bottles of Sarson's White Vinegar. She exhaled, closed her eyes, felt the room keel over and opened them quickly again—and poured herself another gin. She had run out of tonics but the neat gin was fine, in fact, not bothersome at all. She drank less, though the effect was more intense. Less is more, she thought—a nice paradox when it came to alcohol—more is more, being the norm. Yes, of course, she said to herself, picking up her train of thought, she could always go out to the composting bin in the garden and unearth the bottles that she hid there and do a proper count but—to tell the truth—she couldn't care. She didn't actually *care*—she didn't give a fuck.

The television was on with the sound off—she liked that, liked its mute flicker—it made her feel less alone in the house, and the Vale of Health was so quiet at night, hardly a car passing. She took a crisp from the bag in front of her on the kitchen table, topped up her glass to the very brim and carried it upstairs to her study.

The pool of light from the anglepoise illuminated her open notebook with its first few sentences of *The Last Day of Virginia Woolf.* She sat down and read through what she had written and was dissatisfied.

She picked up her pen, unscrewed the top, crossed everything out and started anew.

> Virginia Woolf was dreaming. There was a dog in her dream—a large dog—and it was trying to lick her face. She pushed it away and then, with a lurch, woke up, her hands tangled in the blankets lying over her. She coughed and sat slowly upright, taking her bearings as full consciousness slowly returned, noticing that a pale rhomboid of sunlight was glowing on her bedroom wall. The weather seemed set fair. Her last day on earth would be a clement one.

Much better, she thought, wondering why she had chosen a "large dog" to be in the dream. It was curious how a novelist's brain instinctively and instantly supplied these details. She had known that she was going to start the novel with "Virginia Woolf was dreaming" but then the contents of the dream just came to her, like that. Funny . . .

She took a sip of her gin, aromatic and warm. Ice—that was what she needed. She took her glass downstairs to the kitchen and dug out the ice tray from the freezer, running it under the tap so she could ease the lever device on the top. She pulled the lever back and the ice cubes shattered out, falling and spinning on the kitchen floor. She plopped three cubes into her glass and the gin overflowed. She took two large gulps as a means of lowering the level, feeling the head-reel of intoxication. She was intoxicated to be writing again and the gin, now cold, was better. Colder was better. Less is more and colder is better—let these be her watchwords. She went back upstairs, read what she had written and found it unsatisfactory. She crossed the lines out and started again.

> Virginia Woolf was dreaming. A dog—an Irish setter—was jumping up on her, its paws roughly scratching her forearms, its pink tongue lolling wetly as it panted. She opened her eyes and realised it was her own breath coming fast and she panicked, thinking she might be having some kind of a fit. She sat up in bed and drank water from the glass on her bedside table. A lemony rhomboid of sunlight glowed on her bedroom wall.

> It looked like being a nice day for March. Her last day on the planet would be . . .

Would be what? She crossed out "It looked like being a nice day for March." Banal, and she didn't need to comment on the weather, the sun on the wall said everything required. But the opening still didn't seem right, somehow. The dog-dream was wrong. And why an Irish setter? Where had that come from? She went back to her very first version, still discernible beneath her scorings-out. Maybe it seemed better, maybe she should stick with her first idea. She crossed the lines out and started again.

> Virginia Woolf stirred in her bed, grunted, and opened her eyes. The first thing she saw was a rectangle of sunlight on the wall beside her. She sat up, consciousness invading her, reminding her that today, 28 March 1941, was going to be the last day of her life.

Yes, so much better. More succinct, more telling. "Grunted" was good. Make readers imagine Virginia grunting in her sleep. She liked that image: an elderly lady, sleeping. It made her human, the grunt. Maybe she should fart? No, not quite the right tone. She laughed. The tone of a fart. She picked up her glass and noticed to her astonishment that it was empty. This is what happened when writing took you over. Time, activity, consumption all took place as if on another plane of existence. She stood up and her chair fell over. Fuck it. Carefully she walked back downstairs, glass in hand, feeling a bit unsteady. The sensible thing to do would be to bring the gin and the ice upstairs to her study and eliminate the need for the to-and-fro. Yes, that's what she'd do.

In the kitchen she nearly slipped on the meltwater from the ice cubes that had fallen on the floor. She should have refilled the tray. No matter. She poured some gin into her glass and suddenly found herself thinking of that vile party in Brighton and Reggie and that woman. What was her name? Janet Something. She felt tears warm her eyes. A young woman—with big tits. And she was a writer, she remembered. That was what hurt, stupidly, not the fact that he'd chosen somebody younger and more lubricious but that he'd chosen a writer. He'd betrayed a writer with a writer. She gulped gin. That was what was unforgivable.

3

DO NOT TAKE MORE THAN EIGHT TABLETS IN 24 HOURS it said on the packet of Equanil. She wasn't sure how many she'd taken. Six? She was positive it was six as she counted back—so it was all right for her to have two more. Anny went to the little sink in her caravan, ran water into a glass and took the pills. She had to admit she was feeling a little woozy but that was better than raw anxiety. She peered out through the curtains and spotted Shirley coming up the street towards her. She let the curtain drop—she was already in costume so it must be make-up time. She was the only cast member in these upcoming scenes—everyone was waiting for her.

"I'll be right there, Shirley," she called when the rap on the door came.

"No. We're not quite ready for you. There are two men here who would like to talk to you if you could spare ten minutes, they say."

"It's not a good time. Tell them to come back tomorrow."

"They have to speak to you tonight, they say."

Anny felt the panic attack kick in—the trapped, fluttering bird behind her ribcage. When would the fucking Equanil start working? She thought fast and opened the door.

"Tell them I can talk to them when we wrap tonight. Bring them here to the trailer." She explained further, a plan unspooling miraculously in her head. She knew why they were here and she knew what she had to do.

"Give them a cup of coffee and some cookies, you know. Say I'll be along as soon as I get out of make-up. I may be running a little late."

"Sure. They're happy to wait, they said."

It wasn't a complex series of scenes tonight, Rodrigo had told her. She—Emily—had run off in a state. Night had fallen and she was lost in a strange part of town. She would slowly pick her way along a street, find a doorway, huddle in a corner and fall into a troubled sleep. No dialogue. No Troy. A great opportunity for more great music, Rodrigo said—and then, when she fell asleep they were going to have this amazing dream sequence. A new idea.

"Which is what? Could I know what I'm going to be dreaming about?" she'd asked.

"As soon as it's actually written, honeybun," Rodrigo said.

Night shoots were tedious—so many things could go wrong. Sirens, cars tooting, reflections of headlights from passing vehicles even though the street—the set—was locked down and closed off. Rodrigo ran her through the action. She was to emerge from an alleyway, then be spooked by a passing car that made her hide in a front garden. She would keep hiding as two policemen passed by then she'd make her way along a row of shopfronts until she found a doorway where she could curl up and go to sleep.

"Five set-ups, maybe six," he said. "Doddle."

In fact it was more like ten and the longest one was improvised. He had her looking at her reflection in a puddle until her reflection was distorted by spreading ripples from a solitary raindrop.

Rodrigo made two L-shapes with his thumb and forefinger and held them in front of her face, mimicking the close-up frame.

"Your face, upside down. A big upside-down close-up. Imagine. Then ripples and your face breaks up. Far out!"

"Why would I stop and look at my face in a puddle?" she asked. "I'm terrified, no? Running away, lost."

"Lovely visuals, darling. Academy Award stuff."

She went along with everything he told her to do, half her mind on her developing escape plan. She huddled in the doorway, pretending to sleep, walking herself through the various stages of her plan, making sure the risk element was minimised. Then Rodrigo said it was a wrap for the night.

"Brilliant stuff, babe," he said. "Oh. By the way, I've just been told two people need to speak to you urgently. Police or some such. Is everything OK?"

"It's all under control," she said. "I'm meeting them in my trailer."

"Fine. See you tomorrow."

"I'm not on tomorrow."

"Oh, yeah, that's right." He thought. "Oh, Jesus God, it's Sylvia tomorrow. Wish me luck!"

"Good luck. And then it's the weekend."

"Of course. Brain's packing up. See you next week, sweetie pie. Be good!"

He gave her a hug—he seemed genuinely excited by what he had shot tonight—and she wandered off to change out of her costume and have her make-up removed. Her hair was wild, full of small twigs and leaves from her passage through shrubs and bushes, her face was smudged with dirt and mud—she had to return to normal. While she was in make-up she had a message sent to have her car brought round to the make-up caravan. When she was done, scrubbed and clean, hair glossy and combed, she slipped away, found her car and was driven back to the hotel. She told her driver he wasn't needed any further and she reckoned she had a forty-five-minute to one-hour start on Desmondson and Radetski. She imagined them sitting in her trailer, waiting, being fed coffee and cookies by Shirley. After half an hour or so Shirley would go and look for her in make-up, return and say Miss Viklund had gone back to the hotel. Then her ruse would be exposed and only then would the alarm be raised.

At the hotel, she quickly packed a bag and went down to reception where she left a note for Troy. She had the hotel call her a taxi, giving no destination, and once it arrived she told the driver to take her to Gatwick airport.

She sat in the airport all night—finding a dark corner in the terminal, not risking checking in to a hotel—and managed to doze off for a couple of hours on an upholstered bench before the early-morning cleaning staff woke her up. Then she bought a ticket on the first flight leaving for Paris. She was pretty damn sure no one would have any idea what had become of her.

She only began to truly relax once the plane had taken off. She knew exactly why Radetski and Desmondson had come to the set. They had warned her during their interrogation at Dorian Villiers' party—despite her vehement denials it was obvious they didn't believe her.

"You do understand, Miss Viklund, that Cornell Weekes is a fugitive from justice. A wanted man," Desmondson had said, patiently, as if lecturing a child. "We had an 'All Ports Warning' out on him. That's how we got him."

"A 'most wanted' man," Radetski had emphasised. "He's an escaped convicted criminal. A terrorist."

"I haven't seen him since our divorce," she repeated. "So how could I have helped him? How could I have given him money? He's just trying to incriminate me."

She had known that her shrill refutations of their implicit accusations would only take her so far. She imagined that the information Cornell had supplied about their encounters would have been so precise regarding locations, times, incidental details—the autograph-hunter trick, room service, the decor in her suite—that his claims, his testimony, would have seemed overwhelmingly convincing to the detectives. It was only her good acting and her status as an American film star that had bought her some extra time. They would have to be 100% sure before they accused her of aiding and abetting, then charged her and arrested her. In the event, those couple of days had allowed her to formulate a plan and confirm—via a quick phone call to Jacques—that it was almost impossible to extradite a citizen of the United States of America from the République Française. They could delay it for years, for decades, he said, *pas de problème.*

So she would be safe—that was the first priority—and then she could assess what damage Cornell had done to her life and her future. She sat there, looking at the cloudscape outside the oval window, thinking bitterly that everything had changed for the bad so quickly—that fucking bastard of an ex-husband had gotten his revenge, all right. But where there was life there was hope, she told herself. Where there was hope there was life.

She asked the stewardess for another cup of coffee and thought about the film and her role and what her sudden abandonment of *Emily Bracegirdle's Extremely Useful Ladder to the Moon* would mean to everyone involved. She was sorry. And she was sad—because of Troy and what he would be thinking and feeling about her. One thing she was sure of was that she would see Troy again, come what may. She was absolutely sure about that. It was just a fucking mess. She had been landed in a giant nightmare goat-fuck of a mess that was not of her making, but she owed it to herself not to become a victim, not to be sucked down into the swamp of that mess.

Pire hypothèse. Force majeure. Sauve qui peut. That's what Jacques had said to her on the phone. How would you translate that? Worst-case scenario. Out of your control. Run for your life . . . The noise of the plane's engines changed slightly as they banked and began their descent. Paris, safety and Jacques awaited. She couldn't waste what remained of her precious energies thinking about what she had left behind.

4

"You're making a terrible mistake, Mrs. Tipton. Please reconsider. It's not safe."

"I'm perfectly happy to take full responsibility," Elfrida said.

"We were unable to contact your husband, I'm afraid."

"He's away making a film. Abroad," she lied. Knowing full well why he was uncontactable. "Thank you for everything," she continued, "I'm very grateful for your concern. Goodbye."

Elfrida smiled at the young consultant—she'd forgotten his name, he seemed very young indeed.

"I'm perfectly well," she said. "Don't worry about me, oh no."

She gave him a brisk wave of farewell and made her way through the corridors and stairs of the Royal Free Hospital and found the reception area where she formally checked herself out and stepped out onto Gray's Inn Road, looking around for the nearest pub.

She found one a couple of hundred yards away up the road towards King's Cross called the Heart of Albion. It was suitably depressing and seedy, which was what she asked of pubs. Spirits should be lowered on entry so that spirits could raise them anew, was her rationale. She saw Lincoln-green Anaglypta wallpaper hung with etchings of historic martial triumphs—Trafalgar, Balaclava, the Torres Vedras lines, Blenheim, Dunkirk, Malta GC, Waterloo—all battles, she registered, all to do with war and conflict, as if that was what defined a nation rather than its culture. There was the usual boldly patterned carpet halfway on its long journey to monochrome and in corners bulky gambling machines blinked and beeped. It was just after opening time and the pub was practically empty.

She ordered half a pint of lager shandy simply to gently initiate the old receptors and calculated that she hadn't drunk a drop of alcohol since she had passed out in her kitchen two and a half days previously. It was strange and not a little unsettling to have a blank passage of time in one's personal history, she thought. Two days lost forever. Her final memory was of pouring a shot of gin into her glass (she was definitely going to go to bed after this one, she had told herself) and then nothing. Her consciousness stuttered into life when she woke up in a ward of the Royal Free some forty-eight hours later.

While she was in hospital a young man called Lonnie had come to visit her. He was the man—an Australian, it turned out—who had saved her life, apparently. He was employed by the gardening firm she hired to mow her patch of lawn and deadhead and weed the borders once a fortnight. He had gone into the garden through the side door in the morning and had seen that the TV was still on in her sitting room—the test card showing in the empty room. Thinking Elfrida must be at home and reluctant to surprise her if she was, he had tapped on the glass doors that gave on to the garden. Peering in, he had seen, through the French windows, Elfrida's legs prone in the kitchen. She was lying in a spreading pool of her vomit and urine, so the young consultant had told her, maximising the obloquy and the shame, she thought, in a wholly unnecessary way. Lonnie had called the police and they had broken in, carefully, found her still comatose and had her swiftly swept off to Accident and Emergency at the Royal Free.

Her house was secure, so she was told, neighbours had been alerted to her absence, and—miraculously—she had been provided with her own clean clothes and her house keys were in her handbag. It was as if she had been in a trance, or drugged—two whole days lost to anaesthetic oblivion. She was already feeling better after a couple of mouthfuls of shandy and went to the bar to order a schooner of Bristol Cream sherry. Bristol Cream sherry with a lager chaser provided the fastest route to a wonderful world of carefree lack of responsibility, so an old Welsh writer had once informed her. And she needed to be in that world again, to shut out the facets of her life that disturbed her—at least for a while.

The curious blend of lager and sweet sherry seemed to be working on her. She felt at once calmer, more cogent and more organised. She would stay in this pub for a while and maybe order something to eat, a pie or a sandwich, and then return home, sort everything out and, after a cup or two of tea, resume writing her novel. She had made a start after all—she had put black on white as old Guy de Maupassant had enjoined—she had a subject and she had inspiration. Nothing stood in her way other than the eternal problem of her procrastination and that was a thing of the past, she told herself. Those days were gone. Those ten years of literary stasis and creative inertia were over and done with. What a waste. What might she have written? What a waste of precious time.

She fished in her handbag for her notebook and found it, a fact that made her wonder again how come she had a handbag with her notebook in it and money in her purse to pay for her drinks. It must have been some efficient policewoman or paramedic. No matter, she had everything she needed including her notebook and pen. She opened the notebook at an empty page and started to write.

Novel—finish.
Reggie—finish.
House—sell (money).
Calder—alert (money).
Jessica—hire (divorce).
Future—discern.

Well, that was her life sorted out. She was a bit amazed at the rush with which she had written everything down. She hadn't really thought but, reading back through her list, it looked as if something of a sea-change in her existence was underway. And quite right too. Time to rid herself of this sham of a marriage; time to ponder and envisage the novels she was going to write; time to block out a new happy life that she so manifestly needed. Everything would change.

New life, new novels, new independence, new home, new aspirations. Everything was in her power—she had the agency—right was on her side so she should take control. The sweet sherry and lager chaser had worked its peculiar magic—she now felt ready for a gin and tonic.

5

Ken Kincade telephoned Talbot at his hotel before he had even shaved.

"We're all sorted, chief," Kincade said.

"What do you mean?"

"We're ready to rumble. I know what's happened to your film stock."

He told Kincade to meet him in the dining room of the Grand at nine o'clock and fill him in over breakfast.

"Wilco," Kincade said. "You won't be happy, man. Just a warning."

Talbot went down to breakfast in a curious and apprehensive mood. He felt oddly nervous—what revelation would Ken Kincade spring on him?—and at the same time resigned. This was the story of his life in cinema: ordinary norms of behaviour did not apply.

He ordered his usual breakfast and Ken Kincade appeared at the same time as Talbot's kipper. He was wearing a short black leather jacket and a white t-shirt, black jeans and silver-toed cowboy boots with Cuban heels.

"Hungry, Mr. Kincade?"

"I am actually. I'll take one of them brown fish you're having."

As they ate their smoked herrings, Kincade explained how he'd found out what happened to the missing film stock. He had infiltrated the film store—he didn't specify how—and had indelibly marked all the unused reels of film stock kept there. All reels subsequently found outside the store would be traceable to *Ladder to the Moon*—or not.

"I see the logic," Talbot said.

"The rest was simple surveillance, Mr. Kydd. Very boring, very time-consuming but—nine times out of ten, ninety-nine times out of a hundred—just sitting there on your ass watching, looking on, paying attention, solves the most difficult cases." He went on. "These cans of film are very bulky and very heavy. It struck me that whoever left the film store carrying something that looked bulky and heavy was the man to follow."

"Sounds sensible."

"It is, Mr. Kydd. There's a time to fish and a time to cut bait." He pushed his half-eaten kipper aside. "I saw this guy, this bozo, walk out of your film store carrying a bag that looked like it was filled with lead weights. I followed him home. I followed him to his other place of work the next day."

"But I trust these people," Talbot said, a little aggrieved squeak of outrage in his voice, realising at once how feeble he sounded. "I pay them well."

"You have zero security," Kincade said. "It's like—forgive the expression—stealing candy from a baby."

"What does he—this person—do with the film stock that he steals? Does he sell it to other films that're being made? Undercut the opposition? Agfa? Kodak? Eastmancolor? A kind of black-market deal?"

"I don't think so," Kincade said, mysteriously. "But why don't we go and find out."

They left the hotel and Kincade suggested they travel in his car. Talbot recognised it as a Ford Mustang, all black, left-hand drive, with an orange lightning strike down both sides. He eased himself cautiously into the passenger seat.

They drove to Peacehaven, east of Brighton, and parked in a residential street two blocks away from the South Coast Road.

"Where exactly are we?" Talbot asked.

"Telscombe Cliffs is the name of the area. Eleanor Avenue is where we find ourselves."

Talbot looked at a modest street of modest bungalows and houses, some of them larger, with two storeys. He checked his watch. It was

9:40 on a Friday morning, people were walking their dogs, mothers were pushing prams with babies inside, a municipal lorry with an aerial work platform containing two overall-clad workers was engaged in changing a bulb on a street lamp. It couldn't have been more ordinary.

He and Kincade stepped out of the car and were greeted with the sonic version of the suburban world that they'd just contemplated: a barking dog, the annoying buzz of an electric hedge-trimmer, the chimes of a distant ice-cream van. It was almost parodic, Talbot thought.

"Number 43," Kincade said and they walked towards it, one of the larger houses—two storeys and a high concrete wall around the garden.

"Are you coming in with me?" Talbot asked.

"I reckon it's your rodeo, Mr. Kydd. I'll wait outside. My job is over."

"Fair enough." Talbot thought for a second. What if there was trouble? Fisticuffs? "Stay close."

"A-OK."

Talbot left Kincade on the street and opened a low iron gate and walked up a paved path to the frosted-glass front door of number 43. He rang the bell and waited, glancing back. Ken Kincade had lit a cigarette—he gave Talbot a thumbs-up. Talbot rang the bell again.

A young blonde woman in a dressing gown opened the door a few inches.

"Yes?"

"Hello."

"Can I help you?"

"I think so."

He had no idea what to say next. He wondered if Kincade had got this right. Then the young woman came to the rescue.

"Are you here for the film?"

"I'm one of the producers," Talbot said. It was a near-infallible password, he'd found. Rarely queried.

"Oh. Right. You'd better come in, then. Everyone's upstairs."

Talbot stepped into the hall. The young woman in the dressing gown indicated the stairway.

"Like a cup of tea?"

"I'm fine thanks," Talbot said and climbed the stairs to the upper floor.

On the top landing, two naked men—one very hairy, one very thin—were gently massaging their flaccid penises as they chatted to a naked middle-aged woman with enormous sagging breasts. As far as he could tell they were talking about vandalism in the locality. He heard mention of smashed telephone boxes, washing being stolen from washing lines. The general tone of outrage was strong. He saw thick black electric cables snaking all over the floor and there was an unnatural glare of powerful arc lights coming from a room behind the men.

They looked round as Talbot appeared from below.

"Excuse me," Talbot said. "I'm one of the producers." He held a finger to his lips. The men parted to give him access and Talbot slipped into the bedroom of number 43, Eleanor Avenue, Peacehaven.

Tony During—his director of photography—was hunched over a 35 mm camera, peering through the viewfinder at an unmade bed. Two young women—naked—were lying on it, their arms uncertainly round each other. Three other men stood looking on, chatting in low voices. One of them raised a boom mike over the two in the bed.

"Fucking quiet!" Tony yelled without looking up and the conversation about vandalism ceased outside.

Another man stepped forwards with a clapperboard and clicked it.

"Scene twenty-one, take two."

"I want you to kiss. With tongues," Tony said to the young women on the bed. "It doesn't work if you don't kiss."

"I'm not kissing. You said no lesbian kissing."

"Kiss her neck, then. Look like you fancy her. Then suck her tits. You're meant to be nympho lesbos—Jesus! Action!"

Talbot stood there watching for a few seconds as the two girls on the bed fumbled with each other half-heartedly.

"CUT!" Talbot said in a loud voice. Everyone looked round.

"Who the fuck said—" Tony looked up from his camera and saw Talbot standing there, his look of poisonous irritation dissolving into shameful incredulity in a split second.

"Aw no. Fuck *no.* Mr. Kydd. No, no."

"Yes, yes, Tony, fuck yes. I think the expression is 'bang to rights,' isn't it?"

And then it became all very straightforward and meek and mild. Tony confessed—theft of film stock, of equipment, of malingering, of blatant moonlighting. He seemed almost relieved to have been discovered. Talbot felt like a prep-school headmaster who had caught, red-handed, a trusted prefect raiding the tuck shop.

Then, after the confession, things changed. Tony began to enter mitigating circumstances into the equation. He was heavily in debt, his home was about to be repossessed, his wife had three types of cancer. Talbot's scepticism hardened and Tony sensed it. There was no way out. And as his demeanour became more crestfallen and defeatist so his naked actors and his crew started demanding that they be paid. Talbot found himself confronting the two "lesbians" who claimed they were each owed £20. As their voices became more raised he silenced them by threatening to call the police. He said he had an associate in the street outside who would verify everything that had taken place in number 43. Making hard-core pornographic films was a criminal offence. He advised them to put their clothes on and go home. And so they eventually did, with a certain amount of darkly peeved muttering and hostile looks.

When they were finally alone, Talbot turned to Tony.

"I reckon you owe us between two and three thousand pounds, Tony. Your debt burden has increased dramatically. What am I meant to do in these circumstances? I have my own responsibilities to our film."

"I'll pay you back, sir."

"How?"

"I'll ask my producer. He's got loads of money. He won't want this to get out so don't call the cops, I beg you, Mr. Kydd. We can sort this out, boss. Honest."

"Honest, you'll never work again in the British film industry. Your career is in porno from now on, Tony. Good luck to you. Enjoy, as our American friends say."

"Hoi! Tony!" came a call from downstairs. "What in the name of fuck is going on here? Where is everybody?"

Tony flinched. "Shit. That's him—the producer." He opened the bedroom door and called down. "We're up here, mate."

Talbot lit a cigarette, feeling immediately tense. He hadn't expected this encounter. He clenched his fists. He hadn't physically fought anyone since the war.

And then Ferdie Meares walked in.

. . .

Ken Kincade drove Talbot back to the production office. He had made sure that Kincade was a witness to the moment when he outlined to Ferdie Meares the exact nature of the theft that had been perpetrated and the extent of his responsibilities as the backer and producer of the pornographic film in question. Talbot's silence could be bought only by a swift remuneration of the funds that had been stolen. Ferdie maintained a tone of aggressive resentment throughout, informing Talbot that every British film of note had an equivalent clandestine porn spin-off. When the proper film was released the porn version had a perfect, handy, piggyback. All your publicity became our publicity. What world was he living in?

"Whatever world I'm living in, don't have my director of photography steal my film stock is my advice. Nobody would have been any the wiser and you could have danced to your own porno tune, untroubled."

"I didn't fucking know he was stealing from you," Ferdie said, controlling his evident fury. "He was fucking stealing from me as well. I gave him money for film stock. He trousered that then stole from you. We've both been taken for a ride by that cunt. What do you take me for? Why would I risk stealing your stock? You think I'm some sort of arsehole? This is a proper business. You can make a fortune."

"Whatever you say, Ferdie." They looked at each other, coldly. "What was your nasty little film called, by the way?" Talbot asked, to break the silence.

"We hadn't quite decided. It was going to be either *Sex Ladder to the Moon* or *Ladder to the Sex Moon*."

"I assume you're joking."

"People like you don't know anything about real life, Talbot. You're so blinded by privilege that you make it too bloody easy for the rest of us. That's the whole fucking point."

Talbot sat in his office, recalling his encounter with Ferdie Meares and feeling a little stunned and unsettled. It was only lunchtime yet his morning's events seemed to have provided enough life experience for a week, for a month. Reggie was off filming Sylvia Slaye somewhere, dutifully following the day's schedule, a schedule that established, moreover, that *Ladder to the Moon* had entered its final quarter of filming. Yet he felt troubled and uneasy. Here he was, a man in his sixties, a veteran of the Second World War, an experienced producer of many films with their assorted histories of trauma and disappointments, surprise successes and unforeseen failures. However, in his confrontation with the loathsome Ferdie he had felt—what?—strangely naïve and unworldly, as if a window had opened to a world beyond his comprehension. "Blinded by privilege," so Ferdie had accused him. Maybe he was right, maybe that lofty view obscured so much.

Oh, well, he thought, lighting a cigarette, you live and learn. It's not every day that you stand in a house in Peacehaven arguing with two naked lesbians about proper financial recompense. You had to laugh. Or, at least, you had to try to laugh.

Joe rapped on the door jamb and leant in. Talbot knew him well enough by now to register that he wasn't happy.

"Break it to me, Joe." He assumed Joe was going to tell him that Tony During was off sick again.

"Detective Inspector Desmondson would like a word."

Desmondson was shown into the office, declined coffee, lit a cigarette.

"I'll come straight to the point, Mr. Kydd."

"Please do."

"We think that Anny Viklund has disappeared. Run away."

Talbot almost laughed.

"That's impossible," he said. He looked at the schedule in front of him. "If you show up on Monday morning bright and early you'll find her here hard at work."

Desmondson patiently explained the situation as he found it. They—Special Branch and the FBI—believed that Miss Viklund had given substantial sums of money to her ex-husband, Cornell Weekes, a "most wanted" fugitive who had been arrested trying to flee the country. Desmondson and Radetski had tried to interview Miss Viklund the previous evening after she had finished filming but, having initially promised to meet them, she had left the set and was nowhere to be seen. They discovered she had returned to her hotel where she had ordered a taxi but they had no idea of her destination.

"QED," he said. "*Quod erat—*"

"I know what the initials stand for, thank you." Talbot put his hands palms down on the blotter. "Detective Inspector. Miss Viklund is a young woman. Moreover, she's a young actress. Moreover, plus, she's a significant American movie star. She is very rich. She has three days off work. Do I need to say anything more?"

"She knew last night that we wanted to interview her, that we wanted to ask her questions about her ex-husband."

"And I suspect that's why she decided to slip away and enjoy her weekend instead. I'm sure she'll happily talk to you on Monday morning."

"Is it normal that you lose track of your major actors in this way?"

"I should say 'no' but the answer is in fact, 'yes.' It happens. It is, in its way, normal—if anything is normal in this abnormal business. Look, Detective Inspector Desmondson, it's a very odd job being an actor, anyway. It's even odder if you're a famous actor. You and I wouldn't last twenty-four hours under the unique pressures they experience."

"I believe she has absconded."

"She can't abscond because she has nothing to 'abscond' from."

"She aided and abetted a known, convicted criminal who is a fugitive from justice. We have his testimony."

"And I'm sure you can believe every word he uttered. Come on—you called him a criminal. He'll say anything."

"She gave him money to help him flee abroad."

"There may be another explanation that vindicates her. She's innocent until proved guilty, I assume." Talbot smiled reassuringly, but was in fact remembering Anny's request for $2,000. He suddenly had a bad feeling about this particular episode.

"Yes, of course." Desmondson stood up. If he could curl his lip, he would, Talbot thought. No doubt he thinks I'm blinded by privilege, as well.

"I'd appreciate it if you could use your resources to track down Miss Viklund this weekend and provide us with any information regarding her whereabouts."

The tired circumlocutions of every apparatchik throughout history, Talbot thought.

"I'll certainly make some calls, ask the crew," he said. He stood up himself. "This is all supposition," he said, mollifying his tone. "Wild surmise. You don't understand this business, Detective Inspector. Everything is fickle—beyond fickle—everything is unsure and uncertain. It's like herding cats. She'll be here on Monday morning, full of apologies. I've seen it a hundred times. She had other plans, that's all. Talking to you and your colleague last night didn't fit in. Sorry."

Desmondson stubbed out his cigarette in Talbot's ashtray.

"You won't see her back on this fucking film," he said, coarsely. "She's done a runner. I'll bet you a hundred quid."

"Lucky for you I'm not a gambling man."

Desmondson left and Talbot sat down again, slowly easing his head left and right, trying yet again to relieve the sudden tension in his neck and shoulder muscles. What if Desmondson was right? What if Anny had run away? The disappearance of Anny Viklund would make the confrontation over Ferdie Meares' porn film look like a spat in a playground.

His private phone rang and he picked it up.

"Yes?"

"Ah, Mr. Eastman, it's Mr. Brewster here, I'm the caretaker at—"

"Hello, Mr. Brewster, what can I do for you?"

"The broken window has been repaired and I have paid the glazier."

"Excellent, thank you, Mr. Brewster." There was an oddly sulky tone in Brewster's voice, Talbot thought. "Is everything all right?"

"There's a . . . a difficulty. The cheque that was given to me—by way of reimbursement from Axelrod Scaffolding—has bounced. That's left me out of pocket, Mr. Eastman. Eight pounds, three shillings and sixpence."

"I'll be up tomorrow. Let me deal with it. I'll personally refund your money."

He hung up. Thank God for minor problems, he thought.

6

Back to Rottingdean. In a way Elfrida was happy to be at Peelings again, with its empty rooms, its monkey puzzle trees, its sleepiness, its inertia. After the distress of the fall and concussion in her house in the Vale of Health it was oddly reassuring to be back in this quiet village near Brighton. Reggie had no idea at all what had transpired in London. He'd clearly never bothered to telephone her—in fact she wondered if he'd even really registered her absence.

So here she was back in the kitchen, adding a slug of vodka to her orange juice as if nothing had ever happened and all was well with the world. Time to return to the novel.

> Virginia Woolf was sleeping. On the wall by her bed a pale parallelogram of lemony early-morning sunlight crept towards her face. When the sunlight hit her eyes, she grunted and turned over, but consciousness had indisputably dawned in her brain as well and was urging her awake. Wake, wake. Thoughts began to stir, so she sat up, looking around, blinking. Sunlight on the wall. 28 March 1941. She knew that this was going to be the last day of her life.

Elfrida put her pen down. This was a better opening, she thought: the best yet, punchier somehow, with a more modern feel. She drained the glass of Sarson's and orange and thought about a celebratory refill. Unthinkingly she was rubbing at a long four-inch scratch on the inside of her left forearm. She must have hit something when she fell in the kitchen. In the hospital they had put some gentian violet on it but the purple hue had now disappeared and the scratch was revealed in all its angry pinkness. Why was it like that? she wondered. Was it infected in some way? It didn't look normal.

She held her forearm up to the desk light. It seemed more swollen, somehow. The torn skin was sitting on a little ridge of oedema. She looked closely and to her alarm saw that it seemed to be moving ever so slightly. She put her eye close and with her fingers stretched the skin and she could see—just under the translucent surface—quite clearly, tiny maggots the size of pin-heads pulsing, swarming, writhing.

She felt sick and covered the scratch with her palm, feeling a chilly sweat break out on her brow. Jesus Christ. What had she done to herself? What had happened? How could tiny, near-microscopic parasites be fulminating under a bad scratch on the skin of her arm?

She ran downstairs to the kitchen and opened a drawer where she knew the house's first-aid kit was kept. She found a crêpe bandage and she wound it round and round her forearm, securing it with a pin over her festering wound. She poured herself a tumbler of vodka and took large gulps to calm herself. A complete nightmare! Like something from a science-fiction film or that novel by Albert Camus, what was it called—the name escaped her. *Pestilence* or *Pandemic* or something. Dead rats, that's what she remembered. Rats dying.

The vodka was helping and she began to feel calmer again. What had Reggie told her to do? Any problem, any minor emergency call Joe—yes, call Joe. She found the typed list of the crew with their contact telephone numbers. There he was—Joe Swire, line producer. She put in a call to his office and after a minute or so he came to the phone.

"Joe here, Mrs. Tipton."

"Hello, Joe. So sorry to bother you but I've got a bit of a problem—a medical, health issue. I need to see a doctor as soon as possible."

"Easy as pie, Mrs. T. I'll call you back with the details in five minutes."

Elfrida put down the phone and topped up her drink. This was the marvel of working in the film industry. While the film was underway almost everything in life that you needed was made available to you—

money, transportation, accommodation, food, company, guides, entertainment, restaurant and hotel reservations and, in this case, medical intervention. Her status as "wife" of the director gave her more priority, she knew. If she had called and said, "I've bought a piano and I want it shipped to London," or "Book me a suite in the best hotel in Torquay," or "I've a craving for avocado pears" somebody would be ordered to do what she asked and sort the matter out for her. The trouble was that once the film stopped, all this unquestioned aid ended, and you had to go back to doing things for yourself. It was very spoiling, not to say ruinous, to some personalities. Anyway, at least she would swiftly have an appointment to see a doctor—who was no doubt on some sort of lucrative retainer. He would know that she was "with the film" and therefore nothing would be too much trouble. Perhaps this was the great seduction of film-making, she suddenly wondered. It wasn't about art; it was about making other people do your bidding.

In fact, the doctor turned out to be a "she," not the "he" she had imagined. Her name was Dr. Sarah Ingham and she had a marked Irish brogue. She was a squarely built woman in her forties, wearing a checked tweed suit under her white coat, perhaps a couple of years older than she was. Her surgery was in Hove, just off Lansdowne Road near the cricket ground. She had a strong face, Elfrida thought, as Dr. Ingham examined her scratch with the aid of a magnifying glass, almost carved-looking, with a slightly hooked nose and a clean jawline. Her wiry greying hair was held securely back by a velvet band. Short fingers, no rings. Why did one notice these details? Dr. Ingham said nothing as she examined the scratch, nothing reassuring in any event, and Elfrida began to feel a little afraid of her.

Dr. Ingham put her magnifying glass down.

"You've a bad scratch on your arm," she said. "How did it happen?"

"I slipped and fell. But then these creatures infested it."

"There are no 'creatures,' Mrs. Tipton. You've a bad scratch. Full stop."

"But I can see them—clearly—with my own eyes. I don't need a magnifying glass. Tiny maggot-like creatures, swarming just under the skin."

"We can all 'see' things, Mrs. Tipton." Dr. Ingham sat back and steepled her fingers, looking at Elfrida along the lines of their tips as if she was aiming at her through a gunsight. "I'm here to tell you there are no creatures, no maggots, no nothing. Your scratch will be fully healed within a matter of days. Don't bandage it, let the air get at it."

"So, what am I seeing?"

"You're not 'seeing'—you're hallucinating."

Elfrida decided to say nothing more to this stern, strong-faced woman. She could have her profile engraved on a coin or sculpted on some Soviet war memorial, she thought. Absolutely not the sort of kindly, understanding doctor she needed in her current state.

"I'd like to take a blood test," Dr. Ingham said.

"To confirm the presence of bacteria, microbes?"

"To confirm the amount of alcohol—or other drugs—in your blood."

"I deeply resent that!" Elfrida said with as much feigned outrage as she could muster. She shrivelled inside.

"Do you drink alcohol?"

"Of course. Like everybody else. A sherry before a meal. The odd glass of wine."

Dr. Ingham wrote a note on her pad.

"I think you're suffering from a form of psychosis," she said in her blunt, no-nonsense way. "I'd like you to spend some time in an excellent clinic that we use not far from—"

"Stop right there, Dr. Ingham!" Elfrida stood up. "I'm in the middle of an important new novel. I may admit to a certain amount of stress from overwork but—psychosis? I've never heard such rubbish. Maybe my infection is beyond your experience as a GP—or your competence. Thank you for your time—I will take myself and my problem to . . . To the Institute of Tropical Medicine in London," Elfrida improvised. She stepped back. "I have contacts there, good friends. Good day to you."

Dr. Ingham beat her to the door. She looked at her squarely.

"It's your decision, Mrs. Tipton. I can't force you to do anything. But I can see you're suffering. So, please, call on me again. I may be able to help in all manner of ways."

"I hardly think that will be necessary."

Dr. Ingham placed a hand on Elfrida's shoulder and smiled—considerately, consolingly, Elfrida thought, suddenly annoyed. She didn't want this woman's sympathy: she wanted to be angry at her and her absurd presumptions.

"If you feel any desperation, Mrs. Tipton, remember I am here. There are other interesting options."

Elfrida left the consulting rooms in a confused turmoil of emotions. She was both affronted and grateful. How dare Dr. Ingham aver—no, state—that she was hallucinating and at the same time offer some kind of refuge, a safety net? It was all too distressing and maddening.

She paused at a street corner and took her bearings. Her sense of Brighton's geography was improving and she realised that, as it happened, she wasn't that far away from the Repulse. She felt a sudden and great need for the Repulse and the Repulsives, as she termed her fellow drinkers there, herself included in the collective noun, of course. So, she wandered Repulsewards, looking deliberately about her at the houses and the traffic, taking in the pale stucco, Brighton with its bow windows and its balconies, trying to dismiss her sense of upset and disorientation. Everything had been going so well. The new novel was underway; Calder was in the process of doing her deal but now she had gone and contracted this malign, alien infestation of microbes of some type. How come a doctor couldn't see what she could see?

Once in the Repulse she became calmer. She found a seat, went to the bar and ordered a large gin and tonic from a young man with long hair practically down to his belt. She realised that even after all this time as a patron of this legendary Brighton pub she had no idea who the landlord—or landlady—was. The bar staff, the bar-lads and the bar-lasses, seemed to change on a daily basis.

She paid for her gin and took it back to her seat. As ever the pub had very few customers. There were two middle-aged, stout women with their port-and-lemons; a man in a flat cap and a belted raincoat peering at a newspaper held three inches from his spectacles; two delivery men in overalls drinking lager. She settled down in her corner and looked surreptitiously at her scratch. Yes, the little devils were still there, writhing and crawling the pink length of her scratch, just under the skin.

She reached into her handbag, found her crêpe bandage and discreetly wound it over her scratch, securing it with the safety pin. Out of sight, out of mind—to hell with Dr. Ingham's injunction to "let the air get at it." She repeated the phrase out loud in a strong Irish accent and the two stout women looked round sharply. Elfrida raised her glass to them and they turned away, tut-tutting. Elfrida sipped her gin, feeling hungry. Maybe a packet of crisps or a pickled egg, she thought. But, no—a quick drink or two and then back home to continue with the novel.

*

> Virginia Woolf jerked awake, eyes wide, staring. She had been dreaming—dreaming about the death of a star, somewhere out in the cosmos, a fuming holocaust of incandescence, but it was only sunshine, she realised, sunshine squeezing through a gap in the curtains and printing a lozenge of lemon-yellow light across her pillow. She shifted over a few inches into shade and smiled with relief. And then she remembered: today was going to be the last day of her life and the sun was shining.

Maybe that was even better, Elfrida thought. Somehow more startling for the opening of the novel. Jerked awake? Lurched awake? How exactly did one wake from that type of disturbing dream? Shudder awake? Yes, one would gasp and shudder. Shudder awake, then. She crossed out "jerked" and wrote "shuddered" above the erasure. She put her pen down feeling a slight headache building. She shouldn't have had all those gins in the Repulse but, anyway, here she was, back at her desk, back at work, that was the main thing. Maybe she should make herself some cheese on toast, or something.

She went downstairs to the kitchen thinking, yes, food was the requirement. The incident of the microbes had shaken her up—and then that horrible, judgemental doctor with her horrible, preposterous diagnosis—no wonder she had needed a consoling drink. She searched the fridge for cheese but found none. In a cupboard she found a tin of mulligatawny soup. What sort of beast was a mulligatawny that you made soup from? Some type of eel, or flatfish, or riverine rodent on the large side, like a beaver or a coypu . . . The very thought made her nauseous. She poured a little vodka into a tumbler and added some water. A sip or two—that would calm her.

The phone rang. Yes? No? She picked it up. It was Reggie.

"Hello, honeychild, I'm going to be very late tonight. Sorry. Complicated set-ups."

"Fine. Do you want any supper?"

"No, no. I'll get something here. A sandwich or a burger."

She held the phone to her ear, thinking.

"Are you all right?" Reggie asked.

"Of course."

"Good. See you later, sweetness."

"Bye."

She hung up. She knew exactly what he was up to. Time to gather some hard evidence, she thought.

7

The sitting room in Jacques' apartment wasn't exactly a place designed for relaxing, Anny thought. It was more like a small theatre or an unconventional seminar room. In the centre was a large desk, the size of a double bed, facing two floor-to-ceiling windows that gave on to a view of the boulevard Saint-Germain. There was a single high-backed leather chair at the desk and two angular chrome art deco desk lamps left and right. The walls of the room were entirely bookshelved, filled to overflowing with books. Around the desk in front of the bookshelves were a sofa, a couple of armchairs and a small cane bergère. The floor was blond parquet. When you sat on the sofa or in an armchair it was as if you were waiting for an actor to enter and sit at the desk and proclaim, somehow.

She hadn't been in Jacques' apartment for many months so she was struck anew by its odd, focussed configuration, how the room's priorities led in one direction—to the desk, to the man at the desk, flanked by his two expensive chrome lamps, and—of course—the great thoughts he might be having.

She stood up from the sofa and went to sit on the bergère. Nothing really changed: the view was still focussed. So she went to the window and looked out over the street below. Jacques was in the kitchen preparing a fresh mint infusion for her. Off a small hall were a bedroom and a bathroom and that was the extent of the apartment—the main room was the *pièce de résistance,* with its distant, aslant view of Les Deux Magots and the church of Saint-Germain-des-Prés. Situated here, Jacques was in the swim, she realised. Exactly the kind of swim he wanted.

He came in with her tea on a tray and set it down on a small table by the sofa. Then he sat at his desk, swivelling his leather chair round so he could look directly at her. She was the audience, Jacques was on the stage—the player. She sipped at her tea. There was also a plate of small oval cookies. She picked one up then put it down.

"Feeling better?" he asked.

"Much better. I'm sorry I burst into tears."

"It was relief. You've done the right thing. And, most important, you're safe. The FBI or the CIA can try and extradite you, but it's very difficult here in France. It takes years and years." He smiled. "I could even marry you—then you'd be a French citizen—and here we don't extradite our own citizens." He held up his hand. "We can delay them forever, that's the main thing."

"I know. But I keep thinking about consequences. I keep thinking about the film."

"To hell with the film," he said, making a flipping gesture with one hand. "There'll be many more films. Better films, here in France. You should never have agreed to do that piece of . . . of *merde britannique.*"

Anny thought about arguing with him about the film but decided against it. She was tired. She'd barely slept in twenty-four hours.

"I think I need to get some sleep," she said. "I'm dropping."

"You can't stay here with me," Jacques said. "This is the first place they'd come to."

"Who would come?"

"The press, to start with. Once this news gets out. Everyone knows about you and me. Open a newspaper, a film magazine. You're the movie star who dates a French philosopher."

"I suppose it's a point. But they'll go away."

"And then the lawyers will come. And the FBI. And the British police. No, you'll be much safer with my brother, Alphonse. We need time. We need to see what happens with that *con* you married. Once they lock him up again maybe they won't bother you. But, better to lie down for a while."

"Lie low, you mean." She had said it reflexively, but she could see how he bristled at the correction.

"Apologies for my English. How's your French, by the way?"

"Sorry. Non-existent, pretty much. *Bonjour, au revoir.*"

"Well my brother speaks a bit of English so you should be OK."

"Is he your younger brother?"

"Older. He's a bit boring, but nice. He lives alone."

"Where does he live?"

"In the 13th arrondissement. It's not exactly chic but no one will ever expect you to be there. And it's good you're not blonde. Keep dying your hair."

Jacques stood and spread his arms for her to come to him. He was wearing a loose t-shirt with the slogan MARXISTE—TENDANCE GROUCHO printed on it in thick, black-stencilled type and grey flared trousers. She went over to him and he held her close and kissed her forehead.

"It's exciting," he said. "Having you here. Hiding you. It's like the war. We're hiding you from the enemy."

"What war?"

"The Algerian war. It's the only war I've truly experienced—as a soldier, I mean. But I suppose any war is essentially the same. Terror and boredom. Power and powerlessness. Responsibility and absence of responsibility."

"I don't want to be in a war," she said in a small voice. "I don't want to have to hide from the enemy. I just want to be free."

8

It was most unusual for the Applebys to visit him, Talbot thought. He had tried to arrange an appointment in London but was told they would rather come and see him in Brighton. They had come once before, on the first day of principal photography, to the celebratory dinner—Yorgos had travelled down from London as well and the four of them had dined at a Chinese restaurant on the London Road. But this insistence was out of the ordinary, he felt. A certain apprehension overtook him.

Talbot showed them both into his office. Bob, the younger Appleby, was sallow and burly, wearing a thigh-length camel coat—even though it was a warm day—and what looked like snakeskin shoes. Jimmy was fair and genial, going quickly to fat, with a ready smile and flushed cheeks—rosy cheeks, you would have to say, Talbot thought: apple cheeks. He was wearing a pinstriped suit and a red shirt, no tie. They had been given a courtesy executive-producer credit on the film, because their client was cast in it, but beyond that they seemed to have no real interest in *Ladder to the Moon.* Yet for all their evident good cheer, the smiles, the two-fisted handshakes, the arms-round-the-shoulders bonhomie, Talbot found them a curiously disturbing, threatening pair. They were brothers who looked entirely different, possessed of a worldliness, a *savoir faire,* that made Talbot feel naïve, out of his depth, a boy.

"This is a bit of a shithole, isn't it, Talb?" Bob Appleby said, gesturing at his office, including the whole house in Napier Street with the sweep of his hands.

"We'll be out of here in three weeks. There's no point in anything pricier. It does what we require of it."

"Wrong, Talbot," said Jimmy. "With respect. It's all about perception. Crappy office says crappy film. This place does you no favours. It's all about perception, mate. You should be in a suite in the Metropole."

"Next time," Talbot said. "Point taken."

He had been to the Appleby Entertainment offices on the Euston Road, two floors, high in a glass and steel block. Potted plants everywhere, the corridors lined with portraits of their clients and their gold and platinum discs. He had counted seven secretaries on his journey from the lobby to their offices.

The brothers sat down and gladly accepted the offer of a small whisky. Bob lit a cheroot, Talbot and Jimmy cigarettes. Jimmy leant forward and flattened his palms on the desk.

"Cut to the chase, Talbot. We need a favour."

"Fire away."

The brothers looked at each other.

"We need a song in the film. A Troy Blaze song."

Talbot paused.

"It's a bit late. We have a composer."

"It's never too late, Talbot. For old friends."

"It's not that kind of film, chaps. Rodrigo won't agree."

"Make him agree, Talbot. You're the producer."

"It doesn't work like that."

"Just one song. We'd appreciate it."

"I can ask. But I can't promise anything."

Bob stood up and walked to the window. He spoke without turning around.

"Thing is, Talbot, this is not an 'Is there any vague possibility?' sort of situation, if you see what I mean. Not an 'Is there any faint chance of?' type of enquiry." He turned. "It's a need."

"It's a must," Jimmy added, spreading his hands apologetically. "A definite must."

Bob resumed his seat.

"Troy Blaze needs a hit. Big time."

"That's why we put him in this film."

"I see."

"They're all in films now. Dave Clark, Adam, the fucking Beatles, Lulu. But they all get to sing a song. That's the point."

"You never mentioned a song when we cast him," Talbot reminded the brothers.

"Yeah," Jimmy agreed. "But that was because we was concentrating on visibility."

"But now we want a song. As well as visibility," Bob said.

Talbot realised this was not a negotiation, it was a transaction.

"Maybe we could put a song over the end credits," he said.

"There," Bob said. "We knew you'd come up with a bright idea, didn't we, Jim?"

"End credits is good. Is it?"

"It's an ideal place," Talbot said. "It's what the audience remembers as they leave."

"Let's drink to it," Bob said, holding up his empty glass.

Talbot topped them all up. His mouth felt dry—he needed water, not whisky.

"You won't disappoint us, will you, Talbot?" Jimmy said, smiling widely.

"No. Absolutely not."

"Oh, yes. And there's a Rio in it for you," Bob said.

"A Rio?"

"A Rio Grande. A grand. Get it?"

"It's not necessary."

"Oh, yes, it is," Jimmy said. "It sort of cements our . . . Our understanding."

"Anyway, Yorgos is getting one—why not you?" Bob said.

"You've spoken to Yorgos about this song idea?"

"Yorgos is all in favour. He said you were the man to get it sorted."

"Whereupon we come down to Brighton."

Bob reached into his coat and took out a fat envelope, placing it on Talbot's desk. Jimmy pushed it over to him.

"Have a drink on us. That's what we call it. A 'drink.'"

Talbot looked at the envelope.

"There's no need for this," he said.

"What's your problem, Talbot?"

"It's all a bit corrupt, isn't it?"

"Everything is corrupt," Bob Appleby said, reasonably. "And everybody is corrupt."

"Especially in your world," Jimmy added. "Bloody hell. Talk about corrupt."

"But my world is your world," Talbot said, mildly protesting. "We're in the same business. Entertainment."

"Don't make me fucking laugh," Bob said.

"No, we mean *your* world. We're not part of your world," Jimmy said. He laughed. "Are we, Bob?"

"Fat chance." The brothers chuckled to themselves, amused.

Talbot remembered something he'd once heard—that all Englishmen are branded on the tongue. He saw that, despite the smiles, this wasn't banter. It was a recognition of the barrier that existed between them—between Talbot Kydd on one side and Bob and Jimmy Appleby on the other. A barrier they would never cross.

Talbot picked up the envelope, his Rio.

"Consider it done," he said. "There will be a Troy Blaze song in *Ladder to the Moon*."

9

It had been absurdly easy to find out where Janet Headstone lived. Elfrida had called Joe, the source of all wisdom, and said that Reggie wanted to send a book to Janet.

"We can send it," Joe volunteered, "no trouble at all."

"No, I'll just pop it in the post. It's not urgent."

Joe gave her Janet's address in Brighton, Elfrida wrote it down and thanked him. "Don't tell Janet," she said. "It's a surprise." Then she called her Rottingdean taxi firm and booked a "wait and return." It might be a long wait, she warned them.

Her taxi driver turned out to be a young Asian man who told her his name was Dalgit. He was chatty and Elfrida was pleased to be distracted answering his many questions. He asked her what she did for a living and she said she was a novelist. She wrote books, stories.

"You mean, you just sit at home, make up stories and write them down?"

"Yes," she said. "That's a fair description."

"And you get paid for doing this?"

"Yes. They buy the stories off you."

"Kutsik narak!" He glanced back at her. "I am finding this hard to believe. You sit, you think, you write. And money comes. I'm going to do this. Better than driving a taxi."

"It's not quite as easy as that. They have to like your stories, first, and if they do, only then do they pay you."

"What about writing songs? Write songs for pop music. Much more money, nah."

"Perhaps. But it's just not my thing."

Dalgit parked up in the street across from Janet Headstone's house. Elfrida peered out. An ordinary terraced house but painted purple and with one of those vulgar yucca bushes in the front. She asked Dalgit to park again, further away, where she still had a good view of the house, and he duly did so. Ten minutes passed, then thirty. This is what surveillance is like, she supposed, time dragging by, waiting for something, anything, to happen. Dalgit left the car for ten minutes to try to find something to eat. He returned with a bag of fish and chips—she declined the offer of a few chips—and sat there as he ate, the car filling with the smell of vinegar. She wished ardently that she'd brought a hip flask of Sarson's with her.

An hour passed.

"What is in this house?" Dalgit asked.

"I don't know. That's what I'm going to find out."

At about 8:30—they'd been waiting for over an hour and a half—a saloon car pulled up outside Janet's house and Reggie stepped out, slinging a bag over his shoulder. He strode up to the front door and smoothed his hair down before he rang the bell. The door was opened and he went in but Elfrida couldn't see anything of Janet Headstone.

She felt her body stiffen, now having witnessed Reggie arriving, being welcomed and admitted. The ocular proof had been delivered: what she had imagined had been proved to be real. So much for the night shoot and the complicated set-ups. She exhaled and inhaled slowly, she could feel her heart beating faster, and she noticed that the saloon car remained parked outside the house. Of course, a car and a driver at his beck and call—director's privileges.

She sat back, feeling a muscle spasm in her neck, and, simultaneously, a slight nausea. This had happened with Reggie before. She had caught him out at least five times over the years of their marriage, therefore she suspected that a multiple of two or three (for the times she hadn't caught him) would be a more accurate reckoning of his infidelities. So why was she so bothered by this sneaky little transgression? Because the other woman was a writer—a novelist, like her. It was irrational but that fact made the betrayal all the more bitter. It was as if she had gone and had an affair with another film director. Reggie's ego would take a serious, terminal battering. He would never forgive her. Just as she was never going to forgive him.

"Two minutes," she said to Dalgit, and opened the door.

She had been warm in the car and was struck by the advancing evening's coolness as she walked towards Janet Headstone's house and shivered. She stopped by the saloon car and tapped on the window to wake the dozing driver.

He wound down the pane.

"Excuse me," she said, smiling her broadest smile, "I was just passing but I'm sure I saw that it was the film director Reginald Tipton who you dropped off. Is that right? I'm a huge fan of his work."

"Yes, it was, actually—though he calls himself Rodrigo Tipton, these days."

"Does he live here?"

"No. He's having a script meeting with the writer."

"Right. How fascinating! Thank you so much."

She stepped away, her eyes on the house, and saw lights come on upstairs. For a second, she thought about going to the front door and ringing the bell but she knew, almost instantly, that she would come out of such a doorstep confrontation badly. She would be the one shamed, not Reggie—who would make up some preposterous, ingenious lie and be backed up by his girlfriend. She walked back to Dalgit and his minicab and told him to take her to the Repulse.

It was strange being in the Repulse at night—she had only ever come at lunchtime, she realised. For a start the place was packed, full of young people in their bright sloppy clothes as far as she could tell. And the noise! She pushed her way to the bar and stood there, money in her hand. She was served by a young girl with a fringe as long and eyelash-resting as hers. Large gin and tonic, please. She was served and drank it in ten seconds and held up a pound note to order another.

Drowning your sorrows, she said to herself. If only they could be drowned, like an unwanted litter of kittens. Her gin arrived, she paid and drank, wondering what to do about Reggie and this new—this vilest—betrayal. Do you want to be married to a man who can do this to you? she asked herself. Answer: no. Well, he's living in your house, this interlocuter in her head reminded her. And when this film's over he'll come back to the Vale of Health and recolonise it anew. Will you tolerate that? No. Will you kick him out? . . . She thought about this for a few seconds before she replied. Yes. This time I think I will—but I will choose my moment. Let him dally with Janet Headstone, unaware, until this stupid film is over and then he'll get his comeuppance. On my terms.

It seemed a good plan and she smiled to herself, and said "Yes," quietly. One more gin then Dalgit can whisk me back to Rottingdean.

She saw the young barman with the incredibly long hair and signalled to him.

"Large gin and tonic, please."

He brought it to her.

"Hello," she said. "Remember me? I usually come in at lunchtime."

"Are you with the Salvation Army?"

"Never mind."

She finished her drink and went to the ladies' lavatory where she unwound the crêpe bandage over her festering scratch. There they were, the little creatures, swarming under the skin, feeding off her wound. Little *bestioles,* she thought, the French word suddenly coming to her, proliferating and squirming around her scratch like some kind of loathsome culture in a Petri dish. Stupid, stupid Dr. Ingham. What did she know about anything?

IO

The Disappearance of Anny Viklund. Good title for a film, Talbot thought. A horror film, perhaps. The call had come in from DI Desmondson himself at eight o'clock on Monday morning. Miss Viklund had not returned to the hotel, Desmondson had reported flatly. Her room was empty, unslept in. He was issuing a warrant for her arrest. He thought Mr. Kydd would like to be apprised of the latest situation.

Things go wrong on films all the time, Talbot knew, all the time, regardless of the size or prestige of the film. Dysfunction was in the very nature of the art form that was cinema. But not in this way. In his own experience as a producer he had had to deal with drugs, divorces, physical punch-ups, mind-numbing incompetence, drunkenness on the set, week-long sulks, shrieking anger, the vilest insulting abuse, sexual molestation, scene-stealing one-upmanship—generally the sort of behaviour that a three-year-old would be ashamed of. Even the recent business with Tony During and the theft of film stock seemed run of the mill. But the disappearance of Anny Viklund was something else. Never this. Aiding and abetting a terrorist. This was breaking new ground.

He told Desmondson that he hadn't any idea where Anny Viklund might be. Maybe she'd gone back to America, for all he knew. Meanwhile, on the film, it was time for massive damage-limitation. Shoot around her, he told Reggie, make stuff up, film pick-ups and any amount of "shoe-leather" that he hadn't had time to schedule before. People getting in and out of cars, walking up to front doors, walking away from front doors, driving along, establishing shots, you know the drill. Spend a couple of days filming Troy mooching around Brighton—who could tell, it might come in handy during the final edit. The main thing was that they would track her down and bring her back—she's probably had some sort of brainstorm or panic attack, he said. Everyone would be looking for her and the advantage was that she was a huge American film star—not some runaway adolescent with a drug problem, or a battered wife who had decided to end it all. It could only be a matter of time, Talbot said, reassuringly, but he could see from the panic in Reggie's eyes that he wasn't that confident.

Troy Blaze had been his saviour.

Talbot had been standing at the set where the day's filming had been due to take place—a funfair. This was where Emily and Ben were meant to go after their reunion under the pier. Troy wandered over from his caravan and stood quietly beside him.

"Mr. Kydd," Troy said, "I think you should know. I got a note."

"A note?"

"From Anny."

He showed it to Talbot.

In neat American high-school copperplate Anny had written: "Troy, honey. Gone to Paris for a few days. I have to sort a mess out. Love you, Anny."

Talbot handed it back.

"Bless you, Troy. Don't tell anyone. I'll go to Paris and find her and bring her home. But let's just keep the whole thing between you and me. Right?"

"Got the message, Mr. K. Don't worry."

And then Talbot had an exceptionally good idea.

Ken Kincade buckled his seat belt slowly, as if endeavouring through the process to understand how the simple mechanism worked.

"Fuck me," he said vaguely. "Seat belts. Jesus."

He turned to Talbot, a strange smile on his face.

"I think you should know, Mr. Kydd, that I'm a very nervous flyer."

"You're not alone, Ken."

"Yeah. But I took a couple of—actually, three—Librium in order to get on this plane. I wouldn't be here otherwise."

"I understand. Just relax. It's a short flight."

"It's just that if I don't seem my usual self then it's the Librium talking, not me."

"Of course."

"It's the take-off and landing that does me head in."

Talbot patted Kincade's arm, reassuringly, wondering if his exceptionally good idea was melting before his eyes like butter on a hot griddle.

Ken Kincade was in his usual black suit with his cowboy boots but he had no bootlace tie. He was wearing a t-shirt with the word "SEX?" on the front. Talbot wondered if that had been a Librium-inspired decision, watching him settle back in his seat and close his eyes tightly. He noticed that Kincade had a distinct tremor in both hands, even though they were clamped to his knees.

Talbot turned away and thought about his own problem. How to find Anny Viklund in a city as large as Paris? Furthermore, how to find Anny Viklund in Paris if she didn't want to be found?

He had telephoned Anny's agent in Los Angeles the moment that LA had opened for work and had received a series of abrupt and unhelpful negatives. No. This was not possible. Not Anny. She would never do such a thing. And no, she had no notion of where Anny might be in Paris. The woman—her name was Bernadette Shaw—said she had to step away from her desk for a moment and she would call him right back. Of course, she didn't and for the rest of the day she remained unavailable. After many hours of vain attempts to reach her, Talbot asked her assistant to say just two words to Bernadette Shaw when, if ever, she returned to her desk. These words were "contract" and "litigation." Sure, I'll be glad to pass that on, the assistant said, brightly, and wished him a nice day.

Then Talbot had his brainwave. If anyone could find Anny Viklund in twenty-four hours it was surely Kenneth Kincade (LLB), the man who had so swiftly solved the mystery of the missing film stock.

He called Kincade and explained quickly about the mission to Paris and its extreme urgency and delicacy.

Kincade said that when he worked abroad his fee doubled.

Not the slightest problem, Talbot assured him.

"Looks like we're off to *La belle France,* then, Mr. Kydd. Do please send the travel details to my office."

And so, on Tuesday morning at Gatwick airport, they found themselves on the first BEA flight to Paris.

Talbot and Kincade strode along a wide corridor in the terminal at Le Bourget airport. The plane had been on time, the flight turbulence-free and Kincade had relaxed marginally and asked for a brandy before the fasten-seat-belts sign went on as they began their descent, at which point he retreated into his near-catatonia mode.

"All airports resemble each other, yet there's something indisputably French about this one," Kincade said, musingly. "Don't you think?" He seemed altogether more lively now that they had touched down safely and were back on terra firma.

"Maybe it's because all the signs are in French," Talbot said, wondering if Kincade was still being affected by his tranquillisers or if he was playing his usual provocative games.

"You may have hit the nail on the head."

"But I sort of know what you mean," Talbot said, trying to ease the mood. They seemed to be sparring with each other, rather, and that was all wrong, under the fraught circumstances.

"I've never been to Paris," Kincade said.

"You're not serious, surely."

"No, seriously. Never set foot in France until today." He looked at Talbot and smiled, unabashed. "My interests have always been focussed on the other side of the Atlantic."

"You can practically see France from Brighton."

"Maybe that's the whole point," he said. "I already knew too much. Needed a strange culture. Something new."

"Fair enough. But when it comes to culture France wins hands down."

"That's just your opinion, Mr. Kydd. No, I'm pleased to be here, don't get me wrong. Foreign travel—one of the perks of the job."

As they waited for their luggage Talbot thought it would be civil to ask Kincade more about himself. Here they were on the same mission, travelling together, staying at the same hotel and the man was a virtual stranger. He stirred up some bland conversational starting points in his mind.

"What does your wife think about your trip to Paris? I bet she's jealous."

Kincade glanced at him oddly, as if Talbot had said something exceptionally stupid.

"Is that meant to be a joke?"

"Just an idle question."

"I'm not married."

"What about your girlfriend, then? She'd love to be coming, I bet."

Kincade sighed.

"I'm . . . How shall I put it so you understand? I'm not that way inclined, Mr. Kydd."

"You've lost me. Sorry."

Kincade looked him in the eye. "I'm musical. Light in my loafers. Make my own macaroons. A friend of Dorothy." He paused. "I bat for the lavender team."

"Right. I see." Talbot managed a smile. "Sorry for being so obtuse."

"I prefer the euphemisms," Kincade said, "to the blunter denigrations. You know: queer, homo, fairy, poofter, faggot."

"I know what you mean."

"Of course you do, Mr. Kydd."

"What are you implying?"

"That I'd spotted *you.* Even though you hadn't spotted me."

Talbot saw his suitcase appear on the carousel, took a few paces and hefted it off, glad to have some seconds to collect his thoughts. He now felt he knew Kincade all too well. He should have kept his mouth shut.

Kincade was beside him collecting his own bag.

"I should tell you," Talbot said, quietly, "that I'm a married man with two children."

"Yeah. So was Oscar Wilde. Talking about Paris, I might pop over to Père Lachaise if we've got time to spare." He smiled. "We could go together—pay our respects."

"Let's find Anny Viklund first, before we plan any jaunts, shall we?"

They headed for an exit, customs and a taxi.

. . .

Talbot had booked them both double rooms in a hotel off the rue Notre-Dame-des-Champs called the Hôtel Cardinal. It was a place he knew well, small, but with a dark bar and a perfectly acceptable restaurant—and half the price of the grander, more famous hotels that the city boasted. He and Kincade checked in, were led to their respective rooms and agreed to meet in the bar to make their plans.

Kincade was already established at a small table when Talbot arrived and he noticed Kincade had a glass of red wine on the go. Talbot ordered a Perrier water.

"So," Kincade said, taking out his little notebook. "She's in Paris. That much is established."

Talbot had tried to talk to him on the plane but had swiftly seen it was useless—his fear of flying making coherent conversation impossible.

"We have one other lead," Talbot said. "She has a boyfriend here called Jacques Soldat."

Kincade asked him to spell it and wrote it down.

"What does he do?"

"He's a writer—a philosopher. Quite famous. He was very prominent during *les événements*."

"What's that when it's at home?"

"The riots in Paris. In May. This year, 1968."

Kincade frowned, thinking, clearly unfamiliar with Paris's very recent past. Talbot enlightened him.

"Student occupations, general strike, confrontation, street battles with police. It was a kind of very violent social revolution."

"Oh, yeah," Kincade said, vaguely.

"I don't mean this remotely offensively," Talbot said, "but you did see the fighting in the streets, didn't you? It was, as people said, almost the French Revolution all over again. On TV every night."

"Of course I *saw* it. But I wasn't really engaged with what was going on, not analysing it on a nightly basis."

Again Talbot wondered if Kincade tried to wind him up deliberately. The man was clearly intelligent but sometimes he seemed to want to portray himself as stupid. It was tiresome.

"It was a significant moment in French, not to say European, history," he said. "In twentieth-century history."

"Like I told you, Mr. Kydd, when it comes to 'abroad' almost all my focus, my engaged interest, is on the U.S.A. Ask me anything about the assassination of Bobby Kennedy. Or of Martin Luther King, for example. Did you know that his killer, James Earl Ray, was arrested in London? At Heathrow airport, Terminal 2—"

"All right, all right. I didn't know that. Point taken. Anyway, Jacques Soldat was one of those intellectuals who were very involved in the 'struggle.' If not quite on the barricades then very close on the sidelines. He was an inspirational figure."

Kincade scribbled more notes down.

"So: find Jacques Soldat and we may find Miss Viklund," Kincade said.

"My thinking exactly. That's why I reckoned you were the man to winkle her out. There's one problem, however."

"Which is?"

"His name, 'Jacques Soldat'—it's a pseudonym, a *nom de plume*."

"So he's not likely to be in the telephone directory."

"I just checked. There's no Jacques Soldat listed."

"Have you any idea what his real name is?"

"No."

Kincade made another note. Talbot wondered what exactly he was writing down. Kincade sat back and sipped at his wine.

"He's published under the name Jacques Soldat therefore it would be a fair assumption that his publisher knows who he is."

"Yes. Good point. In fact two of his books are really quite famous. One of them was a kind of international success in the early sixties. The sort of book everyone claimed to have read."

"A bit like *Being and Nothingness.* I remember everyone lugging that around at university."

"Exactly." Talbot looked sharply at Kincade. This was the sort of remark Kincade made, designed to throw him off balance, he realised.

Kincade sat up, as if suddenly galvanised.

"I'll need some cash in advance, Mr. Kydd. I have to buy a few things."

Talbot took out his wallet and handed over a bundle of francs. Kincade shuffled through them.

"How much is this in real money?"

"About one hundred pounds."

"I'll keep an account, don't worry." Kincade stood up. "Shall we meet back here at six o'clock? I can give you a progress report."

Talbot filled his day easily enough. He had a bite of lunch at La Closerie des Lilas and then went to the Jeu de Paume to look at Monet's water lilies, something he always did when he had spare hours to fill in Paris. It was quiet and he found he could spend as much time as he wanted, undisturbed, in front of the huge shimmering canvases. But the Zen-like calm that the lilies usually provoked in him wasn't quite so present today as he found his thoughts returning to the remarks Kincade had made at the airport. How could Kincade have "spotted" him, as he put it, and he not have "spotted" Kincade? Was it a generational thing? What did that say about him and his assumptions? What did that say about his so-called secret life? He wandered back to the hotel in something of a fog of frowning concentration. It doesn't matter, he told himself: you have your life; let others have theirs.

As he strolled up the boulevard Saint-Germain he began to notice a few remaining traces of the May events. Some shops were boarded up, there was a burnt-out cinema and there were still posters here and there and hastily scrawled graffiti. "Lutte Contre Le Cancer Gaulliste," "Nous irons jusqu'au bout," "Flins pas Flics," "Salaires Légers Chars Lourds," "CRS = SS," "La Structure est Pourrie," "Je jouis dans les pavés." As he took in the posters he recognised that some of them were really rather brilliantly designed—very eye-catching. What had he been doing in May? Scouting locations in Brighton for *Ladder to the Moon* with Reggie Tipton. Meanwhile, across the Channel a social revolution had been taking place. Was that what it was like in 1789? he wondered. Distant thunder across the Channel but life plodding on in good old Albion.

He stood for a while looking at what remained of the bleached and tatty posters, remembering the images of the riots in May—Paris under siege, Paris burning. *Tout passe, tout casse, tout lasse,* he said to himself, thinking that there wasn't a similar phrase in English that did the French expression full justice. "All this will pass," was just too weary and stoically resigned. Everything passes, everything breaks, everything tires. Or everything grows weary? A bit unwieldy. He turned and wandered on, trying different versions in his head and finding nothing satisfactory.

Back at the hotel at the end of the afternoon he put in some calls to Joe to see how the production was faring. All seemed well: Dorian Villiers' two days had passed off without incident and now Reggie was filming a lot of Troy wandering the streets, looking out to sea, et cetera. As long as people were being kept busy there was still the illusion that the film was underway, that Anny Viklund's absence hadn't been catastrophic. Yet.

He called Naomi, also, as an act of reassurance. He had told her about Anny's flight to Paris and the potential consequences for the film. She commiserated.

"Poor old you," she said. "Maybe I should come over and cheer you up."

"I'm not good company, darling. We have to find this girl."

"I was joking, Talbot. Relax."

"Sorry."

At six he went down to the bar. Kincade was already there, glass of wine on the table, but entirely changed. He was wearing khaki trousers, loafers, a blue blazer, white shirt and a red tie. He'd had his hair cut short in a crew cut, *en brosse* in the French style, and looked wholly different from the edgy character in his black outfits. He glanced up as Talbot approached. Talbot decided to make no comment.

"Success," Kincade said. "I'm meeting Jacques Soldat tomorrow afternoon."

"Wonderful!" Talbot sat down and Kincade handed him a card. He glanced at it.

Harold J. Hopkins, senior editor, University of South Tennessee Press, it read.

Kincade explained. First, he went to a bookshop and found some of Jacques Soldat's books and from them gleaned the name of his principal publisher—a small Parisian publishing house called Jadis & Naguère. Then he bought himself the clothes he was currently wearing, had his hair cut and presented himself at the reception of Jadis & Naguère and said that the University of South Tennessee Press was interested in publishing new editions of Jacques Soldat's entire *oeu-*

vre. New editions, new translations, new introductions. They were very pleased to meet him, they said.

"I couldn't get *Black Skin, White Heart*—that's already published in the States. But, I got one called *Massacre* and another one called," he glanced at his notebook, "*Pseudo-Citoyens*—I think I've pronounced that correctly. And a couple of others."

"Well done. I appreciate the sacrifice of the tumbling locks."

Kincade ignored him.

"Anyway, I had to wait a couple of hours before I met the publisher. When I started talking money he went away and telephoned Soldat, himself. I said I was only in Paris for one more day so we made an appointment to meet tomorrow morning at eleven."

"Good God, bravo!" Talbot said. Kincade signalled a waiter for more wine. Talbot said he'd join him in a celebratory drink.

"It's the U.S.A., you see, Mr. Kydd. That's what makes the difference. 'The University of South Tennessee Press.' Irresistible. Glamour. The Wild West. If I'd said I was from the University of South Shropshire Press they'd have shown me the door."

Talbot spread his hands in mute admiration.

"I do like the new hair, on reflection," he said. "Maybe you should keep it like that. Makes you look very American."

"Which was the object of the exercise."

"Well, it works. Where did you get the business card?"

"I've got all these blank cards—blank except for a crest on them."

Talbot peered closely. The crest was in colour and embossed: a generic bit of heraldry containing a quartered shield, some oak leaves and acorns and a Latin motto on a scroll: *Dominus Illuminatio Mea.*

"Before you inform me." Kincade held up a palm. "I know where I nicked it from. Latin helps. Then I have my little kit—a child's printing press. I print whatever name and title I want. It does the business but it's the crest that convinces, though."

"I'm impressed."

"It's embossed."

"I noticed. Nice touch."

"And, of course, I spoke with an American accent. A Southern American accent."

"I'm doubly impressed."

"The devil is in the details, Mr. Kydd."

"So I'm told." They finished their wine and ordered more. "What will you do when you meet Soldat?"

"Oh, I won't meet him. I won't show up. He'll wait around for a while and then leave, well pissed off, I should imagine. I'll follow him home. Then you can move in."

"Let's hope Anny Viklund's staying with him."

"Who knows—but at least we'll have the first link in a chain, with a bit of luck."

They decided to eat in the hotel restaurant. Kincade asked Talbot to tell him the whole story of the May *manifestations* in Paris and Talbot did so, as best as he could, trying to remember the sequence of strikes and protests leading to the battles on the streets of Paris and other towns.

"Seeing it was in May—which is a couple of months ago," Kincade said, "and seeing as it was like the French Revolution all over again, as you told me, then what's happened? All I saw today was Paris going about its business, all calm and tranquil. Where is everybody?"

"Good question," Talbot replied, thinking back to his own walk the length of the boulevard Saint-Germain. All he'd seen were a few tattered posters.

"Maybe they've all gone on their holidays," he said, a little lamely. "Fancy a cognac?"

The next morning, at the time of the appointed rendezvous between Jacques Soldat, his publisher and Mr. Harold J. Hopkins of the University of South Tennessee Press, Talbot and Kincade were sitting at a table on the pavement of a café on the rue Saint-André-des-Arts in the 6th arrondissement. They had a good view of the entrance to the small courtyard where Jadis & Naguère were established, their offices occupying the ground floor. All very lovely, Talbot thought, all very French. He couldn't for a second imagine an English equivalent and, moreover, just up the road one of the classic Parisian brasseries—Chez Allard—was situated. How handy for lunch or an early supper. He stopped himself, urging himself to concentrate. He wasn't a French publisher contemplating his lunch, he was an English film producer with a monstrous problem on his hands.

He glanced over at Kincade. He was back in his black suit, black shirt outfit. Talbot hadn't quite accustomed himself to the crew cut, even though it was a sign of Kincade's diligence, his professionalism as an investigator. The cropped hair didn't really suit him, making his lean face look more starved somehow, as if he were recovering from an illness or had just served a term in prison. Still, how many people would have a severe haircut and transform their appearance simply to do a more thorough job? Not many. Score one for Kenneth Kincade (LLB) and Criminality Risk Assessment. He took a sip of his *petit café.* Kincade checked his watch.

"I should have arrived ten minutes ago. They'll start making calls soon."

"Calling who?"

"The Hôtel George V. That's where I said I was staying. And then they'll find I'm not registered."

"What then?"

"Fucking Americans!"

Kincade ordered another coffee.

"I'm getting used to working in Paris," he said. "Bit more enjoyable than Brighton."

"*Quelle surprise.* And you're on double time."

"You ain't paying, Mr. Kydd, so don't get all high and mighty." Kincade chuckled and swatted at a wasp that was hovering around his empty coffee cup. He backhanded it away. "Got you, bastard," he said and looked at Talbot. "Just what is the point of wasps, Mr. Kydd?"

"They must have a function in the mysterious scheme of things, I suppose."

They talked on, waiting for Soldat, content in the mild July sunshine, drinking their coffees. Kincade asked Talbot what other films he'd worked on and was surprised—or feigned surprise—when Talbot told him a few: *Sudden Death in Soho, Cometh the Man, Triple Melody, The Mark of Cain, Sam the Ripper, The Forgotten, The Lost War.*

"I've seen some of those—and here I am sitting with the producer. But what about this one, this *Ladder to the Moon* film? Are you going to make any money?"

"Perhaps. Assuming we get our leading lady back."

"Serious money?"

"One can always dream. As long as I'm paid my fee then everything else is an unexpected bonus. I've got another project, a play—an American play, you'll be pleased to hear—that I have more concrete hopes for."

"Concrete hopes—bit of an oxymoron, no?"

Talbot kept forgetting that Kincade had been to university and had nearly completed a law degree.

"There he is!" Talbot said, suddenly spotting Jacques Soldat exiting Jadis & Naguère's offices, thinking it was strange that they'd never spotted him going in.

Soldat paused at the courtyard entrance and started talking, clearly remonstrating, to someone out of vision. He didn't seem at all happy.

"Bloody American publishers," Talbot said.

"Come on, we're off," Kincade said, standing.

"Do you need me?"

"No one ever thinks they're being followed by a couple."

Talbot dropped some francs on the table and set off after Kincade. They strode on, side by side, Soldat about twenty yards ahead.

Kincade glanced at Talbot.

"You never told me Jacques Soldat was African."

"He's not African. Well, he was originally African—he's from Guadeloupe."

"Slipped your mind?"

"Didn't seem relevant, somehow."

"God help me."

Talbot didn't respond and they followed Soldat up to the boulevard Saint-Germain. He could tell Kincade was a little angry. Good. He didn't hold every ace in the hole. Then he rebuked himself for his pettiness. They were working together—solidarity was all.

They didn't have very far to go, as it happened. After about twenty minutes they saw Soldat go into an apartment building at the angle of the rue des Ciseaux and the boulevard. Talbot looked around. He could see Les Deux Magots in the near distance and the little cobbled square in front of it. Perfect for an *intello,* like Soldat. He turned to Kincade.

"What do we do now?"

"Well you know where he lives. I would confront him."

"This minute?"

"Why not?" Kincade said. "My working maxim is 'Do it now.' DO IT NOW! What's the point in waiting?"

"Yes, I see the logic. Would you come with me?"

"No."

They looked at each other.

"All right," Talbot said. "But please wait outside."

"Wilco. Roger that."

Talbot rang the concierge's bell and was admitted. He asked her in his competent but English-accented French if a tall black African gentleman lived here. They had an appointment. Monsieur Soldat.

"Non. C'est Monsieur Duhameldeb."

"Of course. *Mes excuses.*"

The concierge was straight from central casting: small, stout, grey, humourless—where do they find these people? Talbot wondered, as he waited for her to telephone up. She turned to him and asked him what it was about, this appointment.

"C'est au sujet de Mademoiselle Viklund," he said. That should do the trick. *"Mademoiselle Anny Viklund."*

II

Anny heard Alphonse come in. His apartment was in the 13th arrondissement near the place d'Italie, an area of Paris she'd never visited. The apartment was perfectly comfortable, on the fourth floor of a modern high-rise. She had her own bedroom but she had to share the bathroom with Alphonse, who, however, was off to work at 7:30 a.m. and never returned until after six in the evening.

Alphonse Duhameldeb looked vaguely like his younger brother. He was a tall, serious-looking man with greying hair who worked as a cashier in the Société Générale on the rue de Rennes. He was darker—blacker—than Jacques. Anny asked him about the family back in Guadeloupe and gained the information that Jacques was actually Alphonse's half-brother. Same mother, different father.

In fact, she was quite happy to be shut down and not think. She had asked Jacques to call her lawyer and her agent in Los Angeles and set them to work but he said it was too soon. The fewer people who know where you are at the moment the better. Don't send any signals just yet—it's safer. We'll take our time—our fightback will happen when we want it.

During the day she listened to French radio—playing songs that she could barely understand—snacked, dozed, looked out of the windows. Alphonse returned from work, ate something and went out again. This was clearly on the instructions of Jacques because he routinely appeared ten minutes after Alphonse left. They would go to her room and make love. Somehow the fact that she was on the run and in danger made their relationship flourish sexually again, at least on Jacques' side.

"Why can't I come back and be at your place?" she asked.

"You can, but not now. We have to be careful. All sorts of people will be looking for you. Let's be sensible, let's wait a bit, a few days, a week." He paused. "I've had an idea. It'll wake everyone up. Boom."

She acquiesced; she didn't ask what would go "boom," happy in her limbo at the moment. Sometimes she thought of Troy and worried and wondered what he would make of all this upheaval. She also realised that she was taking more than eight Equanil a day but what else could she do? The time slipped by easier with the Equanil. Sometimes she left the apartment block and went for a stroll. Strangely, the streets around the block seemed full of Chinese people—Chinese people speaking French. She found a café that she liked and would order a Coca-Cola and smoke a cigarette or two, looking around her, watching this unfamiliar world go by—and then go back to Alphonse's place. Sometimes she thought she'd been in Paris for years instead of a few days but nothing seemed to matter all that much, as long as she was safe.

12

Talbot stood outside the door on the second floor where he'd been directed by the concierge. A plastic rectangle above the bell bore the name M. Mehdi Duhameldeb. Talbot rang—and after a few seconds Jacques Soldat/Mehdi Duhameldeb opened the door carefully. He was clearly extremely surprised to see Talbot. He recognised him but couldn't remember his name, obviously.

"You are?"

"Talbot Kydd. We met in Brighton on the film. I'm the producer."

"How did you find me?"

"Ah . . ." He didn't have a ready answer. He improvised. "Anny left your address at the office."

"Why?"

"I don't know. I think she wanted us to send something to you. Something like that. Anyway, there it was." He smiled. "How else would I have found you?"

Soldat peered over Talbot's shoulder as if he expected to find others lurking and, when he didn't, opened the door wider so that Talbot could come in.

In the main room Talbot sat down on a small cane bergère while Soldat positioned himself at his desk, swivelling his chair round to face him.

"What can I do for you, Mr. Talbot?"

"We have a problem, as I'm sure you realise," Talbot said.

"No. What problem?"

"Anny has disappeared. She's 'run away.' We surmised that she might have come to you here in Paris."

"No. Not at all. I can't believe she would do something like that. It's not like Anny."

Talbot thought Soldat's attempt to be disingenuous was pathetic. Still, they would have to proceed with the pretence.

"Maybe she went back to America," Soldat said.

"I doubt it. There's a warrant out for her arrest. Her ex-husband has been apprehended and shipped back to the States. He's in FBI custody. He's accused Anny—claimed she helped him evade capture. That she gave him money to help his escape. It's serious."

"Quel con," Soldat said, bitterly. "I wish I could help you. I haven't seen Anny since I left Brighton."

"Have you spoken to her?"

"Not for a week or so." He stood. "Can I offer you a drink? Whisky?"

Talbot accepted and Soldat left the room, returning moments later with two small whiskies in wine glasses.

"To the swift return of Anny," Soldat toasted. "France is a big country. Maybe she's gone to the south of France. I know she has a friend in Cannes. Maybe you should look for her there."

"Do you know this friend's name?"

"I can find it for you."

Talbot gave him the name of his hotel for form's sake. Soldat's lies were inept. Talbot finished his whisky, sensing that the encounter was near its end. He stood and thanked Soldat for his time, assuring him that the minute he found any trace of Anny he would let him know.

"It's kind of you to offer, but," Soldat paused at the door of his apartment, hand on the knob, "to be honest, I think our relationship—mine with Anny—is over."

"Really? I'm sorry to hear that."

"She was fucking your pop star, what's his name? The Toy."

"Troy. Troy Blaze. No, that's impossible. I don't know where you got that idea from."

"I got the idea from my eyes. From seeing the two of them on the set of your film. I'm not a fool, Mr. Talbot."

Talbot refrained from correcting him.

"I can assure you you're mistaken. I would've known. Instantly. Would've heard. Their relationship was purely professional."

"What is your English saying? 'There are none so blind as those people who will not see.' Use your eyes. It's obvious."

"I see everything, Monsieur Soldat. Nothing escapes me. Particularly on a film I'm producing."

"We all like to think that. It's our unique vanity." He smiled. "Oh no, no one can fool *me*."

He stepped closer, as if he were about to divulge a confidence.

"They are trying to destroy Anny."

"Who?"

"The Americans, the CIA, the FBI. The American state. She's a symbol, you know. Everyone is looking at Anny—what she believes, what she hates, what cause she will follow. If they can smash that symbol it will send a message to many people. This is what's going on, Monsieur Talbot. Be very careful. These forces are powerful. What do you say?—we have to fight fire with fire."

"I think you're mistaken."

Soldat gave him a pitying smile.

"In this world there are people who bow their heads—and people who refuse to bow their heads."

"If only it were that simple. I'm just trying to make a film."

"And there, exactly, precisely, is your problem."

Talbot shrugged. This conversation was going nowhere. Soldat opened the door for him, wished him *bonne chance et bon retour* and Talbot left without a handshake. He slowly descended the stairs, happy to avoid the apartment's open lift with its two sets of rickety, clattering doors. How many lies had Soldat told? It was obvious that he knew where Anny was and, in a way, his oafish denials and his preposterous conspiracy theory were all the confirmation he needed. But what to do now? He was sure Kincade would have an answer. Thank God he'd hired him, difficult, contrary individual though he was.

He stepped out into the street and lit a cigarette, looking around for his investigator. Where was he lurking?

"Mr. Kydd? We meet again."

Talbot turned and saw a man he vaguely recognised. The accent was American. He was wearing a raincoat and a trilby hat.

"I'm Agent Radetski. We met a week or so back."

"I remember."

They shook hands.

"What're you doing here, Mr. Kydd? Looking for Anny Viklund?"

"Yes." Talbot opted for honesty.

"What'll you do if you find her?"

"Try to persuade her to return to her contracted job."

Radetski allowed himself a sceptical smile.

"Have you just met with Mr. Soldat?" he asked.

"Yes. He has no idea where Miss Viklund is. So he says. Their relationship is over, it seems. Ex-lovers."

"Do you believe him?"

"I'm inclined to believe him," Talbot said, equivocally. He had no desire to give any help to Radetski. "I was absolutely sure she'd be staying with him. But, no—not a trace. It's a small apartment—I would have noticed."

"Maybe I should talk to him."

"You can try, but I doubt he'll talk to you. By the way, you and your organisation are the Antichrist, as it were, as far as he's concerned."

Radetski gave a tired smile.

"These intellectuals—Jesus."

"You know you can't extradite her, now she's in France."

"We can try and extradite her—there is a treaty between the U.S. and France—but it seems to take about twenty years, as far as I can tell. We just want to talk to her. She must know a lot. Could be very useful."

"She's just a young, confused actress. You can't—"

"She was married to a terrorist," Radetski said patiently, as if explaining something to a child. "A violent, deadly terrorist prepared to detonate bombs that would kill innocent people. Cornell Weekes is part of an underground terrorist army called the Warning Call. Have you heard of them?"

"The Warning Call? No."

"He's no lone-wolf figure. Your Miss Viklund might be happy to trade some information about the Warning Call organisation for a plea bargain."

Talbot stood there silent, looking at Radetski in his raincoat and trilby hat. Why wear a raincoat when there's no risk of rain? He thought again of Soldat's conspiracy theory and suddenly wasn't so sure it was preposterous.

"I don't think she knows anything," Talbot said. "She's a child."

"With respect, Mr. Kydd, she's no child. Look who she hangs out with—Cornell Weekes, Jacques Soldat. A convicted terrorist. A radical revolutionary philosopher. Come on. We deal with these types every day. They may be deluded but they're not children. She knows stuff, even if she doesn't think she knows stuff. When we talk to her we can analyse what's useful. It's her duty as an American citizen."

"If you can find her."

"She caught a plane to Paris. We've confirmed that. She's in the city."

"France is a big country," Talbot said, echoing Soldat. "Soldat suggested I go and look for her in Cannes."

Now it was Radetski's turn to stay silent and look at Talbot. Impasse. Each with his separate agenda, Talbot thought, but each of them needing Anny Viklund.

"OK. Maybe I'll try Soldat."

"Good luck. By the way, his real name is Mehdi Duhameldeb."

"I know that." Radetski smiled patiently. "See you around, Mr. Kydd. Be sure to let us know if you get lucky."

"I'm heading back to London. I can't do anything more here."

He watched Radetski stroll away towards the boulevard Saint-Germain. Talbot felt a murmuration of worries descend on him as if he were being attacked by a flock of malign starlings. For the first time he had to accept that Anny Viklund's future did not contain the possibility of completing *Emily Bracegirdle's Extremely Useful Ladder to the Moon.* It was a depressing thought.

"You look a bit un-chipper," Kincade said, startling him as he appeared from a nearby doorway.

"I have been in more sanguine moods," Talbot said.

"I like that. I'm going to use it. 'I have been in more sanguine moods.' Classy. Who was that man you were talking to?"

"He's an FBI agent, also looking for Anny Viklund."

"You do move in unlikely circles."

"Not through choice." Talbot dropped his cigarette and stepped on it.

"Any trace of Miss Viklund?"

"Not in that apartment."

"Does Soldat know where she is?"

"I think so. He was lying to me the whole time. Tried to send me off on a wild goose chase to Cannes."

"Cannes? That sounds nice."

"Don't get your hopes up. We're not going to Cannes. What shall we do, Mr. Kincade? Sorry, Ken?"

"I need more money."

They took a taxi back to the hotel. On the way Kincade told him some facts about Jacques Soldat that his publisher had divulged.

"Apparently he was a young conscript in the French army, in 1945, in Algeria. Twenty years old."

"Ah. A soldier. Hence 'Soldat.'"

"Exactly. He was witness to a massacre at a place called Guelma. May 1945. Tens of thousands of Algerians massacred, so I was told. By the French army and French Algerian settlers."

"You sure? I've never heard about this."

Kincade went on to explain that five years later, under the pseudonym of "Jacques Soldat," Mehdi Duhameldeb wrote a book called *Massacre.*

"Made his name. Suddenly he was the intellectual spokesman for the disaffected colonial people of the French empire. Overnight fame. Never looked back. Book followed book."

"*Massacre.* Was that one of the books Harold J. Hopkins was trying to acquire?"

"It was indeed."

"I begin to understand Monsieur Soldat's attitude," Talbot said. "Why he's so permanently aggressive."

The taxi pulled up at the hotel.

"How much money do you need?" Talbot asked Kincade.

"Quite a lot, I'm afraid."

Talbot cashed several travellers' cheques for the sum of £200 and had it converted into francs. He handed the money to Kincade.

"What'll you do with this?"

"I'm going to hire a car. If I'm going to stake out Soldat's apartment I've got to be comfortable. I can't stand in the street all day and night."

"Fair enough. Just keep receipts."

"This plan is all based on your intuition, Mr. K. If you're convinced he knows where she is—then he'll go to her. He won't go tonight because of your visit—not a chance. But he'll probably go tomorrow if he thinks the coast is clear. And I'll be watching." He held up the money. "From the comfort of my hired car."

They stood together in the lobby, Kincade folding the money into his wallet. Unlikely conspirators, Talbot thought.

"Any plans for this evening?" Kincade asked.

"I've got some phone calls to make."

"Exciting. I'm going to a club. Want to join me? I think you'd find it interesting. It's called Inferno. Let me be your guide, your Virgil."

"Some other time, Virgil. I'm tired."

"Fair enough, as you would say." Kincade smiled. "We'll find your precious Miss Viklund tomorrow, I'm sure."

"I'm counting on you," Talbot said. "Have a nice evening. If you can't be good, be careful."

13

"Hello?" Elfrida said cautiously, realising her voice was a bit shaky. She had stood above the phone as it had rung, her hand hovering over it, paralysed with indecision and then, as it showed no sign of stopping ringing, she had picked it up.

"Elfrida, it's Calder."

How is it that three words can convey so much? she thought. She knew from the tone of his voice that there was nothing joyous or uplifting about Calder's call, instantly. She knew that it foretold nothing even bland or neutral of the "How are things going?" variety. Something about the way he said his own name seemed to presage the clear idea that he was the bearer of bad news.

"Hello, Calder," she said, as brightly as possible.

"Bit of a problem, I'm afraid . . ."

"Oh. What?"

"Virginia Woolf."

"Yes. What about dear Virginia?"

He coughed. He cleared his throat.

"Nobody at Muir & Melhuish is very excited about the idea of your Virginia Woolf book, I'm sorry to say."

"Well, they may be excited once they've read it. It's going exceptionally well."

"They're more intrigued by *The Zigzag Man*. Which is something, at least."

"I'll do that next. Get me a lovely two-book deal."

"It's not quite that simple, Elfrida."

"What are you trying to say?"

"It's a bit awkward, but the bottom line is that they don't want your *Last Day of Virginia Woolf* book—that's a definite no—and they won't advance any money on *The Zigzag Man* until they have a completed manuscript."

Elfrida stood there, the phone to her ear, aware she was swaying slightly to and fro.

"Then tell them to fuck off," she said. "Get me another publisher."

"Right. Maybe we should have a talk, my dear. Plot and plan. Set out our priorities."

"Let's talk when you've lined me up another decent publisher. Night, night, darling."

She hung up and headed to the kitchen for the vodka.

14

Talbot had another day to himself, waiting for Kincade to report back. He breakfasted, thought about going to the Louvre but decided against. He wasn't in the mood for concentrating. Instead he went shopping and bought an ambergris silk tie in Charvet and some Chanel No. 5 for Naomi. He lunched at Café de Flore on an *omelette aux fines herbes,* a green salad and two glasses of Brouilly. When he returned to the hotel in the afternoon the porter handed him a message with his keys. It was from Kincade. It read: "Found her. I'm in my room." He called Kincade immediately and he came down to the bar.

"How was your evening?" Talbot asked. He thought Kincade looked a bit tired, a bit shabby.

"Intriguing . . . I left the club early, you'll be glad to hear, and spent the rest of the night watching Soldat's place, just in case." He explained further that, after there had been no activity in the night, Soldat had emerged at around 10 a.m., on foot. Kincade jumped out of the car and followed him to the Métro. On the way Soldat had taken a certain amount of evading action, doubling back, going into a shop and coming out of a rear entrance, all of which made Kincade think that he was heading for Miss Viklund. Eventually he took the Métro to Corvisart and then walked from there to a block of flats on the rue Bobillot.

"The flat is in the 13th arrondissement. I saw him go in," Kincade said. "Followed him in and of course had lost him. But I discovered there was a postbox in the lobby with the name Duhameldeb on it. Bingo."

"His flat?"

"Or a family member's. But I bet you good odds Anny Viklund is in it."

"All that avoiding action is suspicious. Bit of a giveaway."

"You catch on fast, Mr. Kydd."

Once more Talbot was beginning to find Kincade's relentless, sardonic persona a bit wearing.

"What do we do now?" he said, flatly, not humouring Kincade.

"Now comes the fun part. We drive over there in our special hire car and watch and wait."

They drove south-east to the 13th arrondissement. Talbot didn't know this area of Paris. It was like another city, like the suburbs of some provincial town with tatty, dilapidated towers of apartments, and bustling, busy streets filled with cheap shops. They passed a small market selling clothes and vegetables. The people looked poor, needy. They parked the car with a view of the entrance to the apartment block and waited. The afternoon seemed interminable. Talbot smoked three cigarettes in two hours. Kincade went to a superette and bought them fizzy drinks and fig rolls.

"I haven't had a fig roll since I was a boy," Talbot said.

"I think I've become addicted to them," Kincade said. "This is what I do, Mr. Kydd. Sit around waiting and watching for hours and hours and hours. Don't encourage your children to join my industry."

"What do you think is going to happen?"

"At some stage she's going to walk out of that front door, there. Maybe today, maybe tomorrow," Kincade said. "Maybe the next day."

Talbot settled down, thinking that he would give it another twenty-four hours, full stop. Then he would head back home and see if there was any way the film could be saved.

Kincade munched at a fig roll, swigged from his bottle of pop.

"How was your club, your Inferno, last night?" Talbot asked, as casually as he could manage.

"It was excellent. I had sex with a very nice guy called Jean-Louis."

"Jesus Christ."

"Don't you have sex, Mr. Kydd?"

"I'm not about to discuss my private life with you."

"Your choice."

They sat in silence for a while. Kincade ate another fig roll.

"I have been to a club, you know," Talbot said. "In Brighton." He instantly regretted his bravado.

"Oh, yeah? Which one?"

"It's called the Icebox."

"I've been there," Kincade said. "Nice enough place."

"So it seemed. I was meeting a friend. An army friend," he added, as if that somehow brought more propriety to the confession.

"Were you in the army?"

"Yes. In the war. The Second World War, that is."

"I've heard about that one." Kincade closed his eyes for a moment. "See any action?"

"Far too much."

"I'm going to have to adjust my dossier on you, Mr. Kydd. A soldier. The Second World War. Saw action."

"Your dossier is your concern."

"I assume your army friend bats for the lavender team as well."

"If you want to put it that way."

"Did you have sex with him?"

Talbot sighed. "You don't always have to have sex, you know."

"Why go to a club, then?"

"Never mind." Talbot couldn't believe how the conversation had become so wildly uncontrolled, veering around in ways he should never have allowed.

He was aware that Kincade was staring at him.

"Would you like to have sex with me?" Kincade said.

This was typical Kincade, Talbot recognised. Throwing a conversational grenade into the room.

"No. Certainly not. But thanks for asking."

"It was a hypothetical question, don't worry." Kincade swigged from his bottle and belched quietly.

Talbot changed his mind about staying on for one more day. He felt irritated. Kincade had got to him with his brazenness, his provocations. He felt his back itching as if the discomfort was a physical correlation of his mental agitation. He wasn't enjoying sitting in this car any more even if he understood the unique pressures of the journey that had brought him here. He would give it one more hour, then he was heading home. This was getting out of hand. Ridiculous. Why should he, of all people, be putting himself—

"Hello. Here she is," Kincade said quietly.

Talbot looked at the entrance to the apartment block. He saw Anny emerge and walk along the pathway. She was wearing a short cream raincoat, sunglasses and one of those peaked forage caps favoured by folk singers pulled down low over her brow. No one would have recognised her, he thought.

"What do we do now?" Talbot said.

"We? You follow her. My job is over, man."

Talbot stepped out of the car, feeling a little foolish, and set off after Anny, keeping a good distance between them. She stopped at a worn near-grassless little park where some children were playing on swings and a roundabout. There was a decorative pond full of floating rubbish. Then she moved on, turning down a street. He looked for its name—rue de la Colonie. Here there were a few shops—a butcher, a shoe shop, a superette and, on the corner, a large café with a stained chocolate-brown awning and chairs and tables set out on the pavement. Café Couderc was its name. Anny found a table outside and signalled a waiter. Talbot hovered, moving behind her so she wouldn't spot him, his sense of foolishness returning forcefully. A foolishness that began quickly to shade into anger. He was a distinguished film producer and here was his film star hiding incognito in Paris, under contract to YSK Films, jeopardising everyone's work and livelihood, not to mention the art they were trying to create. The film business had landed him in some ridiculous and stupid situations but this one was unmatched. It was time to sort out everything once and for all.

15

Anny looked up from her coffee as a man sat down opposite her.

"Hello, Anny," he said, in a friendly voice.

She stared at him in what she knew was cartoon astonishment. The last person she'd ever expect to see—here, sitting in front of her—Talbot Kydd, her producer.

"Hello, Talbot."

She saw he was wearing a dark grey suit, a pale blue shirt and a thin maroon tie with small badges on it. His white hair was swept stiffly back in two wings on either side of his shiny bald head. As usual, he was looking smart and well dressed, she thought, almost distinguished. He could have been a retired ambassador, or some high-up museum curator art-expert type, or a rich banker, or a count in a minor, sophisticated aristocracy.

"How the hell did you find me?" she said, finally. "I don't believe it."

"It was quite a journey," he said in his clenched, reedy English voice, "but here I am." He gestured at the café and the street. "In this dead-end corner of Paris. What's going on, Anny? You should be in Brighton today, filming your secret marriage with Troy. Not here."

She felt tears fill her eyes.

"I know," she said softly. "I know I should. I'm so sorry this happened."

"Look," he said, more firmly. "We can sort everything out. We have lawyers, we have influence. You didn't do anything seriously wrong."

"I know," she said, "but this isn't about me. It's about Cornell and what he did, what he represents. They want to drag him down and drag me down with him." She paused. "I have to take a stand. I have to speak out against what's happening to me, this witch-hunt."

"No you don't. Just do your job. The one you're so good at."

"No, Jacques is arranging everything. We're going to have a press conference, here in Paris. He's got all his friends in the media alerted. We're going to expose those fuckers. Tell the world what the FBI and the American state is doing. I'm innocent. I've been caught up in this business through no fault of my own and they want to destroy me." She was breathing deeply, she realised; she tried to calm herself.

She saw Talbot purse his lips as he thought.

"I don't think a press conference is a wise idea," he said gently. "It's too public a confrontation. You're inviting them to attack you."

"They're already here in Paris, the FBI—and the CIA for all I know. They've been harassing Jacques. He had to call his lawyer. They want to bring me down, Talbot. We have to fight fire with fire."

"All right, all right, let's talk through the options," Talbot said.

He offered her a cigarette and she took it. He lit it for her, then lit his own.

"There's another way of looking at this problem," he said patiently, "and maybe you haven't thought of it. But you signed a contract and you've been paid a great deal of money to appear in our film. And now you've run away. And the film isn't finished."

"It's not my fault."

Talbot smiled, sadly, it now seemed to her.

"If you don't come back, Anny," he said, "the brutal truth is that you'll never work on a film again. You'll be seen as too big a risk. No one will insure a film you're in and, as you know, you can't start a film without such insurance—a 'bond' as they call them. I'm sure you've never thought of this. So, far and away the best thing for you to do is to come back—come back with me—and we'll sort out this problem with the FBI and your ex-husband. We can say he threatened you, threatened to kill you if you didn't give him money. You were frightened . . ." He paused and took a puff on his cigarette. "But," he went on, "if you don't come back, it'll be . . ." He paused again, thinking about what he was going to say. "It'll be a scandal in our sorry little world. A huge scandal and no one will ever forget it. Or forget you."

Anny felt confused. She'd never thought of this consequence and she felt alarm building in her. Where was Jacques? He said he'd be right behind her. She felt the familiar fluttering bird of panic begin to stir beneath her ribcage.

"I'm sorry, Mr. Kydd—Talbot. I'm sorry for you, for the film, for Troy, but I can't come back. I wouldn't be safe. They'd try to send me to prison, I know. I'm only safe here, in France. They can't get me in France."

"It's the wrong decision, Anny."

"What else is new?" She laughed. "All my decisions are wrong. It's my specialty. It's what I do. I fuck up."

Still chuckling to herself, somewhat shocked by the acuity of her observation, she stubbed out her cigarette.

"What's so funny?" came a voice.

She looked up. Jacques was standing there, staring at her, angrily. Talbot looked round. He stood up. Two tall men facing off against each other.

"What are you fucking doing here?" Jacques said to him.

"I'm trying to persuade Anny to come back with me."

"So she can go to jail in America?"

"She won't go to jail, you idiot. We'll sort everything out and she can finish the film she agreed to make with us."

"This piece-of-shit film—you'd risk her life for that? You'd turn her over to the FBI for that?"

"No one's going to risk anyone's life, Monsieur Duhameldeb—"

Then she saw Jacques strike Talbot in the face, hard, suddenly—he knocked him down with one blow. He fell sprawling to the pavement, uttering a strangled yelp of astonishment, his hand going to his mouth. He shook his head and tried to stand up but Jacques shoved him back down.

"Putain d'Anglais," he said, and spat on him. "You can pay for her coffee. Charge it to your shit film."

He took Anny's hand and led her brusquely away, striding off with her.

Anny looked back quickly. People were helping Talbot to his feet and she could see he had blood coming from his mouth. She felt shame. Why had Jacques hit him? Talbot was a nice man. He was only trying to help, in his way.

Jacques tugged at her hand and she hurried to keep up with him.

ESCAPE

I

The River Ouse wasn't as deep as it had been on her previous visit, so it seemed to Elfrida. Then she remembered it was tidal, here by Rodmell, so the tide must be out, or going out, or had been out and was coming in, she reasoned. Still, it was deep enough for her purposes. She looked around. It would have been better if the day had been dull with perhaps some intermittent drizzle—the pathetic fallacy had always seemed to her an underrated literary tool—it would have been more appropriate to what was about to occur. But instead it was warm and breezy with large gaps of blue sky between the cloud-islands scudding eastwards. A near-perfect summer's day.

She had bought a walking stick at an ironmonger's, a sturdy oak one with a metal ferrule at the end that was proving very useful when it came to prising up large stones embedded in the embankment's turf. Her fur coat smelt a bit mildewy but as it had only cost her a pound at a church jumble sale she could hardly complain. There would have been no point in buying anything more expensive. It was all about symbols: the walking stick, the fur coat, the wellington boots. All she needed now was a decent-sized stone that would fit in a pocket.

She left the river bank and advanced into the meadow, eyes on the ground searching for stones. She spotted one, about the size of a Cornish pasty, and dug it out with the aid of the iron tip of the walking stick. She brushed it clean with the palms of her hands. It weighed two or three pounds, she reckoned, and she assumed it was the same size—approximately—as the one Virginia Woolf had placed in her pocket. It had to fit in a pocket, after all. Calculating further, as she rammed it into the right-hand pocket of her fur coat, she realised that it must have been the sodden coat that would have really weighed Virginia down—not the stone—the sodden coat would have been far more effective. Funny that no one else had elaborated this theory, she thought. Try swimming in a fur coat. Even for Virginia Woolf the stone was more of a symbol, a symbol that this was her clear intent to end her life—that she was not victim of an accident, hadn't slipped and fallen in. Because of the stone, they wouldn't be able to rewrite the story of her life more comfortably. Poor, brave, mad woman.

With the stone now snug in its pocket, Elfrida walked, in a somewhat ungainly way, back up the embankment and stared at the river again. Should she jump in? Or should she slither down the bank on her bottom and wade in? Whatever she decided, she would deliberately leave the stick on the bank to indicate where she'd entered the water. She looked downstream to the bridge at Southease wondering vaguely where her body would end up. She didn't care, in fact: she was at the end of her tether, she admitted to herself, the very end. Her marriage was a shameful farce; she seemed incapable of writing more than a few lines of the novel that was going to redeem her, cancel out the years of silence and revive her reputation. Add to this the fact that her arm was infested with tiny parasites feeding on her skin. It was more than one person could take. She was pleased that as a side consequence of ending her own miserable existence she'd also drown these vile microbes.

She reached into her left pocket and removed her bottle of vodka. She took too large a swig and coughed, harshly. And she was an alcoholic, let's not forget that, she told herself. All in all, oblivion would be a blessing. Then she heard, as if in answer to her cough, a distant laugh.

She looked upriver towards Lewes and saw a small group of ramblers wandering along the Ouse's bank on her side of the river. Fuck. Just when she was ready. She'd have to let them pass, now, and no doubt nod and smile and say, "Lovely day, isn't it?"

As they drew nearer she saw that the group was all women—five women—but led by a man in khaki shorts with a rucksack on his back and a guidebook of some kind in his hand.

She leant on her stick and stared out over the river as if in a contemplative reverie. Maybe they'd just walk on by and not disturb her trance. She'd pretend they weren't there.

She heard their excited chatter draw nearer. She closed her eyes. Please, just keep going. Ignore me, leave me alone.

"My goodness," she heard the man say. "What an extraordinary coincidence!"

She turned, vaguely recognising the man in shorts, then absolutely recognising him as she spotted his yellow-grey Abraham Lincoln beard. Maitland Bole, of all the people on this earth. She almost felt like crying.

Bole halted his little group and stepped towards her.

"Yes, what a coincidence," Elfrida said as they shook hands, trying to raise a smile. "Just doing some research."

Bole gestured at her fur coat. "Getting into the spirit, eh?"

"I mustn't keep you."

"We've walked over from Charleston," he said. "We call it the Vanessa to Virginia walk. We'll go up to Monk's House via the church and that'll be that. Time for a tankard of foaming ale in the Abergavenny—not for me, of course. You're very welcome to join us." He lowered his voice. "I should explain. These guided tours are another sideline. *Du Côté de Chez Virginia Woolf.* Increasingly popular."

"Some other time, perhaps," Elfrida said, faintly.

Bole swivelled round to face his group of women. They were mainly middle-aged, Elfrida saw, with stout walking shoes and anoraks. Three in bright headscarves, one in a straw hat and the fifth—the only youngster—who looked Japanese. They were all staring curiously at this fur-coated, rubber-booted woman on the banks of the Ouse in midsummer, Elfrida thought, with good reason.

"Ladies," Bole said, raising his voice. "This is an extraordinary coming-together. As we retrace the route from Charleston to Monk's House, Virginia Woolf's last home, who should we encounter on the way but the *new* Virginia Woolf—Elfrida Wing, the novelist."

One of the women gave a little squeal of recognition and the others applauded, as if this were some tour-guiding masterstroke of Bole's. Elfrida wanted to crack him on the head with her walking stick, the ridiculous little man! But she managed a smile and raised her hand to confirm the identification.

"We will leave Miss Wing to her literary musings and look forward to the eventual tome."

Bole turned back to her, smiling.

"Do get in touch if you need any more information. Come on, ladies!"

He led his group away—they all said a polite goodbye to her, the Japanese girl bowed—across the water meadow towards St. Peter's Church.

Elfrida tugged the stone out of her pocket and threw it in the river. Bole had ruined everything, everything. Stupid man, why had he identified her like that? He and his ladies were now witnesses. How could she drown herself now? How could she just slip away into the Ouse, like Virginia, lucky Virginia who had been able to die unwitnessed? The death of Elfrida Wing would become notorious. Police would interview Bole and his ramblers about her demise, all of whom had seen her preparing for it. Oh, yes, she was wearing a fur coat, funny that. We thought it was one of Mr. Bole's clever ideas. No, she seemed very friendly—we had no idea what she was about to do. What a shame, poor lady. It was absurd, now, everything was wrong, she felt. Wrong, wrong, wrong. She took out her bottle and had another few shuddering gulps of vodka, feeling a sense of bitter disappointment invade her. What could she do now? She felt forlorn, inconsolable, desperate . . .

She lowered the bottle from her lips. Desperate. Dr. Ingham . . . What had Dr. Ingham said to her? "If you feel any desperation remember I am here. There are other options." What other options? she wondered, trudging back towards Rodmell, through the knee-high grass of the meadow. She flung her walking stick away, angrily. What was she meant to do with her useless life now?

2

Talbot signed his name on the bottom of Kincade's cheque. Now, a couple of days later, it seemed far too generous a sum, given that the mission to Paris had failed entirely. However, Kincade's accounting and the receipts he had amassed had been meticulous. After all, Talbot had agreed to the doubling of his fee and Kincade had warned him whenever extra expense was required—the American-publisher disguise, the hired car—so he couldn't really complain. But still the rancour persisted, though perhaps it was nothing to do with the money, he reflected, more as a consequence of the man in black sitting opposite him—provocative, sarky, unsettling. Kincade had got under his skin, he admitted.

He waved the ink dry and handed Kincade his cheque—who then gave it a thorough examination as if it might not be genuine. There, my point exactly, Talbot thought, always stirring in his sly way.

"Happy? Is that the right amount?"

"Perfect. We did our best, Mr. Kydd. I'm just sorry I wasn't there when that bastard Soldat hit you. How's the lip?"

Talbot reflexively touched the prominent scab on his lower lip. It had been well and truly split by Soldat's fist and was now an unsightly, crusty black stripe, just off centre.

"It's fine, thank you."

"No, thank *you,* Mr. Kydd. It was an education—honestly. In fact,

I've taken a bit of a shine to Paris. I'll be going back, that's for sure." He stood up. "We made a good team, I thought. You were the brains, I was the muscle, as it were. You evolved strategy; I was agency."

"Yes, well, be that as it may."

"Kydd and Kincade." He chuckled. "Sounds like the title of one of your films."

"Most amusing."

"If you ever need my help again you know where to find me."

"I won't hesitate."

Kincade moved to the door. He paused, and stared intently at Talbot.

"Seriously, Mr. Kydd, if I could give you a piece of advice. I think you should—"

"I don't need any advice from you."

"I think you do. The trouble with you is you won't accept the fact that—"

"Nice doing business with you, Mr. Kincade."

"Yeah . . . Yeah, OK. See you in the Icebox, one of these days."

He smiled and left, closing the door quietly behind him. Ken Kincade . . . Talbot found he couldn't summon the animus he wanted any more. Kincade had actually been invaluable, both of the times he'd been employed. The fact that Talbot found his presence and attitude somewhat irritating and perturbing wasn't Kincade's fault. Kincade's breezy self-assurance was in strong contrast to his own diffident, secretive nature, he knew. What was that French expression? Kincade was *bien dans sa peau*—he was at ease in his skin in a way that Talbot felt he could never be. And now he began to wonder about what "piece of advice" Kincade had been going to offer him. It might have been interesting. Too late now.

He glanced at his watch. Reggie wanted him out at some country location. He had sounded very excited on the phone.

The unit car drove him a short way out of Brighton towards, according to the driver, a small village called Tanyard Malling. They turned off the road to Lewes and bumped along a single-track lane that seemed more of a cart track than a minor road. The lane descended into a narrow valley thick with beech trees and through the trees Talbot could make out a squat ancient church with a few houses set close to it. Tanyard Malling was more of a hamlet than a village, Talbot thought. They turned off the lane into a harvested field where the usual caravanserai of vehicles awaited them. The driver parked and opened the door for Talbot.

"They're all down by the church, guv'nor," he said.

Talbot crunched through the stubble and headed down the lane, passing as he did so the yellow Mini that Ben and Emily drove around in. Its windscreen was smashed open, he saw as he walked by, as if a body had flown through it.

The church—small, flint, with lancet windows—seemed to be the centre of activity. Talbot spotted Troy sitting in the wooden porch reading his script. By the stubby bell tower a trestle table had been set up and, to his astonishment, Talbot saw Janet Headstone sitting at it, typing. In all his years as a film producer he had never seen a writer on set—let alone on set, actually writing. He was about to go over and greet her when Reggie intercepted him. He seemed in a very good mood. Something must be going well, at last.

"Talbot, glad you came. You have to see this for yourself for it to make sense." He pointed at Janet. "That woman is a fucking genius. We've solved our problem. We don't need that flaky bitch, Anny Viklund. Janet's come up with a marvellous idea."

"Calm down, Reggie. Talk me through it slowly."

They turned and wandered back up the lane to the damaged Mini, Talbot listening hard to Reggie's rush of words as he explained.

"The last scene we have with Anny and Troy together is under the pier, right? They're reunited after she's run away, got lost, et cetera. In a long shot we drop in a voiceover line from Troy: 'Meet me at St. Saviour's Church. I've got something to give you.'

"Yes. I'm with you."

He went on. "Then, we cut to Troy—to 'Ben'—waiting by the church." He pointed back to Tanyard Malling's church tower. "That's St. Saviour. He opens a velvet box that contains a golden wedding ring. He's going to propose."

"Yes, I follow. But wouldn't it be an engagement ring? A diamond?"

"We need a gold ring. The symbol of the simple circle."

"Fine. Whatever you say."

"Janet had remembered we'd shot all that footage of the yellow

Mini driving through the country lanes. She said, why don't we use that?"

"What's that got to do with Troy proposing?"

Reggie explained. "We'll assume," he continued, "that Emily is in the Mini, driving to meet Ben at St. Saviour's."

He waved his hands about.

"We have a shot, a great shot of the Mini, at some speed, moving fast along a sunken lane. Then it turns the corner. Out of sight. SMASH! Are you still with me?"

"Yes, Reggie."

"Back at the church, Ben hears the noise. A crash! Oh no! He runs up the lane and finds the Mini, up against a tree, the windscreen smashed, and lying there in the middle of the road is Emily. Dead."

"Dead?"

"Isn't it brilliant?"

"You said we didn't need Anny."

"We use her double. Face down."

"Ah. Right. Go on."

"Ben is poleaxed with shock, devastated," Reggie continued. "He can't believe cruel fate has killed his fiancée-to-be as she was on the way to receive his proposal of marriage. Insane with grief, he drags Emily's body into the car and tries the engine. It starts."

"Then what?"

"This is Janet's next stroke of genius."

"Enlighten me."

"He drives to Beachy Head."

"Ah-ha." Talbot's huge scepticism began to diminish. He began to see the logic.

"Then," Reggie said, "we cut inside the car at Beachy Head. Ben at the wheel, Emily's body slumped over beside him, heading for the cliff edge—faster, faster." He paused. "We have to shoot that new stuff this Monday, by the way, after the weekend."

"And Emily's face won't be visible, of course."

"No. She's sort of hunched over. Ben is weeping, hysterical. The car hurtles towards the edge of the cliff. And this is Janet's third stroke of genius." Reggie's face was screwed up in a grimace of mad jubilation, his fists clenched. "Ben—Troy—turns to Emily's body and says: 'We'll be OK, Emily. We'll always be together. We've got our ladder to the moon.' The yellow Mini goes over the cliff edge. Disappears. The end. Cue music. Not a dry eye in the house."

Talbot thought. It could work, it might just work.

"And," Reggie went on, "from your producer's point of view the film is effectively over. We might have a few pick-ups, but, to be honest, we've shot miles of stuff while we were waiting for bloody Anny to come back from her Paris jaunt. We have our film, Talbot. And the title actually makes sense."

He started babbling on about possible interpretations. Was it fantasy? Was there indeed "A Ladder to the Moon"? Was there a kind of hypothetical lunar heaven for young lovers? Or was it a simple act of grief-stricken suicide provoked by this confrontation with intolerable loss? Gloss or grit. Bingo. He started mentioning names like Adorno and Freud and the Frankfurt School but Talbot stopped listening, thinking about the logistics. One thing was for sure: the massive, apparently insurmountable problem of Anny Viklund's disappearance had suddenly gone away.

Talbot and Reggie walked slowly back into Tanyard Malling talking about the practicalities of shooting the car going over Beachy Head cliff.

"What happened to your lip, by the way?"

"I was punched in the face by a French philosopher."

"No, come on, what really happened?"

"I walked into a door."

"You want to be more careful, Talbot."

Reggie told him he wanted to physically launch the Mini over the cliff and allow it to crash into the sea below. It would be pricey but worth it, he argued. Talbot agreed immediately. This new ending was saving them a great deal of money, anyway. One wrecked Mini was of no consequence. He was about to go and congratulate Janet when he saw Troy signalling to him from the porch. He went over.

"Did you find her, Talbot?"

"Yes . . . But she wouldn't come back."

Troy clenched his jaw and managed to hold his face together, Talbot saw, as he took in the bad news.

"She's too frightened of being arrested," he said. "She's safe in France, you see. She feels safe there. It's almost impossible to be extradited from France, apparently."

Now he saw tears in Troy's eyes and his chin dimpled. The boy was profoundly upset and Talbot remembered Soldat's accusation about Anny and Troy . . . Maybe there was some truth in it, after all.

"Jesus," Troy said, huskily. "What a fucking mess." He held up the new pages of his script. "That explains this, then. You can finish the film without her."

"Yes. Necessity is the mother of invention."

"What's that supposed to mean?"

"It means we had no choice. I begged her to come back, told her we'd sort everything out with our lawyers. But she wouldn't."

"It's that fucking French geezer, isn't it? Soldier, or whatever his name is. He's got a hold on her."

"He does seem to be organising everything," Talbot said, deciding not to mention the press conference.

Troy exhaled noisily and eased his shoulders, throwing his head back, looking up at the sky. He glanced again at Talbot.

"What happened to your lip?"

"I slipped getting out of the bath."

3

"Somerset?" Elfrida said. "I don't think I've ever been to Somerset. Ever in my life. How odd."

"It's not as far away as you think," Dr. Ingham said. "Bath's in Somerset."

"I've been to Bath."

"Well, there you are. This place is near Taunton. Three hours or so on the train, but it seems like another world. I think it would do you a power of good. I think it would be the saving of you."

"You think I need saving, do you?"

"I would say so."

"Well, anything has to be better than my status quo."

"But you'll have to stop drinking," Dr. Ingham said, reasonably. "How much have you drunk today?"

"Goodness. I had a glass of white wine with my lunch."

"Well, even that's too much." She wagged an admonitory finger at her.

It was curious, Elfrida thought, how rapidly her opinion of Dr. Ingham had changed. From fizzing resentment and hostility to a kind of passive warmth and easy obedience. She wanted to entrust her future—her life—to this strong Irish woman: so practical, so sensible. So . . . There was only one word for it—so *nice.*

"I can set everything up for you in a matter of days—say the middle of next week. Will that allow you to get your affairs in order?"

"Yes, absolutely," Elfrida said instantly, not thinking, just wanting to move as fast as possible away from the abandoned "Ouse Solution," as she termed it, towards this new one. There was a plan and a purpose and that meant everything. "How can you arrange things so quickly?"

"Because I've resorted to this process once or twice before, so I know what's what. And my sister is in charge of . . . Of the visitors. That's what they call you. 'Visitors.' It's not a life sentence."

"Ah. Connections."

"Family connections. Even better."

Dr. Ingham walked her to the door.

"It's not free, you know," she said. "I assume you have sufficient funds."

"Oh, yes. I have—or will have—plenty of money," Elfrida said, confidently, another plan forming.

Dr. Ingham squeezed her arm and, to her own astonishment, Elfrida spontaneously kissed her cheek.

"Thank you," she said. "I think you may have saved my life."

"We're just at the beginning of a process. No need for high drama."

"Of course." Elfrida paused. "Those pills you gave me," she said. "They will kill those creatures in my arm?"

"Oh, yes. In twenty-four hours. I'll call you with any further details about your stay. Just pack an overnight bag. You won't need much once you're there."

4

Anny stood at the door, apprehensively. She knew the FBI men and the CIA men were now aware that she was in the flat, so Jacques had told her. They were watching the apartment block. But Jacques had also told her that they couldn't arrest her because they had no jurisdiction. They just wanted to interrogate her—but that was her decision, only she could comply.

"Who is it?" she said.

"It's me, Troy."

She opened the door. Troy stood there, wearing his suede jacket and blue jeans. She quickly checked the corridor behind him—there was no one. He stepped in and she double-locked the door behind him.

They kissed. She hugged herself to him, liking the way he clenched his arms around her back.

"I can't believe this," he said. "I can't believe I'm here, that it's you."

"It's me. Did you see anyone outside? Watching the place?"

"No. I waited twenty minutes like you said. I couldn't see anyone."

"OK. Maybe no one saw you."

"Shall we talk first or go to bed?" he asked.

"Do you have the money?"

"Everything I could lay my hands on."

"OK. Thank you. Let's go to bed."

Afterwards, Anny insisted that they dress, just in case Alphonse returned for some reason.

"I can explain why you're here," she told him, "but I couldn't explain why we would be in my bed, naked."

Troy didn't protest. She thought he seemed a little subdued, even though his lovemaking had been as strenuous and enjoyable as ever. She tried not to think of Jacques.

"Are you all right?" she asked.

"I miss you," he said. "So I'm not really all right. No."

"I had no choice," she said. "If I wasn't here in France I'd be in jail."

"Talbot Kydd said he could fix everything for you. You'd be OK."

"He's just a producer. He wants to finish his movie. He doesn't care about me or my life. Or my safety."

"We finish on Monday, you know."

"What? How, for fuck's sake? How can you finish without me being there?" She had taken an Equanil while she waited for Troy and was finding it hard to concentrate.

"They've thought of a way of finishing it—without you." Troy carefully explained what the new ending involved.

"So, they kill me off," she said, quietly. "I die." She thought of her dream and her daily waking thought. Maybe that was what she had been prefiguring—her movie death. Somehow it didn't make it seem any better.

"I die too," Troy said. "We die together."

"Well, that's something." She reached out and stroked the back of his hand. "Good."

"And then we go up our ladder to the moon."

"And what does that signify?"

"Anything you want, I suppose. Rodrigo has about ten explanations."

"I suppose he's a nice enough guy but he's full of bullshit. Pretentious bullshit."

"I think he's shagging the new writer," Troy said.

"Wouldn't surprise me." She paused. "Where's the money?"

Troy crossed the room to his jacket that was hanging on the back of a chair and fished in the pocket. He handed her a thick envelope. She looked inside: it was full of notes, British money. She had called him at the hotel, told him where she was living and had asked him to bring her as much money as possible.

"How much is there?" she asked, taking the wad out.

"About nine hundred pounds. It's everything I could get. I can get you more but just give me some notice."

In her head Anny converted the pounds into dollars. It was more than enough. It would last her until she could find a way of accessing her own money in the States. She stuffed it back in the envelope and set it down on the table beside her.

"I'll pay you back," she said.

"I don't want you to pay me back. It's a gift."

"I'll pay you back."

"OK. If you want to." He reached out and pulled her off her chair and into his lap. He kissed her throat and she gripped the hair on the back of his head.

"I've written a song about you," Troy said. "Would you like to hear it?"

"Sure."

"It's called 'The Man You Wanted.'"

He cleared his throat and sang, in his husky tenor.

I knew I'd never be the man you wanted
I knew I'd never be your Mister Right
But all the same my life is haunted —
My heart's marshmallow, yours is anthracite.

"Stop," she said. "I can't listen to any more."

"There are three more verses."

"I can't listen to more. You'll make me cry."

"Don't worry. But I'm hoping they'll use it in the film. At the end, over the credits, they say."

"What's anthracite?"

"It's a kind of coal. The best type of hard coal. It burns with a smokeless, blue flame. I found the word in a rhyming dictionary."

"I don't have a heart of coal."

"Then why don't you come back with me?"

"I have to stay here. I explained."

"With Jacques."

"Yes. He protects me."

"I'll protect you."

"I can't, Troy." She kissed him again and he hugged her.

"Come back," he whispered. "Come back with me."

"I will," she said. "One day."

5

Gary Hicksmith was fifteen minutes late. Talbot was, in a way, rather relieved—it gave him some more time to compose himself. He felt strangely nervous, as if he were going to an important interview, or was about to meet some grand actor who might deign to appear in the film he was producing. How absurd, he remonstrated with himself, kindly get some perspective. The young foreman of a scaffolding firm was coming to apologise and reimburse him for a bounced cheque. He told himself to calm down.

The doorbell rang—at the main door—and Talbot stepped into the hall to answer it. Gary was in black jeans and a charcoal-grey windcheater with a red t-shirt underneath. He looked crisp, clean and well-shaven, something of a contrast to the man Talbot had known in his work clothes.

Talbot led him back to the flat where Gary proffered a £10 note as reimbursement, no change required, profound apologies from Axelrod Scaffolding Ltd. for the embarrassment.

"It couldn't matter less," Talbot said. "Anyway, everything's sorted out now. All's well that ends well."

"True," Gary said, looking around the flat with frank curiosity. "You're sorted, Mr. Eastman, but I have to tell you I'm still up to my neck in other problems."

Talbot sensed he wanted to unburden himself. He looked at Gary with a sympathetic smile. Gary, tall and slim, scrubbed up, his dark-blond hair curling over his ears, hands in pockets, troubled.

"Listen," Talbot said, "can I buy you a drink? There's a nice pub down the road—the Swan. A problem shared is a problem halved, and all that."

They walked down the road towards the Swan, Talbot detouring so that they could pass the Alvis—he'd left his chequebook in the glove compartment. He unlocked the car and fetched it out. Gary was walking around the Alvis, wonderingly.

"This is yours, I take it," he said.

"It's an indulgence. But I do enjoy it."

"I'll say. God. Bet you that costs a pretty packet."

"It did, rather." Talbot laughed. "They make very few of this model."

"An Alvis. Wow. Must have cost thousands."

"Shall we wander on?"

They walked on to the pub, Gary taking one last admiring look at the car before they turned the corner.

The Swan was an old pub, eighteenth century, so it claimed, rather over-revelling in its purported antiquity, Talbot thought: low ceilings, uneven, dark-stained, wide-planked floors, wooden booths and a quaint little door between the snug and the saloon that you had to duck through. Behind the bar dozens of bashed pewter tankards hung. Everything was polished, glass winked brightly. The pub's venerable history justified a corresponding hike in prices in everything from the beer, the booze to the food on offer, the implication being that you wouldn't come to a pub like this if you didn't have the financial wherewithal. Consequently, its clientele was comfortable North London middle-class and middle-aged. Sepia pictures of famous cricketers hung on the oak-panelled walls. The landlord was smug and famously arrogant, liable to refuse to serve customers if he didn't like the look of them.

Talbot sensed Gary's instant, instinctive unease as they walked in and they found a booth as far away from the bar as possible. Gary asked for a pint of lager; Talbot opted for his usual gin and tonic. It was early on a Saturday lunchtime. There was just a quiet susurrus of conversation and the occasional snorting laugh.

"Cheers," Talbot said, raising his glass. "Thank you for coming round. And for the reimbursement. Much appreciated."

"I shouldn't be telling you this, Mr. Eastman, but I'm paying you back out of my own money. Axelrod Scaffolding's going bust. Any day now. Bankrupt."

He explained further. Mr. Axelrod had a chronic gambling problem. The firm seemed to be doing well but in the last year or so it had become apparent that in fact it was limping along, overburdened with debt. They had tendered for huge jobs—office blocks, bridges, cantilevered and slung scaffolds, heavy-duty support scaffolds, temporary roofs—that were beyond their capacity and so they had been obliged to subcontract, thereby reducing their profit margins. Axelrod had gambled away the firm's profits. And, final nail in the worm-eaten coffin, they were being sued by Camden Town Council.

"It's a full-on nightmare," Gary said. "But I personally didn't want you to be a victim of Axelrod's fuck-up. Apologies. We did the damage to your house—we should pay for it."

Talbot asked what was going to happen, what was he going to do?

"Well, to be honest, I'd like to set up on my own," Gary said. "I can pick up the stock and material very cheaply when he goes belly up. I would start small, you know—one lorry, a small yard, got all the metal." He mimed a rectangular sign with his hands. "Hicksmith Scaffolding. Start with all the little numbers the big boys don't want. Domestics, paint jobs, shoring. You do it well, it pays well—prompt. You buy another flatbed, more tubes, couplers, boards. Hire more scaffs. Jobs get bigger, money gets bigger."

"Good luck to you," Talbot said. "Makes a lot of sense." He was happy watching Gary talk in his quietly intense, passionate way. "What does your wife think about it all?"

"I'm not married."

"Sorry. I somehow got the impression you were. What about your girlfriend?"

"I'm, ah, single at the moment. The last 'relationship'—well, didn't work out."

"Well, he travels furthest who travels alone."

"Yeah, but I ain't been paid for a month. Know what I mean? None of us have. We're all skint."

Talbot had an idea; he saw an opportunity present itself from nowhere.

"Here's a thing," he said. "What would you say to fifty pounds for an hour's work?"

"I'd say thank you very much. When do I start?"

"You know I'm a photographer," Talbot said, improvising quickly. "I've been given a rather nice commission."

He was surprised at his quick-wittedness and his eloquence as he constructed his story for Gary. He had been commissioned by a "glossy magazine," he said, to take portraits of Londoners. He could offer his subjects, whoever they were—taxi drivers, barmaids, High Court judges, nurses, politicians—a fee of £50 if they posed for him. "Even scaffolders," he said.

"You'd give me fifty quid to take my photo? I'm on."

"It's not a snapshot. It would have to be at my studio. It takes about an hour—hence the fee to pay for your time."

"I'm available, Mr. Eastman. Fifty pound is fifty pound."

"What're you doing, ah, tomorrow afternoon?" Talbot asked, trying to seem as unperturbed as possible.

"Nothing that can't be shifted."

"Why not come round about four o'clock? We'll have you done before the pubs open."

He saw Gary's smile broaden as he calculated his good fortune.

"Come round to the garden gate," Talbot continued. "You know, off the mews, where we first met."

"Got you. Do I have to look smart, like?"

"No. Come as you are today. It's your face we're interested in."

"I'll be there. Four o'clock. On the dot."

"You've got a very good face, Gary. Perfect for the job."

"Have I? Who'd have thought? So much the better."

"Fancy another pint?"

"Go on then, don't mind if I do. What happened to your lip, by the way?"

"I . . . I was playing squash. Racquet hit me right in the mouth. Ouch."

6

Alphonse counted the notes twice, expertly, with the deft hands of a practised teller, concentrating, pausing to lick the palp of his middle finger from time to time. It was as if he couldn't really believe what he was holding—5,000 francs; 5,000 francs, moreover, for his old 1962 ultramarine Renault 4. Anny had asked him how much it would cost to buy his car and he had replied, 3,000 francs. Anny said she would give him 5,000 if he didn't tell Jacques for twenty-four hours. Alphonse agreed instantly. Anny sensed that Alphonse and Jacques were in fact not that close. She had changed Troy's pounds for francs in a bank the day before and emerged with great bundles of notes; 5,000 francs was about $1,000, she reckoned, maybe half the money Troy had given her. The car was the big expense, but it would take her safely and incognito to Spain where she could live cheaply. At this stage having her own car was key—was everything, she calculated. She didn't need to depend on anybody else.

They were standing by the Renault in the underground car park of the apartment block.

"Why do you need a car?" Alphonse asked.

"It's better that you don't know," she said. "I just do. I need my own car."

"OK. For sure," he said with a shrug and handed her the keys.

"Do you need insurance?" he asked. "I have a friend who can make you a deal."

"No. I don't need it. I'm insured to drive any car."

"How is this?"

"It's an American thing," she lied.

Anny opened the rear door and slid her bag onto the seat. She was ready to go.

"You leave now?"

"Yes."

"Your American friend said he would come back tomorrow."

"He's not my friend."

"He say you his friend."

"He's an American spy. *Espion.*"

"I tell him—no, she is no stay here."

"Good. Thank you, Alphonse. I'm going now. Tell Jacques I'll call him."

"Where do you go?"

"Amsterdam."

She shook his hand and thanked him again and climbed in behind the wheel. Then she saw to her alarm that the gearstick was mounted in the dashboard. Alphonse spent five minutes explaining how the push-pull mechanism worked. She started the engine, put the car in gear and slowly drove out of the car park, up the ramp and onto the street. She drove on by instinct, following the large-lettered signs that directed her out of Paris. At the first petrol station she saw she pulled in and filled the tank and bought a large, detailed map of France.

She plotted her route south: Orléans, Tours, Poitiers, Angoulême, Bordeaux. From Bordeaux she could reach Spain in a couple of hours or so. San Sebastián, Bilbao, Pamplona—any of these towns would be good to hide up in and make plans.

Plans. Jacques had scheduled the press conference for the next day in a large concert hall in the middle of Paris. The whole French media would be there, he said. And some Americans. He was talking about dozens of journalists, it would be like a bomb going off when she told her story, he said. It would be a global news story, he said. "And it's you, Anny Viklund, movie star. You're the victim of this plot. You're the target of the FBI. They won't dare try to extradite you after we do this. Cause célèbre—it always works, the best way."

He had been very passionate, almost as if he were the one in the spotlight, being asked to present himself, defend himself to the world's press. He hadn't even asked her if she wanted to do it, she had realised with mounting alarm, and that was what had freaked her out. It was entirely his plan. That was why she knew she had to start running again.

First, be alone, then shake off the FBI, then start making calls. Call who, though? She needed advice. Troy would always send her money if she needed more. She would be safer on her own, hiding. She needed Troy, not Jacques, now.

Outside Tours she stopped by a hypermarket, a Carrefour, and bought a tartan blanket and a pillow, as well as some packs of cookies and bottles of water. She managed to drive on as far as Poitiers before she felt tired. She parked in a side street near a school and settled down for the night in the rear seat with her blanket and pillow, locking the doors. She slept badly, waking every half-hour or so, and as soon as it was light she was on her way once more—*direction* Angoulême. The little Renault wasn't speedy but it seemed to run well. She wasn't in any hurry, after all—if she reached Spain in two days or five, it didn't matter. The main thing was that not one single person in the world knew where she was.

7

“This is where our visitors stay,” Sister Lamorna said, leading Elfrida across the wide lawn behind the convent towards a building set around a courtyard.

“It used to be the stable block,” Sister Lamorna went on, gesturing. “But we’ve converted it into little units.” She smiled. “A bedroom and a shower room in each one. You eat your meals with us.”

The convent of St. Jude and St. Simon the Zealot was a converted country house, quite large, ashlar-faced with a four-column portico. A simple, plain wing had been added with dormers and symmetrical windows. To one side and separate was a large and rather ugly Victorian Gothic chapel built in variegated brick, charcoal grey and burnt orange. The house was set in its own generous grounds, some 200 acres, ringed by a high dry-stone wall. It wasn’t far from Taunton. Elfrida had caught a train there and a taxi had brought her from the station to St. Jude’s in about twenty minutes. Yet the impression she gained, once she entered through the gates past the lodges, was one of near-total isolation. Tall oaks and chestnuts blocked out much of the surrounding view and standing on the gravelled forecourt in front of the porticoed entrance and looking around her she could make out only a couple of distant farms. Deepest, darkest England, she thought. Perfect. It was a breezy, cool day with only brief bursts of sunshine. The great leafy mass of the trees ringing the estate shrugged and shifted as they were hit by the gusts of wind—almost animate and restless, it seemed to her, as if they were huge arboreal giants keen to make a move.

She and Sister Lamorna went through an arch into the stable yard. Some farm vehicles were parked there and half of the buildings seemed converted into workshops of various kinds. The short-pitched, dry sound of a hammer on metal came from one of them. On two sides were evenly spaced grey doors with numbers on them, one to six.

Sister Lamorna opened the door to number two and Elfrida stepped in, seeing a bare white room with brown linoleum on the floor. There was an iron bed, a wooden chair and a chest of drawers, painted white. A small ebony cross hung on the wall. A door led off to a neat tiled bathroom with a shower. It looked like a cross between a room in a hospital and a cell, Elfrida thought. She turned to Sister Lamorna and smiled.

"This is exactly what I was hoping for."

Sister Lamorna was Dr. Ingham's sister, though there was little resemblance. Lamorna was lanky with a small round face under her bonnet; she lacked Sarah Ingham's handsome, chiselled sternness.

"How many other 'visitors' are there?" Elfrida asked.

"Two others currently. We're rarely full up. It's not to everyone's taste."

Elfrida glanced again at the small, stark room. This would be her world from now on, for £100 a month.

"It seems ideal," she said.

"Let's go back and sort out the administrative bits and bobs," Sister Lamorna said. "Perhaps this would be a good time to meet the Mother Superior."

The Mother Superior, the Reverend Mother Matilda, turned out to be a tiny person with a pronounced dowager's stoop. Osteoporosis had its iron claws into her, Elfrida saw, but she seemed unperturbed by her awkward posture. She had bright gleaming eyes behind round wire-rimmed spectacles. She was dressed like Sister Lamorna in the Zealottine's typical forest-green belted tunic but beneath her white bonnet she wore a coif and a wimple across her bent shoulders.

They chatted about the few formalities of becoming a "visitor." Elfrida would wear a green tunic, always with an apron and a headscarf of her own choosing as long as it wasn't too garish—this would signify that she wasn't a novice Zealot. She was free to roam anywhere about the grounds—even go into Taunton if she wished (always in Zealottine garb, however)—and choose any form of manual work she felt inclined to do, in the kitchens, the gardens, the workshops or the home farm.

"Do I have to go to church?" Elfrida asked.

"Good heavens, no!" the Reverend Mother said. "We're not here to convert you—and we don't want any heathens in our chapel." She found this notion amusing, as did Sister Lamorna. They both laughed, hands over their mouths. "Of course, if you want to worship, you're more than welcome."

She would eat with the nuns when they ate (at a separate table) and if she smoked she could smoke in her room.

"You're not a prisoner," the Reverend Mother said. "You're our paying guest. A 'visitor.' Like all visitors if you want to leave we won't stop you."

Elfrida saw the wisdom behind this licence. Your redemption as a visitor—physical and mental—wasn't the responsibility of the institution, as it would have been in a hospital or a detox clinic—it was entirely your own business, paid for by yourself and, if it worked, a product of your own efforts. All they did was provide a safe context for that redemption to occur—if it could.

"How would you like to be known? Sister Elfrida? We call all our visitors 'Sister.'"

"I'd like to be called 'Sister Jennifer,' please," Elfrida said.

"Sister Jennifer it shall be."

She was taken by Sister Lamorna to an office, the bursary, as it was called, where she filled in and signed forms and completed a standing order for her bank to pay her monthly rent. The business over, they returned to the front door where her taxi was waiting.

"Give my love to Sarah," Sister Lamorna said. "Will you be seeing her?"

"Yes, I will," she said. "I have to report back. I'll settle my affairs in London and should be down next week."

"Grand. Give us a tinkle on the telephone and we'll have your unit ready and waiting."

Elfrida said goodbye and climbed into the taxi. They pulled away down the short drive and passed through the gates between the twin lodges. After five minutes, Elfrida asked the taxi driver to stop. They were on the crest of the hill and they had a good view of the wide long valley below and the convent set there in its park and farmland. She let her eyes follow the modest inclines and declivities of the valley floor—its swales and ridges, hollows and hillocks—pulled into a kind of shapeliness by the hand of human beings with its superimposed grid of lanes and hedgerows: random nature subdued by an easy and unthreatening order. Larger woods bulked where the land began to climb and couldn't be tilled—agriculture ceding ground to heath and rocky outcrop—and beyond the summits of those encircling hills was a blurry frieze of other plum-hazed hills in the very distance. She hadn't any fixed sense of her geography yet. These hills and woods had ancient names, like the farms and the hamlets she could see, and one day soon she would learn them but now, in her innocent ignorance, she felt embraced by a vision of perfect English countryside, steeped in its history and seasonal cycles.

As she looked out over the view and the place that was to become her home, Elfrida felt a strange, almost spiritual moment occur. It seemed a form of exorcism to her, as if Elfrida Wing, novelist, the new Virginia Woolf, was departing her corporeal state and her body would now play host to a new persona, Sister Jennifer. It was a kind of inorcism, she thought, if such a word existed. She had a strong conviction—and a strong conviction was all you could really ever be sure of in life—that she was going to be all right.

8

The spotlights were in position, casting their powerful beam, as was the stand with its vinyl backdrop—a stippled "old master" white—unrolled between the two tall windows with their wooden shutters closed. There was a stool for Gary to sit on. Talbot checked the frame through the viewfinder of the Rolleiflex then fitted a pentaprism so that the Rollei's lateral reversal would be corrected. There was nothing more to do other than wait for the model.

He poured himself a small calming Scotch and soda. This ridiculous pop song was in his head—the park, the cake, the rain, the sweet green icing flowing down, the bloody missing recipe—and one key line repeated like some loop on a tape recorder. "Pressed in love's hot-fevered iron, like a stripèd pair of pants." He never remembered popular music, it was like the noise of traffic to him, or aeroplanes passing overhead, but this song had a strangely powerful grip on him. Maybe it was that line, like something from a gimcrack metaphysical poem with its preposterously accented adjective and, he acknowledged, he had to admit, its particular association with the very day he had met Gary Hicksmith. He had popped out to buy a pint of milk and some biscuits in case Gary wanted a cup of tea. He went to the small grocer's in Meadowbank, that appeared to be open twenty-four hours a day, seven days a week, and that song, the song of his summer of 1968, had been tinnily playing on a transistor radio by the till, haunting him with its plangent, ghostly refrain. The park, the cake, the rain, the sweet green icing flowing down. And the stripèd pair of pants, of course, pressed in love's hot-fevered iron.

He heard the garden-door bell ring and he hurried down to admit Gary. He opened the door, diminishing the welcome of his smile in order to seem more professional and disinterested—not like some panting lover on a tryst.

"Come in, Gary, come in," he said. He suddenly wished Gary wasn't called Gary, that he had a name like Tim or Sam. Fool, he thought, snob—be careful.

Gary was wearing the same clothes as yesterday—the pale jeans and the blouson—but had changed his red t-shirt for a white one.

"Is this outfit OK, Mr. Eastman?"

"Perfect. But we won't go any further until you start calling me Talbot."

"Talbot it is. Talbot."

They went in and climbed the stair to the main room, Talbot leading the way. He could see that Gary was impressed with the array of lights and the evident professionalism of the set-up. Talbot offered him a drink—tea, red wine, whisky?—and Gary opted for red wine, thanks, Talbot.

Talbot handed him an envelope with a cheque for £50 inside.

"This is for your time. The commission."

"Oh. Fantastic. Thanks." He folded the envelope and quickly slipped it into a pocket without looking at its contents.

The exchange of money somehow altered the mood, Talbot immediately thought, irritated with himself for introducing it so early, as if the transaction had robbed the occasion of its informality. He went to fetch the wine—maybe that would help—as Gary wandered around taking in the room.

"It's a great flat, Mr.—Talbot. Great. It's, you know . . . It's very good taste, if you know what I mean."

"Thank you. I just wish I could spend more time here."

He opened the wine and poured two glasses.

"My God! What's that? Fort Knox?" Gary said. He had seen the door into the gallery with its heavy padlock.

"I keep my cameras and lights there," Talbot said, handing him his glass of wine. "Expensive stuff. Thousands of pounds. When I'm away I have to feel it's secure. So many people are in and out of this place."

"Don't blame you." Gary smiled. "When you're worth a few bob you've got to keep it safe."

"Precisely. Shall we make a start?"

Gary took his seat on the stool and Talbot made a fuss of minutely adjusting the lights, turning the stands an inch or two this way or that way, enhancing or reducing the luminosity.

"You can take your jacket off," Talbot said. "The t-shirt's fine."

Gary slipped off his jacket and Talbot hung it over the back of a chair. Then he took up his position behind the Rollei and peered down into the viewfinder, sharpening the focus. He saw Gary's young, strong face in stark chiaroscuro, ready to be captured. A vein on Gary's neck pulsed visibly, the light shadowing its cursive path along the muscle. Talbot felt the paradoxical inverse of the old fear—that conviction experienced by primitive peoples who were sure that, being photographed, their souls were stolen by the malevolent photographer with his magical camera-machine. In this instance the subject was innocent, unconcerned and ignorant. Now the photographer was the knowing soul-stealer. In the next few seconds Talbot would steal the soul of Gary Hicksmith from him, thanks to the expensive stop-time device he was employing, mounted on its tripod before him.

He could see Gary was a bit tense, not at ease.

"Think of something else, Gary. Ignore the camera. How did the Arsenal play this Saturday?"

"I don't know. I'm not that interested in football to tell the truth."

Click. He wound on the film with the Rollei's little handle. Got you.

"So what did you do on Saturday afternoon?"

"Went fishing."

Click.

"Catch anything?"

"Couple of tench. Two-pounders."

"Have them for supper?"

Click.

"You've got to chuck 'em back in."

Click.

"Really? That seems unfair."

Talbot kept up the flow of questions, all banal, interspersed with a few posers—"Ever fished with a dry fly?"—that had Gary frowning before he replied. The camera captured the moment, stopped time and Gary Hicksmith was held forever. Talbot finished the roll and wound it on to the take-up spool.

"Let's take a break," he said, and topped up their wine glasses.

"This is really tasty," Gary said, sipping his wine. "I'm not really a wine drinker, in actual fact."

"It's a burgundy," Talbot said. "Comes from a tiny vineyard in the east of France, in the Saône Valley. Just a few acres. They make this exquisite wine." Now he felt a bit pompous. "It'll get you drunk, though, if you give it a chance." That sounded false, as well.

"Costs a fair bit, I don't doubt," Gary said, holding the wine up to the light.

"Worth every penny."

"If you've got the pennies."

"Of course."

"You could teach me a thing or two, Talbot, I'll bet." He pouted, thinking. "I left school at sixteen. Wanted to earn some cash so I started as a scaff. My dad was a scaff. And that was that."

"You've got plenty of time, Gary. You're young."

"Yeah. But I'm not educated. And I know it. And I want to start my own business—but I don't know nothing—apart from scaffolding. And fishing."

"Well, if I can ever be of help . . ."

"You've already helped. This fifty quid you paid me—it'll be my deposit. I found a small yard in Muswell Hill. Hicksmith Scaffolding Ltd. We're on our way, sort of. Soon as I can afford a lorry."

"Bravo! Shall we have another session?"

Talbot went through the motions of taking another roll of film, knowing he had everything he needed. Gary's face, perfectly lit, perfectly printed, would be hanging in the gallery in a day or two.

He stepped back from the camera feeling a form of listless contentment overtake him. Was he a bit drunk? Perhaps it was the burgundy and the darkened room affecting him, Gary Hicksmith spotlit at its centre.

"I think we have it, Gary. Let's finish the bottle, shall we?"

Talbot lifted the bottle off the table and started towards Gary but, as he did so, the toe of his left shoe caught in the creased corner of the rug on the floor and he stumbled, the bottle flying from his fingers, and he crashed into the camera tripod going down heavily on one knee, breaking the force of his fall by rolling over onto his back.

He sensed Gary leap from the stool and in a second he was standing over him.

"Talbot! You OK? You all right?"

"Silly bloody fool that I am. Yes, I think so."

Gary reached down a hand and Talbot grabbed it, thumbs interlocking for better purchase, and Gary took his weight and hauled him easily up, Talbot lurching forward again as he regained his feet.

In that half-second their faces were suddenly very close—an inch or two—Gary startled, concerned, Talbot breathing heavily—and Gary steadied him with a strong grip on his bicep. Talbot swayed. Gary's face, large and focussed. So close. So very close. It was almost an embrace, chest to chest, hands gripping.

In that heedless moment Talbot thought he would kiss him. He leant forward. Gary recoiled.

"Your lip's bleeding! Jesus!"

Talbot reared back, feigning more imbalance.

"Sorry! Sorry about that!"

There was blood on his chin, dripping. Talbot's hand went to his mouth and his fingertips came away—red, slick. The scab on his lip must have broken in his fall.

"Jesus Christ! You all right?"

"I must have banged it when I fell. I'm sorry."

Gary was staring at him, very strangely.

"What's going on, Talbot?"

"Let me get a cloth," Talbot said and ran to the kitchen, thrust a dishcloth under the tap, wet it and held it to his mouth. He closed his eyes, trying to blank out what he'd almost done. For some reason he thought of a line of verse—"The awful daring of a moment's surrender"—why? What song, what poem? One, two, three. He went back in.

"I think they call that a 'clash of heads' on the football field," Talbot said, forcing a smile.

Gary still looked at him strangely. Talbot dabbed at his re-split lip and glanced at the cloth in his hand, at the blood-blots.

"Many apologies, Gary. I probably should have had a stitch in that cut. Bloody hell!"

Absurdly he found himself thinking of Anny and Jacques Soldat, of Soldat's hard blow. The blow that had produced this scab. This scab that had broken at the vital moment. What life was that? he thought. In what universe did that occur?

"My apologies, Gary," he repeated. "God, *Sturm und Drang.* Must watch that bloody rug."

"Yeah, well, no harm done," Gary said, his voice quiet, thrusting his hands in his pockets, evidently uncomfortable. "You're the one what's bleeding. How about you?"

"I'll survive," Talbot said, imagining he could almost hear Gary's mind racing, re-running the last few moments, trying to comprehend what nearly happened there. Keep talking, keep talking, he told himself. "I think I need something stronger than wine," he said, with forced heartiness. "Something medicinal."

He went to the cupboard and took out the bottle of Scotch and two glasses.

"Not for me, thanks," Gary said.

Talbot poured his whisky carefully, again glad to have something to do as he collected his thoughts and wondered where this ghastly, awkward situation might lead. What had he been thinking of? Awful daring. Madness. Insanity. He drank a small mouthful of the whisky, his lip stinging, watching Gary slowly pace the room.

"All's well. Thank you, Dr. Glenlivet."

"Actually, come to think of it, I will have one," Gary said. "If you don't mind."

Talbot poured an inch of whisky into a tumbler and handed it to him.

"You sure you're all right?" Gary said. "It can shake you up, a fall like that."

"I'm fine. Nothing broken." Talbot sat down on the arm of an armchair. "What drama."

"You almost knocked your camera flying. Rocking to and fro—managed to grab it."

"Now that would have been a disaster."

Gary stood there, deep in thought, and took a sip at his whisky. He put his glass down with a clunk, as if about to make a speech or a proclamation, it seemed.

"Yeah . . ." he said to himself, as if making a decision. "Yeah . . ."

"What is it?" Talbot asked, trying to sound neutral.

"In fact, Talbot, I was just on the point of asking you something," he said. "Just then."

"Oh, yes? What?"

"A favour."

Talbot smiled. "Anything I can do to help."

"It's a 'money' favour . . ."

"Oh." Talbot felt a quick sadness envelop him. A falling away, as he suddenly remembered all the remarks Gary had made about money in their short acquaintance, as if assessing him, auditing him. A money favour . . .

"I won't mess about," Gary said, flatly, as if trying to mute his embarrassment. "Cut to the chase, and all that. I need two hundred pound. It would be down payment on a flatbed lorry. I was wondering if I could borrow it off of you."

Talbot sensed a little keening note of worry start in his ear, a kind of sonic tingle of disappointment. He tried to ignore it. He also thought he detected a change in the tone of Gary's voice—suddenly a little hoarse, deeper, somehow more insistent and controlling. Was that worry—or nerves—or an implicit threat? . . .

"I'm sure a bank will lend you two hundred pounds," Talbot said, lightly, logically.

"I already borrowed from my bank."

"Right. I see."

There was a silence that Talbot wasn't going to break. Gary spoke again—again with that unfamiliar rasp to his voice.

"If you could, you know, see your way to lending me two hundred pound it would make all the difference. I'll repay with interest, no problems. But I need that lorry—can't start the business without one."

"It's a lot of money, Gary."

"Of course. I know. It's a lot of money to me. But—no disrespect—not to you."

Talbot took this implication in, reluctantly. The easy, complacent assumption provoked a little squirm of anger in him. Talbot "Eastman"—rich man. Rich man for the plucking. The keening note in his ear was growing more shrill. He wasn't befuddled with wine, or with the unforeseen adrenalin rush of the fall—he knew exactly what was going on. He stood up.

"So you want me to 'lend' you two hundred pounds."

"Exactly. I'd be most grateful. You see, you're the only person I know who I could ask. You seem like a nice man. You've already been very kind to me. So I thought I'd—"

"You thought you'd just try and pressure me into a loan."

Gary looked baffled. A studied bafflement, Talbot thought.

"What? What 'pressure'? It's a simple request."

"It's a simple request but it's the *timing* of your request that interests me. It won't work."

"I don't know what you're talking about."

Talbot felt his facial muscles tightening. He found it impossible to maintain his smile.

"I know what's going on, Gary. I'm not a fool. Please don't take me for a fool. I can read between the lines."

Gary held up both palms.

"Hey. Talbot, please. Mr. Eastman—it's just a simple request. You can say no, or you can say yes. Full stop."

"It's the opposite of simple. It's full of nasty little complications. Ifs and buts. Hidden 'or else's.' What if I decide not to lend you the money? What then? Well, what would you do? Mmm? I wonder. Et cetera, et cetera."

"Et cetera what?" Gary's voice was rising now. "What're you going on about?"

"You are trying to make something out of absolutely nothing. It won't work. Sorry."

"Talking Chinese, Talbot."

"Translate it."

"What are you fucking trying to say?"

They were facing each other now, two feet apart. Talbot was aware of his chest heaving, semi-breathless with the accumulated emotion gathering around this unexpected, unwanted confrontation. He craved oxygen, he almost felt light-headed. How could he have got himself in this situation? Stupid, misguided, tragic old fool.

"I think you'd better go," he said, as calmly and as neutrally as possible. “You have your fifty pounds. You earned that. I promise I won’t stop the cheque.”

“I still don’t know what you’re talking about.”

“I think you do.”

“Is it because you wanted to—”

Gary stopped. He looked at him, his face slightly contorted, clearly disgusted as Talbot’s inferences suddenly became plain to him. Then he took the envelope with the cheque in it from his pocket. He tore it in two, then in four. He threw the pieces up in the air.

“Keep your fucking money. I don’t want it.” He pointed a shaky finger at him, anger making his features flinch and twitch.

“Fucking nutter. Fucking weirdo,” he said, grabbed his jacket and walked out. Now Talbot could breathe. He swallowed. No, he realised immediately, no, he had read this all wrong—this had gone hideously awry, stupendously, mind-bogglingly wrong.

He went to the window and fumbled like a dotard with the captain’s hook on the shutters, his hands were trembling so badly he could hardly perform the elementary operation. He flung them apart and looked down into the garden to see Gary striding across the patch of lawn to the door and wresting it open.

He knocked on the glass. Rapped his knuckles hard on the pane.

“Gary!” he shouted. “Wait! Please! Wait a second!”

But Gary didn’t look back and was gone in an instant.

9

It was after she left Angoulême that Anny became aware of the car following her. Two cars, in fact: one was black and the other was silver. They were taking it in turns to keep her in view—keeping quite far back, hoping she wouldn't notice. She turned off the Route Nationale and waited an hour in a village before returning to the RN and continuing on to Bordeaux. But there, twenty minutes later, in her rear mirror, were the cars interchanging, staying back, keeping their distance. Black car, silver car.

She tried to keep her panic at bay, thinking that Alphonse—that piece of shit—must have told Jacques. But Jacques wouldn't have alerted the police, no. Therefore it must be the FBI or—what was the French version?—the Sûreté. She remembered the name from some script she'd read. But how would they know? They had come to the apartment, yes, Alphonse's apartment. Maybe the phone was bugged—and then if they heard Alphonse's call to Jacques it wouldn't be difficult to track down the details of Alphonse's car, its type, its colour, its number plate.

She felt sick. How could they be following her so soon? What would they do if they caught her? They couldn't arrest her—she was untouchable in France. And then thinking on, she realised that what she needed was a lawyer in France. She'd been relying too much on Jacques—but, as her father used to tell her—the only person you can really rely on is yourself. Yes, she thought, once she was secure in Spain she would call her lawyer in the States, get him to find someone in Paris, or Madrid, someone who could handle her case in Europe. She'd need money for that but Troy would send her money until she could unlock her own funds. She was rich—she had plenty of money—money wasn't a problem. The problem was trust. She trusted Troy—she realised that she could rely on Troy—and the thought made her sad. Only Troy.

Then she saw a sign for Bordeaux airport—Mérignac—and she had a sudden idea. A good idea, she thought. Dump Alphonse's Renault and hire a new car. That would buy her more time. They would figure it out eventually but by then she'd be across the Spanish border and out of harm's way for as long as she wanted. She waited until the next sign indicating the exit to Bordeaux airport and, at the very last moment, turned sharply off the Route Nationale and accelerated away.

At the airport she parked the Renault in a long-term car park and walked to the arrivals hall, where the car-hire firms were. She chose one of the smaller ones, S-O-L, Sud-Ouest-Locations, and she hired a Simca 1000 from them. She felt a little apprehensive as she handed over her passport but the girl behind the counter made no reaction as she noted down her details. Anny was given the keys and told where her car was parked but, as she turned away with relief, she realised that she'd left her big map of France in the Renault. She hurried off, striding quickly back to the car park. However, as she approached the Renault she saw two men standing by the car, peering in and talking, gesturing to each other. They were both wearing leather jackets and were young, with short hair. She turned around without lingering further, her throat tight, feeling a sudden weakness invade her, making her think she'd fall over, hadn't the strength to stay standing. What should she do? They were closer than she had imagined. She returned to S-O-L and was given a map of the Bordeaux area. Anny decided to wait this out for a day or so and see if by staying still—by not running—she could confuse them further. And it would give her time to think and plan. She was finding that harder, thinking clearly. Maybe she should cut down on the Obetral . . .

So she sat in the Simca for a good half-hour, telling herself to calm down, forcing herself to think logically. They would assume, first, that she'd caught a plane—the abandoned car at the airport would suggest that, and that would be their initial check, looking for any passengers called Anny Viklund. Or maybe they might think she'd met someone—an agreed rendezvous with a friend, an accomplice—and not even think of a hired car. She swallowed hard, coaxing saliva into her mouth. What should she do? She needed time. Stay still, don't move. If you don't move they can't follow you.

Forcing herself to look at the map she saw that there was a long promontory near Bordeaux, a thin spit of land that formed the ocean-side of a large bay. The promontory, the cape, was called Cap Ferret and looked thinly populated, with just a few small villages situated here and there. Somewhat remote, then, and with only one road in or out. Using a kind of inverse logic, she supposed that no one would expect anyone running away to deliberately choose a dead end as a place to hide. No. That would fool them. Maybe that was the ideal spot to hole up, she thought to herself, free of pursuit and its attendant panic. It would give her time to figure out what to do—time, that's what she needed—time to choose her moment to slip into Spain and safety.

It was late afternoon as she motored through the pine forests of Cap Ferret and encountered the first of the chain of little villages that dotted the headland, moving down towards the tip of the cape itself and its lighthouse. She recognised their names from the map she'd studied—Le Petit Piquey, Piraillan, Le Canon, L'Herbe. After L'Herbe the road turned west to skirt the Atlantic side of the headland. She stopped the car at a picnic area, stepped out, stretched and decided to follow a sandy path through the aromatic pines that led her to the dunes and the ocean. She wanted to see the ocean, for some reason.

But here, she was a little stunned to see vast grey concrete blockhouses set squarely in the dunes overlooking the wide beach. Gun emplacements from the Second World War, she realised, now emptied of their weapons and scribbled over with graffiti. This must be the remnant of Hitler's "Atlantic Wall," she remembered. She wandered down a path between two of the bunkers to find herself on the immense, immaculate beach. On the beach she could count the blockhouses, looking south and north as far as the eye could see, still menacing somehow, almost a quarter of a century later, permanent reminders of the conflict, ugly and awful monuments, she thought.

The tide was on the turn and the foaming breakers were crashing and spreading themselves higher up the sand. The evening was warm and there were still a few families and sunbathers reluctant to admit that their day was ending. A fisherman sat on a folding canvas chair, four rods planted in the sand in front of him, their lines stretching far out beyond the ranks of rolling waves. Anny walked down to the surf's edge, feeling the ocean breeze fresh on her face and, for a moment, experienced a powerful urge to strip off her clothes and rush into the battering, exhilarating embrace of the breakers. She stepped back from the final fizzing, lazy spill of the waves as they smoothed the sand in front of her. She couldn't linger—she knew she had to find somewhere secure to settle down for the night. Jesus, what was happening? How was this happening to her? She looked out to the horizon, the sun beginning to go down, the light burning soft and gilded. Next stop the U.S. of A., she thought. And thought further—how could she ever go back?

In the village of Cap Ferret itself she stopped at a shop and bought some more cookies, water and two packs of cigarettes. She drove down to a small ferry port with a sturdy wooden jetty. There were a good few cars parked here and she reckoned one more Simca wouldn't be noticed. She saw the tracks of a narrow-gauge railway and soon the little train duly appeared, arriving at the jetty, trundling tourists and bathers between the beaches and the ferry point. There was a lot of activity—perfect. She pulled into a gap between a Peugeot van and a Fiat 500. This would be her base until it was time to drive to Spain.

She sat in her car and smoked cigarettes and ate cookies until it grew dark. She urged herself to run through the various options that she thought she had available to her, but the arrival of night affected her mood and the hopelessness of her situation began to seem more and more overwhelming. Options. Plan B. Plan C. Should she go back to Paris, to Jacques? What about his crazy idea of a press conference? She couldn't go through with that, she knew. Or maybe she should just turn herself in and take her chances. Or could she ask Troy to come and rescue her and take her back to England? She knew he would come if she asked him. But what about those men following her? And the men peering into her car at the airport? Who were they and what was their agenda? How far away were they? And what would they do if they ever found her? . . .

She stepped out of the Simca. The warmth of the day was disappearing and a cooler breeze was evident from the ocean side of the promontory. She could hear the heavy slap of water on the piles of the jetty as the tide came in and a thin, jaunty sound of music carried from a bar in the town. Suddenly, as she stood there, she realised that she had no idea what to do next. No idea where to go or who to turn to. Jacques? Troy? . . . Her brain wasn't working. Maybe she should have listened to Talbot. But that was way too late now. If she could have gone back . . . She stopped herself. It had been a mistake to come to Cap Ferret, this dead-end promontory with no way out. She was at a dead end, that was it. And what did you do when you were at a dead end? An answer came to her suddenly and she thought about it. She acknowledged its rationale and with that acknowledgement came a sense of absolute calm. What she would do, in this instance, was entirely within her power and would solve every problem she faced. She could defy all the potential unhappy futures that fate had waiting in store for her.

She slipped back into the car and opened her grip. In her sponge bag she found all her pills—the tranquillisers, the sleeping pills, the diet pills—her Equanil, Seconal and Obetral. She emptied them into her lap and began to swallow them all, in small handfuls, taking big draughts of water to wash them down. When she'd finished, she clambered into the back seat, locked all the doors of the car and lay down, pulling her tartan rug around her. She settled there, blinking slowly in the darkness, contemplating this course of action that she had initiated and feeling, as she thought about it, an intense, overpowering relief. All her troubles would soon be over. It would just be like going to sleep, she told herself. And then, as she began to feel very strange, and she sensed her grip on consciousness begin to slip and slide, tilt and turn, she thought she heard hushed voices. Was she imagining them? Were the drugs making her hallucinate? But, no, she was sure there were men talking quietly, standing by her car. And then someone tried to open the door. Please leave me alone, she said out loud, leave me alone! And she pulled the rug over her head, shutting out the world and its agitations forever.

10

An ordinary Monday morning in high summer, Talbot thought, strolling along Great Marlborough Street towards YSK's offices. Monday morning and the last day of principal photography on *Emily Bracegirdle's Extremely Useful Ladder to the Moon.* Today they would film a weeping Ben inside the car with Emily's dead body alongside him in the passenger seat, and then, once that was in the can, three cameras would be positioned to capture the one-time-only shot of the windscreen-less Mini being catapulted off the cliff at Beachy Head. There was even a fourth camera on a boat offshore to record the impact as it landed in the sea.

Talbot supposed that he really should have been there but more urgent matters claimed his time this morning. If all went well—if all passed off as he hoped—then perhaps he might make it down to Beachy Head in time for the Mini's launch out into the blue in the late afternoon. He paused at the door to the YSK building and lit a calming cigarette. The reverberations of the appalling debacle yesterday with Gary still rocked and disturbed him. Gary had walked out and had left him feeling—what? Vulnerable and shamefaced, was the answer, stupefied by his own idiocy and bothered by a persistent unease—not so much guilt, but self-reproach of the most severe and unforgiving sort. He wouldn't quickly forget the expression on Gary's face as he ripped up the £50 cheque. As rebukes went it was devastating, not to say adamantine. However, one of the consequences of the grotesque misunderstanding was that it had somehow sharpened his focus.

Later, as he sat in his gallery with his whisky after Gary had left, trying to calm down—looking at his portraits of his models, male and female, at their shadowed faces and the guileless, classic nudes—he rebuked and cursed himself for hours. He remembered how, once, some clever person—some screenwriter or film director he was talking to—had said to him that, as an adult, all the emotions you experienced were unconsciously measured against their adolescent equivalents—and found wanting. Desire, longing, hatred, revenge, love, shame, frustration, jealousy, yearning, and so on—all your adult emotions failed to equal or come close to the intensity of those emotions that you experienced as an adolescent. Which was why, the argument continued, adults were always searching for a repeat of that level of experience, that emotional truth, because they already had a touchstone, a template, that they remembered vividly. But they searched in vain, because the original experience—the vivid, heartfelt one—was always out of their reach, buried deep in their past, unrecoverable. And this was why they fucked up their lives. This vain search applied to both men and women, so this clever person had said, offering this argument as a defence of the adolescent spirit, much maligned for its selfishness, illogic, irritations, inadequacies and frustrations. In this displacement, in this unbridgeable disconnect between adolescence and adulthood, all our emotional, personal, sexual problems lay, so it was claimed.

Yes, of course, how true, how perspicacious, Talbot had agreed, unreflectingly. But, later, thinking back, he found himself disagreeing. As far as he was concerned his adolescence was a forgotten history—like the Etruscans or the Neanderthals. For him, all his emotional intensity had come from his adult life, once he had confronted and accepted its nature. Only as an adult had he sensed and savoured true desire, burning disappointment, sexual excitement, lasting regret, unfulfilled longing, and so on. The fervency and immediacy of his emotional life as an adult had completely overshadowed and obscured what he'd felt and suffered as a teenager. Why was that? he wondered. And he answered himself by recognising that what he felt as a grown man was sophisticated, nuanced and understood—not raw, pulsing and baffled. He had moved on from those inchoate states of being and he was happier as a result.

Anyway, realising he had been a total fool with Gary Hicksmith, he had determined not to be fooled in turn—particularly by Yorgos Samsa. Throughout that Sunday, as he thought and mentally probed, relived and winced, berated and punished himself long into the evening, hunkered in his shuttered flat, drinking whisky after whisky, he had constructed a plan that was going to solve everything, or so he thought. A plan that no one would imagine Talbot Kydd could conceive.

He stood on his cigarette, took a breath and looked around. To his surprise, parked up the street, twenty yards away, was a Rolls-Royce with the number plate 1 AP. He recognised it instantly as Jimmy Appleby's Rolls. What was it doing here? No matter. It was time to act. He pressed the buzzer, was admitted and pushed through the door.

Yorgos seemed unusually smart, Talbot thought, wondering if he was going on somewhere that demanded special sartorial protocol. He was wearing one of his wide-chalk-striped double-breasted suits and a floppy navy-blue bow tie with white polka dots. It was as if he had dressed specially for the occasion. His face looked glossily moisturised and there was an expensive scent of some cologne about him. He seemed very relaxed and Talbot hoped his own nerves were not in evidence. A great deal of super-confident bluff would be required of him in the next few minutes.

Yorgos had everything ready. Three duplicate contracts for *The Smell of Burning Leaves* lay in a neat row along the edge of his desk, facing Talbot, a silver pen at the ready.

"I know what this may look like to you, Talbot," Yorgos said in his reassuring bass. "But, believe me, this is the only way to make the rights secure from the estate, to protect us. The Luxembourg company will own the rights and only we can unlock them. So if the estate tries to sell to others, if the estate sues us, to try to block us making this film, our hands are clean. They can do nothing."

Only *you* can unlock them, Talbot silently corrected him, smiling. "It's all very clever, Yorgos. I could never have figured it out, myself. Where do I sign?"

"Have you explained to John Saxonwood? Every stone must be turned over, in case there is a rotten truffle."

"Exactly. He's happy. He understands it all."

Yorgos turned the pages of the contract and indicated where Talbot should sign and what clauses he should initial. He did so, swiftly conveying his part of the film rights in *Burning Leaves* to FUMODOR S.A. (Lux). He looked at Yorgos's slack expressionless face but thought he could sense, all the same, little inward tremors of exhilaration.

"So. This means I—we—don't own the rights any more. Theoretically."

"In name only. Officially, legally we don't. But we can get them back when we want—and then we make disgusting amounts of money."

"Ah, yes, money."

"Think what you may do with it all, Talbot. Money is the root of the good times at the end of the rainbow."

Talbot smiled.

"I thought I saw Jimmy Appleby's car parked outside. Is he here?"

"Appleby? No. Maybe he's doing some shopping."

Something about Yorgos's terse denial and the easy excuse gave him pause. Sometimes it was the very lack of curious follow-up questions that was the giveaway. Mentioning Appleby's name should surely have triggered a few offhand remarks, an anecdote, a recollection, an opinion. But nothing. Yorgos didn't want to talk about the Applebys. Talbot suddenly had a convincing vision of an Appleby/Samsa collaboration in the matter of the *Burning Leaves* complexities. It didn't concern him any more—he had his escape plan, whoever else was involved.

"Yes, probably shopping in Oxford Street . . . Anyway, talking about money," Talbot went on, trying to keep his voice level and emotionless. "I think the time has come, Yorgos, for you to buy me out of YSK Films. I want you to buy my shares. You can have the lot for a fair price."

Yorgos's smile faded then disappeared. He frowned, thinking fast, getting nowhere. Completely outflanked, Talbot thought. This was not part of the Yorgos plan.

"What? A buyout? Are you crazy, Talbot?"

"No. I'm very sane."

"You just signed the contract."

"I know. And I know what's going on. I want you to buy my 49% share in the company for £200,000." He smiled. "Or else."

"It's very, very smart of you, Talbot," John Saxonwood said admiringly, rubbing his jaw, thinking. "Yes, inspiringly clever. I wouldn't have thought it of you. But very risky."

"All reward comes with some risk."

"But this risk is impossible to quantify, to assess."

"I'm not so sure. I actually didn't think there was much risk in it. My scheme only works because of the very strange, curious and paranoid nature of our business," Talbot said. "If it merits the name business."

"I'm a bit surprised you didn't run it by me first."

"Because if I had you'd have forbidden me from doing it."

"True. But all's well that ends well, it seems."

Talbot had explained in some detail. If there is one thing the film industry hates, detests and despises above everything else, he reminded John Saxonwood, then that is litigation—even the vaguest threat, the slightest whiff of litigation circling round a project is anathema. He had known exactly what he was doing in allowing Yorgos to defraud him. Yorgos and his sleeping partners now had the extremely valuable asset that was the film rights in *The Smell of Burning Leaves* but it would cease to be valuable—or its value would dramatically diminish—if there was any taint of scandal attached to it. Talbot's threat had been very simple, he told John Saxonwood, and was one that Yorgos would understand and evaluate immediately. Yorgos had a straightforward choice. He had to buy Talbot out for the price mentioned—there would be no negotiation—or else Talbot would sue him.

"But you signed the fucking contract," Saxonwood said, baffled. "You'd lost your leverage."

"And, paradoxically, that gave me more power. Yorgos's 'fraud' was in place, in print, in legalese." He went on, explaining further. Why else are successful films bombarded with plagiarism suits? he asked rhetorically. Because the plaintiffs know that, rather than go to court and jeopardise the timetable or the viability of the film under attack, the studios, the producers, will pay money to make the problem go away.

"So my 'or else' to Yorgos was the threat of a massive lawsuit. All guns blazing, the full majesty of English law."

"So what? You'd signed."

"It doesn't matter. That's the beauty of it. And, remember, he *was* actually defrauding me. My lawsuit against him would have buggered up the potential film of *Burning Leaves* completely. No financier would invest in the film—in any film—with a big, public lawsuit pending, even a half-baked lawsuit, even one that might get thrown out of court. And, moreover, a lawsuit initiated by the other partner in the production company. Pure, lethal poison. And Yorgos knew that. It might take a year, or even two—and I'd appeal any judgement that went against me. Yorgos knew that—he *knew* I'd got him. The film community would know that Yorgos Samsa was being sued by his former partner for fraud. Talk about a 'taint' of scandal. Very bad news for YSK Films and FUMODOR S.A."

"I take my hat off to you, Talbot. Nerves of steel, all the same. Bloody hell."

"For good measure—as extra insurance—I threatened to remove my name as producer from *Ladder to the Moon*. That would have set more alarm bells ringing, also. Nasty smell. And I said that if I took my name off then Andrew Marvell—the first writer—would also take his name off. Another problem. The nasty smell getting more noxious. With all this smoke the film business would wonder where the fire was."

"The smell of burning leaves," Saxonwood said.

"Exactly."

"Right. It is a funny business."

"So Yorgos's simple option, his simple solution, was to buy me out. End of problem. In a flash. Problem gone. Talbot gone away forever. He knew that. It took him about ten seconds to agree." Talbot shrugged. "I'm pretty sure the Applebys are behind this, colluding with Yorgos. They want to move into the film business but only with like-minded people. And I don't fit that description, as they made very plain to me the other day." He paused. "Yorgos and the Applebys baked the cake that was the FUMODOR S.A. version of *Burning Leaves* and they decided they didn't want to give me a slice. But what they didn't know was that I had the recipe. But, still, I didn't want to take it, didn't want any part of their cake." He smiled. "So I came up with this plan, this way of having my cake and eating it—but without the cake, if you see what I mean." He could see that John was looking bemused.

"You know that crazy pop song that's playing everywhere," Talbot said, thinking it might help. "The one about the green cake in the park, melting in the rain?"

"Are you feeling all right, Talbot?"

"Never felt better. I think I understand what it means. The song, that is."

"You've lost me, old fellow."

"It was a fair price anyway. Not too much over the odds. I didn't ask for a million. I wasn't being greedy."

"How much was it, again?"

"Two hundred thousand pounds."

"That should keep you going for a few years."

"That's what I thought. I could join the idle rich for a while. Become a remittance man. I could get used to it."

"What made you make up your mind?"

Talbot wondered how much he should tell John. He decided to keep the explanation vague.

"I had an experience this weekend that shook me up, rather," he began. "Stripped veils from my eyes, if you know what I mean, and made me rethink my priorities. Made me rethink the direction my life was going."

"Maybe you'll tell me in more detail one day."

"I will, don't worry."

"Shall we drink to your Machiavellian tendencies?"

"Yes, please. A large one."

II

She kept it on a small shelf beside her bed as a reminder of her old life—of her old self—an empty bottle of Sarson's White Vinegar. Sometimes she unscrewed the cap and sniffed, although she knew vodka had no smell and there would be no trace, but, fancifully, she imagined that some atom, some molecule, might be inhaled. It would be a tiny souvenir, a memory of what it had been like to be Elfrida Wing, novelist.

As Sister Jennifer, she had adapted to her new life with astonishing ease, or so she thought. It was—though she disregarded the religiose undertones—like being born again. She rediscovered her schoolgirl talent for sewing and spent many hours in the convent's sewing room making repairs to the nuns' tunics and aprons. She started designing better aprons to her own pattern, cut from heavy linen with extra pockets, that proved very popular. She had even repaired the Reverend Mother's wimple. Also, she rediscovered the bracing, restorative properties of strenuous manual labour. She picked apples and other fruit in the orchard, she swept leaves from the lawns and the pathways, she helped repair breaches in the dry-stone walls around the estate. She stopped reading books, newspapers and magazines. She never watched television or listened to the radio. Any news from the outside world came to her by hearsay, second- or third-hand. She went to bed tired and slept well. If she found she had time on her hands she simply went to one of the more senior nuns and asked for a task: polishing the brass in the chapel, typing letters in the administrative office, changing a tyre on the Reverend Mother's old Vauxhall Velox. The days passed in tranquil order, seamlessly, happily.

Only one person knew where she was, her friend and lawyer, Jessica Fairfield. Elfrida had given Jessica full power of attorney and she was engaged in initiating her divorce from Reggie and selling the Vale of Health cottage, the profit from which would ensure she could remain a "visitor" at St. Jude and St. Simon the Zealot for as long as she wished—perhaps even for the rest of her life. Reggie, Jessica told her, was being surprisingly accommodating, keeping the moans and grumbles to a minimum. Elfrida wasn't surprised—Janet Headstone was doubtless looming ever larger in his life. Elfrida had sworn Jessica to absolute secrecy but it hadn't been necessary, Jessica reminded her, as she was fully protected by the legalities of lawyer/client privilege. The right attaches to you, darling, Jessica had said, not me. Only you can waive it.

Apart from Jessica no one in the world knew where she was . . . As she lay in her narrow bed at night this was the thought that sustained her. Elfrida Wing had effectively disappeared from the face of the earth. How marvellous! She found the concept entirely liberating. To her astonishment she realised she was happy again.

12

Some vestiges of his old life did remain, Talbot realised, flicking through weekly *Variety* at the breakfast table, catching up on all the film industry news at home and abroad. It was now almost four weeks since his confrontation with Yorgos and three weeks since £200,000 had been paid into his bank and he had formally renounced his partnership in YSK Films Ltd. He was still the titular producer of *Ladder to the Moon* and from time to time calls came in, there were documents to sign and he was occasionally required to pop in to the post-production office in Frith Street in Soho where everything was being readied for the film's eventual release. Even Janet Headstone had written to him sending him a copy of the new draft of *Turmoil.* He took a sip of tea and turned the page. He wasn't missing his former life, he had to admit. He looked up to see Naomi sitting opposite him doing the *Times* crossword—to set her morning brain in gear, she said. It took her ten minutes or so. She was frowning, biro poised—then pounced.

Talbot turned and scanned another page. Ah, yes. There was always something of interest.

Here under a gossip piece about "hot" UK helmer Rodrigo Tipton was the news that his latest film *Moonladder*—that was unforeseen—was scheduled to screen at next year's Berlin Film Festival. Tipton, moreover, was about to move straight on to the hugely anticipated film version of the Broadway smash-hit play *The Smell of Burning Leaves.* Script by Janet Headstone. Stella van Fleet and Dorian Villiers attached. Yorgos hadn't wasted any time. Talbot investigated his feelings, now he knew the facts. He felt nothing. Well out of that, he thought to himself, tossing *Variety* aside.

"I'd better be going," Naomi said, standing up. "Want *The Times*?" She passed it over. "Governors' meeting—give me strength."

"Give 'em hell, darling," he said.

She came over and pecked him on the forehead.

"You all right? Not getting bored?"

"Boredom is one problem I'll never experience."

She left the room, Talbot realising that her instincts were shrewd: he was a bit bored. He had mown the lawn twice this week. He'd played squash, joined a swimming club and had investigated doing a degree in comparative literature as an extramural mature student at University College London. He had started reading *A la recherche du temps perdu* for about the seventh time. All the indications of a man with too much leisure time to fill.

He heard Naomi's car drive away, made himself another cup of tea and idly picked up the newspaper. Mayhem and street-fighting at the Democratic Convention in Chicago. Warsaw Pact invades Czechoslovakia. God, 1968, he thought, what a year, and we still have a few months to go. He turned a page and his eyes were caught by a headline: "AMERICAN FILM STAR FOUND DEAD." Who was it, he wondered: Greta Garbo? Lillian Gish? He read on:

Bordeaux, 27 August 1968

The body of the American film actress, Anny Viklund (*The Yellow Mountain, Aquarius Days*) was found in a car on Thursday in the village of Cap Ferret, near Bordeaux. Based on forensic examination of the corpse, French police speculated that her body had lain there unnoticed for about three weeks. Miss Viklund (28) had recently starred in the British comedy film *Moonladder* but had fled the country as a result of a Special Branch/FBI investigation into her links with her ex-husband,

Cornell Weekes, also a fugitive from justice, recently charged and found guilty of terrorist offences and conspiracy to murder.

Miss Viklund's body has been taken to Paris for a post-mortem.

At the time of filing, French police declined to confirm a verdict of suicide. A spokesman for the FBI denied any involvement in the pursuit of Miss Vikland or any connection with her "tragic" death. French police say there were signs of a struggle and that Miss Viklund's car had been broken into. They say suspects in a potential murder case are being actively sought.

Talbot put the newspaper down feeling a palpable cold shock spread through him, remembering vividly his last encounter with Anny in Paris, as she sat outside that café in her raincoat and forage cap, how he lit her cigarette for her—before that lout of a boyfriend punched him in the face. Poor, poor girl, he thought, very shaken at this news. What an awful thing to happen to her. What were they implying—that she had been assassinated by the FBI or the CIA? Anny Viklund? It seemed inconceivable. The complicated ramifications of *Ladder to the Moon* had rippled far beyond Brighton.

He stood up and wandered unhappily through the open French windows into the garden, hands in pockets, wondering futilely if he could have done anything different, could have changed things. No, he thought, he had begged her to return, promised her every legal assistance. It was no consolation to think that if she had returned she would still be alive. What must Jacques Soldat be thinking? Maybe his stupid, perverse idea of a press conference had been the final pound of pressure on poor Anny Viklund . . . Then he thought of Troy Blaze and wondered what the collateral damage would be on him. Jesus, what a fucking mess. How horrible and unnecessary. We cannot control most aspects of our lives, he thought, but those we can try to control, or at least influence, we should protect and cherish.

He paused. He suddenly knew exactly what he wanted to do next. A firm kind of certainty and conviction took hold of him, a different confidence in his judgement that almost surprised him in its audacity, suggesting a course of action that the old Talbot of a month ago would have dismissed in a second as both risky and potentially undignified.

He found it strange that it had taken the news of Anny Viklund's death to set him on this course. What was it about Anny's miserable lonely death in a car park in south-west France that had suddenly cleared his vision? In her short, baffled, beleaguered life maybe she had inadvertently arrived, at its desperate but willed-for end, at a truth about her existence—and therefore, by extension, every human being's. Talbot understood what she meant by that act, that cry of pain.

He strode back inside, picked up the phone and dialled Directory Enquiries.

"Hello," he said. "Do you have a number for Hicksmith Scaffolding Ltd.? Muswell Hill, London. Yes."

Talbot called the number he had been given and a young woman's voice answered the phone with a perky, "Hicksmith Scaffolding! How can I help you?" Talbot said he needed to speak to Mr. Hicksmith and was told that he was out of the office on a job in Chalk Farm. I've got a big contract for him, Talbot lied, and was immediately given the address where Gary and the crew could be found.

He drove up to Chalk Farm in the Alvis and parked a street away from the address he'd been given. He took a few moments in the car to compose himself. He realised that, if what he hoped was going to happen next actually happened, then his secret life wouldn't be secret any more, or for very long. But that would be the right thing. That would be good. It was the protection that his secret life had given him that had now brought him here to Chalk Farm, here to Gary Hicksmith. The flat, the gallery, his photographs, his models, his solitude, being Mr. Eastman, had served their purpose. He had wanted to know who his real "self" was and now he did.

He stepped out of the car, locked it, and walked circumspectly round the corner to where Modbury Gardens was to be found, not wanting to be spotted by Gary before he was absolutely ready for their encounter. It would be decisive, one way or another, he knew. It had to be. And that was exactly what he wanted.

The job turned out to be a modest terraced house that needed repainting. One of the "small domestics" that Gary had said he would be starting out with, his essential bread and butter. A couple of scaffs were on the second floor finishing off the job, one of them affixing the sign "Hicksmith Scaffolding Ltd." to a high tube.

Talbot saw the flatbed lorry parked opposite the house. Gary was sitting in the passenger seat, the window wound down, punching numbers into a calculator, frowning. Talbot walked over to him.

"Hello, Gary," he said quietly.

Gary looked up and almost managed to hide his total surprise.

"Jesus . . ." he said.

"How are you? I see you're up and running."

"What the fuck do you want?" Gary said.

"I want to apologise."

Gary sat back, put down his calculator and rested his left forearm on the windowsill. With his right hand he ran his fingers through his hair.

"Yeah, yeah. Forget it, *Talbot.*" He emphasised his name, as if to underline some remembered impatience. "It's well over."

"Good to see you're underway." Talbot gestured at the house opposite. "Hicksmith Scaffolding. Tremendous."

"No thanks to you."

"So much the better, don't you think? Did it all on your own, no help from anyone."

Gary looked up at the ceiling of the cab and allowed himself a rueful smile and a small chuckle, half incipient laugh, half throat-clear.

"Yeah. It's a point, I suppose." He tugged at an earlobe, thinking again, his eyes unfocussed, half-looking at something through the windscreen at the end of the street. Talbot saw that he hadn't shaved for a day or two.

"Listen, Gary." Talbot took a step forward. They were closer now, no one could hear what they might say to each other, but still he dropped his voice a tone. "I want to say how sorry I am. How sorry I am that I got everything wrong—that day at my place. I don't know what I was thinking, what stirred me up. It was . . . It was unjust. And stupid of me. I felt I had to see you again—simply to say that."

Gary was about to reply but Talbot held up his hand to pre-empt him.

"You don't need to say anything. No need to respond," Talbot said. "Just 'message received,' that's all I need to hear."

Gary frowned, and pouted in that way Talbot now recognised as something Gary did when he was considering an answer or a course of action, with due seriousness. The fingers of his right hand drummed on the steering wheel.

"All right," he said. "Message received."

"And I owe you fifty pounds," Talbot said. "And a print of the photograph, if you want it. It's very good. Or so I think."

Talbot hesitated—and then he gently placed his hand on Gary's forearm. He wanted to touch him. It was a test. Gary didn't flinch or draw his arm away. Talbot felt the warmth of Gary's skin heat his fingers. He squeezed gently.

"Will you accept my apology."

"Nothing to apologise for, Talbot. All forgotten."

They smiled quickly at each other, Talbot feeling a sense of pure relief flood through him.

"And, well, fifty pound is fifty pound. Could be useful," Gary said.

"I owe it to you. I'll pop it in the post."

"No, I'll swing by," Gary said. "I'd like to see the photo, and all."

"Right. Great," Talbot said, removing his hand. "I'm around at the weekend. All weekend," he added.

"I'll call you next Saturday," Gary said. "Thanks."

They made their easy farewells and Talbot turned away, heading back to where he'd parked the Alvis. He felt a strange buoyancy about his person, as if he were suddenly lighter, filled with helium like a balloon, suddenly standing an inch or two taller. A hand was placed upon an arm. The warmth of that contact—palm on arm—was registered. And the arm was not removed. It wasn't a lot to go on but he would settle for that. He closed his eyes and opened them. Yes, it was the same old world and he was still walking down a road in Chalk Farm towards his car. It was late August, 1968, a cloudy, cool day.

13

It must still be August, Elfrida thought—surely?—though it was a cloudy, cool day. She had lost track of the days of the week and now the months were becoming hard to remember. A small late-summer storm had whirled through the valley in the night and she was out with her rake gathering the torn leaves into piles and breaking up the deadwood that had fallen into kindling-sized pieces ready for winter and the convent's open fires.

She picked up a small dry branch, ripped from an oak tree, and started snapping it briskly into bits. Her hands were calloused and her nails were short and dirty, she saw. She enjoyed being busy, doing mundane tasks, and she found herself wondering if that was why Virginia Woolf liked doing housework. Don't think of Virginia, she told herself, that was your other life, Elfrida's. Once you've finished here, you've got to get the Allen Scythe out and attack the long grass and the nettles in the orchard. She placed the kindling twigs in the wheelbarrow and went to drag away another branch that had fallen on top of the boundary wall. A rook or a raven was cursing raucously; somewhere, something must have disturbed it.

And then she heard a kind of indeterminate cheeping noise in the air all around her and looked up to see the sky above the oak trees filled with flashing, darting birds. Swifts.

Swifts. All at once, she remembered an incident that had occurred on a holiday—was it Cyprus? South of France? Crete? Anyway, she had been alone by the swimming pool in the villa they had rented, Reggie and the friends they had invited were off on some jaunt but she had decided to stay behind and work on a book review that she had promised to deliver. It was midday and hot, she remembered, as she sat with her book in the shade by the pool, and there had been a mid-day crescent moon in the blue sky above, a thin translucent sickle of moon. The pool was limpid, as clear as mineral water. Suddenly a flock of swifts—a scramble of swifts, a flurry of swifts—appeared overhead, their treble cheeping very audible as they darted about.

And then, one by one, the swifts dived down to the pool to drink. She sat and watched them, amazed and mesmerised, as, oblivious to her presence, they banked and fell, barely decelerating, to skim the surface of the pool, making a million micro-calculations so that they were able to dip their beak into the water as they swooped. Ripples spread from the split-second contact. When they dived to drink they stopped their thin, high calls, and all she heard was the percussive thrum of their wings as they pulled up and out from the pool—after their miraculous manoeuvre, their vertiginous dive to drink—and swerved off and away into the empty blue sky again.

Gratitude and Acknowledgements

THE FILM-MAKERS

Scott Meek, Dame Joan Collins, Ashley Luke, Frederic Raphael, Richard Attenborough, Jack Gold, Jim Clark, Luca Mavrocordato, Mark Tarlov, John Fiedler, Frazer Fennell-Ball, Suzi Fennell-Ball, Pat O'Connor, Steve Clark-Hall.

THE IN-CROWD

Dr. David T. Evans, Christopher Hawtree, Gudrun Ingridsdottir, Thomas Mogford, Alison Rea, Theo Fennell, Louise Fennell, Derek Deane, Bruce Frankel, Peter Peterson, Nicholas Maddison.

A NOTE ABOUT THE AUTHOR

William Boyd was born in 1952 in Accra, Ghana, and grew up there and in Nigeria. He is the award-winning author of sixteen highly acclaimed novels and five collections of stories. He divides his time between London and France.

A NOTE ON THE TYPE

This book was set in a modern adaptation of a type designed by the first William Caslon (1692–1766). The Caslon face, an artistic, easily read type, has enjoyed more than two centuries of popularity in our own country. It is of interest to note that the first copies of the Declaration of Independence and the first paper currency distributed to the citizens of the newborn nation were printed in this typeface.

Typeset by Scribe,
Philadelphia, Pennsylvania

Printed and bound by Berryville Graphics,
Berryville, Virginia

Designed by Soonyoung Kwon